K.A. Barker is a twenty-something author from Brisbane who writes books about imaginary places and impossible deeds. She is fond of dirigibles, good books, shower singing, cheesy adventure movies, and time periods not her own.

N.M. Barker is a twenty-something author from Brisbane who writes books about imaginary places and impossible deeds. She is fond of dirigibles, good books, shower singing, cheesy adventure movies, and time periods not her own.

THE BOOK OF DAYS

K.A. BARKER

PAN
Pan Macmillan Australia

To my mother and father, for their unconditional love as I discovered who I am.

And to anyone who's ever looked up at the night sky and asked themselves the same.

First published 2014 in Pan by Pan Macmillan Australia Pty Ltd
1 Market Street, Sydney, New South Wales, Australia, 2000

Cataloguing-in-Publication entry is available
from the National Library of Australia
http://catalogue.nla.gov.au

Typeset in 12/15.25 pt Garamond Premier Pro by Midland Typesetters
Printed by McPherson's Printing Group

ACKNOWLEDGEMENTS

Graeme and Jenny Barker – for encouragement, plot tennis, sway hugs, baked dinners and reading the darn thing in all its forms.

John Marsden – for your amazing quote and believing enough in my first chapter to recommend me to Pan Macmillan.

Bianca and Jim Reynolds – for your never-ending blind belief in me.

Charlotte Ryland – for your fantastic website skills and much-appreciated shared geekery.

To my fabulous editors: Jo Lyons, Vanessa Pellatt, and Julia Stiles – thank you so much for your work on *The Book of Days*. Not only did you transform it for the better, you always supported me on the long journey to publication. Also, your editing notes made me laugh.

And especially to Claire Craig . . . without whom this book would still be a half-finished, unrecognisable mess. Thank you for your passion, your patience and, most importantly, your belief in *The Book of Days*.

The Seething Sea
Roqda-Maai
Saqira
Daluk Shakti
Sahir
Aqira
Qahosh
Dragonshead Point
Al-Tarah
Yeswahiis
The Sea of La'Haia
Keshlahar
Baslann
Khast
Territory of the Shining Ones
The Petrified Forest
The Bay of Wenslas
Ormonde
The Crossroads
Bittertongue
Belborough
Cordale
The Widowmere
Tarrant
Tarranton
The Pomegran Grove
Beggars End
De Kena Lands
Tantallon
The Unreality House
Aleria
Aslamere
Varley
De Valko Lands
The Mallowmere
Witherstoke
Tanglewood
Ordenvale
The Realm of the Under-Elders
Voltemande
Grimholt
The Rime

N
W
E
S
THE VANISHING ISLANDS
THE SILK SEA
SKAA - THE WASTELANDS
HIYEMOR RANGE
THE ANTIEL
URANTIEL
RO
THE CROOKED STRAIT
ERISHORE
OLNESTRI
YÄEL
AVE
YU SHEMAY
AELANI GORGE
THE TRI-CITY REGION
TIAMA
TORDESTIIN
YANA'EST
CORTE
TIAMATA
JYN
SYLPHAEN
THE SEA OF LAMENTATION
LINMOORE
THE FIN
NEW HALLOWHYME
FALLAM
EASTREACH
DOFFLE
LANNAWOOD
THE SENTINELS
SHIPWRECK BAY
THE SEA OF SOULS
ALDHAVEN
RAVENS REACH

CHAPTER ONE

Most people believe the best way to forget someone is to throw them down a well. Or lock them in a room with eight keys, or bury them at a crossroad in the thirteenth hour. But they're wrong. The best way to forget someone is for them never to have existed in the first place.

Madame Marisol's Unreality House was where you brought people to make that happen.

It was a harsh October evening when the strange young man showed up at Madame Marisol's door. This wouldn't have been strange in itself except that no one ever made the journey across the Whispering Plains after dark; and yet here he was, standing on her front landing with the nerve to drip on her welcome mat.

He was so tall that the top of his hat was cut off from her view as she peered through the peephole, while a blue woollen greatcoat swathed the rest of him, and so she was no better off at guessing his identity or purpose than she had been when his knock had first disturbed her.

The rain fell in diagonal sheets, splattering against the weathered timber of the House and half-soaking the stranger every time a vindictive flurry of wind found its way underneath the veranda.

Madame Marisol pulled back from the peephole and calmly reached for the loaded musket she kept propped up in the umbrella stand. Then, with equal poise, she put down the book she'd been reading to the occupants of the Unreality House, opened the door a crack, and aimed the musket at the strange young gentleman's face.

'You have sixty seconds, sir,' she said, cocking the gun, 'before you no longer have a head. Use them wisely.'

He took a step backwards, tilted his head to the side as though formulating the fastest way off her veranda, and raised a sodden arm in feeble defence. 'You can't be serious. I'm Lord of the Fifth Quarter, you know.'

'And I'm the Lady Fortuna,' she remarked, taking in the bare patches on his greatcoat. *The Fifth Quarter.* He might as well have said he was from north of the Seething Sea – both places were equally imaginary. 'Did Sterling send you?'

The hat he wore quivered in what could have been a laugh. 'Last I heard, he was chasing up recruits out in the provinces. Besides, do I look like a daybreaker to you?'

His sass didn't impress her. Time was, someone who answered back to her in such a manner would find themselves seated in one of the deceptively innocent chairs in her drawing room – the one with the really big spike in the unfortunate position and the lovebird cushions – to be tested on *The Little Blue Book of Basic Etiquette*, and Days help them if they got an answer wrong. 'Just for that,' she said, 'you've got ten seconds left.'

He looked from her face to the musket held steadily in her hands and then back again, and she could almost see the thoughts humming away in his head. *Just how good is she with that musket? Could I make a dash for it?* She met his eyes, silently daring him to try as her finger twitched against the trigger. The furthest anyone had gotten was the lightning-struck tree by the gate. That gentleman's false teeth were still embedded in the bark. 'You could be taking this time to compose some suitable last words, dearie. I've heard some corkers.'

'No doubt.' Despite her hopes, he paused for another second, and finally drew off his hat in a swift movement, revealing mismatched eyes of blue and brown, a strong brow, and white teeth set into his dark face in a conciliatory grin. 'There. And may I say what a pleasure it is to meet such a beautiful hostess.' He bowed, and then paused as though waiting for her reaction.

She stubbornly refused to give him the satisfaction. With his wide-brimmed hat swept up just so, revealing his close-cropped hair, the greatcoat falling open at the chest to show just a hint of an embroidered waistcoat, and his handsome face smiling up at her, it was true that he cut a fine figure. But the entire effect reminded Madame Marisol of men she had seen in her youth, waiting in alleyways with cards or dice or cups-and-shells.

'Oh, don't try your tricks on me,' she told him. 'I'm too old to be charmed by the likes of you. What is your name, daybreaker?'

To his credit, the only hint of his disappointment was a slight twitching in one of his little fingers. 'My name is Quintalion,' he said. 'And though I may own to being cunning, self-absorbed and rather too loose with the truth for some people's comfort, I can't yet add "murdering zealot" to my list of vices.'

She settled the musket into a more comfortable position against her shoulder and squinted at him. 'How do *I* know that? Just because you say you're not and you've got a nice smile? Daybreakers have teeth too, you know.'

'True,' he conceded, 'but I doubt they have this.' He reached into the innermost recesses of his coat and pulled out a piece of parchment, little larger than a calling card, which he held out to her between two fingers. His greatcoat had protected against the worst of the weather, but segments of the card were still damp, the green ink blotched and running.

'Days preserve me,' Madame Marisol said in the most sarcastic voice she could muster. 'A piece of paper. Welcome to my humble abode, kind sir. Would you like tea and biscuits?'

The strange young gentlemen who called himself Quintalion huffed out a breath. 'Take it,' he said. 'I hope you'll at least look at it before depriving me of a head.'

With one hand still pointing the musket where it could do the most damage, she took the offered card and stared at it suspiciously.

'It's an invitation,' he said, as though she didn't see the very words in front of her. 'Completely genuine, I think you'll find.'

It was all there on the parchment: the green ink of the invitation, sealed with a charm that warded off copies and other tricks; the golden sigil of the Unreality House ingrained into the paper; the words she remembered as well as her own name. *The bearer of this invitation is offered full rights of entry to my House according to the ancient codes of welcome.* She'd written so many of them over the years: scraps of paper that she'd pressed into the hands of distraught family members who'd brought their loved ones to her House to forget about them rather than face the agony of grieving. Most people never found their way back to her door, having forgotten why they visited the moment they left, which was for the best. Precious few of her souls faced a life outside her walls that would be filled with anything other than pain and death. Better an eternal sleep than a life of torment.

'Where did you get this?' she asked him sharply, gesturing at him with the barrel of the musket.

He stared at her. 'Where does one normally get them? It was delivered to me one morning and I assumed I had visited your House to drop off one of my . . .' He paused. 'Oh dear,' he said in a deadpan tone, 'I do hope it wasn't Uncle Balthazar.'

It was true that she sometimes sent out invitations to the families she thought were ready to accept their loved one's passing, or on rare occasions the miracle of having them back again, but she hadn't sent one in years, not since before . . .

She turned the card over. There, written in handwriting she knew almost as well as her own, were five words: *Wake me when it's safe.*

'When was it delivered?' Madame Marisol said, fear making her words harsh.

'A year ago? Three? I don't remember. A man can't be running about after possibly dead relatives all the time. Why does it matter?'

'You don't understand.' She tried to keep her voice calm, but she was afraid that the girls in her weekly whist club, were they to hear her now, would be gleefully reminding her to use her indoor voice. 'The girl pertaining to this particular invitation, she . . .'

'Oh, a girl, is it? I didn't know I had a sister, but I suppose that's the point.' As Quintalion craned his head, trying to snatch a glance of the House beyond her shoulder, Madame Marisol began to have the sinking feeling that the musket was no longer providing effective dissuasion.

We'll see about that when he finds himself short a toe, she thought.

'And I'm sure you're well aware of the wording of that invitation: full rights of entry, and final decision to remove said possibly dead relative if I wish it. So lower the frankly intimidating musket, please, and I take my tea with two sugars and a dash of lemon.'

Madame Marisol reluctantly lowered the barrel. *Think of page 63 of* The Little Blue Book. *It is the height of bad manners to kill someone simply for being unpleasant.* 'I suppose you'll be wanting to come in then.'

His mouth opened into a grin. 'Only if you're offering.'

The musket went back into the umbrella stand, but she kept her eyes on the gentleman as he followed her in out of the rain. It paid to be careful. Not many travellers found their way to her House these days – magicians mostly, influential families that still kept to the old ways, and, of course, her weekly whist companions. Invitation or not, this man was still a stranger, and strangers were made to be distrusted.

At the moment, however, he seemed more interested in scraping the mud from his boots than in doing anything underhand.

'You won't believe the nonsense I went through to get here,' he said, leaving a large chunk of mud and grass on the lintel of the door.

She shut it against the rain, pleased when he had to leap to one side to avoid catching his foot. 'Oh, yes?'

'Blockades everywhere. The daybreakers have been swarming around the borders for a month now. Don't want a repeat of what happened up north, I'll wager.'

'I don't blame them,' she said, remembering how many extra guests she'd had during the horrible years of the Saturday Wars. She'd contemplated lining the keeping-houses up in the hallway. 'How many died?'

He shot her a dark look. 'Too many. They say war is never over, but some people are taking it too literally for my liking. It's bad for business.'

'Follow me, then,' she said, and led him further into the House. She snuck a glance over her shoulder as she pattered over the stone floor. When people heard of a house that contained the souls of those caught between death and life, she doubted they imagined a modest little homestead with a fireplace that smoked, cheery wallpaper, and a pianola in the sitting room. And sure enough, her guest was so busy looking around him, one eyebrow raised in disbelief, that he tripped over a rug by the fire.

'Be careful there, dear,' she said, 'that rug's genuine chimera and you can't get its like for love nor money these days.'

The House was arranged around the large, two-storeyed entrance hall, which was something of a nonsense since she kept little in it besides the stone fireplace to the left, rugs to warm her old bones, and paintings that the House switched over when it wanted a change. But she had lived here for so long that she wouldn't have had the House any other way: the sitting room at the front and to the left, the dining room to the right, the kitchen at the back, and the bedrooms up the wooden staircase on the second floor. Everything was where it should be.

Including the room she was leading him to. They walked underneath the second floor landing and into a small passageway at the back of the House. The shadows choked the little light that made it through from the entrance hall, and all she got was a glimpse of white hair and the rose-pink fabric of her favourite dress as she passed a mirror on the wall, before turning away to face the door opposite it.

Madame Marisol felt it before she saw it. Even after all these years, the power of the room and its sleeping occupants still left her breathless. They were the heart of the House; their presence reminded her that, however much she might have felt at home here, she was still and would always be just the caretaker.

She hesitated, her hand hovering above the ruby handle. 'Is it safe out there for her?'

'Not my problem,' he replied quickly. 'I, Madame, make a point of avoiding situations that can get me killed. I'll try my utmost to do the same for this girl, whoever she is.'

She could hardly trust the word of a man she'd just met. He wouldn't be able to guarantee the girl's safety, not with the daybreakers apparently growing in number. But she had no choice: as the bearer of the invitation, he had the House-given right to take the girl away, however much Madame Marisol herself protested. But that didn't mean she couldn't give him a run for his money.

'Why are you here, really?'

He shrugged. 'I had an invitation and an inclination to find out why. Besides,' he pulled aside the bulk of his coat to reveal the ivory handle of a pistol peeking out above the holster at his hip, 'I'm very much hoping this is worth the trouble.'

So he's one of those types. Madame Marisol rested her hand against the door in a vain effort to quell the anger rising within her. 'You do realise, my dear,' she said, and it took all her concentration to keep her voice calm, 'that if I hear that you hurt a single hair on that girl's head, I will have to come after you with all I've got?'

Quintalion flicked the cuff of his greatcoat, spraying droplets of water everywhere. 'Thank you for the warning,' he said. 'I would hate to face up against doilies, cat hair and the faint smell of regret.'

Madame Marisol dug her fingernails into the wood so hard that she felt splinters under her nails, but when she turned back to him, she wore a smile on her face. 'Never underestimate a woman with knitting needles, dearie. Now,' she added, and pulled the door open with a flourish, 'would you like to come inside?'

*

No matter how many times she set foot into the room, Madame Marisol always breathed in that first breath of air like a drowning soul. It tasted of wind and lightning, and seemed to fill her up right from the bottom of her toes to the top of her head. It was like waking up after a good night's rest, and she automatically whispered, 'Good morning, my loves.'

The hundreds of keeping-houses lit up all as one, throwing a soft light against the faces of their sleeping occupants. Some were young, barely yet alive, and some had beards that coiled around the bottom of their keeping-houses like blankets. There were peasants and kings, dairymaids and court ladies. Some looked merely asleep, and others as though they would never wake again, with gashes and limbs missing and the pale milky complexion of delayed death.

She knew all their stories. Most were sad. The Unreality House was a place to bring people to escape their fate, be that death or dishonour, and those with happy lives rarely graced her doorstep. Madame Marisol could remember when each of them had arrived at her House, carried on stretchers and funeral biers, or, in one particularly heart-breaking case, entwined in each other's arms.

There was only one, in all the thousands of souls she had kept safe over the years, who had found her way to Madame Marisol's House by herself.

Beside her, Quintalion drummed the fingers of one hand against his leg as his head moved from left to right to take in the room. 'It's not . . . it's not possible. The room must be half a furlong from wall to wall, but it's not *possible*. Have we gone underground?'

Smiling to herself, she shook her head. 'Not at all, my dear. We're still in the Unreality House, of course. Would you like me to define "unreality" for you?'

Without waiting for an answer, she set off past the first row of keeping-houses. Years of experience had left her with knowledge of the twisting paths, but folk had been known to get lost in the room. The House had a way of ridding itself of undesirables.

They walked in silence for a few minutes, the *tap*, *tap*, *tap* of Quintalion's boots on the marble floor the only indication that he was following along behind her, and, since it felt wrong to cheapen the revered quiet of the room with small talk, Madame Marisol contented herself with humming a little ditty.

Another right, a left, and a complicated half-turn later and they'd almost reached the girl's resting place. When the girl had first come here, Madame Marisol had placed her close to the back for two reasons: it meant less of a chance that unfriendly eyes would find her, and there was also a group of other young people of good families for her to associate with. Although they spent their time in the perpetual sleep of the Unreality House, Madame Marisol was the last person to claim herself an expert on what went on inside the keeping-houses, which is also why she insisted on reading proper literature to them all every night.

'I really must remember to put a bookmark in *The Tale of Amiens and Aemilia*,' she said absently. 'Amiens is about to get stabbed with the poison dagger and I would hate for my duckies to miss it.'

'That would be tragic.' Quintalion had wandered over to one of the keeping-houses and was peering at the soul encased inside, his nose almost touching the glass.

'I've heard the great heroes of the past are here,' he said. 'Sir Tristan the Valiant, the seven sisters, Alaric and his fool, Sylvain the Swordsinger. Of course,' he added with a carefully timed cough, 'that's ridiculous.'

'You'd be surprised, dearie,' she said lightly. 'I've met my share of heroes. They're a strange breed – tramping in without wiping their boots, eating all the scones, insisting to their companions that they're fine when they've got half a quiver lodged in their chests. I've never really cared for them. Now,' she added, 'I think you'll find who you're looking for just over here.'

The girl hung suspended in the pale glow of the keeping-house. She was an odd thing: a girl to *forget*, frozen halfway between childhood and womanhood, and as gawky as Madame Marisol herself had been at that age. She had a long straight nose set in an otherwise unremarkable thin face, hair the colour of bark that hung in shaggy tendrils to her knees, and a beanpole body. In her most generous mood, after a sherry or two, the most Madame Marisol could have said in her favour was that she was interesting looking.

'This is the girl,' she told Quintalion. 'As she came to me with no name, I called her Tuesday.'

It wasn't exactly the truth, but she wasn't about to go spilling all her secrets of that night or the letter that she had hidden in her lanterloo table.

'Let me guess . . . she arrived on a Tuesday?' Quintalion raised his eyebrows.

'You're just full of insight, fine sir.' She watched as he circled the girl's keeping-house with a quick step, once, twice, and then a third time, his hands positioned behind his back. It was taller even than he was: a rectangular box, *or coffin*, she thought darkly, made out of rosewood on three sides and with a glass door on the fourth. 'Do you know her?'

He looked down at his dark skin and then back up at Tuesday. 'She's certainly no sister of mine.' He made one final lap and paused in front of the girl, saying softly to himself: 'And yet he had the invitation . . .'

Madame Marisol had tucked it away up her right sleeve, but now she pulled it out and stared at it again, hoping that a second look would reveal some obvious sign of fraudulence, but it looked more and more authentic the closer she studied it. It even had the second watermark she'd hidden up in the right-hand corner to trick forgers. But something didn't feel right about the man standing in front of her. She couldn't decide what it was exactly – his restless fingers or his shark-like smile – but the very air around him smelled *wrong*, as though the House was trying to warn her about him.

She ran a thumb over the invitation. 'The funny thing is,' she said in a deliberately calm tone, 'I never actually drew up an invitation for Tuesday.'

She had told herself many times over the last ten years that she really ought to get around to it, but every time she sat down to pen the invitation, something always seemed to come up, or she received news of more skirmishes in the borderlands or that Sterling and his daybreakers were on the prowl, and the invitation remained unwritten.

Quintalion didn't even bother to look away from the girl's keeping-house before replying: 'And yet I have one. Surely that indicates one of two things: you're growing forgetful in your old age, or I'm lying through my teeth. I'm going to go with the former . . . but of course I *would* say that.'

Or that she didn't trust me as much as she claimed, Madame Marisol added silently.

'So what will this Tuesday be like, anyway? I'm not going to have to teach her how to use the privy, am I? Because that doesn't quite work to my schedule.'

Seven sisters, give me patience. Madame Marisol joined him next to the keeping-house and purposely refused to look at his face, for fear she might forget the rules of invitation and smack him about the ears for his impertinence, instead sweeping the frame of the keeping-house with her eyes: fir branches, splayed open in a delicate pattern, and a nameplate down the bottom, the name mostly hidden by grime. 'Oh, she'll be able to tell you what a cup of tea is and hold a decent conversation about the weather, but if you want much more, you'll have to be patient.'

He snorted through his nose. 'Not one of my many qualities.'

'Tough,' Madame Marisol said. 'You're the one trouncing up to my House in the middle of the night. If you're claiming that invitation of yours is real, then it's your responsibility to look after her. Which would include not selling her to the highest bidder.'

'My dearest Madame Marisol, as if I would sell my beloved little sister.'

They were clearly no relation, so the fact that he was claiming kinship spoke more of mockery than any real feeling, and it set her teeth grinding.

He must have noticed, because he added, 'Fine. If it will put your heart at ease, I promise not to sell her.'

Madame Marisol was sure she heard a *right away* dangling at the end of his sentence, but as she had no authority to refuse him, she let it slide, and gestured to Tuesday. 'Then it's time to wake her up. Be careful, dear, the lock sticks.' *And I know precisely where to stick it . . .*

His eyes narrowed. 'How do I do that, exactly?'

'Some give a good old kiss, though that's a little too forward in your case, I'm sure. Contact is the key. Go ahead. Press her hand and be done with it.'

Madame Marisol watched as he fiddled with the door, smirking when he let out a curse at the stubborn latch, before he finally wrestled the glass open, releasing a waft of musty air that smelled like mothballs.

The day that Madame Marisol had first come to the House, so long ago that she barely remembered when, there had been no keeping-houses, just an empty room waiting to be filled. The keeping-houses had gone through many different designs over the years, but she'd ordered the current model from a casket maker in Bittertongue, who had no concept of aeration, it not being a concern of his usual clients . . . or her duckies either, if she cared to think about it.

Quintalion paused with his hand hovering just above Tuesday's skin and took one long look at her. 'What was he doing with her?' he muttered, softly enough that Madame Marisol had to lean in to hear him. 'Ah well, there's no accounting for taste.'

Not for the first time, she wished that she'd never introduced the invitations. The ancient codes of welcome were one thing, but they did make it far more difficult to stab someone without the House disapproving.

Quintalion reached out, not for her hand as Madame Marisol had suggested, but to brush his fingers lightly against her left cheek.

The nerve . . .

Golden light bloomed where his fingers touched her skin.

Quintalion let out a strangled hiss, and cradled his hand to his chest. 'That . . . hurt,' he said, his breath coming in gasps. He wavered for a moment, leaned over with his eyes screwed up, and then straightened again to look at the white marks he had left behind on the girl's cheek. 'I do believe my heart stopped beating for a second there.'

Ah, she thought, her suspicions confirmed, but all she said was: 'Nothing to worry about, dearie. It happens to the best of us. Now off to the kitchen with you. I'll not have you blabbering about daybreakers and hearts stopping when she wakes. There's half a cold chicken in the larder. Help yourself to anything else, but I'd avoid the chocolate cake if I were you. The last gentleman to eat a slice grew an extra head.'

'Thank you for the warning,' he said dryly, and turned to leave.

Cursing her snap decision to tell him about the cake, Madame Marisol waited until she heard the door shut off in the distance before she turned her attention back to Tuesday.

The golden light had spread to cover her entire body. It pulsed through her veins and shone out behind her teeth to spill from her slightly opened mouth.

'There now, my love,' Madame Marisol told the girl, who was now beginning to vibrate with the throbbing energy and magic that filled her body, awakening every muscle and shooting fire through each nerve ending. 'It's just you and me. Show me those pretty eyes of yours.'

Tuesday glowed all over with golden warmth, nowhere brighter than the still visible fingerprints on her cheek.

They'll leave a mark, Madame Marisol thought. *I hope she doesn't mind.*

The light surrounding the girl's body fluttered faster and faster until she fairly hummed with unreleased energy, like the string of a plucked fiddle. Just when Madame Marisol thought she might have to give her a gentle tap with the paddle she kept for just such occasions, the girl's eyes flew open.

She gasped, scrunched up her nose in confusion, said, 'Wh . . . what . . . ?'

And then she fainted.

'Welcome to existence, dear,' said Madame Marisol with a slight smile. 'You'll get used to it.'

CHAPTER TWO

Silence. Just the fevered dreaming of a soul still asleep. Then, like a star on the horizon, a touch. And, oh, the possibilities . . .

The world exploded into being with enough force to take her breath away. She gathered the air in large gasps and felt her chest expanding with every frantic gulp, until she grew greedy and swallowed too fast, which left her coughing. *Too much*, she thought. *Too much . . . everything.*

Something soft and gentle caressed her back. 'Not to worry,' came a voice. 'It happens to everyone. Best give yourself a moment to take it all in.'

She focused on the feeling of the figure eights going from one shoulder to the other, and gradually her breathing calmed enough for her to gingerly move her head from the marble to find the owner of the voice. It turned out to be a wisp of a woman wearing more pink than Tuesday would have thought possible. She had a shock of white hair and kindly eyes, and stared down at her with a smile on her wrinkled face, her hand still resting on Tuesday's back.

'Welcome to the world, Tuesday,' the old woman said.

The joy of discovery thrilled through her. *My name is Tuesday?* she tried, but her voice came out as a cross between a croak and a puff of air, so she was forced to simply stare up at the woman, moving her lips in silence, and hope the white-haired woman understood what she was attempting to say.

The old woman's eyes twinkled. 'Indeed it is, and mine is Madame Marisol. It is a pleasure to meet you again, my love. Do you think you're ready to get up?'

Tuesday nodded. She didn't know whether her body would agree with her, but when she thought about moving her toes, they gave a little wiggle that left her grinning in delight, so she assumed everything was in working order.

Madame Marisol put an age-spotted hand underneath her elbow and, with her pulling and Tuesday concentrating on moving *this* leg and pushing herself up with *that* arm, the two of them managed to get her standing.

'Well done,' Madame Marisol said.

Tuesday smiled and then clutched desperately at Madame Marisol's arm. Her legs had apparently decided that they were sick of this standing lark and buckled in protest. But thankfully Madame Marisol, despite being little more than half her height, was able to keep her upright with minimal fuss, and it wasn't long before Tuesday could let go of her and stand unassisted.

'Well, aren't you a bright little thing,' Madame Marisol said proudly. 'It normally takes all morning. I had one, bless him, who wouldn't get up for a week. I had to feed him broth with his legs sticking up in the air. It didn't half make a mess.'

'Wh . . . why?' It was a pathetic breath of air, expelled through chattering teeth, but at least it was understandable.

Madame Marisol laughed and patted her on the arm. 'I don't know, really. It just takes some more time than others. Not you, though. Look at you – already burning for the world. You remind me so much of . . .'

'Who?' Tuesday said, vaguely aware that she was progressing through the five Ws in rapid succession. *The five Ws . . . how do I know that?* She remembered soft words breaking through the fog: words that lightened the darkness and made her dream of knights and quests and romances and, strangely, that she should never go out to meet a gentleman without a chaperone.

'It doesn't matter, my love. When you're as old as I am, you've got more years behind you than in front of you, and it's easy to get lost in them, let me tell you. Now come with me, dear.'

Slipping and falling with legs that kept wanting to skew out in different directions, Tuesday let Madame Marisol lead her through the room. The tall boxes on either side of them drew her attention; each one was filled with a face that seemed familiar to her, though she couldn't understand why. She inched closer to Madame Marisol as they walked.

'They'll not hurt you, my love,' the old woman said. 'You were like them for a very long time.'

'But now I'm alive.' The words startled Tuesday. It was the first full sentence she could remember speaking, and since her voice had decided to settle into her body, she sounded more like herself. Not that she knew who that was.

'Now you're alive,' Madame Marisol repeated. 'And sixteen or so, if I know years. And when you've seen as many as I have, duckie, you get to be intimately acquainted with them.'

'*Really* alive.' It was mind-blowing. Not long ago she'd been trapped in the darkness of a sleep that was more than sleep, and now the world had opened itself to her. Her heart thudded in her chest. 'And sixteen. I . . . I don't know what to do.'

'Well, to start with, how about a nice cup of tea?'

*

The tea burned her tongue when she sipped at it, her chair was lumpy and covered in cat hair, and the biscuits Madame Marisol offered her had melted into one sticky, congealed mass, but to Tuesday it was the best afternoon tea she'd ever had. Even if it was, as the grandfather clock in the hall had pronounced, eleven at night and not normal afternoon tea at all.

'Evening tea,' she said quietly to herself, cradling the scalding cup against the blanket Madame Marisol had covered her with. 'Midnight tea.'

As Madame Marisol puttered about with sweet-smelling kindling and matches for the small wood-burning stove that sat in the corner of the sitting room, Tuesday settled herself deeper into her armchair, drawing her long hair up out of the way as she tucked her legs under her and wrapped the blanket tighter around her to draw off the chill. She gave the chair a few experimental bounces, which only resulted in expelling a lifetime's worth of dust and even more cat hair, if that was possible.

Madame Marisol's head snapped up from where she had been going through matches in attempt after attempt to get the damp wood to do anything other than smoke furiously. 'Have another chocolate,' she said. 'Goodness knows it's been too long since I got the chance to spoil anyone.'

Tuesday looked at the pile of chocolates in the centre of the tea stand. A fine layer of cat hair covered them. Oddly she hadn't yet seen a cat. She hesitantly took another, patted the worst of the cat hair off it, and dunked it in her tea. Three little hairs backstroked through the liquid.

Mercifully, Madame Marisol saved her from having to come up with a reason why, after three sweets, two-and-a-quarter biscuits, and a squashed pastry, she was suddenly allergic to chocolate. 'Put down that cream caramel if you don't mind, my love – I have to test some things.'

Tuesday had never been happier to obey in her life.

So, with fingers still sticky from the treats, she let Madame Marisol run through a series of increasingly odd tests: she flicked her ankles with a small silver instrument; asked Tuesday to poke out her tongue and commented on the colour and whether it shouldn't be just a little bit spongier for good measure; she inspected her ears, delightedly noting that Tuesday had attached lobes, as though that bit of knowledge were as important as the fact that she had two earlobes to begin with; she plucked one of Tuesday's underarm hairs and stood, inspecting it under a three-lens magnifier; she got her to hum a variety of notes, some at the same time; and, after asking Tuesday whether she could easily say 'She sells seashells on the seashore', she wrote for a long time in a large book.

'What are you doing?' Tuesday asked, once she'd finished off the rest of her now cold tea, dipped her hands in the finger bowl and pushed the stand of biscuits to a safe distance.

From where Tuesday sat, Madame Marisol's cramped handwriting looked like a spider's web. 'Just taking my usual measurements,' she said, her brow furrowed in concentration. 'Each time one of my duckies is woken, I like to make sure that everything's come back as it should. Sleeping so long can turn a person's head. It wouldn't do for one to sing soprano when before they were a bass.'

'Before?' Tuesday asked. 'You mean there was a time before the darkness?'

'Of course,' Madame Marisol replied. 'But it has never done anyone a lick of good to bury their head in the past, so I don't want you to think about it, all right my pet?'

She said all this very quickly in a bright voice, but when Tuesday opened her mouth to ask why, Madame Marisol shot her a look that silenced her.

'*Because*, my dear,' she said as she finished writing and closed the book. 'Sometimes that's all there is to it.'

While Madame Marisol began to chat about the abysmal weather they were having lately, Tuesday let her mind drift in an attempt to remember what her life had been like before she'd woken up. It was easy enough to shut out Madame Marisol's lilting voice, but when she closed her eyes to concentrate better, it hit Tuesday that the voice she had heard, the one that had told her so many stories and lightened the darkness that had been her entire world, belonged to Madame Marisol, and she felt guilty enough that she found herself saying the first thing she could think of in the general topic of weather, just to make up for ignoring her.

'It's very dark tonight.' *It's very dark tonight?* She inwardly shuddered, but Madame Marisol only nodded and started telling her about how she lived at the edge of the Whispering Plains and no one had settled there for fear of the de Kena clan, who were by Madame Marisol's account, 'fairly hard to get along with, it must be said, but sweethearts once you get to know them'.

She spoke so quickly, and with such an insistently cheerful tone of voice, that Tuesday couldn't help but think she was trying to hide something. Despite vague warnings in the back of her mind about the rudeness of interrupting, Tuesday burst out, 'What was I like before?'

Madame Marisol paused with her teacup hovering in the air halfway to her mouth. 'Beg pardon, dear?'

Tuesday twisted a shaggy lock of hair in her lap, suddenly awkward. For her, the only solid memories she had to cling to were of this night, of her abrupt awakening and the events thereafter, but a tiny voice deep inside her whispered that there must be more. If she cast her mind back beyond the fog of the keeping-house, she saw nothing but flashes of light and a feeling that she had to run, run and never look back, but the more she grasped at the glimpses of colour behind her eyelids, the more they darted away, and she opened her eyes to find that she had balled her fists.

'I don't know,' she finally said. 'I must have had a *before* . . . but I can't find it. Whenever I try, it keeps flitting away. I can't hold on to the memories. It's like . . . it's like they don't want to be found.'

Madame Marisol's cup had been tilting to one side as Tuesday spoke, the tea getting closer and closer to spilling, but now she sighed and righted it, putting the cup on the tea tray beside her with a deliberate clatter. 'You're right about that, love.'

There was a drawer hidden among the lacquered decorations of the lanterloo table upon which Madame Marisol had set their tea. She leaned over, pulled the delicate handle, and produced a letter from the depths of the drawer, before handing it to Tuesday.

'I think you should read this,' she said.

Tuesday stared at the letter. It had been folded and turned so that the parchment also acted as an envelope, but snippets of words peeked out at her – *you* and *nothing in your past* and *promise*.

Tuesday ran her thumb over the rough parchment, apprehension thrumming through her with every breath, and then she turned it over, broke the seal and began to read.

Dear

And here the ink grew blotchy, with several dots marking the stark parchment, as if the writer had put the quill to paper and then removed it several times.

It is my sincerest hope that you now have another name, and another life to go along with it, and I needn't have penned this letter at all, but since I have already sent the invitation out, I know myself better than that.

No doubt you are wondering what you were like before you woke in this rather marvellous House.

Don't.

There is nothing in your past but pain and regret. I willingly lay down my life so that you may start a new one. And that is the only promise I would ask you to make: forget me.

Build a new life, a better life. A life filled with love that is not oppressive, dreams that do not warp and turn bitter, and a future that is finer than your past.

I wish you nothing but the joys of discovery. Never look back.

With hope,

The name was left blank. Tuesday stared at the piece of parchment, hoping that if she looked at it for long enough, the name she desired would suddenly appear. She pinched her thumb and forefinger together and traced the looped words with an invisible quill, trying desperately to copy the way the letter writer had produced her *l*s and her gently looping *g*s, but they remained locked behind a door she didn't have the key to.

'Who . . . who wrote this?'

She knew the answer before Madame Marisol gave it, and yet still trembled when the words fell from her lips: 'You did, my dear.'

'No.' It slipped from her before she could stop it, as did the tear that fell on the open parchment, blotting the writing. She shook her head in a silent refusal of the truth. If she had truly written the letter, then her life before must have been filled with little else but, as she wrote, pain and regret. Tuesday blinked away the moisture in her eyes, looking up at the ceiling as she cast her mind back, wanting nothing more than to understand why she would have chosen the oblivion of the keeping-houses over what was outside the House, because whatever it was, it had to be better than the un-life she'd been living.

But it was like looking through frosted glass: images floated through her mind, snatches of conversations and memories, but without any context they were little more than incomprehensible blurs.

'Was I really so sad?' she asked.

Madame Marisol leaned over the armrest and clasped Tuesday's cold hands within her own. 'Sad and desperate, with no place else to run,' she said softly. 'So you came here to give yourself a fresh chance at life.'

She squeezed her hands, drawing Tuesday's gaze to her. 'Which is why I beg you, pet, to take it. Take the chance you gave yourself and live. *Live*, my love, and never look back.'

'I can't remember,' she said, the parchment rough beneath her questing fingers. 'Why can't I remember?'

'Who you were before,' Madame Marisol began, 'well, she came here because she had no other choice. She expected death, welcomed it in fact, and yet here you are. I think it would be best to view your life as beginning the moment you woke from your sleep. There is only Tuesday now . . . and Tuesday needs to get dressed before she catches her death of cold.'

CHAPTER THREE

Getting dressed proved to be more difficult than Tuesday had expected. While she vaguely understood the concept of socks and shifts and stays, she'd never actually had the opportunity to test out her theories about placement and order . . . which meant that she soon ended up with a sock on one arm and an inside-out blouse on the other.

It didn't help that Madame Marisol kept popping in and out of the upstairs bedroom she'd led Tuesday to, flinging moth-eaten skirts and frocks at her and keeping up an endlessly cheerful commentary about the weather, which, Tuesday rapidly realised, was her favourite topic.

'It'll be cold out there . . .' she was saying as she disappeared out the door.

Tuesday pulled off the pair of drawers that had just landed on her head and placed them on the growing pile of clothes that threatened to swallow the bed whole.

She'd put the letter on the bed as well, and every couple of seconds her eyes wandered to it of their own volition, checking that it was still there. Though every muscle twitched with the desire to grab it and read it until the words flowed from the page and into her memory, she forced herself to leave it be, and instead amused herself with examining the room around her.

It was large enough to be comfortable, but the gaslights that lit it threw onto every wall silhouettes that made Tuesday inch closer to the bed. *You're sixteen*, she told herself. *You shouldn't be frightened of shadows.*

The rain didn't help. As it was a corner room, the rain pounded against the half-length windows; it sounded like fingernails skittering on the glass, and Tuesday was torn between wanting to throw the lacy curtains open to see what was out there and calling for Madame Marisol.

Instead, she forced her hands to cease their nervous picking at her hair and let her attention wander to the inside of the room. It held fewer horrors than the unknown outside, but fewer fascinations as well: just a chest of drawers, painted with pastel flowers, a hip bath beside it, a hopefully unused chamber pot, and a folding screen lacquered and inlaid with gold. The room had been painted in what Tuesday guessed was intended to be a sky blue, but the gaslight washed it out to a dull brown.

She continued her categorical exploration of the room until her eyes lighted on something flashing in the light of the flame: a mirror.

Tuesday dropped the sock and the blouse onto the bed and crossed over to the mirror, yelping when her feet hit the cold wooden floorboards at the edge of the room. The mirror was small, oval and framed in simple white, and the glass had a crack right through the middle that distorted the image, but Tuesday didn't care.

'Hello,' she said to her reflection. She traced the line of her brow, down her long nose, and brushed a finger across the three pale marks on her left cheek. They almost looked like fingerprints, but that couldn't be right.

The reflection's grey eyes narrowed and the nose scrunched up. She smiled to see that her mirror-self apparently shared her confusion.

The fingers ghosted across her face and absently tucked a strand of hair behind her ear. It was the colour of bark: a muddy brown with hints of gold that shone through in the gaslight, and long enough to reach her knees.

'You're not what I expected,' she commented to her reflection. A face flittered in the darkness of her memory, staring back at her with those same grey eyes, but otherwise so different to anything she saw before her.

'And what did you expect then, dearie?' came a voice.

Tuesday turned to find Madame Marisol standing at the open door, gazing at her indulgently. A blush worked its way up her mirror-self's cheeks. The image in her mind disappeared like a wisp of smoke.

'Nothing,' she said quickly. 'It doesn't matter.'

She *had* hoped that the moment she saw herself in the mirror, everything would suddenly click, and the blurred lines of her past would come together to form a picture of herself that she would recognise. But the girl standing before her was just as foreign as ever.

Her eyes fell to the floor in disappointment, so she didn't see Madame Marisol approach her until one hand lifted her chin with a strength Tuesday hadn't thought the old woman possessed. 'Do you want to hear a secret?'

Tuesday tried to turn away, but Madame Marisol's grip on her chin increased until she gave up and distracted herself with looking everywhere but Madame Marisol's face, because a traitorous dampness had begun to well in her eyes and the last thing she wanted was for her new friend to think she was ungrateful for the life she'd been given.

She didn't voice the thought, however, but simply nodded in response to Madame Marisol's question.

'You're everything you should be,' the woman whispered, leaning in so that their heads were almost touching, which gave Tuesday the feeling that she'd just been told something important.

'But ... I don't remember,' she attempted. 'I thought I would . . .'

'Don't, my love.' Madame Marisol's voice was firm. 'There is nothing in your past worth the trouble of looking back. Take this chance you've been given and live.'

Madame Marisol's hand abandoned her chin and came to rest on her naked shoulder, squeezing so tightly that Tuesday bit the inside of her mouth from the pain. '*Live*, child,' she said. 'There is no greater gift than that.'

Tuesday nodded, and absently rubbed at the pale marks on her cheek.

'I'm sorry about that,' Madame Marisol said, all business again. 'I'd hoped Quintalion would be careful, but sometimes these things happen. They'll be permanent, you mark my words, but if you want, I'll give you an ointment that'll get rid of the worst of the marking. Wouldn't want to spoil your pretty face.'

She's being kind, Tuesday thought as she gazed at herself over the top of Madame Marisol's head. The girl in the mirror was nothing extraordinary. If Tuesday had passed her on the road, she wouldn't have given her a second glance. But the marks . . .

they were at least something distinctive. 'Don't bother,' she said. 'I like them.'

'Wonderful.' Madame Marisol held up a pith helmet, which she'd been concealing behind her back. 'I don't suppose you'll need this. You're not planning on heading any expeditions, are you?'

Tuesday shrugged and walked back over to the bed and its pile of clothes. 'I don't know. Will I be?'

Madame Marisol threw the pith helmet over her shoulder – a loud crash out in the hall signalled that it had discovered something expensive to destroy – and began to wrestle a cape into a brown leather satchel on the bed. 'That's up to you, my love. You can go anywhere you like, though I'd recommend staying away from the daybreakers.'

'The what?' she asked, sorting through a series of increasingly flimsy shifts for one that wasn't made up of more lace than material.

'Daybreakers,' Madame Marisol returned promptly. 'They come from Voltemande, which explains a lot if you ask me: the country hasn't been right since they stopped banging their heads on rocks and discovered industry.'

'Oh,' Tuesday said, not sure what she was expected to say, but Madame Marisol carried on regardless.

'They're a band of thugs dedicated to wiping out the old ways – magic, Days, *me* if the truth be told. Very unpleasant. They smell, too.'

The lawn shift Madame Marisol slipped over Tuesday's head muffled her excited exclamation. *Magic!* It couldn't be possible. Tuesday pinched herself hard on her arm, expecting to be lost in one of her dreams of magicians and grand quests, but all she got for her trouble was a sore arm and a mouthful of material.

She spat it out and said, 'Magic? Really?'

Madame Marisol smiled at her. 'Of course. What do you think kept you asleep all those years?'

'I don't know,' she said, and then realised what her new friend had said. 'All those years . . . how long *was* I asleep?'

'Ten years, give or take a couple of months. But with the magic of the House here, it could have been a hundred for all you'd know.'

'Ten years,' she breathed. 'I never really thought about how . . . but real magic! What's it like?'

'Temperamental,' Madame Marisol replied promptly. She straightened the shift over Tuesday's shoulders and held out a pair of knee-length drawers for her to step into. 'It's like quicksilver. Many an amateur magician has lost his eyebrows from spells blowing up in his face. But most people don't hold by it anymore, in the east especially. You'd be hard-pressed to find more than a hundred conjurers in the land, and those that still practice magic have started to call themselves *thaumaturgists* to sound more modern.'

She buttoned the drawers in a particularly vicious way that told Tuesday exactly what she thought of these modern thaumaturgists.

Two petticoats followed the drawers, one for warmth and one for show, then whalebone stays that pinched and pushed in places that really shouldn't be pushed, and finally thick woollen stockings that had to be pulled on with Tuesday lying ramrod straight on the bed, as Madame Marisol had *forgotten the cardinal rule of dressing*.

'Stockings and shoes first, *then* stays,' she said, when Tuesday asked what the rule was. 'Saves a world of grief.'

The promised shoes quickly followed: a pair of stout grey kid boots that were a toe too long just in case Tuesday grew any more.

'Almost done,' Madame Marisol told her. 'You'll be fit for society.' She paused and added, 'Just avoid having any adventures, dear. Stays and adventures don't go so well together.'

Tuesday endured the prodding and the fussing without complaint, because her mind was already far away, through the rain bucketing against the windows, over the dales and out into the world. It was a blank map to her, but she filled it in with all the topographical delights that a life spent dreaming could conjure: mountains tall enough to touch the sky, caves so large that you could spend your entire life exploring them without ever seeing the light, houses made of trees, and rivers of every colour to dip her toes in.

Yes, she thought, remembering the words of the letter on the bed. *I could happily spend my days in discovery.*

But then a dark thought rained over her pleasant ones, turning the landscape of her mind cloudy and dull. 'What happened to me? What was so bad that I thought I couldn't escape?'

Madame Marisol stuck her head out of the wardrobe she was rummaging around in. 'Oh, my dear,' she said. 'I told you I didn't want you to think about that.'

'But it must have been bad, or else I wouldn't have come here.' The stays shifted in protest when Tuesday sat up on the bed, and she began to understand what Madame Marisol had said about them not going well with adventuring.

'It wasn't you, Tuesday dear. I need you to understand that. You began the moment you opened those pretty eyes of yours. Don't spend your days worrying about a stranger's life.'

She wanted to do what Madame Marisol asked of her, but the more she tried to forget the dreadful letter, the more the words echoed through her mind. *Funny*, she thought suddenly. *My life is a blank slate, yet I can remember those words perfectly.*

Madame Marisol pulled a light-blue travelling dress over Tuesday's head and made a great show of getting her up, tugging it down past her chest, fitting the belt properly, and checking that the three-quarter sleeves were wide enough not to be a bother.

She then ruched the dress up to her hips and tied what looked like a small pillow to her waist, turning the contraption around so that it rested against the top of her drawers.

'I believe a bustle is the fashion now,' Madame Marisol told her, giving it a final tug to situate it correctly before pulling the dress back down. The blue fabric puffed out at the back, away from her legs. 'But if not, you can just slip it off and use it as a pillow instead.'

As Madame Marisol scurried around her, tying up *this* cord or fastening *that* button, Tuesday leaned over and picked up the letter, and stared at it as though she could unlock its secrets by sheer willpower. Nothing was crossed out, so she'd obviously been thinking of what to say for some time, but the words were blotched and messy, as if she'd been in a hurry to get them down on paper. What could have made her rush through the most important letter of her life? Especially if, as Tuesday assumed, she'd written it in the safety of Madame Marisol's House.

She had to know more. That was all there was to it. A deep hole existed inside her, and nothing would fill it but the knowledge of her old life. She felt like a husk, empty and insubstantial, and if she weren't careful, a strong wind would blow her away.

'No,' she whispered to herself. 'I am Tuesday. I won't just disappear.'

'Of course you won't, my dear.' Madame Marisol produced a pair of silver scissors from the chain on her belt and began to slice chunks of Tuesday's hair off, humming a tuneless ditty as the tresses fell away.

Tuesday snatched out a hand to catch a lock and rolled the spray of hair back and forth between her fingers, frowning as she did so. She'd only just formed a picture of herself, and now it was being changed into someone else's idea of her, like the stays and the stockings when she'd rather just stay bare. *Is this what it will always be like? Am I a blank canvas?*

The last bit of hair drifted down through the air, brushed up against Tuesday's knee, and stubbornly clung to the fabric with such tenacity that she almost felt bad for brushing it aside. She grasped her remaining hair to find it shorn to just below her shoulders, but then Madame Marisol gently moved her questing hand and started to twist and pull at her hair until tears came to Tuesday's eyes.

'There,' Madame Marisol said, guiding her over to the mirror. 'You're done.'

And so Tuesday, who had never been clothed in so much as a sock, now found herself trussed up, itching and ramrod straight. The girl peering out at her from the mirror wasn't the same girl she'd seen earlier that night. Tuesday stared at herself, desperately hoping for some speck of familiarity, but there was nothing. Then her eyes caught the three white marks on her cheek and she smiled.

'I'm still Tuesday,' she said.

'Of course you are,' Madame Marisol replied, and for the first time Tuesday had the distinct feeling that Madame Marisol was only listening to the things she wanted to hear.

She watched, her camisole sleeve slipping down her shoulder and her boots nipping at her ankles, as Madame Marisol handed her the bag she had been holding. It was small, just a satchel with long thin straps.

'There's a cape for the cold weather, and some money.' Madame Marisol pulled out a small pouch and spilled its contents across her palm. Gold and silver coins sparkled in the lamplight, along with a generous helping of dust and lint, which she blew away with an embarrassed cough. 'The golds are helions, and worth more than the luns, which are –'

'The silvers,' Tuesday interrupted, picking up one of each. The helion had the face of a man stamped into it, staring directly at her, while the lun had the aspect of a woman, half her face hidden in darkness. On the other side of the helion was a sun, and on the lun, a moon.

'Just so. They were minted back when the Days were still in power, so places like Voltemande and Tantallon won't have a bar of them.' Madame Marisol emptied the coins from her palm back into the pouch and then held her hand out for Tuesday's. 'But they'll be honoured by any countries that still cling to the old ways – mostly west of Tantallon, and some of the borderlands – so I think you'll have enough to start yourself up somewhere nice and safe. Mind you, if you get any change, it's likely to be local, so make sure you spend it before you cross any borders.'

Tuesday's confusion must have shown on her face, because Madame Marisol added, 'Just ask Quintalion if you get stuck, duckie. He'll have no qualms about spending your money for you.'

She dropped the last two coins into the pouch and replaced it in the satchel, which she slipped over Tuesday's head so that it rested comfortably across her shoulders. 'Speaking of Quintalion, we'd better be going before he beats down my front door.'

'Quintalion?' she asked, remembering that Madame Marisol had spoken that name earlier in the evening. It sounded foreign on her tongue.

'He's the one who woke you, dear.' Madame Marisol fiddled with the strap of Tuesday's satchel. 'He's charged with escorting you safely to wherever you wish to go. I'd suggest Ormonde. It's lovely this time of year, and about as westerly as you can get, so the daybreakers won't be bothering you.'

Tuesday peered out of the window into the darkness beyond. The storm was passing, but it was still too dark to make out much beyond the indistinct plains. 'What am I to do out there?'

'Find somewhere safe and enjoy your new life, of course. Travel, learn a trade, find a house and live in it until you're as old as I am. The world is before yo–'

Her words were interrupted by a bell, ringing deep in the bowels of the House. Below them came the sound of footsteps and then the crash of a door being opened, closed and then opened once more in rapid succession.

Tuesday remembered what Madame Marisol had said. 'This Quintalion . . . he's strong enough to beat down your front door?'

Madame Marisol laughed, a fruity sound that came from deep inside her. 'No, but he might well talk it open. Either way, the House thinks it's time for you to be off, so we must make haste.'

*

They arrived downstairs to find the front door perfectly safe, and a man Tuesday assumed was Quintalion pacing back and forth in front of it. He appeared to be in his early thirties, though Tuesday knew she probably wasn't fantastic at guessing ages, seeing as she'd only learned her own a couple of hours ago.

He wore an emerald-green waistcoat, with golden threads woven into it in a pattern of figure eights, brown leather trousers cut high at his waist, a white shirt and cravat, black-and-brown boots up to his knees, all of which was swamped by the blue woollen greatcoat he'd shrugged on over his shoulders. He was the most elegant thing she'd ever seen.

'I thought I heard bells,' he said by way of greeting. 'Surely it's not dawn yet? Even so, I find myself with the greatest desire to leave. Now.'

'Whoever came up with such a bothersome method for keeping time deserves my foot on their britches,' Madame Marisol remarked. 'But you're right – you two should go. Though it wouldn't be proper without an introduction first.'

Madame Marisol manoeuvred Tuesday, who was still clumsy in her new boots, over to Quintalion and placed her directly in front of him.

'Tuesday,' she said, 'this is Quintalion. He's going to be looking after you for a while.' She shot him a look that matched the thunderclouds outside. 'And he knows what he's going to get if he doesn't.'

‘I can imagine it’s pointy and unpleasant,’ Quintalion said. He bowed straight from the hip in an abrupt motion that had Tuesday skittering back so he wouldn’t smack his head into hers, and then, coming out of his bow, met her gaze for the first time. His eyes narrowed.

Tuesday dropped her eyes and fiddled with the straps of her bag. His stare went right through her. She didn’t know why he was looking at her as though she’d said something rude, but the air seemed to grow cooler between them as the seconds stretched out and he kept staring with those strange mismatched eyes.

But then the moment passed and Quintalion smiled at her instead. ‘Might I just say what an honour it is to meet you.’

‘Tuesday,’ she said, still shaken from his silent scrutiny. ‘My name is Tuesday.’

‘I know,’ he replied swiftly, extending his arm to her. ‘Shall we be off?’

Tuesday slid a hand into the satchel. She’d slipped the letter inside an inner pocket when Madame Marisol hadn’t been looking, since she hadn’t been certain how she would react if Tuesday asked outright to keep it, and she had no wish to insult her only friend. The smooth paper crackled against her fingers, and she imagined she could feel the velvet green ink.

With Madame Marisol’s gentle encouragement and the knowledge of the letter bolstering her courage, she took Quintalion’s offered arm and walked with him to the door. The rain seemed to be letting up, though there was no sign of the dawn he had spoken of through the floor-to-ceiling windows on either side of the door. The light from the entrance hall only extended several feet out, painting the veranda in dancing shades of browns and golds, and the world could have ended after the front steps for all Tuesday could see.

Madame Marisol followed them to the door, but before she opened it, she turned and did something Tuesday hadn't been expecting: she threw her arms around her and squeezed her tightly in a hug. Tuesday stood there awkwardly for a couple of seconds and then closed her arms around Madame Marisol, who was soft and warm. White lace tickled Tuesday's nose where she rested her head against the woman's neck, bent over awkwardly to accommodate their difference in size. She had a fleeting desire to stay with her forever, but then Madame Marisol withdrew from the hug, patted her hand and said: 'I'm sorry, my love. I'm not usually so weepy when my babies leave. And you'll be fine. I know it.'

'How do you know?' Tuesday asked.

Madame Marisol whipped a handkerchief out of her sleeve and made a great show of dabbing her eyes, before saying, 'My House is where you take those who have no hope, be it of life or love or both. It is a graveyard, filled with sleeping souls – most of whom never wake again. But *you* did, my sweet, though you never expected to. And that is why you'll do wonders.'

'Thank you,' Tuesday whispered, hugging her again. She inhaled into Madame Marisol's cardigan: she wanted to remember everything about her, like the way she smelled of talcum powder, every crease in her face, and her softness as she embraced Tuesday back. *I'll tuck every inch of you away in my heart.*

'I'll never forget you,' she said out loud. 'I promise.'

'And I won't forget you.'

It *was* a promise, a covenant, and as Tuesday squeezed Madame Marisol's hand one final time, she thanked whatever gods there were that they had sent someone to watch over her.

Then Madame Marisol pressed a packet of something into her hand and whispered, 'If you ever need help or just want to talk, brew some of this tea and think of me. We'll meet in our dreams.'

Tuesday wrapped her fingers around the packet and nodded into Madame Marisol's wispy hair. 'Thank you,' she said, and meant it. 'I will.'

Quintalion coughed pointedly, and just like that the moment was over.

Madame Marisol broke away from Tuesday with a little sniff, and marched over to Quintalion, staring up at him with such ferocity that he stepped back, still towering over her. 'Don't hurt her,' she said to him.

Quintalion's eyes flicked from Tuesday to the door and then back to Madame Marisol. 'I have no intention of doing anything of the sort.'

'Good,' Madame Marisol replied cheerfully. 'Because if you do and I find out, no amount of sweet words will stop me from ripping your tongue out, so help me Days. Do you understand?'

'Fully and painfully.' Quintalion's hand brushed the skin at his jaw, which he wriggled from side to side as if testing whether his tongue was still there. Then he held out his right hand for Madame Marisol to shake. 'Fare you well, Madame. Thank you for your unparalleled hospitality.'

Madame Marisol looked at him like he'd stepped in something foul-smelling, but begrudgingly took his offered hand. 'Yes, well, you've got the rifle to look forward to if you ever come back.'

'I wouldn't dream of it.' He clasped her arm and then slid his left hand down in an enthusiastic double handshake. When he broke it off, something small and white disappeared into the sleeve of his greatcoat, before he smiled at Tuesday and said, 'After you, girl.'

It's Tuesday, she said silently, and then looked to Madame Marisol for permission before slipping the package of tea into her satchel, grasping the door handle, which was cold from the early morning air, and turning.

Fresh air swept past her. She drank it in, sucked it deeply into her lungs, where it filled her with so much excitement that there was no longer room for fear. A fierce wind blew a trail of leaves into the House and tangled the skirts of her dress around her ankles. It brought with it a tangy, bitter scent that Tuesday breathed in so wholeheartedly that her mouth began to taste of the rain. Before she even had time to think, she grabbed the lit lantern by the door and ran out into the darkness.

Tuesday didn't know where to look. At first she tried to point the lantern everywhere at once, but that just left trails of light dancing behind her eyelids, so she forced herself to slow down and take things in one at a time. The flowers in the garden were a riot of colour, blues and oranges and yellows all mixed together, but the lone tree by the fence around the House also commanded her attention, as did the gentle mist of the rainstorm retreating to the west, and the sky, which remained dark and impenetrable, no matter how high she raised the lantern.

'It's perfect,' she finally said.

'Good,' Quintalion cut in, 'because you're going to get a lot more of it where we're going.'

'Oh,' Tuesday said, turning back to him, 'and where is that?'

The lantern cast shadows about his dark face as he loomed over Madame Marisol on the veranda. 'Out into the wild world.'

CHAPTER FOUR

As it happened, *the wild world* seemed to be composed entirely of ankle-deep mud that took an almost gleeful pride in swallowing boots.

Quintalion had barely spoken to her since they'd left Madame Marisol's House, preferring to tramp along in front of her with his shoulders shrugged up against the cold and his wide-brimmed hat pushed down low over his face.

She didn't yet know what she thought of him. Madame Marisol trusted him enough to let her leave with him, yet she'd made no secret of her disdain for him in the veiled looks and sugary-sweet comments. *Should I follow suit?* she wondered. *Or would it be smarter to play along?* Madame Marisol had promised a painful death if he hurt her, but that didn't mean he wouldn't just run off and leave the rest of the world to do the hurting.

Would it be so bad if he did? There were a hundred new discoveries to occupy her while she mulled the thought over: the grass beside her as she walked was the most delicate shade of lavender; each bristle scratched and tickled at her skin as she trailed a hand through the stalks; her boots left imprints in the mud for other travellers to read her journey; the wind whistled around them in such a haunting melody that the first time she heard it she spun around, certain that they were surrounded by some kind of mysterious nocturnal musicians; and, finally, an orange light broke up the darkness of the night sky.

'What's that?' she asked Quintalion, pointing to the glow.

'That felicitous light,' he said as he stopped so that she could draw even with him, 'is civilisation. Beggars End, to be precise. Somewhere I have absolutely no desire to end up, if you want the unequivocal truth.'

'What's so bad about it?' She bent down to rescue one of her calfskin boots for what felt like the four-hundredth time. The mud had turned the leather a dingy brown, which consequently turned *Tuesday* a dingy brown as she tried to scrape it off, making her feel glad that she wouldn't have to explain to Madame Marisol how she'd managed to get filthy so quickly.

Quintalion lowered the lantern for her until she'd finished scraping off her boots, though she didn't need the flame so much anymore, for a pale light streaked across the eastern skies. 'Let's just say that I've made a couple of friends there who would very much like to run into me again.'

'Well then, we should go. I'm sure it would be nice to see them.' She'd been holding her petticoats up out of the way with one hand, but now she let them fall again, and shook her many layers back into place.

Quintalion strode forward, saying over his shoulder: 'No, I don't think you understand. If I happened to see these particular friends again, they would be the last things I *would* see.'

She frowned as she hurried along behind him; he was taller than her and his stride ate up the miles. 'Why?' she asked. 'You're not sick, are you?'

He barked out a laugh. 'You really are the most infuriatingly obtuse girl.'

She understood the words, but she'd never heard them placed together in such a fashion – they gave her the feeling that she was being insulted. 'I'm not!' she replied hotly.

'That invitation could have been for anyone – kings, heroes, dashingly charming scions of an ancient house. But no,' he gesticulated wildly, almost smacking Tuesday in the head, 'I have the greatest luck to draw you from the proverbial barrel.'

He made one last violent gesture, pointing at Tuesday with a vigour that shook his greatcoat and caused a small card to slide out of his sleeve and flutter into the mud.

Wanting to save it from her boots' fate, Tuesday snatched it up before it hit the ground.

'Leave it!' Quintalion cried.

But it was too late. She'd already glanced down at the card in her hand. It was a little larger than her palm and bordered in gold. She read the words eagerly and then flipped the card over, still not completely understanding but realising that it was important. *Wake me when it's safe.*

It was in the same looping handwriting as her letter. Excitement shortened her breaths as she smoothed the green ink. 'This is mine,' she said. 'From before.'

Quintalion snatched the card out of her hand. 'Well, that's very interesting, but I don't see why you need to give it any more thought.'

Had they known each other before the darkness of the keeping-house? She had obviously trusted him enough to wake her up. Had he stolen the invitation from whoever its owner was? Or perhaps the bearer had cared so little about her welfare that they had given the card over to Quintalion's trust.

She chewed at her lip and watched Quintalion hide the invitation back in his greatcoat. She would have liked to look at it for longer, but he had already started walking again, so she hurried along to catch him up. 'If I wrote that,' she said, 'why did I ask you to wake me when it was safe? Is it not?'

He drew the lantern up so that it was level with his chin; the flames dancing around his face. 'Not for people like us.'

The wind howled through the grass. The storm now lay behind them, in the west, but the threat of rain still hung heavy in the air. She shivered. 'What do you mean?'

Quintalion turned away from her and continued on down the path, tossing a single word over his shoulder: 'Daybreakers.'

'Daybreakers?' she whispered. 'Madame Marisol said they were bad. They want to destroy the old ways. But what could they want with me?'

'Oh, I don't know,' Quintalion said, his tone light. 'There's the fact that you've just woken from slumber in a *magical* House run by a woman they've been wanting to get their hands on for years –'

'I'd never betray her!' Tuesday burst out.

'Perhaps you wouldn't – at first.' Quintalion shrugged. 'But I've seen what's left behind after they're finished with a person. I know what they do. If you're lucky and they don't want any information out of you, they'll break your neck first: give you a quick death. If you're not – and believe me, you won't be – it'll be the fingers first, then the toes. They don't want to start on something big, you see . . . people have an annoying tendency of dying too quickly that way.'

The pale lights of Beggars End silhouetted him as he turned on his heel and advanced on her, his mismatched eyes bright in the shadows. She took a step back.

'The legs next, hobbled with mallets usually, but sometimes dragged behind their iron airships if they really take a disliking to you. Most people crack at this point; spill all their secrets to listening ears and die with words of thanks upon their lips. But the stubborn ones stay their tongues. Are you stubborn, Tuesday?'

Tuesday had been lost in the story of pain and desperation, and so she flinched to find Quintalion's face not an inch from her own. She leaned as far back from him as she could without falling into the long grasses behind her. 'I . . . I don't know.'

'Pray to the Days that you're not,' he continued. 'Pray that you give the daybreakers all they want to know. Because if you don't, it'll be the arms next. They'll break the bones at the elbow and wrists.' His cold fingers brushed against her wrist and when she recoiled from him in horror, he laughed.

'That's not the worst of it,' he said. 'The daybreakers will leave you after that, for a day or an hour until they come for you again. Leave you with your fears and the knowledge of your fate.'

He was staring past her face now and into the darkness beyond the circle of light that the lantern provided. Though he kept his words light and conversational, Tuesday had the feeling that he wasn't speaking to her anymore.

'When they return,' he continued, 'the fun really starts. The ribs will be the first, each one shattered with an expertly placed punch, or perhaps one of their new steam-driven devices. Oh, the shoulder or a hipbone might be next, but by now you're already dead. See, a good punch will smash your ribs inwards:

into your heart, your lung. Death is slow but certain at this point. I once heard a man choke on his own blood for an hour before he finally died.'

His gaze shifted back to her face and his mouth curled upward into the ghastly parody of a grin. 'Or sometimes,' he said, 'if they're feeling particularly lazy, they'll just shoot you.'

Her heart thudded in her chest. The darkness loomed up at them. She wanted to run back to Madame Marisol's House and throw herself under the bedcovers. She wanted to find the daybreakers and destroy them, to break them like they'd broken so many others. But all she did was let out the breath she'd been holding and whisper, 'How do you know?'

She already knew the answer – she'd guessed the truth halfway through Quintalion's terrible story – but it didn't prepare her for what he did next.

Quintalion silently lowered the lantern to the ground, stepped back, and held out his right hand. The two smallest fingers were a knot of scar tissue.

'They . . . they did that to you? They hurt you?'

He raised an eyebrow. 'They tried, before I taught them that those of the old ways also know how to be cruel. And our methods are not half so civilised.'

'Good,' she said, and balled her hands into fists. 'They deserved it. Someone should break *their* bones.'

Quintalion barked out a laugh. 'And I suppose you're the one to do it. No, girl. If you have any sense in you at all, you'll stay far away from them. Set yourself up somewhere safe, if any place can earn the name. I'll even take you there myself. Call it charity.'

It was almost exactly what Madame Marisol had told her to do, and yet she shook her head in disgust. She'd barely seen anything of the world, and now she was expected just to find somewhere, some hole to hide in and never come out again? She *couldn't* . . . not when she longed to follow the road ahead as far as it would take her and beyond. 'No,' she told him.

'No?' he said in disbelief. 'Understand that I'm under no obligation to take you *anywhere*, so I'd think twice before rejecting my offer. You're unlikely to find a better protector.'

She narrowed her eyes at him. 'Why should I believe you?'

'Because, despite my claims to the contrary, you're not stupid.' He picked the lantern up and swung it in the direction of Beggars End. 'With the daybreakers patrolling the border towns, you've got about as much chance of making it to safety as there is of a Saqiran walking away from a fight. That is to say: none.'

'So you'll take me wherever I want to go?' Possibilities had begun to swirl around the edges of her horizon. She could travel to the furthest edges of the map – could see the world – and with Quintalion protecting her, the daybreakers wouldn't be able to hurt her.

'Hold up there. I didn't promise that,' Quintalion said. 'As far as I'm concerned, letting you tag along with me is charity, and charity is very much not my style. Name a town and I'll take you there, but unless you can make it worth my while, that's where you and I part ways.'

He rubbed his fingers together to demonstrate his point.

Tuesday wondered whether he was cold or possibly just trying to snap his fingers.

'Huh?'

'I may,' he said slowly, 'be revising my earlier estimation of your intelligence.'

She suddenly realised what he was talking about, and dug around in her satchel to pull out the purse of coins that Madame Marisol had given her. 'I've got this,' she said, breathless with triumph. 'If you keep me safe from the daybreakers and take me where I want to go, I'll give it to you.'

'A purse,' he replied. 'A *small* purse.'

Her fingers were stiff from the cold, which caused her to fumble with the drawstrings, but eventually she untangled the knots and tipped a handful of the coins into the palm of her hand. 'I don't know what these are worth, but if it's not enough, I'm sure I could ask Madame Marisol for more. She'd give me more. I know she would. She wouldn't want the daybreakers to get me.'

Quintalion's eyes followed the coins sparkling in the lantern light. 'I'm wounded that you would think me so easily bought.'

She shook out a few more coins from the purse.

Quintalion's hand darted out and he snatched one of the coins and bit it between his teeth twice before saying, 'You've got yourself a deal. Give me that handful now and the rest later, and I'll protect you from all the daybreakers you could wish for.'

None, Tuesday thought. She gave the rest of the coins in her hand to Quintalion, who quickly dropped them into a pocket in his vest and bowed to her.

'You,' he said, 'have engaged the services of Quintalion: rogue, swindler, pickpocket extraordinaire, with more lives than a whole litter of cats, be they black, mottled or otherwise.'

'Insufferable blowhard.' She didn't know where that had come from; the words slipped out of her before she could stop them. She turned to Quintalion, ready to apologise, but he raised his hands to silence her before she had the chance.

'Was that . . . attitude? It was, wasn't it.' He shook his head and covered the lower half of his face with one of his big hands, but Tuesday still caught the smile before he hid it away. 'This job might not be completely dull, after all. So, she of the hidden depths, where are we off to first?'

It was a good question. But without a map to consult, Tuesday found herself utterly unable to answer it.

'Come on, come on.' He snapped his fingers at her. 'The bells for dawn will ring. I have no desire for the de Kena to find us wandering their territory. Their methods of execution might not be as cruel as the daybreakers', but they're far more inventive.'

'Beggars End.' Tuesday blurted out the first name that came to mind. 'I want to see it. Will you take me there?'

'Are your ears still asleep?' he said, with a flourish of the lantern for emphasis. 'I thought I told you that going there was a bad idea.'

'No, what you said was that you have no desire to end up there, but *I* do.' She started to walk again, moving forward with a confident stride. A half-lit dawn, however, was less than conducive for assured striding, and she stumbled more times than she would have liked before Quintalion caught up to her.

When she flicked her gaze to his face she saw the conflict storming in his eyes. She could guess what he was thinking. Beggars End was dangerous, she believed him when he said that. But if he left her now, he'd be forfeiting their agreement, and that would mean giving back the gold.

He struggled for a few more moments and then the clink of gold in his pocket won out. 'Fine. To Beggars End we go.'

CHAPTER FIVE

The wall stretched as high as the sky. Tuesday stood with her hand pressed against the stone, marvelling at how the blocks fitted together with barely a groove between them. The morning sun had not been out long enough to warm the stone and, standing in its imposing shadow, Tuesday shivered.

She rested her ear against the wall, ignoring the chill, and listened. Somewhere deep inside came the sounds of a city waking up: the muted voices of people still half-asleep, the soft thud of shutters being removed from shop windows, the low rumble of early morning carts being driven through the streets.

'Listen to this,' she told Quintalion, smiling at the sounds of life.

Quintalion, however, marched right up to the gates and gave them a swift kick. 'Hey!' he shouted, and craned his head far back to look up at the top of the wall. 'Open the gates.'

Tuesday stepped away from the wall and joined him. The gates were made out of logs of strong dark wood stacked horizontally on top of each other and reinforced with vertical strips of metal that didn't seem entirely necessary, but were probably there to give intruders pause before they attempted entry. They certainly gave Tuesday pause. 'Do you really think you should yell like that?'

Quintalion withdrew his leg. 'The gates come up when the bells ring for dawn. Well, the sun has graced us with its presence and yet we find ourselves without either bell or entry, which gives me reason to believe that the guardsmen are shirking their duties.' These last three words he shouted for the benefit of the apparent guardsmen, though Tuesday couldn't see anyone standing at the top of the wall, no matter how far back she craned her neck.

'You're wasting your time.' The voice came from a pile of rags that Tuesday had assumed was rubbish thrown from the ramparts until it sat up and rearranged itself into a spindly-armed man, a tin cup quickly appearing in front of him.

'Oh, we are, are we?' Quintalion said. 'And how, in all your wisdom, do you know that? Are you a seer? A great magician? Fortune has clearly been good to you for you to end up here.'

Tuesday could have cut through the sarcasm with a knife, and was about to apologise when the man shrugged and said, 'Nah. I just heard the guards talking is all.'

He wiped his dripping nose on the back of an arm and nudged the tin cup conspicuously. 'If you can spare a brass or two, I'll tell you why.'

Ignoring Quintalion's dark look, Tuesday took her purse out and shook a couple of the coins into her hand. She tipped them into the man's cup and watched as he stared down into it with wide eyes.

'Two helions and a lun?' he said incredulously. He bit down on one of the helions and, seemingly satisfied in its authenticity, doffed his cap at Tuesday. 'Thank you, miss. I'll dine well on these for the next week. Pork pies, roasted pigeon, and some of those pastries with the little fiddly bits of crusting on the top . . .'

'Less recipe, more information,' Quintalion said. 'Or I'd be happy to take them back and hire someone to kill you messily instead. I wonder how roasted tramp tastes.'

'All right, all right,' the beggar said, and the coins magically disappeared into the folds of his rags. 'There was another attack last night . . . from over there.' He nodded in the direction of the Whispering Plains to the west. 'The patriarch has ordered all but the South Gate closed. Travellers have to show their papers upon entry as well. He didn't half choose a bad time for it, what with the Feast of the Ashes tonight.'

'Thank you,' Quintalion replied, and then turned to Tuesday, drawing his arm around her and leading her away from the beggar, who settled back against the wall.

'This might be a problem,' he told her. 'I bought my papers in Jyn: very well done, seal in place and lettering to die for. The forger is one of the best I've ever known. Pity he's dead. But you, my little sleeping beauty –'

'Papers?' She'd been following the conversation feeling more and more lost, so she said the first word she'd caught on to.

Quintalion took a deep breath. 'Seven sisters,' he muttered, 'but I forget how much you don't know. The Saturday Wars divided this land of ours straight down the middle: the west to those who still follow the old ways, and the east to those in favour of, well, brutally killing everyone who still follows the old ways.'

'The daybreakers,' Tuesday guessed, earning a nod from Quintalion.

'Among others . . . though most of the countries are thankfully keener on modernisation than murdering. But with modernisation comes bureaucracy and –'

'Papers,' she finished, feeling a little like a broken music box, always playing the same tune. She reached into her satchel and pulled out her letter. 'I have papers here, if they'll help. Or the invitation. Surely that will explain everything.'

Quintalion threw a look over his shoulder at the tramp, who was now noisily recounting his culinary plans to a stray robin that had happened to alight on a nearby stalk of grass. 'Lower your voice. Even the walls have ears here.'

'They do?' She looked past Quintalion to the great walled city of Beggars End beyond, which, if its outside was anything to go by, could have heard a lark's cry a thousand leagues away.

'Of course.' He led her away from the beggar and along the path in the shadow of the wall. 'Now what's that bit of paper you have there?'

Lowering her voice, she said: 'It's a letter that I wrote to myself. I mean, before I was . . . well, what I mean to say is . . .'

'You wrote it to your future self before you went to sleep. I get the basic conceit,' Quintalion said. 'And if you have any sense in that head of yours, you'll never show that letter to another soul.'

'Why not?' she replied. 'If I show it to the guards, they'll have proof of who I am and they'll let me in.'

'And hand you straight over to any nearby daybreakers,' Quintalion said darkly. 'Beggars End is far more tolerant of the old ways than some cities, but a letter and invitation from the Unreality House itself skirts past tolerance and into wilful ignorance. No, I think the only way we're getting in is with a little bit of ingenuity.'

They walked onwards, leaving the gate behind. At first they walked in silence, with little to disturb them but the wind through the grass and the chirps of birds as they woke for the day, but as they went further south, Tuesday began to hear voices, laughter and the creak of carts.

When they rounded the corner, the crowd appeared. They travelled on foot and in wagons drawn by oxen, on horseback, or by palanquin, and wore clothes of every colour and type: dresses with hems trailing in the dust, breeches and coarse shirts, ruffs starched and standing to attention, and even clothes made out of grass and shells.

'So what's your plan?' Tuesday asked as she pushed her way closer to the large South Gate.

Quintalion nudged someone out of the way with his elbow. 'Not a plan so much as some good old-fashioned bribery.'

The rest of the crowd pushed in around them, growing larger by the second, and soon Tuesday found herself pressed with her hands up against the wall of the city.

'Keep close to me,' Quintalion said in her ear. 'I'm not being paid to let you get yourself squished against the wall.'

'Can that actually happen?'

'It can and it has,' he told her, tucking her behind him so that he took the brunt of the crowd's jostling. 'And it's the Feast of the Ashes today. That always draws in a big crowd.'

'The Feast of the Ashes?' She had been curious when the beggar had first mentioned it, but Quintalion had drawn her away before she could ask him.

'An old superstition,' he said, and shoved a farmer to their right out of the way, ignoring the man's loud cursing. 'Every year people gather here to record who they are on special pieces of paper. Then they burn the paper.'

'Why?' she asked him.

She felt him shrug against her. 'It started as a prayer to the Days. *This is who I am and I'd really like to stay this way for the next year, if you don't mind*, sort of thing. Back when you were liable to get a poleaxe in the eye just because you looked twice at your neighbour's cabbage, it was probably as good a safety measure as any.'

'Who are the Days?' Something stirred in her memory before being pulled back under the murky waters of her past.

'Seven sisters, girl,' Quintalion spat out. 'Madame Marisol said you'd know the basics, but clearly she was being optimistic. The Days are the gods of this land . . . or, at least, they were.'

She felt like a tree left too long without water, absorbing all this new information and yet still thirsty for more. 'Really? What were they like?'

Quintalion shot her an incredulous look. 'You think someone like me cavorted with gods? Flattering.'

'Their names, at least,' she said. She was keen to learn all she could about the world she'd woken into, and gods had to be a pretty big part of that. Perhaps they could even help her on her travels. Gods and goddesses were always interfering with the lives of mortals in the stories she remembered being read.

Shoving someone else out of the way, Quintalion sucked in a breath. At first he looked like he wasn't going to tell her, but then he quietly said, 'Minden was the patron of knowledge, of the old ways especially. Thaïs watched over the travellers. Wenslas, who was a barrel of laughs, so I've been told,' he added, sarcastically, 'was the patron of tears and the sea. His twin sister, Thestia, watched over warriors and the home.'

'A strange combination,' Tuesday remarked.

'You'd be surprised how often the two correspond. Frey was the patroness of the very old and the very young. Mourners still invoke her name at funerals. Satyr . . .' he paused and cleared his throat, straightening his greatcoat. 'Satyr was the god of all that's wild. And the youngest was Sannen, who encouraged industry and invention. Voltemande loved him, as you can imagine. He's the only one of the Days they didn't want to destroy. I'll bet you can still find a couple of old artisans in Voltemande with flints in their pockets that have been blessed in his forge. So there, that's the Days. Meddling do-gooders, the lot of them.'

Something that he had said disturbed her. 'You said that they *were* the patrons of all those things. What are they doing now?'

'Who knows?' He grabbed Tuesday's arms and pulled her away from where she'd been about to step in a pile of droppings. 'They disappeared. No one's seen them in a hundred years. But they'd fallen out of fashion long before that. The people changed, as people do. They started getting *ideas*.'

The way he spat out the word made it clear just what Quintalion thought of ideas. He continued: 'It started with murmurings – that the Days were oppressive, were purposely holding them back. Then came the mobs and the riots, and the sword through the rising sun. Voltemande broke away first, to no one's surprise. They had their mechanisms and fires and industry; they had no need of the old ways. Tantallon followed, as it always does, and its principalities, and then before you knew it there was a war.'

‘The Saturday Wars,’ she breathed.

‘Indeed,’ he replied. ‘War is all I remember. Old ways against new and everyone dying the same no matter what they believed in. Fantastic for graverobbers and soldiers, but not so great for anyone else. In the end, the Days were forced to take desperate measures to stop it. And for the past twenty years or so, it seems that everyone’s decided to just draw a big line down the middle of the land and ignore each other.’

Tuesday glanced to her left. For a moment she expected to see a black line running across the countryside, but then she was beginning to understand that people didn’t always mean what they said. ‘Does it work?’

‘Yes, for the most part. Nobody wants a repeat of the Saturday Wars. The old ways to the west and the new to the east, and never the two shall meet,’ he said in a singsong voice. ‘But Beggars End just happens to be in the borderlands, and borderlands are messy.’

‘You’ll get us in, though, won’t you?’

‘Of course,’ Quintalion replied. ‘It’ll be a walk in the park.’

*

‘Absolutely not,’ the guard said, scratching the tip of his nose with his cudgel. ‘I let you in, and soon half the city’s gold is missing and you’re tearing off into the distance on a suspiciously heavy wagon.’

‘*Half* the gold?’ Quintalion said with an eyebrow raised.

The bells were ringing for dawn, great peals of sound, and the crowd had surged forward. The guard shook his head and moved Quintalion out of the way, nudging him over into the mud at the side of the track.

'And as for you, miss.' The guard turned to Tuesday, who had kept silent during the exchange. He was taller even than Quintalion, with a mess of red hair that stood straight up from his head as though he'd just been struck by lightning, but his broad face was kind.

'What kind of scam has he got you involved in, eh? The Corte Shuffle, the Serpent with Two Heads? Judging by the state of you,' he added, gesturing to her mud-stained hem, 'I'd say you were going for the Forlorn Beggars and Their Box of Tricks, but as I can't see a unicycle, dog or accordion, you're making a pretty poor showing of it.'

Most of the words the guard said went completely over Tuesday's head, so she latched on to his general meaning. 'Not a scam, sir,' she said. 'I just want to get into the city, please. You see, I just woke up from being asleep for –'

'Three days,' Quintalion interrupted. 'She's a heavy sleeper. We're working on it. Anyway, what would you say to letting me and the girl into your fair city?'

'I'd say no,' he replied, and shifted his gaze back out over the rest of the crowd, who were rapidly entering the city before the gates had even been fully raised.

'Of course you would.' Quintalion sidled up to the guard and only just managed to avoid a cudgel to the back of the head. 'But perhaps, Peytar Botwright, you could just turn your back for a moment and the problem would go away. Your beautiful wife and your little babe at home would appreciate it, I've no doubt. It was a girl, was it not?'

The guard's eyes flashed, dark and dangerous. When he spoke, it was a whisper, but he said the four words with such intensity that Tuesday could still hear him: 'Is that a threat?'

'I wouldn't dream of it.' Quintalion held his ground, even though Peytar's face was inches from his own. 'Of course, a few words from me, and it could be. A promise, even. A captain of the guard makes a lot of enemies.'

'Leave.' The vein at Peytar's forehead pulsed.

Quintalion stared up at the guard. Tuesday could feel the tension, thick in the morning air. It was obvious that neither of them was going to back down, so Tuesday, not wanting to start a fight, tugged on Quintalion's arm to get him to move.

'C'mon. I don't need to see Beggars End. We can go somewhere else. Ormonde, maybe.'

'Get out of here,' Peytar said to them, his voice quiet. 'Just leave.'

Quintalion, however, seemed to have no intention of leaving. He stood staring down Peytar, who didn't give an inch, and Tuesday was forced to drop her entire weight onto Quintalion's arm before she could half-drag him away.

'It *had* to be Peytar Botwright on duty,' he muttered. 'At a hint of gold, any other guard would have let us into the city with open arms, but I have the misbegotten luck to get the only honest one of the lot.'

'Would you really have hurt his wife?' she asked him when she'd successfully steered him over to the side of the road.

'Of course not, but that's not the point.' He took a deep breath and the tension seemed to leave his body in one long stretch. 'If you take to heart anything that I say, girl, let it be this: words have power. More than anything in the world, in fact. A man can be the most hideous thing that's ever slithered out into the midwife's arms, but until you let him know it, he'll just continue on his miserable existence in ignorant bliss. For example . . .'

Before Tuesday could reply, Quintalion took two quick steps away from her and patted the shoulder of a man waiting in line who was dressed in leathers and had a long, sharp face. 'Excuse me,' he said, 'but I just heard that farmer there call you a filthy horse-loving savage.'

'*What?!*' The man's face turned red. He strode over to the man Quintalion had pointed at, a farmer drawing a cow along on a threadbare rope, and, without another word, punched him directly in the middle of his pockmarked face.

The farmer clutched his nose, stared at the man as though he couldn't believe what was happening, and then launched himself at his attacker with such vigour that he lost one of his shoes.

Quintalion strolled past the brawling men and the crowd drawing around them and stopped in front of a group of merchants all wearing bright silks and attending to a cart laden with birds of all colours. He sidled up to the man in front of them in the line, draped his arm over his shoulder, and when the man roughly shoved him off, said: '*Of course* they're not jumped-up, sap-sniffing, back-laced dandies. What a horrible thing to say!'

The man turned, but it was too late – the merchants descended upon him. The last thing Tuesday saw before Quintalion dragged her away from the mayhem was the heel of a jewelled boot heading towards the man's jaw.

'Oh for the love of . . .' Peytar the guard streaked past them, followed by the other four guards who had been standing at the gates to the city. When she snuck a look back, she saw half of them desperately trying to unwind a leather whip from the farmer's throat and the other half throwing themselves into the melee of fists and colours, with Peytar landing a good right hook before being taken down by a long-beaked bird that one of the merchants had let out of its cage.

'Welcome,' Quintalion said, as they walked through the gates unchallenged, 'to Beggars End.'

CHAPTER SIX

It was all Tuesday could do not to gasp in wonder as she followed Quintalion into the city. People streamed around her, pushing and shoving and chatting loudly about everything from the cold weather to their plans for the week.

A whole herd of cattle thundered past, so close that she had to jump back to avoid being trampled. They were driven by a boy with a whip that he would lightly touch against their flanks when he wanted them to move in a certain direction. It didn't seem to be working so well, because the cattle were traipsing all over the road, earning the irate shouts of several of the other pedestrians, one of whom dropped what looked disturbingly like a human head in a jar and then made a rude gesture at the cattle boy's back.

People stopped to talk at the numerous open fire pits set up at random intervals in the city, warming their hands above the coals while they lit pieces of paper on fire. Tuesday watched as one scroll burned away to ashes. The woman who had dropped it into the fire turned to her companion, adjusted her bonnet and said, 'Well, that's me for the year. How about we meet up at the Tippler for a nosh-up when you're finished?'

'Love to,' her friend replied. She was balancing a piece of paper on her knees and scribbling away onto it with a long fountain pen that she had to refill every couple of seconds from a pot of ink perched on the edge of the fire pit.

'What are they doing?' Tuesday asked, intrigued, but Quintalion was already several paces ahead of her, trying to navigate a path around two burly men who were carrying an entire sheep between them.

She hurried to catch up with him. A large roast boar had been skewered on a spit above one of the fires, with the entrepreneurial owner charging tuppence for a plate of juicy meat. The line behind the man crossed over the path before almost doubling back on itself, and there was a continual stream of *Excuse me*s and bumping elbows as those heading further into the city tried to nudge past.

The noise around her was louder than anything she'd heard before: people shouted conversations at each other from opposite sides of the roads between houses; pigs squealed while they were herded through the grass-strewn streets, which seemed to be playing host to an impromptu farmers' market; women with the mark of the eye above their tents shouted out for customers.

'Watch it there, lass,' a pot-bellied man rumbled at her as he took two quick steps to avoid running into her.

She backed up, but that just landed her directly in the path of a couple of boys dragging on the reins of a white horse with two stubby horns growing from its forehead, and their father, who was cheerfully encouraging them to get a move on by swatting at each of them when they failed to move the stubborn horse.

The walls overshadowed everything. They curved around in a semicircle, and when Tuesday walked on after Quintalion, she could see that there were further walls beyond the outer ones, intersecting the city like a knife. There were guards everywhere, too: leaning against the bales of purple grass that had been propped against the walls of the ramshackle houses, or walking side by side with their cudgels hanging menacingly from their belts. Remembering how they'd entered the city, Tuesday stopped in the shadows to pull her cloak from her satchel and slip it around her neck, pulling the hood over her head as much as she could to hide her face.

Quintalion was waiting for her in the shadows of an open door. He waved her over and she hurried to join him inside, blinking to acclimatise from the bright sunshine outside to the darkness of the hovel.

'Stay here,' he said. 'I won't be long. I just have to procure some suitable papers for you. You don't mind being classed as brown-haired, do you?'

'No, I suppose not.' She blinked away the shadows to reveal a room empty of all furniture, but with a pile of the purple-tinged grasses of the Whispering Plains heaped on the ground. Someone or something snored gently in the corner.

'Good,' Quintalion replied.

He was halfway out of the door when Tuesday thought to say: 'What about . . . you know?' She inclined her head in the direction of the snorer.

'Him? He won't harm you. This is the Fifth Reach, girl – you have to expect a couple of beggars.'

'The Fifth Reach?' She eyed the sleeping beggar with distrust. He smelled like he'd been rolling in dung.

Quintalion nodded. 'Five Reaches, five walls. This city learned long ago not to trust their lives to a single wall . . . not with the de

Kena as neighbours, anyway. There have been skirmishes going on for thousands of years. Beggars End is right on the edge of the proverbial line between east and west, you see? Well actually,' he revised, 'you're probably the only person who doesn't.'

His sharp tone of voice stung her into action. 'Actually, I *do* see,' she told him. 'The Saturday Wars, the civilised countries versus the old ways – I do have a memory, you know.'

'And a temper, apparently,' he said, but when he shifted, which caused the light to throw his face into sharp relief, she saw that he was smiling. 'Just stay here, all right? The daybreakers will be skulking around somewhere – they always are – and there's my old friend Peytar as well. The last thing we need is him throwing you in the lockup just to spite me.'

'Is he likely to do that?'

'I have no idea,' he said, pulling his coat tighter around him. 'That's the problem with people with morals.'

She nodded and watched as he paused by the door, glanced in both directions, and then skulked outside. Soon, despite being a head and shoulders above everyone else, he was lost to the crowds.

*

She meant to stay put, she really did. She even sat herself down on a dry pile of hay a little way from the door and amused herself by watching the people walking by. None of them seemed to be staying in the Fifth Reach, she noticed. Oh, there were those that busied themselves with taking part in the festivities of the Feast of the Ashes, but they were few and far between, and most of the crowd streamed past her door, heading for the next wall and further into the city.

Sitting on a pile of grass listening to the dulcet snores of the beggar asleep in the corner didn't keep her attention for long, and she soon found herself scooting closer and closer to the door, straining her neck to catch every single activity going on in the streets.

A group of men and women in bright fabric and leathers called out to passers-by in a tongue she couldn't understand. Their cart was so filled with goods – leather whips and pots of foul-smelling ointments – that it groaned in complaint. Tuesday breathed through her mouth as they passed her, though that was hardly an improvement, for now she could taste the bitter scent as well as smell it.

A man wearing striped trousers and a straw boater called out as he walked past. 'Books here. Get your books. Picture books, scripture books, books that'll make you cry and books that'll bleed you dry. I've got books more dangerous than the Book of Days itself, and books that'll read *you*. A duke's head for one, a king's for five – cheap at the price.'

He had a shelf of books attached to a rope around his neck, and stopped when he caught sight of Tuesday in the doorway. 'Care for a book, my lovely?'

She shrunk back into the darkness of the house. 'Oh, no. Thank you.'

The man took a step closer, stared at her, and said, 'No, you're probably right. You've got much more important books to be worrying about.'

Then, without another word, he turned back and continued on his way, leaving Tuesday to wonder what he had meant until another familiar voice interrupted her musings.

''Ere,' it said. 'What's a girl with a purse of helions doing in the beggars' city?'

She looked up. The beggar from the west gate stood in front of her, with his begging cup tucked under one arm and his hands in his pockets.

'Oh, hello,' she told him. 'I'm waiting for a friend. He told me to stay here.'

'That friend wouldn't happen to be that cove you were with before, would it? Him with the glare?'

She smiled at his apt description of Quintalion and nodded.

'Well, I'll give you ten to one that he's off and left you, sweetheart.' He reached up and pulled the cap he wore further onto his greasy head. It was knitted with a pom-pom on top.

'He wouldn't,' Tuesday said, picking at a bit of stray grass in her lap, which stained her fingers purple.

'Enough with that,' he said gently. 'You're not a beggar, so it would be a shame to get the beggars' blush so young.' When he leaned down to take her hand, she saw that his own skin was the dark purple of a bruise.

She took his hand instead, turning it over into the light so she could see the colour better. 'What happened?'

'Ah, it's nothing a good scrubbing won't fix.' He shrugged and ran his other hand across his brow. 'The grass stains, you see. The auldermen of the city, in all their generosity, leave the Fifth Reach for us lot – the downtrodden of society. A place to sleep at night and grass to lay our heads on. What more could we need?'

The purple had seeped into every inch of skin that Tuesday could see, which was admittedly not a lot, as he kept himself bundled up in an array of ill-fitting and stinking jackets, doublets, and one very patchwork cloak that looked as though the mice had been at it. 'So,' Tuesday said, beginning to understand, 'all these houses . . . they're all empty?'

He nodded. 'The genteel folk moved out the second the de Kena started hammering at the walls. You'd have to get past the guards and the walls to at least the Third Reach to find any of them toffee-noses again. But let me help you up, young 'un.'

'I don't know,' she said, glancing past him to the streets outside. The flow of people had calmed now that the gates had been open for a while, but there was still a smattering of townspeople travelling against the flow of the traders, heading towards the fire pits, and Quintalion *had* told her to stay here.

'I'll not harm you, if that's what you're worried about. And with those bits of grass sticking out your cloak, you'll look like just another beggar to them. They've trained themselves not to notice *us*.'

Her hands twitched in her lap. She'd promised Quintalion she'd stay put, but she didn't know how long he was going to be; it probably wouldn't hurt to have a quick look around the Fifth Reach, not when she could be back safe in the little house before he even knew she'd left. She held her hand out to the beggar.

His grimy face split open into a grin as he took her hand and gently pulled her to her feet. 'That's the spirit, lass. The name's Col, by the way,' he said.

'Tuesday,' she replied.

'Ah, a foundling, right? Them childerhouses sometimes name their babes after the days of the week. And months, too. I once met a man called Friday March – no prizes as to his origins, eh?'

She joined in with his laughter, mostly to let him think that he'd guessed right.

'Well, Tuesday,' he continued, 'I suppose you've come for the Feast of the Ashes?' He wiped his nose on one stained sleeve and continued on without giving her time to answer. 'Come with me, my dear, and I'll show you the best spot for it in the whole five reaches.'

She let him lead her out of the hovel and through the streets. Now that the sun had risen, the place had begun to stink. A glance at the ground revealed why: mounds of garbage and waste lay to the sides of the dirt streets. Wilting lettuce, rotten vegetables, scraps of cloth too ripped and threadbare for anyone to wear, and even dead cats and dogs lay mixed with the ever-present grass. The people around her didn't seem to notice. They hurried past in their frock coats and wide-skirted gowns, their only concession to the squalor the handkerchiefs pressed to their noses and the length of their clothes, which all ended just above the ankle on the ladies and mid-calf on the men, revealing legs covered by dark-coloured stockings and thick-soled shoes.

Tuesday stopped for a moment to watch one of the women, whose shoes were so high that two servants had to help her wobble along.

'Pattens,' Col said to her with a disgusted sigh. 'They're all the rage now. Came from the Tri-City Region, so I hear, where they might actually need them, what with all their swamps and lagoons. But the nobles of Beggars End'll take to anything new … no doubt they don't want the stink of living on the border washing off on them.'

'You're not from Beggars End, then?'

He let out a guffaw that caused several heads to turn in his direction. 'No, lass, no. But all of us end up here, one way or the other.'

His hand darted up in the direction of the wall. The breath left Tuesday's body: three bodies hung from gibbets at the top of the wall, their skin waxy and their eyes staring out over the reach, blank and black in death. 'What did they do?' she asked once she'd gotten her breath back.

'Spies.' Col spat on the side of the road. 'Or so the guardsmen claimed. The Saturday Wars might be history, but they never ended in most folks' hearts.'

'What about the border skirmishes?' she asked him, remembering what Quintalion had said. 'Surely that means that some people aren't ready to stop fighting.'

'Well no, lass. Once you get generations of folk all killing each other, it doesn't take much to start it back up again. But officially there's a truce. I heard tell that the delegates all met together and signed it on paper, all official-like. Not that paper means much out here, unless you're planning on burning it.'

He led her through the streets, making his way towards the towering wall to the west. It was quieter here, with hardly any of the hustle and sounds of the main thoroughfare, for which Tuesday was supremely grateful. Still, she kept glancing back at the road behind them. The hairs on the back of her neck itched.

'And the . . . daybreakers?' she whispered.

Col stopped stock-still in the middle of the street. 'You don't want to go getting yourself tangled up with the likes of them, young miss,' he said, still facing away from her. His ragged cloak quivered and he sniffed. 'Least not for as long as you can avoid it.'

'But there's a truce now, you said there was. Surely they wouldn't attack anyone during a truce.'

He turned to face her. His hand shook so hard that the coins rattled in his begging cup. 'They don't care for truces or peace. All they care about is hate. Trust me, my dear, if you're a follower of the old ways, they'll slit your throat just as wide in peacetime as they would in war.'

She swallowed down her fear. The dryness of her mouth choked her. 'It's a good thing, then,' she said as she forced the tremor from her voice, 'that I'm just an orphan from Tantallon.'

He stared at her for a long moment and then finally nodded. 'Aye, it's a good thing.'

*

They eventually emerged at the base of the wall. The early morning sun hadn't yet chased away the chill of the night, and Tuesday hugged her cloak tight about her body, silently thanking Madame Marisol for insisting on dressing her in more than one petticoat. A couple of people stood warming their hands by the coals of a smouldering brazier, and the only others to be found were high above, walking three abreast at the top of the wall or climbing by means of a rope ladder. One lady had left her cane hoops at the bottom of the ladder with a friend who held the rope steady, and was ascending with her dress wrapped around her legs and tucked into her belt like a pair of slops.

'Here's where I must leave you,' Col told her. 'Lots to see, money to be made.'

'Must you?' She cringed at the longing tone in her voice.

The beggar only gave her a gap-toothed grin in response. 'That's the burden of being a free spirit in a city of bells – time waits for no man, as they say.'

He nodded in the direction of the ladder, where the woman had finished climbing and was now being hauled onto the top of the wall by the man in front of her. 'But if you want the best view this side of the Silk Sea, just head up that ladder there. There's a brazier at the top for those who like to send their wishes to the skies with a view. And here,' he rummaged around in his pockets for a second to produce a creased piece of paper and a pencil, which he held out to her, 'take these too. You can't come to Beggars End on the day of the Feast of Ashes without burning something.'

She took the offered paper and pencil, holding them awkwardly in front of her as she stared at them. 'But what am I supposed to do?'

'Write out who you are, my girl. Then burn your words and send them up to the sky as ashes. The Days may have disappeared, but it's the thought that counts.'

'What if the daybreakers see me?'

'What if they do?' He knocked her hood from her head and ruffled her hair affectionately. 'They can't very well kill every person with a pencil and paper in hand or this'd be a city of corpses. Whether they like it or not, Beggars End has always been tolerant of the old ways. They have to play nice.'

She glanced down at the paper Col had given her. It looked so very blank. Her hand twitched with the desire to tear the paper into a thousand pieces and scatter them on the wind, anything to stop its mocking whiteness. For a moment she thought that she might copy the letter in her satchel onto the paper, but she quickly dismissed the idea. The letter may have been written for her, but it was a *her* who didn't yet exist, a question mark in the air. Those words had nothing to do with who she was now.

But the problem was that she couldn't find a single word to describe who that was. *Alive* was nothing but a medical state of being, *A Single Day's Existence Upon This Earth* was confusing and technically incorrect, and *Young Female, Tall, With Brown Hair and Grey Eyes* sounded more like the matrimonial advertisements Madame Marisol had occasionally read to them.

None of them described the feeling she'd felt upon waking: the ache to do and to see and to *live* that still throbbed inside her with every breath she took.

'Are you all right, Miss Tuesday?' She looked away from the paper to find Col staring at her in concern, one stained arm extended towards her.

She swallowed back the sob and choked out, 'I'm fine. Thank you for the pencil and paper. I hope you have good fortune.'

'I will.' He grinned at her and shook his begging cup. 'After all, you did give me the moon and sun.'

'Will I see you again?' she asked, unwilling to leave her new friend after she had known him for such a small amount of time.

Before he turned away from her, she caught the edges of his sad smile. 'I shouldn't think so, lass, and you should be grateful for it.'

'How could I be?' Tuesday said. 'You've been nothing but kind to me. You showed me around, you gave me all of this . . .' She raised the paper and pencil in demonstration.

'Aye, that I did. And I wish you good sport with them.' Col shifted and looked anywhere but her, even as she tried to catch his eye. 'But I'd move on soon, if I was you. I'd find that ill-tempered friend of yours and get as far away from this city as you can. Beggars End is where goodness comes to die. Someone with a face as sweet as yours doesn't belong.'

He loped away from her before she could respond, and was soon lost to a bend in the road.

It was most likely flattery – more of the honeyed words that he seemed to delight in – but his compliment warmed her inside. A sweet face. From her short glance in the mirror, she wouldn't have called herself sweet. Had someone else called her so, she wondered, back before the Unreality House and the darkness?

She staggered, overcome with a thought that suddenly flashed through her head. *What if I find out who I was?*

It was so perfect she laughed at herself for not thinking of it sooner. She clutched the pencil and paper so tightly that her fingers turned white. 'How can I be expected to know who I *am* if I don't know who I *was*?'

Excitement bubbled up inside her. That was it. That was her reason for being alive. She'd go and tell Quintalion that he had to take her somewhere she could find out about her past. The only clue she had was the letter in her pocket, but paper was common and words even more so, and she would find few enough clues from it. No, she needed more than just pleas to make her own way in the world. Hadn't she understood, as she was then, that it would never be enough? That veiled warnings would only incite her imagination and leave her even more determined to unravel the mystery at the centre of herself?

It made so much sense that she couldn't hold her elation in anymore, and did a queer little shuffling dance in one spot that caused a bedraggled woman sitting by the roadside to get up and hobble away, probably for fear of catching the madness that had infected her.

'Yes,' she said, revelling in the certain tone of her own voice. 'I *am* mad. I am mad and I am alive and I am Tuesday. And there is nothing better in all the world than that.'

She was still celebrating when a shadow fell over her. She glanced up to see a large ship hovering above the city.

Tuesday took a flying leap and flattened herself against the wall, causing the ladder-holding man to let out a surprised: 'Thaïs's trousseau!'

The ship broke through the smoke above the city like a knife through butter, a great metal beast of gun turrets and rivets. Clouds of soot and smog belched out from its engines, obscuring most of the craft from view, but Tuesday could still see the symbol etched on its sloping bow: a rising sun pierced through by a sword.

'Daybreakers,' she whispered in horror.

CHAPTER SEVEN

'Bloody hell,' the man next to her said. He dropped the set of hoops he was carrying so quickly that they bounced when they hit the ground, and took off at a jog in the direction of the inner reaches, ignoring his companion's shrill cries from the wall above.

As the shadow of the ship crept over the city, the streets cleared of people almost instantly. Tuesday, frozen with fear against the wall, heard the sound of doors slamming shut all over the Fifth Reach as the beggars took shelter anywhere they could. She wished she could join them, but her legs were wobbling too much to even support her weight let alone carry her to safety, and she sank to the ground, her back still pressed against the wall. *Perhaps*, she thought, her fear turning her thoughts fanciful, *I can melt into the stone.*

The airship above her halted in its slow surveillance. Metal shrieked against metal; several sections of the ship shifted, turning a full one hundred and eighty degrees to reveal enormous arrow bolts chained to the ship. If Tuesday squinted at the towers, she could just make out the hint of a helmeted head and the beginnings of a torso at each of them: clearly a man sat at each post, but she couldn't tell why until, all at once, the four arrow towers moved and there was the most horrible sound of shrieking. She clapped her hands over her ears, but it didn't help. Her whole body shook. *Where is Quintalion?* She knew she had to run, to at least try to escape, but her legs didn't want to obey her.

Something whistled through the air. An arrow bolt smashed through one of the hovels close to her, wood and tiles flying everywhere as the entire structure shook. Someone inside screamed and then fell silent. The arrow was attached to a massive chain, which swayed and then, with a shriek of metal – chain links and gears – it drew taut.

Up on the airship, several men threw themselves over the edge, landing on the chain and sliding down with sure-footed precision.

Tuesday scrabbled to her feet before they could reach the ground. She ran.

Another arrow slammed into the dirt in front of her. She leapt over it before the men above could pull it tight.

The first of the men hit the ruined roof of the hovel several streets away.

Tuesday stumbled over the hem of her dress. She snatched it up in great handfuls, freeing her legs from the bulk of her petticoats as she ran, switching directions through the narrow streets as much as she could to throw off the daybreakers.

She paused for a second underneath the sloping roof of a house on the corner of one of the smaller roads and the main thoroughfare. Expecting to hear boots thundering after her, she was surprised to find the city quiet. Her heart laboured in her chest. She didn't want to breathe in case each shallow pull of air alerted them to her location.

In the cover afforded by the roof, Tuesday tried to think through her situation logically. There was no way they could be here for her specifically. If Quintalion was right, then they hated all followers of the old ways, and Beggars End *was* on the border between the two worlds. They might be here to arrest a magician or one of the de Kena clan he kept talking about, or even just to stop for a nice cup of tea.

A nice cup of tea? She shook her head in disbelief. Panic was working its way up her aching body and into her mind, and if she didn't get to safety soon, she was afraid that she'd lose all reason and simply reveal herself to the daybreakers, whether they were hunting for her or not.

'Come out.' The voice reverberated off the rotting beams and walls around her. She flicked her head around, expecting to find one of them right beside her, but she was alone save for the eyes that followed her every movement from the darkness of the surrounding houses.

'There is nowhere to hide. We *will* find you. Give yourself up and we will be merciful.'

The voice sounded tinny and amplified. Closing her eyes, Tuesday waited for it to come again. She didn't have to wait long.

'If you don't, we will be . . . less merciful.'

Less merciful probably means breaking all of my bones instead of just my arms. She tried to shove the image of Quintalion's broken fingers to the back of her head and focus instead on where the voice was coming from.

'Don't be scared. We have your friend. He wants to say hello to you.'

There! Although the twisting streets muffled the voice, it definitely came from somewhere to her left, from the direction of the main road. And then the words hit her.

The daybreakers had Quintalion. It hit her straight in her gut and she doubled over, unable to draw a full breath. They had him. She didn't know why it hurt so much to think of him standing out there, in pain and silenced, but it made her vision grow blurry with tears, which she wiped furiously away. It wouldn't help him to fall apart now.

'We have your friend,' the voice called out again. It sounded male and strangely musical, deep and layered with a harsher tone. 'Things will not go well for him if you don't come to us now.'

'Oi! That wasn't part of the deal.' Another voice, male also, but definitely not Quintalion. There was the sound of flesh on flesh followed by a muffled curse.

Tuesday inched her way along the wall and then poked her head around the corner to find Col standing in the middle of the main road, one hand pressed against his bleeding nose. He was surrounded by daybreakers, but Tuesday found her gaze drawn to the man standing next to him, a hand on his shoulder.

The man sighed, and the sound came out as a harsh whistle through the speaking-trumpet he held to his lips. 'We wish you wouldn't make this difficult.'

'I'll bleedin' well make it difficult,' Col said, lashing out at the man. He missed his face by a good six inches. 'You promised me gold if I gave you a follower of the old ways. Well, the girl had coins – old coins, from the west. Where's my money?'

The man stared down at him. Tuesday couldn't see him clearly from where he stood, but she felt a strange desire to go to him, and had stepped forward, almost out into the open, before she stopped herself.

'Indeed we did promise that,' the man said, speaking only to Col, though the speaking-trumpet picked up his words.

He removed his hand from Col's shoulder and dug through his pocket, quickly pulling out a leather pouch that he dropped at Col's feet. The cord came loose and spilled coins out onto the street. 'There,' he said. 'We are not a liar. You have your gold, newly minted with the face of the High Lord.'

Col ducked down and used his arm to sweep the coins into a pile. He was so preoccupied with his task that he didn't see the leader gesture and one of his men pull out a gun from his belt.

'Though,' he said, almost regretfully, 'you'll have no need for gold in the grave.'

'No!' The word leapt from her. She dashed out into the street, her arms held high against the daybreakers who suddenly raised their guns at her. She slowed down to a walk, but didn't stop, just kept coming towards Col and the daybreakers despite a voice screaming in her head for her to run.

She stopped just outside of the circle of daybreakers. 'Don't hurt him,' she said, and then added, 'Please,' just in case it would help.

'Sir, should we take her now?' One of the daybreakers, a brute of a man covered in tattoos, broke formation and addressed the man in the centre of the circle, his eyes never leaving Tuesday.

The man stared at her. Now that she was closer, she could see that he was tall, with shoulder-length brown hair he'd tied back into a ponytail with a length of blue ribbon. He wore the same uniform as the others: a dark tunic with a high collar that buttoned down the right side of his chest, and a pair of pants with a stripe up both sides of the legs, but he wore it better than them. He looked like he belonged in it, whereas the other daybreakers were clearly uncomfortable in the confining uniform. The badge pinned to his chest – the same sun and sword from the ship – shone in the sun.

The speaking-trumpet dropped to the sand at his feet. His hands curled into fists by his side, his entire focus on Tuesday.

His eyes. They were the brightest green she'd ever seen. He stared at her as though she was an oasis in the middle of a desert, taking in every inch of her, and she blushed to feel his penetrating gaze.

'It's you,' he said, so softly that Tuesday had to lean in closer to hear him. 'We weren't expecting . . . we didn't think we'd ever see you again. We had forgotten for so long . . . but it's really you.'

'Sir?' the tattooed daybreaker tried again. 'Commander Sterling?'

The man blinked twice and seemed to wake from his dream. He grabbed hold of Col, who had been surreptitiously trying to edge his way out of the circle, and spun him around harshly, then shoved him forward so hard that he staggered to his knees.

'We thank you,' Sterling said, 'for your help, but your services will no longer be required.'

'What?!' Col looked around at the others, still on his knees, but hastily trying to push himself to his feet. 'You said . . . you *promised*.'

One of the daybreakers raised his gun, not three feet away from the beggar. Tuesday watched, still not sure what was going to happen. She knew she should run while their attention was elsewhere, but she felt as if she was stuck to the ground, drawn to the scowling green-eyed man before her, and she remained standing inside the circle.

The crack of the gun deafened her. A patch of bright red appeared on Col's chest, just above his heart. He raised a hand to it and then looked at his fingers in wonder – the red and purple mixed to create a muddy brown – and then toppled over in the dirt at her feet.

For a moment, everything was still. And then the reality of what had happened came roaring back to Tuesday. She ran.

The shouts of the daybreakers followed her. It was only when a bullet ricocheted off the beam of a house next to her that she realised they were shooting at her as well.

Her body was so numb that it was all she could do to keep stumbling forward. Any second now they would be on her. She could hear the sharp tread of their boots behind her. Eyes watched her from the shadows of the houses as she ran.

'Help!' she called out.

A saddle lay in her path, but she didn't see it until it was too late. She tried to jump over it but her heel caught the pommel and she fell, all the air leaving her body when she smacked into the ground.

Where is Quintalion? A bullet whizzed over her head – if she hadn't fallen, it would have hit her. The men were less than ten paces from her. Fear rippling through her, she pushed herself up, only to collapse in a heap when she tried to put weight on her ankle.

'Somebody help me.' Her words were choked and less than a whisper.

The daybreakers rounded the corner. One of them kicked out at an unlucky beggar cowering against the side of a shanty.

The blow connected with the man's face and he pitched backwards with blood on his cheek.

Defiance swirled in Tuesday's heart. She crawled away from the daybreakers on her hands and knees. Each movement sent a jolt of pain through her ankle, but she ignored it, gritting her teeth with the determination that, if they were going to kill her, at least she wouldn't make it easy for them.

A boot landed squarely on her back, pushing her into the dirt. She choked and gagged as she inhaled a mouthful of dust, and then she found herself eased over onto her back, looking up at Sterling. He stepped over her so that both feet straddled her waist. Tuesday, her heart so loud in her ears that it overpowered even the mechanical sounds of the airship above, had a wild desire to plant a boot between the fork of his legs, but the sabre pointed at her head stopped her.

She raised her hands in surrender.

The rest of the daybreakers skidded to a halt beside the first. One of them, the same one who had kicked the man by the stall, drew his leg back. Tuesday shut her eyes, expecting to feel his foot slam into her, but the blow never fell. Opening her eyes, she found Sterling with his arm across the other daybreaker's chest.

'Enough!' he spat out the word in a furious whisper. 'She must be taken alive. You would jeopardise the entire mission?'

'Nossir, sorrysir,' the second man replied, but he didn't look happy about it.

'Let me go,' she whispered. She tried inching forward, but Sterling rested one foot firmly on her stomach, halting her progress.

'Let you go?' A third daybreaker laughed and elbowed one of his companions jocularly. He had a death's-head scarred on both cheeks. 'Let her go, the creature says. That's rich. After what she did.'

'I haven't done anything.' She shrank down into the sand. Comprehensive thoughts refused to form, just an endless litany of horror. *PleasenoanythingpleasehelpnoQuintalion* . . .

Sterling shifted his sabre slightly and stared at her. His eyes were confused. 'You're not what we expected. You look just like you did when you ran from us on the shore of the Silk Sea, and yet that must be ten years ago now. How is it possible? But it *must* be you . . . only death can open that door.'

He seemed to be speaking more to himself than to her, his gaze soft, but just when she was beginning to think she might be able to ease his boot off her and crawl away while he was distracted, he reached down and dragged her to her feet. She yelped and grabbed at his wrist, but he was as strong as an ox, and she couldn't break his grip. The hand that was wrapped around her neck was white and pocked with scars. She tried to recoil, but he wouldn't let her go. His cold skin brushed against her chin. Bile rose in her throat.

'Why do you not say anything?' He gripped her shoulder with his free hand and shook her lightly.

Her teeth chattered in fear. 'I don't . . . I don't know what you want me to say.'

'Ah, but a murderer should always be given the chance to confess. Did she struggle, our love? Tell us, did she suffer?' He jerked back from her, and his hands on her shoulder shook with a pent-up emotion that barely registered on his face. 'Tell us!'

Tuesday dug her fingernails into his arm, but that only made him squeeze harder. 'I don't,' she said finally, as blackness dotted around her vision, 'know . . . what you're talking about. I . . .

I come from Madame Marisol's . . . I've never killed anyone . . . I swear it.'

'Your name,' he whispered, stricken. His fingers beat time against her shoulder. 'What is your name?'

The word slipped from her with ease, despite the terror locking her jaw. 'Tuesday.'

'You mock her?' For one fleeting second she thought he would release her, but one hand remained tightly around her throat. The other let go of her shoulder and reached for the sabre at his belt. He withdrew it and rested the tip directly against her heart. The gold handle drew her gaze until it was all she could see: an hourglass design etched into the brass with two hearts and the words *Solus mayetvos* engraved beneath them.

'The woman we love gave us this sword,' he said to her, his voice little more than a whisper. 'It carries a deadly poison on its blade. Would you like to feel its sting?'

Tuesday flinched, closing her eyes as she expected to feel the kiss of cold steel against her neck, but the pain never came. Instead, the sharp retort of a gun echoed through the streets.

She cracked one eye open just in time to see one of the daybreakers crumple to his knees and then pitch forward, slumping against Sterling's leg. The man stared blankly at Tuesday. There was a small neat hole in the middle of his forehead.

The six remaining daybreakers looked around wildly, falling into a box formation around Sterling, who pulled Tuesday in front of him, his breath loud and hot against her neck.

A dark-haired woman stood no more than twenty paces away from them. She was outlined by the light of the sun, but through her haze of fear Tuesday could still see the long musket she held to her shoulder and the puff of smoke as she fired.

Crack! Another daybreaker down, smacking into the ground before he could even go for his weapon.

'What the hell . . .' the death's-head daybreaker said. 'It's that northern woman!'

The woman raised her musket and took aim again. The man beside him dropped without a sound, his blunderbuss falling from nerveless fingers. He hit the dirt head askew.

The death's-head daybreaker cursed and ducked down. He pulled a flask of gunpowder from his belt and poured it down the barrel. All around Tuesday, men were doing the same: measuring out gunpowder and loading shot with hasty precision. One of them dropped to his knees, raised his blunderbuss and fired.

'Try your luck, boys,' the woman called out, after three more had emptied their shot in her direction. 'The blunderbuss has a range of four feet or so. Who wants to bet that you'll still be standing when I get that close?'

'We know that voice . . .' Sterling said quietly. Tuesday winced as his arm tightened around her neck. 'Hester St Clare.' He spoke the name like a curse.

The death's-head daybreaker suddenly rose to his feet, his blunderbuss raised high and murder in his eyes. 'You want to try me, you little savage?' he shouted. A speck of spittle flew from his lips. 'Take your best shot!'

He lurched towards her. The woman – Hester – whipped the musket down from her shoulder, rested the butt against the road, and began to reload. The daybreaker bore down on her with a furious speed. Tuesday almost couldn't bear to watch since surely Hester couldn't reload before he reached her.

He was eight feet away, then six. He squeezed the blunderbuss between shaking hands.

Hester wouldn't make it in time. She fumbled with the ramrod, fiercely pumping it down the musket barrel.

Tuesday called out a warning, but Hester didn't look up from her weapon.

The daybreaker was five feet away, and then four. *The blunderbuss has a range of four feet . . .*

'Hurry!' Tuesday screamed. The sun backlit the scene so that all she could see was the daybreaker's back as he advanced, and the outline of the dark-skinned woman yanking the ramrod out and stashing it behind her.

The death's-head daybreaker laughed. 'Looks like Lady Luck is on my si–'

His voice cut off suddenly. Tuesday blinked against the light to see him fall to his knees, revealing Hester standing behind him with smoke still rising from her musket. 'Not today,' she said.

Suddenly Sterling grabbed Tuesday around the throat again. His large hand squeezed her neck so tightly that she struggled to take a breath, but before she could even raise her arms to try to pull him off her, he pressed the edge of his sabre against her cheek.

CHAPTER EIGHT

Hester stopped where she stood.

'Good day, Hester,' Sterling said casually. 'We must say, since we thought you were dead, seeing you here is . . . disappointing.'

'Sterling.' She nodded in acknowledgement and lowered her musket, resting it against her leg. The three remaining daybreakers shifted nervously.

'Orders, Commander?' one of them said.

'Hold off,' Sterling shot back. 'We wish to know what she wants.'

The daybreaker frowned, but held his position, kicking one of his dead comrades out of the way.

'I would think it obvious,' Hester said. 'Let the girl go, Sterling.'

Tuesday wrapped her fingers around Sterling's arm, but his thick tunic protected him from her scratches, and all she could do was keep one hand on his arm and the other on top of his hand at her throat, trying to pry him off. Her chest moved in and out in a futile attempt to draw air into her lungs.

'No, we don't think we will,' he replied. 'We haven't yet finished with her.'

Hester's eyes narrowed. 'Whether you think you've finished with her or not is none of my concern. If you do not hand her over, those will be your last words. And they are not very good ones.'

'You're not still bitter about your brother, are you?' Sterling said, letting out a dry laugh that sounded like the rapping of a fist on wood. 'Or is it the loss of your leg? We see you've found a replacement.'

He pointed to her right leg, which was wooden from the knee down, her trousers rolled up to reveal a complicated system of pulleys, gears and a line of metal that ran up the sides of both her stump and the wooden leg and ended in a brace at her waist.

'Too bad replacing your brother will be a little more difficult,' he continued.

She spat on the ground before him.

Tuesday could feel Sterling smirk against her hair as the sabre slipped against her cheek. 'Is that a curse?'

'A promise,' Hester told him. 'Before this year is up, one of us will die.'

'Let's look at this logically, shall we?' Sterling continued. 'Assuming you can get past our men, curse or no curse, you'll never be able to get to her before our sabre does.'

His fingers tightened on Tuesday's neck. She gasped, her vision blurring. The sabre was a cold weight against her cheek.

'Perhaps you've heard the stories?' he said to Hester. 'Our blade never misses and a cut,' he spun Tuesday around so that she was looking up into his eyes, 'just a single *scratch* brings death.'

She tried to edge her head away from the blade, but he followed her movements, keeping the sabre tucked up against her cheek. A hint of extra pressure would break the skin.

'You won't kill me,' Tuesday said, her voice barely a whisper.

'Oh, won't we?' His breath was hot and sour against her cheek. 'Why not?'

She said the first thing that came to her head, though she hardly knew why, for the words were foreign to her: '*Solus mayetvos.*'

Sterling's grip around Tuesday's neck loosened. In one swift movement she drew his hand up and sunk her teeth into the fleshy base of his thumb.

Sterling let out a cry and pulled his arm away. The sabre swung wide. Heart pounding, Tuesday slipped underneath it and elbowed him in the stomach. His eyes closed and he doubled over, wincing. *Serves you right* briefly flittered across Tuesday's mind before she was kicking off the ground and pushing herself away from him.

Something silver and small flashed past her. The knife hit Sterling in the right shoulder, making him drop his weapon with a cry of frustration, but he remained standing with one hand wrapped around the blade, a crescent of blood blossoming in the sharp crease of his tunic.

'Kill her!' he shrieked. 'And bring the girl to us.'

But Hester was already striding confidently past Tuesday. She flipped the musket upside down, took hold of the barrel and smashed the butt of the gun across the closest daybreaker's cheek. The man dropped like a sack of potatoes.

The second daybreaker's blunderbuss went off in a cloud of smoke, but Hester wasn't there anymore. She twisted to the side and clubbed the man straight in his right elbow. He swore and dropped his weapon.

Sterling slashed at her, but he was forced to wield it left-handed, and though the blow would still have split Tuesday up the middle, Hester sidestepped it. Sparks flew as the sabre glanced off the metal holdings of her wooden leg. She grabbed hold of the knife in his shoulder and twisted. Sterling groaned.

Letting go, she ducked beneath the final daybreaker's gun and swung her own straight at his legs. He fell hard, his head hitting an old broken cobblestone, shuddered, and lay still.

'Come, child,' Hester said to her, walking away from the prone daybreakers. 'Now is a prudent time to leave.'

Tuesday waited for Hester, still in shock. Her neck ached from where Sterling had grabbed her – she wouldn't be surprised to find a handprint. Tears pricked at the corners of her eyes.

Hester loped off down the path, so she forced herself to take a deep breath and follow.

'I have to . . .' she said, before a sob found its way out of her throat. 'I have to find my friend. He'll be looking for me.'

Hester walked stiffly, favouring her right leg. The mechanisms whirred softly in time with every step. She silently pulled out a handkerchief and handed it to Tuesday, who took it gratefully.

'Come,' she said. 'I'll take you to him.'

Tuesday glanced back at Sterling, who was holding a jacket from one of the dead daybreakers against the wound in his shoulder and staring daggers at them both.

Her hands shook and she almost dropped the handkerchief twice before she managed to dab at her eyes. 'How can I trust you?'

The dark-haired woman smiled. 'Look at it this way – do you have any choice?'

'No,' she admitted.

'Then I'm glad we've sorted that out. I give you my word that no harm shall come to you while you are in my care.'

Col's dead staring eyes flashed through her memory. He'd betrayed her, had sold her out to the daybreakers, and yet she couldn't help but feel sorry for his fate. 'And how can I trust *that*?'

Hester swung the musket across her shoulders and rested an arm on the barrel as she walked. 'My word is my bond. It is all that I am.'

Tuesday turned, wanting to see Sterling once more before he was lost to the twisting road. He'd abandoned the rest of the daybreakers, who were either dead or unconscious in the street or crawling after him and trailing blood, and he had made his way to the closest arrow bolt; he kicked it loose and stepped onto it, looped his good arm around the chain and nodded. The airship slowly pulled him and the arrow back up into its depths.

'I'm sorry,' Tuesday said, realising what Hester had said, 'but who *are* you?'

'Under the blessing of the sacred moon goddess, Aqira, I was named Hassar San Khalar. But that woman is dead. You meet me now as Hester St Clare.' She bowed from the hip, her right leg straight out in front of her.

Tuesday may not have known much, but even after running for her life, being trampled, shot at and strangled, she knew basic manners, and the words easily left her: 'I'm pleased to meet you, Hester. My name's –'

'Tuesday,' Hester interrupted. 'I know, child. But do not repeat it. There are those who would sell their mothers into slavery to put a name to your face. Just this past night, Sterling himself was asking after a girl with your description. Though he seemed to think you'd be older.'

The ship hovered above them, casting a shadow over the Fifth Reach. 'He said I killed someone.'

'And did you?' Hester said, somehow managing to look down her aquiline nose at her despite being a good foot shorter.

'No!' Tuesday burst out. 'I mean, I hope not. I don't remember.'

'Then that is all I need to know. Come. Follow me. I will take you to your friend.'

We have your friend . . . Sterling's voice echoed through her mind. Tuesday glanced behind her at the scene of carnage they were rapidly leaving behind. Col lay sprawled in the dirt. A crowd of beggars had gathered around the bodies; several small children had begun rifling through their pockets, and a woman with twigs in her hair was cracking open the mouth of one of the daybreakers with a pair of pliers.

Tuesday looked away. Col had betrayed her – had turned her in to the daybreakers – and yet she wished he hadn't come to such an end. No one deserved to have their belongings examined and squabbled over like that.

Hester was far ahead of her. She had paused at the end of the street, and Tuesday hurried to catch up. 'Why,' she said, once she had joined Hester at the intersection of two roads, 'are you helping me?'

Hester stared down at her, and for a moment Tuesday thought she wouldn't answer, but she finally said, 'The daybreakers killed my brother. I live now only to thwart them.'

'Oh,' said Tuesday. 'I'm sorry.'

Hester inclined her head, and her glossy braided hair bobbed in response. 'I thank you. Now come. Your friend awaits.'

Hester led her through the twisting streets of the Fifth Reach, and soon they lost the macabre scene to a bend in the road. The rest of the reach had begun to come alive again. Beggars gingerly shuffled out of the gloom of the hovels, brushing grass off their hands and knees, and stared at Tuesday and Hester as they walked past. The bird merchants, whom Tuesday thought must have long ago headed further into Beggars End for the safety of the inner reaches, emerged from behind one of the ruined houses, their birds squawking fiercely and throwing themselves at the bars of their cage in such distress that it took one of the merchants, a dark-haired young man with a cheeky grin, several seconds of playing a lullaby on his pipe for them to settle back on their perches. Even a few of the guards slunk out of the shadows, where they'd been sharing a swig of something in a leather flask, and straightened up as they started their patrols again.

Tuesday followed Hester towards the large, straight wall on the western border of the city. They left a narrow lane to find that they'd emerged at around the same spot Col had taken her to, the one with *the best view this side of the Silk Sea*. She wondered where the Silk Sea was, and what was so beautiful beyond it.

The ladder still hung from the top of the wall. The lady who had previously been traversing it was nowhere to be found, and had apparently taken her hoop skirts with her. Hester rested her gun against the metal brace around her waist and steadied the swaying ladder with one hand. 'After you.'

'What's up there?' she asked, remembering Col's betrayal. She had no reason to trust Hester, after all, and it was entirely possible that the only reason she wanted her to climb the wall was to push her off it.

'You'll see,' Hester said, and offered her a sharp-toothed smile that did nothing to dispel the worrying images Tuesday had of herself flailing wildly as she fell through the air.

But she had no choice. Quintalion still hadn't showed up, and without him she felt adrift and far too small. 'I don't . . .' she murmured, realising something far more practical. 'I don't know how to . . .'

'You've never climbed a ladder before?' Hester sounded incredulous.

Deciding that it might be better to keep her past secret, Tuesday simply went with: 'Not to my knowledge.'

'It's simple.' Hester nudged her in the direction of the ladder, and Tuesday, who hadn't been expecting it, tripped on her swollen ankle and had to grab at the rungs to keep herself upright. 'Like most things in life, you just put one foot in front of the other and let nature take its course.'

One foot in front of the other . . . The rope felt coarse against her skin as she grasped it tightly and stepped up onto the first rung. Even with all her weight off the ground, the ladder barely swayed at all, since Hester kept it lying flat against the wall. She may have been small – at least a head shorter than Tuesday – but she was strong.

Tuesday took the next couple of rungs with a rush of elation that only ended when, pink-cheeked and grinning, she ascended too quickly and lost her footing, sliding down a couple of feet and only saving herself by snatching at the ladder.

'Don't die,' Hester called out to her. 'It'll look bad on me.'

Shutting her eyes, Tuesday forced herself to even out her breaths. *One, two,* she thought. *In, out. One, two. Just like the staircase in Madame Marisol's House.* She set off again up the ladder, only this time she concentrated on each step she took, climbing in a controlled manner, and soon she was above the houses.

From her perch on the wall, she could really see how the Fifth Reach would have looked when it had been a village, before the walls of Beggars End swallowed it up: the paths followed the contours of the land, the houses were grouped together with no rhyme or reason in a way that spoke of long years of growth, and there were even the remains of a mud-daubed wall way out on the opposite side of the city, running along in pieces just inside of the stone wall.

'Take your time. I'm sure the daybreakers will enjoy taking pot shots.' Hester's voice startled her and she swung around on the ladder until she faced the stones again, breathing hard. The beautiful view had almost made her forget that she was clinging to a thin cord halfway up a wall, but the mention of the daybreakers brought it all rushing back to her.

The ship still hovered over the city, but it hadn't started firing again. Tuesday wondered if they'd managed to lose the daybreakers in the winding streets. The ship was large enough to cover half the Fifth Reach, and when Tuesday climbed higher up the ladder, she began to feel the steam from its engines break upon her skin, damp and unpleasant. The men still sat at the arrow-bolt turrets, turning left and right as though they were searching for something.

From her vantage point on the wall, she could see more of the upper side of the ship, which was hidden to the city below. The surface was mostly flat, unlike any ships she'd ever heard of, with space for the men to walk around. A long gun port ran along the side of the ship, with cannons peeking out of every hole.

The mid-deck converged with an observation tower, through which she could just make out several men in uniform. It was too far away to know whether Sterling was among them.

I'd know if he were, she thought to herself, though she couldn't say how. She climbed higher until she was almost at the top of the wall, and caught sight of a massive balloon hanging above the entire back half of the daybreaker ship. It was tethered to the ship with chains, and every so often plumes of flame would rise from the three enormous furnaces that sat in a line down the middle of the deck. At the stern, propellers spun lazily on either side of the rudder.

The ladder swayed suddenly. Far below, Hester had begun to climb with her musket strapped into its holster across her back. Though climbing with her wooden leg must have been difficult, she ascended so quickly that Tuesday was forced to take the final couple of steps in a rush so she wouldn't catch up.

When she stumbled out onto the top of the wall, two hands steadied her.

'Quintalion!' she cried, straightening up to find him in front of her. He'd swapped the emerald waistcoat for a yellow one and had slicked his short hair back with pomade.

'What a surprise to see you again,' he told her. 'Did you have fun playing with the little boys in their jumped-up flying machine?'

'Playing?!' Tuesday squeaked. 'I almost died.'

'Yes, and whose fault was that? If you'd just stayed put like I told you to, none of this would have happened.' He ran his fingers down the front of his coat and hooked his thumbs in the pockets. 'Thankfully, I happen to be incredibly clever and sent the redoubtable Miss St Clare out after you.'

'*Captain*.' Hester heaved herself up over the side of the wall with a deft flick of her wrist. The wall was wide enough for all three of them to be able to stand abreast.

Quintalion breathed out through his nose, closing his eyes for a moment before opening them again and treating Hester with a bright smile. 'Forgive me . . . Captain.' He then turned back to Tuesday. 'You see, girl, while you were playing chasies with the commander over there, I not only found you some decent papers, but a ship and a captain to go with it.'

'A ship?'

'I may be wrong,' he continued, 'but I was under the impression that you wouldn't want to spend the rest of your life in this cesspit.'

'I don't!' she said. 'That is . . .'

'What? Out with it. I don't have time for your lollygagging.'

She reached into her satchel and drew out the letter that Madame Marisol had given her. 'This,' she said, holding it up to show Quintalion and Hester, while keeping it firmly out of their reach, 'is all I have from my former life . . . from the time before I woke up. I want to know who I was. Can I do that in Beggars End?'

'Not unless you were a vagabond in that former life of yours,' Quintalion remarked. 'What does Madame Marisol think about your great scheme? I can't imagine she'd be too happy.'

Tuesday bit her lip and lowered her gaze to the letter in her hand. 'She doesn't know.'

'What? What did you say?' Quintalion raised a hand to his ear in a pantomime of hearing difficulties.

'I said she doesn't know, all right!' Tuesday exclaimed. A blush worked its way up her neck. She hadn't meant to yell.

'The girl has spirit.' Hester smiled into the back of her hand.

'That's what I'm worried about,' Quintalion muttered. 'So you're going behind your beloved Madame Marisol's back, eh?'

Tuesday twisted the letter between her fingers. 'Not exactly. I mean, I'm not doing it on purpose. I just didn't think to tell her, and there's hardly any point going all the way back to her House now, is there? Not when we've come all this way.' She was babbling, she knew, but she couldn't seem to stop until Quintalion raised his hand and said: 'You'll be wanting to go to Fortune City, then.'

'You think that wise?' Hester, who had been studiously fiddling with the clasps on her leg brace as the two of them talked, now lifted her eyes to them both, challenging them to meet her gaze.

'What choice do we have? If she wants answers, then the Lady Fortuna is the one to give them to her. Nothing happens in the skies without her knowing about it.'

'The skies?' Tuesday repeated, feeling out of her depth in the conversation. 'I thought you said we were going on a ship.'

Hester's eyebrow quirked and she jerked a thumb in the direction of the daybreaker ship. 'I thought you'd have realised by now that not all ships sail the seas.'

She crooked a finger at Tuesday and began to walk along the wall, several sections of which had partially collapsed, affording them a glorious view of their surroundings. The Whispering Plains stretched far into the distance, their shimmering lilac fields broken only by a river that wound through them, disappearing into the little valleys before reappearing as the plains opened up the closer to Beggars End they got. From the way Quintalion had spoken about the two sides – the old ways and the new – Tuesday had almost expected to see a physical line at the edge of the plains, marking east from west, but there was nothing but a few scraggly plants and some women with baskets on their backs, bent over and hacking away at the grass with scythes.

I'm sorry, Madame Marisol, she thought, picturing the little house lying far to the west. *But I just have to know.*

Hester stopped suddenly and gestured at the crenellations. 'My ship and my services are yours for as long as you need them.'

'It's amazing what the promise of a bloody revenge will buy these days,' Quintalion said quickly. When Hester reached up to touch the barrel of her musket, however, he suddenly became deeply interested in a loose thread on the sleeve of his greatcoat.

'I don't understand,' Tuesday said. 'I don't see a ship.'

The corner of Hester's mouth turned upwards into a smile and she whistled once, sharp and clear on the morning breeze.

A ship rose up out of nowhere. Masts appeared above the wall like spires, and then white triangular sails, rippling against their restraints, and finally the hull and a pointed bow with a figure-head of a boy, captured in mid-laugh with the wind streaming through his curling hair.

'Welcome,' Hester said, 'to the *Zephyr*.'

CHAPTER NINE

Tuesday stood at the edge of a field. No, that couldn't possibly be right. She'd been on Hester's ship a second ago – she *remembered* climbing the gangplank and breathing in the fresh smell of wood and the faint hint of spices that lingered around the *Zephyr* – and yet here she was, alone and utterly bewildered.

No, not alone. Someone stood beside her. He was conversing with another man who stood by his side, so she could only see his back, but she would have recognised the voice anywhere. It was Sterling.

She twisted away, ready to run, but her body didn't want to obey her. Her legs remained rooted to the spot as she stared out at the field. The dirt was freshly turned, as though someone had planted something recently. She shifted her gaze downwards, relieved at this small victory over her own body, and was surprised to find that she no longer wore the travel dress and cloak that Madame Marisol had picked out for her, but rather a tunic and tight riding trousers, both soiled from the dust of the road, and a set of elaborately engraved armour on top of them: breastplate and vambraces that laced all the way up her arm with leather thonging.

But it all felt right. Everything from the tilled earth, to the clothes she wore, to Sterling – especially Sterling – who was pressed up so close to her that she felt a thrill down her arm when he accidentally nudged her, felt unavoidably, uncontrollably *right*. She breathed out a sigh of relief without even meaning to.

'Darling.' Sterling turned to her then, clasping her hand in his for a moment before pulling away. 'We should leave. Our reports say they're drawing near.'

'And miss the entertainment?' The voice was hers, but the words weren't. 'Where's your sense of adventure?'

Doubt flickered across Sterling's green eyes, but then he laughed. It was nothing like the embittered sound he'd made back in Beggars End, but an open chuckle that brought a blush to her cheeks. 'Very well,' he said. 'I can deny you nothing.'

'As it should be,' she replied archly. 'And you should remem–'

A loud trumpet muffled the rest of her words. Suddenly her heart was beating loudly in her ears as she gripped Sterling's hand, but Tuesday couldn't tell whether the fear and excitement bubbling through her came from herself or the phantom woman that she'd become.

Something moved at the edge of the field. Trees veiled the entrance, their branches heavy and bowing with fruit – pomegranates, her mind supplied, and she marvelled at herself for worrying about such a small detail when the very ground itself shook with the force of what approached.

A line of men and women broke through the trees. They were dark-skinned, all, and wild-looking, with the sun gleaming off the copper armour they wore on the front of their chests. Beside her, Sterling took a step backwards.

They charged towards them, wave after wave. There must have been a thousand of them, a battalion of warriors with blazing eyes, all moving as one.

And what was even stranger was that she felt no fear as they thundered out onto the churned earth, only glee.

*

Tuesday shot upright. The world swam around her and she gulped in huge pulls of air, terrified that when her vision came back she would find herself in the field still, but soon the darkness receded and a blue sky crossed with the pink-tinged streaks of sunset greeted her. She stretched a hand out to find coarse netting beneath her and then gasped when she almost overturned a half-full cup.

I'm on the ship with Hester and Quintalion, she thought. *It was a dream. It was just a dream.*

'And what a dream!' Quintalion remarked from where he crouched, leaning against the main mast for support.

Tuesday blushed. She must have spoken the words aloud and not realised. She felt drained, somehow, as if she'd run a mile . . . and yet it was only a dream that even now began to fade from her mind.

Quintalion slanted his head towards her with a cynical grin. 'You were tossing and turning so much that I almost felt inclined to take bets with the captain here as to when you'd tumble over the edge of the ship.'

'A bet I'd never take,' Hester called, 'as I, unlike your friend, girl, have an ounce of honour in me.'

'You flatter me, Captain,' he shot back.

She let the rest of his words wash over her as she picked up the cup. She could still feel the warriors' thundering footsteps below her, and she half-expected to see them crest the side of the ship. *But it was just a dream*, she reassured herself. Memories of the day rushed back to her. As soon as she'd settled herself on Hester's marvellous flying ship, she'd begged a cup of boiling water from the captain and steeped the tea that Madame Marisol had given her. She'd wanted to talk to Madame Marisol, to reassure herself that she wouldn't be too cross with Tuesday's plans to discover her past, but as the tea took hold and fatigue swarmed over her, her thoughts had turned to Sterling. Perhaps that was why she had dreamed of him instead.

'Tuesday?' Quintalion said loudly.

She shook her head to dispel the last of the dream. 'Sorry?'

'I said that I thought you might want this.'

He threw a small booklet of papers at her. Her coordination skills were apparently taking longer to wake up than the rest of her, because, when she went to catch it, the booklet simply bounced off her hand and dropped into her lap.

Tuesday slowly sat up, stretching as she did and attempting to ignore the aches shooting through her arms and legs. Though the dream had seemed to last mere minutes, she must have slept for hours. The afternoon was drawing on and the sun lay low on the western horizon.

When she had sat up, the booklet slid out of her lap and onto the deck by her side, and now she picked it up, smoothing out the battered leather cover. In stamped red letters, it read: *Papers for the proof and purpose of individual identification, as authorised by the High Lord (ruler of Tantallon and its territories, everlasting majesty, rook-king, long may he reign).* She smiled as she imagined the kind of person who would have written that: a small man, she decided, with a round body, a balding head like an egg, and hands permanently stained with ink, no matter how hard he scrubbed at them.

'Well?' Quintalion's voice broke into her thoughts. 'Aren't you going to say thank you? You're lucky I'm not charging you extra – five helions and a lun just for a bit of forgery. Highway robbery!'

'Thank you, Quintalion,' she said absently as she flipped open the thin book. It was bound with scarlet cord that made a pleasant *shhh* sound when it rubbed against the parchment pages. The first page contained only a picture of a sallow man in a crown that seemed to wear him, and not the other way around. The High Lord, she guessed.

In the background, Quintalion loudly complained about *certain people's lack of gratitude these days*, but Tuesday easily tuned him out. She was starting to learn that he liked the sound of his own voice, not that this was a bad thing. It gave her a chance to practise distinguishing between important conversations, and conversations that she could *ah* and *yes, that's very interesting* her way through, while focusing on other essential things.

Like the name on the paper in front of her. 'Dagny?' she asked, stopping Quintalion's ranting cold.

'That's unfortunate,' Hester remarked.

'It's a perfectly legitimate name, *Tuesday*,' he replied.

Tuesday attempted to school her face into a neutral expression, but her nose kept wrinkling up every time her eyes rested on the page. 'But . . . Dagny? I don't want to be a Dagny. I want to be Tuesday and . . . well, I don't know who, but I know I'm not *that*.'

'You are now.' His lips quirked and she swore she could see the calculations going on behind his eyes before he slowly said, 'Dagny.'

'You want me to shoot him for you?' Hester said from the helm.

'Um, no thank you.' Tuesday wasn't sure whether Hester was being serious, but she didn't want to take any chances.

'Your loss.' She turned the helm to the right, causing the *Zephyr* to shift easily beneath them.

Ignoring Quintalion, who was chortling to himself, Tuesday stood, tucking the papers into her satchel, which she then slipped over her head. The twinge in her ankle reminded her that she'd taken a tumble when she'd been fleeing the daybreakers, and so she walked on it only lightly, wincing as the movement jarred it.

It took her a second to acclimatise her body to the constant pitching of the deck, but when she got the hang of it and made sure to put only the slightest of weight on her injured ankle, walking wasn't that difficult. For the first couple of steps, she threw her hands out as a counterweight to the motion, but by the time she made her way over to the railing, she could walk normally with little interruption.

Tuesday leaned out over the railing and then drew back suddenly. Clouds whipped by underneath them in white swirls and, way below, the ground rolled out in waves of fields and cities and woods. All annoyance at the horrible name she'd had foisted upon her disappeared on the wind. 'We're flying,' she whispered. 'We're *actually* flying.'

She'd seen the *Zephyr* pull away from Beggars End, of course, but she'd been too worried about what Madame Marisol might think of her venture to really appreciate it.

'It's marvellous,' Quintalion said in a monotone. His hand clenched and unclenched at his side.

'Don't you like it?' she asked him.

'It's all I could ever dream of,' he replied. 'Now get away from the edge before you fall. You'll get no answers from Fortune City if you arrive there in a shroud.'

The wind blew in from behind the ship. It brought with it the heavy smell of soil and manure, the stink of garbage, the fresh scent of a recent rain. She took one last deep breath and retreated from the railings.

Following the line of the planks as she walked, she said, 'What's it like?'

'Dangerous,' Hester threw out darkly. She stood at the helm and looked down upon them from the raised deck, occasionally turning the wheel slightly left or right without ever taking her eyes from the two of them.

Quintalion pulled off his hat and began to play with it, turning it over and over in his hands. 'She exaggerates. Just because a few people have been thrown off the city . . .'

'A few?' Hester turned the wheel and the ship lurched in response to her touch. 'When I was last there, I counted twenty-seven, and I was docked for just an hour.'

'Wait, what? Thrown from the city?' Tuesday said. 'How?'

'With little effort, and hopefully after they're dead.' Quintalion jammed his hat back on his head and pulled it forward so that the brim shaded his face. 'Now go bother Hester – I haven't slept in three days.'

Annoyance flared in Tuesday, hot and sharp. She huffed out a breath but he pointedly ignored her and rolled over with his head against the mast, his back to her.

'Come here, child,' Hester called to her. 'I will tell you all you wish to know of Fortune City.'

She limped over to the captain, pretending that it took her so long because she was admiring the *Zephyr* and not that every misstep awoke fiery agony in her throbbing ankle, though in truth, the ship *was* impressive.

It was small, maybe sixty-five feet from prow to stern, with two triangular sails that rippled like silk when they caught the wind. The deck was clear but for a single lifeboat, the nets she'd slept on, and a few barrels and chests that had been firmly tied down against what Tuesday assumed was the captain's cabin; she supposed that, for a flying ship, it was safer to have the cargo strapped down in case of turbulence. The rest of the cargo, if indeed the *Zephyr* was a cargo ship, must have been stashed underneath the hatch in the middle of the deck. She didn't venture down into the dark depths, preferring instead to investigate the captain's cabin on her way to Hester.

It had diamond-paned glass windows on either side of the yellow door. Tuesday wandered over to them and pressed her hands against the glass to peek in when Hester wasn't looking, but the room beyond was dark and she could only make out a vaguely lumpy shape that might have been a bed.

It was only when she'd taken in every inch of the lower deck – from the bowsprit jutting out from the prow, to the brass stampings of the secured chests, some full of sails and rope and others, oddly enough, full of pomegranates, and all spelling out exotic places that she longed to visit: *Daluk Shakti* and *Corte* and foreign letters she couldn't even read – that she ventured up to the bottom of the quarterdeck stairs.

Hester watched the horizon. She nodded when she saw Tuesday hovering, but otherwise said nothing.

Tuesday took this as invitation enough and climbed the steps, wincing as she accidentally put too much pressure on her aching ankle. The quarterdeck was as bare as the main deck, without even a table or chest to hold the navigational instruments Tuesday guessed Hester would need to captain the ship, just the helm and the second mast, several long slots cut into one side of it the only concession to storage.

'See the map?' Hester said. 'There, below the star charts. Get it out for me, would you?'

A large rolled-up piece of oilcloth stuck out from the lowest slot in the mast, among other papers, round leather containers, two curved blades, and a broken sword with a tiger's head for the hilt. Tuesday slid the map from its resting place and took it over to Hester.

'Good,' the woman replied. 'Unfurl it. I must check our bearings.'

Tuesday looked around for some way to fulfil Hester's request, but she couldn't see any place to unroll the map besides the floor, and she wasn't eager to jolt her ankle any more than she had to, so she stood clutching at it until Hester clucked her tongue at her, locked the helm into position against her wooden leg, and took the map, spreading it out across the wheel.

'This,' she said, tapping her small hand lightly against the oilcloth, 'is the known world. My people speak of a lost land to the north, but that is nothing but tales told to children who will grow up to regret that there is nothing left to explore.'

Tuesday leaned in closer, eager to see the world she'd found herself in. The map revealed countries drawn in vibrant blues, greens and reds, with their names written out in a precise hand in golden ink that shimmered in the dying light. One big landmass covered most of the left half of the map, with a smaller island to the right, with none of the rivers, cities and mountains that covered its sister to the west.

'I do not think you've seen this before, eh?' Hester said slyly.

Tuesday looked up to see the captain staring at her through her long eyelashes.

She knows, Tuesday thought. *Or at least suspects.* Quintalion would urge her to be cautious and not share any more of her story than she had to, but he was snoring on the main deck, and so Tuesday went with her gut feeling. She trusted Hester St Clare, though she couldn't say why . . . Of course, saving her life that day might have had something to do with it, now that she thought about it.

'No,' she finally said after a pause that felt like a lifetime. 'I haven't.'

She raked her eyes down the map, passing borders and mines until she found what she was looking for. 'I come from here,' she said, pointing at the tiny symbol of Madame Marisol's House. 'It's all I know.'

'Then it's true,' Hester breathed out. 'You are one of the undying. Those that live and are born again.'

'I suppose.' She shrugged. 'I mean, I don't really know much about it. But yes, I have lived another life. That's why I want to go to Fortune City: to find out who I was.'

The images of her dream rushed back into her memory then – the warriors running towards them, and she and Sterling side by side, facing death head-on. She shuddered.

Hester just stared at her.

Tuesday began to squirm beneath her sharp gaze. She was about to say something – anything – to break the silence, when

Hester spoke again, with a voice that was little more than a breath of air.

'And is it true that, in your Madame Marisol's House, those who've died may yet live again?'

The intensity of Hester's gaze was becoming uncomfortable, so Tuesday glanced down at the map in front of them to escape it, tracing the tiny house absently. 'Maybe,' she said. 'Why?'

'No matter.' Hester gave her a swift smile and clapped her hands together, loud in the gathering dark. 'Let me show you where I hail from.'

She ran a finger over the map, up, up past Beggars End in the centre, past the Crossroads, where four roads joined in the shadow of a large tree, over the Petrified Forest, and past the sand dunes to a country that took up almost a quarter of the landmass.

'Saqira,' she said, her voice fond. 'Ever will I love it.'

It was the northernmost land on the map, bordered by the Seething Sea to the north and the Vanishing Islands to the east. Tuesday couldn't even pronounce half of the city names, but she traced them with her fingers anyway. 'What's it like?'

Hester smiled. 'The date trees grow heavy in the summer – the children have races to see who can climb the highest. In the north, the sacred twin cities of Sahir and Aqira shine gold in the sun. And it is said that dragons still live in the heart of the desert, buried deep beneath the sands. But I can never return.'

'Why?' If she'd found a place she loved as much as Hester seemed to love her homeland, she wouldn't let anything keep her away.

'I made a promise to myself,' Hester said softly. Her fist clenched on the map, but then she spread her fingers wide and rested her hand against the parchment with a sigh.

'But look!' she said. 'I have found my bearings. Now we must find Fortune City.'

*

Fortune City, it turned out, wasn't a city at all. Well, that wasn't entirely true. It *was* a city, but it wasn't bound by land to one location like Beggars End or the other places that Tuesday eagerly read on Hester's map: it was a flying city, made of metal and smoke, that travelled with the trade routes up and down the countries, unburdened by the laws of the land.

This made it, as Hester said, 'the home of every villain, blackguard and scoundrel from here to the Seething Sea.'

She scowled as she spread out a circular piece of oilcloth and gestured for Tuesday to help her flatten the edges over the wheel and the map that still rested against it. There were holes stitched into the oilcloth at several even points; Hester showed her how to slip them over the knobs on the edge of the helm so that the entire oilcloth lay taut. Instead of the lushly painted lands and cities of the map Hester had shown her, it was covered in columns of numbers and dots of light. Only small sections of the map could be seen beneath it.

Tuesday ran her fingers over the numbers, enjoying the feel of the slightly raised writing against her skin. 'What is it?' she asked.

'The way to Fortune City,' Hester replied, studying the oilcloth intently. 'It is a star chart of a different sort.'

Tuesday couldn't make head or tail of the strange numbers and constellations. 'Why don't you just use a normal map? Then everyone could read it.'

'*Because* everyone could read it,' Hester said. 'Fortune City was once the pride of Voltemande.'

'I know,' Tuesday cut in, excited. 'Quintalion spoke of Voltemande. He said its people were good at industry.'

'They were.' As Hester spoke, her eyes flicked from the writing on the star chart to the actual stars themselves, glittering in the darkening sky. 'They were so skilled at the metal arts that they fashioned a city in the skies, a place of escape should the gods grow jealous of their talents.'

Tuesday was pretty sure she knew how stories like this usually went. Madame Marisol had read enough of them to her while she slept, and though she couldn't remember the exact words, she still remembered the gist of the tales . . . and more than she ever wanted to know about Amiens and Aemilia.

'And the gods – the Days,' she corrected herself, remembering the proper terminology of the land, 'they waited until everyone was in the floating city and then sent a lightning storm or a hurricane and blew it out of the skies? Proving that it was the Voltemandians' hubris in their own talents that destroyed them.'

She felt quite pleased with herself for that, but Hester only shook her head and said: 'You've read too many stories. My brother would have liked you. Narvi always had his head in a book . . . if he wasn't slipping scorpions down the back of my father's robes. He would have called you his Kharkarum.'

The word sounded pleasing to Tuesday's ears, all guttural and whispered. She was about to ask Hester what it meant, but Hester got there before her.

'It is the language of my people, the Saqirans. "Two-hearts, one soul." But you are completely wrong about Fortune City,' she continued. 'Your gods did not rain terror from the skies. The Lady Fortuna, a powerful magician, liked the look of the floating city and stole it in the dead of night.'

'And now she lies at its heart, consumed by the very city she named as her own,' a deep voice spoke. 'They are linked. If one falls, so does the other.'

Quintalion appeared at the top of the stairs, stretching his lanky frame from toes to fingertips. 'We've all heard the stories. Honestly, Captain, I thought I could take a short rest without you filling the girl's head with nonsense.'

'*You* deal in nonsense, not me.' Hester sent a glare in his direction. 'I was merely providing some local colour.'

'Well, don't. If you keep telling her things, she'll get attached.'

'To what . . . the world?' Hester shot back.

Tuesday thought back to the thrill she'd felt in her bones when she opened the front door of Madame Marisol's House to let in the fresh night air. She'd known even then that she'd been born to breathe that air and travel the distant roads wherever they took her. She breathed in the same air now as it slipped up over the prow of the ship, and her feelings hadn't changed. 'I think,' she said slowly, 'that it's a little too late for that.'

'Excellent,' Quintalion said. 'See what you've done, Hester? You've got her involved. Next thing you know, she'll be searching for the Book of Days with the rest of the fools and dreamers.'

Hester just shrugged, her back to them as she lit the lanterns that hung from the mast, effusing the deck with a gentle glow that drove back the night.

'The what?' Tuesday asked. Her stomach flipped over with the thought of new discoveries, making her feel slightly ill and yet wonderful all at the same time.

'Oh dear, what have I done?'

If Tuesday ever wanted to study human emotions, she'd need only to spend a day in Quintalion's company: two hours with him was more than enough time to turn the slowest student into a master of sarcasm. Not that she'd want to learn. If she ever heard that world-weary tone in her own voice, she'd jump off the top of the nearest available building.

'You've filled the girl's head with nonsense, that's what you've done,' Hester replied, echoing Quintalion's words. 'The Book of Days? Pah. It doesn't exist except in the minds of parents desperate for stories to lull their children to sleep.'

She turned back to the star chart and studiously avoided eye contact with either of them, giving Tuesday no choice but to turn to Quintalion once again for information.

'Please,' she said, wishing that she'd been woken by a more willing storyteller, 'I'd like to know.'

'You might as well tell her,' Hester said. 'If this chart is correct, we'll be flying through the night to get to Fortune City. It has anchored up north near the Crossroads.'

Quintalion threw his hands up in defeat. 'Fine, fine,' he said. 'You win. I am a slave to your curiosity.'

Not even the prospect of her first full night was enough to deter Tuesday from questioning Quintalion about this Book of Days. She watched him walk away from her, and was about to trail along after him when he returned with a handful of nets, dropped them into a pile near the helm, and settled himself on them with his legs crossed and his elbows on his knees.

Tuesday seated herself beside him silently, for fear that even a single word would break the spell.

'There is little enough to tell,' he began, 'and doubtless not enough to satisfy you.'

'Try,' she told him. The cold had burned away the clouds and left the stars diamond bright in the darkening sky. Tuesday flopped onto her back so that they filled her vision as she listened to Quintalion. Her satchel made a suitable headrest and, if she pulled her hood far over her face, she could pretend they were the only people in the entire world, sailing through a sea of stars where the daybreakers would never find her.

'Well,' he said, coughing awkwardly, 'where to begin . . .'

CHAPTER TEN

'I find the beginning is always a good place.' Hester made one final adjustment to their course and then, unexpectedly, came to sit in front of them on the deck, with her wooden leg laid out in front of her. 'I know little about your myth-stories,' she said, loosening the clasps on her leg, 'but I would imagine this one begins with the Book of Days.'

'I thought you didn't believe in it,' Quintalion said, shooting her a sideways glance. 'I thought that it was nonsense.'

'I said *myth-stories*, did I not?' She shrugged. 'Besides, it is always pleasurable to pass an evening telling tales . . . no matter how fanciful they may be.'

Fanciful or not, Tuesday wished that Quintalion would get on with the story. She was about to tell him so when he stretched, sighed and finally said, 'Then you're right. It does begin with the Book of Days. But perhaps the better beginning is how the Book of Days itself came into being.'

'If it is a book,' Tuesday said, her time being read to by Madame Marisol making her feel an expert on the topic, 'then it was written.'

'Ah,' Quintalion said in a gleeful tone, 'but it isn't just any old book. It contains the knowledge and experience of the Days themselves. If you were to read from the Book of Days, you could learn how to become the greatest warrior the world has ever seen, or build impossible buildings, or fly. It is even said that Frey whispered into it the secrets of coaxing life from death.'

'Ridiculous,' Hester barked out. 'The dead cannot return to the land of the living. It is impossible.' She bit her lip and turned away, hugging her body, though the night was mild enough for Tuesday to remove her cloak and lay it next to her on the deck.

'Perhaps,' Quintalion conceded, 'but that doesn't change the fact that it's dangerous. I've seen the Shining Ones and lived to tell the tale. I know what it can do.'

'The Shining Ones?' Tuesday asked.

Quintalion waved her question away. 'I'm getting ahead of myself. If you don't want to be here all night, you won't interrupt me again.'

But Tuesday wouldn't have minded if the story continued all night and through to the morning. Her thoughts raced with each new piece of information about the world around her, and she tapped her foot impatiently to hear more. It was like a tapestry: she might marvel at the colour and pattern at first glance, but only when she looked at each individual thread could she truly appreciate its complexity. She nodded for him to continue.

'The Days created the Book when they had no other choice,' he said, 'or else they wouldn't have risked it. A great shadow stalked the land – like a night without the promise of dawn. No one knew where it had come from – deep beneath the ground, most assumed, or bearing down from the north and its impassable seas – but there were whispers that it was not of our world at all. It had no name. People began to call it the Mora –'

'Trampling death,' Tuesday said. She didn't know how she knew the translation, but she just *did*, deep inside of her.

Quintalion nodded. 'The Days fought this evil, but its power was too great. Only by combining their own strength could they have a hope of defeating it. So they poured all their knowledge and power into the creation of this Book, though it left them little more than us mere mortals.'

His face twisted into a sneer. 'Stupid of them, really, but what are you going to do when a creature of darkness threatens the lands? And technically it worked: with their powers united in the Book of Days, they finally banished the Mora from our world.'

'My people have similar legends,' Hester cut in. 'A fire-djinn, all consuming, turns our fertile valleys to sand. Of course, being a Saqiran tale, the story does not end so happily. The djinn is banished by a warrior scholar, who reads the rains down from her magical book of life, which drown both the warrior and the djinn alike.'

'A true party pleaser,' Quintalion remarked dryly.

'I liked it,' Tuesday said, and shot Hester a quick smile.

'Well, you *would*, wouldn't you? Now where was I? Ah, yes.' He lay down on his back on the deck and pillowed his head in his hands. 'Years passed, and the days turned into nights and back again, as they are wont to do. The Days knew that they could never let their Book fall into the hands of a mortal.'

'Why?' Tuesday blurted out.

'What did I tell you about interrupting?'

She looked over at him innocently. 'And *you're* wasting even more time scolding me for it. Just tell me why a mortal can't read the Book.'

Hester, who had been rooting around in the storage spaces cut into the mast, choked out a laugh. 'She's got a point.'

'How did I know you would side with her? Oh, very well. The Book contains too much knowledge for a single mind. No one can know *everything* without going insane. Think about it, if it contains all the collected wisdom and experience from seven immortal gods, how many words do you think it's going to take for your brain to explode?'

'None,' she said promptly, 'because I wouldn't read it.' *But you would*, a little voice in the back of her head told her. *And you'd know everything and live and wouldn't that be grand.*

'That's possibly the first intelligent thing I've heard come out of your mouth. Well done, Tuesday.'

Hester pulled out a dark-coloured bottle that had been hidden behind the swords in the mast. 'Get on with it, Quintalion,' she said. 'There is mead to be drunk.'

He frowned at her under the brim of his hat, but continued on: 'The Days, knowing the curiosity of the mortals, which if it is anything like a certain girl I know, gave them quite a headache, swore never to let the Book of Days out of their sight. They took turns guarding it and using its power – helping the crops grow, healing the sick – and everything was just dandy.

'But the Voltemandians were a proud people. They refused the Days' help and resented those who accepted it. And it wasn't long before the chieftains, eager for war, fanned that resentment into white-hot hatred of the Days and all those who still worshipped them. In those days, Voltemande was just a collection of little backwater mountain towns, barely deserving to be called a country. It wouldn't have had a hope against the Days if not for Sannen's moronic bragging. When it was his turn to guard the Book of Days, he couldn't help but show off to Voltemande. "Look at how much better my furnace is than yours. You call those iron-forged weapons? *This* is how you forge weapons." Call it accidental teaching by taunting. And in a hundred years, Voltemande went from a country of goat farmers to the most disciplined and well-equipped army in the lands.'

'South of the Burnished Plains, I think you mean.' Hester raised an eyebrow.

'Of course, my dear lady,' Quintalion said, bowing his head in her direction. 'Tantallon, a peaceful farming country and the breadbasket of the world, was the first to fall to Voltemande. Then, once Tantallon was defeated, Voltemande's army turned its full attention to the west. They struck with wave after wave of soldiers, overpowering those who had rallied under the banner of the Days. It was at the Crossroads that the Days made their last stand.'

'I heard they had no more than a hundred souls against an army of many thousands,' Hester said, carefully uncorking the bottle.

'Not half so many,' Quintalion said. He stretched out on the deck, and his eyes shone bright in the light of the solitary lantern. 'Voltemande had them surrounded. The only thing keeping them alive was Voltemande's fear of the old ways. They knew that the Days still had the Book, cornered as they were, and a trapped wolf is twice a terror. So they held back. But the longer that the Days didn't call down lightning and fire from the skies, the bolder they grew, and soon Voltemande's forces were little more than a hundred feet away. The Days knew that there was no choice. Once again they would have to turn to the Book. They argued among themselves how best to end the war: Thestia and Satyr were all for imbuing their own warriors with the strength of ten men and slaughtering the Voltemandians where they stood; Wenslas wanted to call up a mighty wave and wash them away.'

'It would not have ended well,' Hester said with a knowing look.

'In the end, it was Thaïs who came up with the idea. Their people were tired, and hopeless, and scared. Surely Voltemande's army was as well. Thaïs suggested that they use the Book of Days to amplify that fear and hopelessness. Surely, she thought, if the invading army were too scared to fight, then peace must follow.'

'But it didn't,' Tuesday said. She had heard enough stories in the darkness of her keeping-house to know how these things turned out.

Quintalion sat up suddenly and wrapped his arms around his long legs. His greatcoat fluttered in the light breeze. 'No, it didn't. Satyr was guarding the Book of Days, so it was his final decision. Thaïs had always been his favourite sister, and so he agreed with her plan.'

'What happened?' she urged, a shiver passing through her. Something deliciously terrible was on its way.

'If you cease these infernal questions, I'll tell you,' he said, and shifted impatiently. 'Instead of bringing peace, it drove the Voltemandian army mad. They tore at their clothes and fell onto their own weapons, out of their minds with wild, animalistic fear. They destroyed each other, and would have attacked the Days' army also, if Satyr hadn't had the first good idea that day and ordered a retreat. Their fear incited them to lash out at those around them; their hopelessness tore away their self-preservation. They were the perfect killers, fighting without reason, hope or mercy.'

He drew his coat tighter around himself. 'Over the years, they became known as the Shining Ones, because the glint of sun or moon off their armour was the last thing you'd see before you found yourself a permanent guest of the City of Lost Things. There's fewer than a hundred of them left now, I've heard. So I suppose, in the end, Thaïs's idea worked. Voltemande never came as close to defeating the Days as they had that moment, and the Saturday Wars petered out not long after. We've had skirmishes, of course, over borders and lands, but the fighting was never as fierce.'

'What happened to her?' Tuesday breathed. 'To Thaïs?'

Quintalion shrugged. 'Who knows? After that, the Days faded out of everyday life. They were seen less and less as the years dragged on. Eventually people began to think them long dead, if they'd ever existed at all.'

'That is not the way I've heard it told,' Hester said. She had prised the cork off with one of her knives and now took a swig of the contents of the bottle. A sweet smell drifted through the air. 'It is rumoured in the taverns and alleyways that your Thaïs waited until it was her turn to guard the Book and disappeared with it. That it has not been heard of since. Of course,' she added with a haughty sniff, 'it is all utter rot.'

'So you keep saying.' Quintalion exchanged a look with Tuesday, and then slapped his palm down on the deck. 'Now let's have that mead. I wish to spend our journey to Fortune City completely forgetting about why we're going to Fortune City.'

Did she really run away? Tuesday thought as Hester passed the bottle to Quintalion. If she had done what Thaïs had – accidentally turned loyal soldiers into a pack of merciless killers and unleashed them on the world – then perhaps she would have run too. But it all seemed so sad to her. *She didn't mean to hurt anyone. She was just trying to save her family and her people.*

She wished to hear more, but Quintalion shook his head when she asked him. The next couple of minutes passed in a silence broken only by the swallows of Quintalion and Hester, who shared the mead between them, both of them frowning when she refused a mouthful.

'It is bad luck to turn down a drink, girl,' Hester told her.

'I'll have the next one,' she replied, still deep in thought.

Gradually, though, as the night drew on around them, the mead loosened her companion's tongues, and the tale of the Book of Days led to other stories.

Hester spoke of her childhood growing up in Keshlahar, a desert oasis; Tuesday was drawn from her thoughtful melancholy by the sound of the woman's laughter as she told the story of her brother lacing the communal meal with the red peppers that grew at the edge of the encampment, and how the entire council of elders fell over each other to drink the oasis dry.

And when Quintalion regaled them with his first theft, begrudgingly at first, and then, once Hester uncorked a fine flask of small ale, with increasingly animated hand gestures, Tuesday forgot all about Thaïs and the Book of Days, and even took some of the ale, though she swallowed too quickly and the liquid bubbled up her nose and burned her lips. She shoved the flask back at Hester, who laughed her rich, fruity laugh and said something about being young in the ways of the world and how she should treasure it, but the world Hester spoke of was blurring at the edges, and when Quintalion, demonstrating how he'd made his daring escape dressed as a woman, accidentally nudged Tuesday clean over, she tumbled into an ale-induced giggling fit.

With slurred words, Tuesday told them of waking up – ignoring Quintalion when he complained that he'd lived it already and didn't need a recap, thank you very much – and also of her strange dream. Hester went still and silent for a while after that, but then Quintalion started up on how Tiamatan wine was better than Aqiran wine, which of course caused Hester to bring out a bottle of the two to compare, and the three of them sailed all the way to Fortune City in a happy, muzzy mess.

*

Ow. Other thoughts refused to form, beaten into submission by the pounding headache in the back of her ... everywhere. *Ow, ow, ow.*

Tuesday dragged herself into a semi-upright position and opened her eyes. The sun had the audacity to shine directly in her line of sight, causing her to wince, grasp her head and wonder why she now felt like she had two men with sledgehammers competing to see who could split open her skull first.

She'd been on a boat. Only it wasn't just a boat ... it flew. And there'd been words, words that pierced behind her eyes when she tried to make any sense of them. And drink. Lots of drink.

'Oh.' She exhaled it in a single long syllable. That explained so many things, like why she currently wanted to stab herself in the eyeballs with the closest sharp instrument, and why the stars had deserted her for the cruel sun.

'Are we there yet?' she asked.

'Yes, girl,' came a voice that was entirely too cheerful given the circumstances. 'We have arrived at Fortune City.'

Tuesday turned to find Hester at the helm, though she kept listing to the side. Or so Tuesday thought until her right shoulder hit the deck and she realised she'd slid back down without noticing, giving her an excellent, if unwanted, view of Quintalion snoring on his back next to her. His arm shaded most of his face except for his mouth, from the side of which a single line of drool crept with aspirations of freedom.

Suddenly Hester was right in front of her, helping her to sit up again and pressing something into her hands – a warm something in an iron mug.

'Drink this,' Hester told her. 'It'll make you feel better.'

Tuesday shifted her legs underneath her so that her dress wouldn't get caught when she stood. 'What is it?'

'Willow bark tea.' Once she was sure Tuesday had a proper hold of the mug, Hester let go and straightened back up. 'My grandmother swore by it. Slower than a camel's kick and just as unpleasant.'

Tuesday scrunched her nose up when she took a sip of the tea, remembering the strange dream Madame Marisol's tea had left her with. The bitterness rushed straight into her mouth and down her gullet without leaving her time to process it, and she spluttered and coughed half the first mouthful back up onto the deck and down the front of her dress. 'I have to agree,' she said, grimacing, 'with your grandmother.'

Hester smiled. 'Most folks did, if they didn't want a slap in the face.' She turned back to the helm and said over her shoulder, 'When you're feeling up to it, I thought you might want to view the city before we dock. It is a real sight.'

Pinching her nose, Tuesday swallowed the rest of the tea in three large gulps. The dregs were the worst part. They coated her mouth in foul-tasting slime that left her wishing she'd never heard of mead or small ale. Soon enough, though, the ferocious pounding in her head began to dim.

The sledgehammer competition must be ending, she thought as she pushed herself to her feet, still keeping her eyes squeezed almost all the way shut against the light.

Remembering her twisted ankle, she gingerly tested her weight upon it. The pain flared and then simmered down to a manageable level. She leaned over and, turning away from the others, peeled one of her stockings down from her thigh, wanting to see how bad her ankle was. It had throbbed terribly yesterday, but she was relieved to find that the night's rest must have helped, because, though still swollen, it gave her little trouble when she took a few cautious steps.

She rolled up the stocking, fastened her garter again, and walked lightly across the deck.

'Kick your friend while you're at it,' Hester called to her. 'It is time for him to wake as well.'

'I'll have you know,' came a voice from beneath Quintalion's arm, 'that I've been awake for hours.'

'Ah, so the snoring coming from your direction was clearly just a trick of my hearing. Forgive me,' Hester said, sharing a secret smile with Tuesday.

Quintalion eased himself into a sitting position with a remarkable amount of grace for someone who'd been drooling not two minutes before. He rubbed his hands over his face and stretched out, catlike.

'We're here,' Tuesday told him. 'That is, I haven't seen Fortune City myself, but Hester says we're here, so we must really be here, right?'

'If you'd look starboard, you'll see that we are.' Hester pointed to the right.

Tuesday, who had just taken a step to the left, turned back on herself and tottered over to the side of the ship. When she spotted the city floating before them, she blinked three times very hard and then rubbed a fist over her eyes, sure that she was still dreaming.

'Oh my,' she breathed. Fortune City was like nothing she'd ever seen before. It was as if someone had dumped four cities on top of each other: the buildings twisted around, and sometimes through, each other in a chaotic, smoke-filled mess of brick and steel. Seven towers loomed over the city, so tall that their upper levels peeked out of the choking black smog like chimneys.

A constant stream of ships of all kinds made their way to Fortune City, docking in the many floating platforms that had been tethered to the edges, and narrowly avoiding the flames licking up from the engines that must have kept the whole city afloat.

And the noise! Clanking and whirring and metallic shrieks. The whoosh of the many flames beneath the city. And underneath the sound of machinery, an endless bass thrum that reverberated around Tuesday's head. She clapped her hands over her ears.

Hester laughed. 'The first time I came here, you would have found me in the same position. The drums of Fortune City, as they call them, take a while to get used to.'

'What are you talking about?' Quintalion joined her by the railing, shrugging on his greatcoat. 'I hear only the dulcet tones of opportunity.'

'I think Tuesday here wishes the dulcet tones of opportunity would take a day off.'

'No, thank you,' Quintalion said. 'I have no wish to fall to my death today.'

Hester eased the wheel forward. The *Zephyr*, ever responsive to its captain's orders, surged down, and they sailed into the smoke and the noise that was Fortune City.

CHAPTER ELEVEN

The understreets were a twisting, stinking maze of paths and tunnels that wove in and out of the buildings, filled with smoke and dust and darkness. The sun had dawned brilliant in a pale blue sky, but it might as well have been midnight for all the good it was doing.

'I tell you, it's going to get looted,' Hester said, worrying at her lip. She had reluctantly left the *Zephyr* in the care of the harbourmaster in a dock to the east end of the city, but not before packing her musket and hiding several knives about her person, claiming that they would do more good with her than in the harbourmaster's pockets.

Despite Hester having pinned the man against the mast and promised him a swift and gruesome death should anything happen to her ship, Tuesday had to agree with her. He had licked his chapped lips when he'd spotted the chests on the *Zephyr*'s main decks, and though Tuesday wanted to believe the best of him, he'd seemed a little too interested when they'd told him they'd be gone for at least a day.

'And I say it won't.' Quintalion strode ahead of them, not even breaking his pace when he ducked to squeeze through an area of road where the houses on either side leaned over so much from age and disrepair that they were almost touching.

Tuesday hurried after him. The smoke was even thicker on the streets and she didn't want to lose him in the blackness. It was hotter here in the north, so she'd left her cloak on the ship, but she covered her mouth with a sleeve to breathe in as little of the acrid smog as possible.

Everything in Fortune City was black, as if someone had painted it on with a brush. Tuesday ran a finger down the nearest house, a little stained dwelling with greying washing strung from the windows: it came away streaked with soot.

To the side of the street was a shrine, so dark with grime that she could barely make out the statue in the alcove, which was chipped and faded. Melted candle wax covered the base of the figure, hardened into a black tar that almost obscured the patina-fogged nameplate: *Sannen, patron of innovation and industry.*

'Why is it so dirty?' she wondered aloud. This was a shrine to Sannen, one of the Days. Surely it deserved a more dignified fate than rotting in some forgotten corner.

'The city runs on steam,' Hester told her as she glanced at Quintalion, who walked even further ahead of them now, disappearing in and out of the mist. 'But do not bother with broken-down shrines of old gods. They can no longer take offence.'

Still, she felt sorry for the shrine, silent and still in the rush of the city. She dug around in her bag and pulled out a coin, and placed it at the base of the statue, avoiding the worst of the congealed wax. It may not have been a candle, but hopefully Sannen wouldn't mind. She needed all the help she could get.

Hurrying to catch up with Hester, who had started off after Quintalion, she noticed that it wasn't only the buildings that were black. The smoke got into every crevice. It settled on clothes and skin in fine layers that smeared when Tuesday tried to rub them off. The people jostling past her must have been used to it, for they all wore clothing of blacks and greys: trousers, sweat-stained shirts and caps or battered top hats for the men, and scarves and dresses hitched up in their belts for the women.

They all seemed to have things to do and not enough time to do them in. They hustled along mostly in packs or, if they travelled alone, they kept one hand on their belts and wove through the crowd with their heads lowered and their eyes on the ground before them.

Tuesday, who had been looking every which way, accidentally smacked into a tall man coming the other way, eliciting only a rough, 'Watch where you're going,' as he ploughed past her.

'They're a friendly lot, aren't they?' she commented.

'If you want friendly, head somewhere you can pay people for their smiles.' Quintalion appeared in front of her out of the smoke. 'You won't get it here. It's bad for their reputation. Now hurry up – I want to get to the court before the bells ring for nine.'

He led them through the twisting alleyways and up a flight of stairs cobbled onto the outside of a building. They creaked as Tuesday ascended them; she looked down to find that they were made out of old fruit crates and barnacle-covered planks.

There were metal railings above them, barely discernible in the murky light. The sun did its best, but it couldn't penetrate the choking smoke here at Fortune City's ground level. The most it could manage was a weak ray of light that brightened the very tops of the seven tallest towers, but they looked hazy and indistinct from below.

Strange carriages zipped along the railings, ducking around the buildings, and even occasionally going straight through open windows, ruffling the many items of clothing that had been left – somewhat optimistically, Tuesday thought – to dry in the light breeze.

'What are they?' she asked.

'Our transportation.' Quintalion stopped at the top of the rickety stairway, and Tuesday followed him closely, only looking back to make certain that Hester still followed them. Sure enough, the woman brought up the rear of their little party with her musket draped casually across her shoulder in a manner that almost invited trouble.

A small carriage was perched on the rail running past their makeshift platform. It swung to the right suddenly as two gentlemen in bowler hats and cream suits emerged from the carriage, fussing with their identical black umbrellas. The driver, who sat on the front wearing goggles and thumbing through a newspaper, held his open hand out to them without looking up from the article he was reading, and silently took the two coins the gentlemen gave him.

The gentlemen then departed through a door in the side of the building, so engaged in a heated discussion about the price of silk cravats that they didn't notice when three grubby-faced youths made off with their pocketbooks.

Tuesday was about to shout out to them when Hester grabbed her arm. 'Don't,' she said. 'This city is free from the laws of the grounded. There is a code.'

'Besides, they deserved it,' Quintalion said, waving the carriage driver on. 'Swanning around in the lower levels with their silk and their cream linens. They were lucky it was pickpockets and not a nobbler.'

He *had*, however, done up the buttons on his own greatcoat so that his pretty waistcoat couldn't be seen beneath the plain wool.

Quintalion let another four carriages rattle by them in quick succession. They were all different from the first carriage. One was a pig cart that had been fitted to the railings badly enough that Tuesday heard it squealing along before she saw it. It raced by them with a family of four clutching desperately onto the back. Two more lacked roofs or doors, and another wasn't a carriage at all, but a pitiful little chain of seats held together by rope and peddled along by the driver, who sat on a bicycle and mopped at his face with a polka-dotted handkerchief.

'There's no fixed transportation here,' Quintalion told her when she asked why they were all so different. 'Any old louse with a couple of wheels and enough money to grease the right palms can set up shop.'

He finally settled on the fifth carriage, an open-air vehicle. It was so small that Tuesday had to hop up onto the hobble seat at the back, but it shone with a new coat of blue paint and lacked any bits that looked like they were about to fall off. It even had a footman, clinging to the back of the carriage.

'All aboard,' the driver yelled. He threw a look over at Quintalion. 'Where to?'

'The Lady Fortuna's court. And there's an extra copper for you if you get us there before the next bell.'

The driver nodded and reached down to his right to tug at the throttle. A plume of choking black smoke shot out of the end of the carriage into the unfortunate footman's face.

'Any luggage?' he asked through a mouthful of soot.

Quintalion raised an eyebrow at him. 'Do you think I'm a fool?'

'Couldn't say, sir,' the footman replied cheerfully, wiping his face with the back of his torn sleeve. His eyes darted to Tuesday. 'Would a fool understand that there are those who'd give their eyeteeth to know the location of the girl you've got with you?'

Tuesday shrank back. The hairs on her arms rose and, despite the oppressive heat of the lower levels, she suddenly felt cold. She glanced around, certain she'd see daybreakers lurking in the mist or Sterling's piercing eyes staring out at her from a dark corner, but there was only the endless rush of bodies passing by on the streets beneath them.

'Perhaps,' Quintalion said, more to stall for time than as an actual answer, Tuesday thought. When he next spoke, his words were quiet and thoughtful. 'But a *wise* man would know that he never saw her. Last the wise man heard, she was heading out west to Ormonde.'

'West?' The footman coughed out a laugh that sent a black cloud of smoke shooting into the air. 'She'd be killed. Do you know whose territory we're flying over?'

'We have no care of spears and horses and the horns of war.' Hester rested the barrel of her musket against her knees. It was so long that it poked Quintalion in the thigh before he shifted around to find a more comfortable position.

'Well, I do,' the footman said, adjusting his cap. 'The Shining Ones give me the willies. They'd have her clean out of her bones before she had the time to scream. A wise man'd say she was headed south. The border cities are a sullen lot, but they at least won't devour her essence.'

Tuesday felt the knife against her throat. She raised a hand to ward against the blow, but there was nothing there. 'No,' she said quietly. 'I can't go back.'

The carriage lurched forward and they began to gain speed. Tuesday grabbed onto her wooden seat with one hand to keep from flying off as they accelerated, but kept the other resting on her collarbone in defence against the knife, even if it was only in her mind.

'So the girl is heading south.' Quintalion apparently hadn't noticed her fears. He was too busy digging through his pockets.

There was a flash of gold in the darkness and then the footman doffed his cap, said, 'Right you are, mister,' and tucked himself in against the back of the carriage to avoid the worst of the smoke.

'You won't make me go back there, will you?' Tuesday asked Quintalion. Her fingers beat a tattoo against the column of her neck. 'I mean, I want to find out who I was, but not if I ever have to see that man again. His eyes . . .'

'Of course not,' Quintalion said. 'Now when we get to the Lady's court, let me do all the talking. We've an understanding, her and I.'

'I want nothing to do with any of your understandings,' Hester said darkly, hugging her musket.

'Will she know how to find out who I am?'

'For a price, no doubt. The Lady has the good sense never to do anything for free.' Quintalion turned the lapels of his greatcoat up against the wind.

Tuesday copied him, pressing her sleeve against her face. The carriage was zipping along the railings now and, without a roof, the choking dust blew directly into their faces. *But it's all worth it*, she thought. She'd climb mountains or swim the seas if the Lady Fortuna told her it would help her to discover her past.

They shot along the railing, skirting past houses and towers and – once – straight through the middle of a heated game of billiards. Quintalion just missed being impaled by the cue.

Flocks of pigeons followed them everywhere. They squawked and squabbled over the rooftops and makeshift walkways that ran from house to house. Besides the pigeons and a marmalade cat curled up on a windowsill, the only other living creatures were the rats. They scuttled along the rails before the carriages, occasionally squealing as they fell to their deaths if they weren't fast enough to avoid the oncoming traffic. There must have been other animals, she pondered as they did what felt like the third lap around the same tower, because to her knowledge pigeons didn't eat rats. Or maybe the pigeons in Fortune City did.

It certainly seemed like that sort of place. It was a city of thousands built for hundreds, and so the people had made space wherever they could. When their carriage suddenly dipped below the street level, there were even people there, crowded in the darkness at the edge of the lamplight.

Tuesday had thought Fortune City was only its streets and its clusters of buildings, but here beneath the ground, there was a whole other world. The driver took them past endless rooms, effortlessly switching tracks every couple of minutes and throwing them all into steep curves that made them cling onto their seats for fear of being flung out into the darkness. It was like a honeycomb, with rooms so small that you'd hit your head on the ceiling, and great halls that took them ten seconds to cross even at the speed they were travelling.

And everywhere in this subterranean world was life. The people huddled together in families, sharing hunks of broken black bread, playing cards, singing songs or, to Tuesday's shock, picking over the bodies that had found their way to the lower levels, all in clear view of the carriages going past.

The people glanced at them with disinterest as they rode on by. They lived in public, they conducted their business in public, and they died in public. Tuesday wouldn't have been surprised if the most cherished item in Fortune City wasn't jewels or gold, but an empty room; she'd been in the floating city for only a couple of hours and yet she already burned for the space and fresh air they'd left behind on the *Zephyr*.

'Is it always like this?' she asked Quintalion as they dashed past a funeral procession in lavender silks, mourning with their hands raised over their heads and fat tears rolling down their cheeks.

'Like what?'

'This,' she replied, and waved her arm to indicate the scenes around them.

He laughed. 'Privacy is for those with nothing to hide. What's a few hundred extra friends when there's sport such as this to be had?'

Quintalion inclined his head to the right, and Tuesday turned from her precarious seat to see a cockfight in full progress in a room that couldn't have been larger than Madame Marisol's sitting room, the men crowded around the ring and the frantic birds nipping at each other until the blood and the feathers flew.

And then another turn in the rail hid the scene from view. The driver stopped pedalling and their vehicle began to slow down, finally pulling to a stop outside some stairs carved into the rock that led up to a closed metal door guarded by two men with pikes.

'The Lady Fortuna's court,' the driver said, and held out his hand.

'Yes, yes.' Quintalion impatiently flung a coin in his direction and then opened the carriage's half-door and stepped out onto the rock.

With his weight gone, the carriage leaned precariously to the right, and Hester scrambled to the left to compensate. Tuesday threw herself off the top seat in a single leap, afraid that, had she stayed any longer, she would find herself hanging upside down with the rest of the unbalanced carriage.

'Now remember,' Quintalion said as Tuesday dusted herself off the best she could, 'don't say a word when we enter. Don't even look at her, you understand?'

'Yes, Quintalion.' She chewed at the inside of her lip before adding, 'But surely it would be better if I brought my own case to her?'

'Not a peep,' he said, and then turned and bounded up the stairs two at a time to talk to the guards. Their conversation had a lot of hand gestures and, though Tuesday couldn't make out what they said, several exclamation marks by the sound of Quintalion's raised voice.

After another minute or so of arguing, the guards began unlocking the great door, as a very smug Quintalion looked on with his arms crossed. And then he and Hester gestured to her, and she tripped up the stairs and into the Lady Fortuna's court.

CHAPTER TWELVE

Like the rest of Fortune City, the Lady Fortuna's court teemed with life. It was a small room, hardly larger than the hovel Tuesday had hidden in back at Beggars End, and yet it contained what looked like fifty or sixty people, all standing shoulder to shoulder in a pushing, sweaty throng that smelled of unwashed silk and smoke.

Above them, hanging from the ceiling, were all manner of bottles, glass oddities and vials, but Tuesday didn't spare them a second look, for she was more interested in the Lady Fortuna herself. Though she stood on her tiptoes, she was at the very back of the crowd and couldn't make anything out but the backs of heads, which were very interesting but hardly what she had come to see.

'Here,' hissed Quintalion. He'd already manoeuvred himself to a less dense area of the crowd.

Tuesday hastened to join him. In her head, she was already rehearsing the words she would say to the Lady Fortuna, if Quintalion gave her the chance to speak. *Honoured Lady*. She had heard that in a book Madame Marisol had read to her and had always liked the way it sounded. *Honoured Lady . . . I have come here to beg your help.*

Tuesday hurried over to Quintalion, who silently gestured for her to slip through the gap between a woman with a nose ring and the man next to her who was standing on an empty box of Johnson's Soap.

The man seemed to have found a good vantage point, and she half-wanted to join him, but the murmurs of the crowd blocked any chance she had of hearing the Lady Fortuna, and so Tuesday instead ducked down and pushed between the woman and the man on the soap box, apologising as she jostled them. Hester followed her, not bothering to duck, but rather sweeping aside the people in her way with her musket, which she wielded like a staff, leaving behind a chorus of complaints and indignant cries. When she looked back, Tuesday saw that Quintalion was swanning along in Hester's wake, and soon all three of them made it almost to the front of the room.

'Where is the Lady Fortu–' Tuesday began, before trailing into silence as a booming female voice sounded in the air.

'You bring the man known as Sebastian Sol to the Lady Fortuna. What, pray tell, is his crime?'

If Tuesday snuck between the two people in front of her, and twisted her neck to the right, she could just make out a man kneeling, flanked on either side by two men. Though he faced away from her, Tuesday knew he was crying, for his whole body shook with the force of the tears. *What has he done?*

One of the men doffed his cap and shifted nervously before something that Tuesday couldn't see. 'Begging your pardon, milady, but I don't like to bring it up before an honourable court such as yours.'

'And what is a court if not to condemn crimes?'

Quintalion appeared at Tuesday's elbow.

'I thought you said this was a lawless place,' she said to him, and then turned to Hester, who stood on her other side. 'That it's filled with every blackguard, villain and scoundrel.'

Quintalion shrugged, so close to her that she felt the movement against her own shoulder. 'Even criminals have their codes.'

Up the front of the court, the man turned his hat over in his hands. 'Right,' he said, 'well, Sol here was seen by my cousin, who's a merchant sailor what deals in hay when the times is good and a little bit on the side when they ain't so good, if you know what I mean . . .'

'Kindly get to the point,' the voice said again, 'or you might find yourself before the court as well . . . and I won't be so lenient.'

The man's ears flushed red. 'Sorry, your worship, your eminence, milady . . .'

'Sol was seen entering the daybreaker outpost in Belborough, Lady.' The man to Sebastian Sol's right took over from his companion, who had finally stuttered into silence.

'Was he now?'

'I didn't say anything, I swear it!' The accused man clasped his hands in front of him in entreaty. 'It's just my wife is ill – it's the smoke, you know, it gets on her lungs – and they said they could help her. They've got doctors there in the east . . . *real* doctors. I never told them anything.'

'You expect the Lady Fortuna to believe your silence?' The voice was scathing, hard as metal.

Tuesday moved to the right and darted into a spot that had just been made vacant courtesy of Hester's musket in the ribs of the man in front of her. The Lady Fortuna was seated at the front of the room. The man's coat still obscured most of her, but Tuesday could just make out the restless movement of her knee as she beat her leg in time with the engines thrumming beneath them.

'It's not for me to say whether you believe it or not, milady, but it's the truth, I swear it.' Without warning, Sebastian Sol lurched to his feet. He made it a couple of paces, pushing through the low-hanging vials, before his legs crumbled and he collapsed, sobbing, on the ground. Several of the bottles smashed to the ground. He curled his body around one of them and then shied away when the two guards grabbed him and hauled him to his feet back before the Lady.

'Your crime,' the Lady Fortuna said to the unfortunate man, 'is great.'

'Mercy,' he muttered, his words distorted by the sobs that tore themselves from his throat. His blond hair tangled in his eyes. He could have been considered handsome but for his contorting face as he cried.

'Mercy?' She laughed, but it was not full-bodied and uproarious as Madame Marisol's had been, nor even the sly chuckle that the mead had drawn from Quintalion, but rather a cold sound that echoed in the silent hall. 'I grant no mercy for those who threaten my city.'

'I would never . . . I swear it on my children's lives . . .' His shoulders quaked, but the tears on his face had dried. He slumped against his captors, who, after looking to the Lady for confirmation, spun him around in front of the crowd.

Tuesday ducked underneath the elbow of the man before her, who wasn't even watching the proceedings but darting nervous glances behind him at Hester. Ignoring Quintalion's frantic whispers for her to *get back here this instant*, she turned to one side to slide past a corpulent man with a row of medals pinned to his blue sash, and excused herself as she passed his equally large wife, who had a hairdo almost as tall again as she was. Three more people and she'd be through to the front. She'd never considered herself particularly tall – not after travelling with Quintalion – but now for the first time she noticed how difficult it was to push through the rustling skirts and pressed trousers of the court without causing a commotion.

Someone shifted before her. The Lady Fortuna's arm came into view, immobile against the armrest. Tuesday had to stare at it for a moment before she could distinguish it from the chair: it was the same golden colour, shining in the light of the lanterns above, and locked into position by three bars that ran from one side of the chair to the other. *Is she a prisoner too?*

'The Lady Fortuna has heard enough. I am ready to pronounce my sentence.'

'I hope it's better than the last one,' someone whispered to her right. 'Beheading wasn't any fun at all.'

'Beheading?' she repeated to herself in horror.

'The one before that was good. When was it . . . a week ago, two? The one where she broke all her bones? Most amusing.'

Tuesday couldn't believe what she was hearing. A chill sank into her. The crowd pressed tighter and tighter as they surged forward to hear the Lady Fortuna's judgement, and the closer they got, the more her chest tightened, locking her breath in her throat.

'Sebastian Sol,' the Lady Fortuna said, drawing ripples of anticipated tittering from the crowd. 'My pronouncement is thus: for the rest of your natural life, you will be condemned to dream of your death. And then, at the moment of your death, you will wake and find that your death has deserted you.'

'No!' The cry tore itself from Tuesday. She pushed aside those before her, the crowd already parting at the disturbance.

'Fantastic.' Quintalion's voice came from somewhere in the background.

Tuesday threw herself before the throne. 'You can't!' she said, hardly believing that the words were her own. 'I hate the daybreakers as much as anyone, but you can't do that to him. It's not right.'

But it was too late. To her right, Sebastian began to shake. His eyes rolled back in his head and he let out a shriek that turned Tuesday's blood cold, flinging his arms up wide against unseen foes.

The two guards backed away from him, staring at his twisted face, and then ran. They disappeared into the crowd, which was rippling with people pushing each other to better see the spectacle before them. Whispers filled the room.

'Why did you . . . ?' Tuesday shrank back from the quivering man at her feet and suddenly found herself face to face with the woman sitting in the chair. The words died on her lips.

The Lady Fortuna bled. She bled from a thousand cuts all over her body, and the blood flowed into the chair, and the harness that held her strapped into it. The oldest wounds were scabbed over, the skin around them mottled and flecked with bronze, but the newest, some deep enough to be fatal, dotted her bare neck, upon which a single metal prong looped around and pinned her to the back of the chair, like some perverted necklace.

The skin not covered in blood was deadly white, and the way that tiny tremors continuously ran over her body made Tuesday think that the only reason Lady Fortuna was still upright was the chair and its metal shackles around her neck, chest, waist, hips and ankles. She wore a white dress stained with blood. Her black hair was tied in a long braid that coiled around her shoulders like a snake. Her face was ageless but for the lines around her pale eyes as she frowned down at Tuesday.

'And what is this?' she said. 'Can the girl-child not stomach the price of power?'

Tuesday tried to tear her eyes away from the bleeding woman, but she couldn't. She sputtered into silence, all thoughts of why she was here melting away.

'I'm extremely sorry, my lady. You have my utmost assurances that she won't interrupt you again.'

Quintalion. Her thoughts were sluggish, and it wasn't until he was pulling on her arm to raise her from her supine position that Tuesday even realised Quintalion had moved.

'You,' the Lady Fortuna said to him. 'I thought I killed you years ago.'

'It's good to see you too.' Quintalion tugged on Tuesday's arm more insistently.

In a daze, she let him pull her to her feet, and then Hester was in front of her as well, shooting a suspicious look at the Lady Fortuna as she looped one of Tuesday's arms over her shoulder.

'Come,' she murmured into her ear. 'Let us go. I do not think you wish to meet such a fate.'

Sebastian Sol had stopped shrieking, his eyes fallen shut. They moved rapidly beneath his eyelids, however, and every couple of seconds he let out a whimper.

'Wait.' Tuesday put her hand on the front of Quintalion's greatcoat and tangled her fingers in the fabric, which effectively stopped him shepherding her down the stairs. She shook her head to clear it. 'I'm here for a reason. I can't go yet.'

The Lady Fortuna laughed sharply. Her rib cage struck the harness and the laugh turned into a grimace. 'Well, what does the girl-child want with the Lady Fortuna?'

It almost looks like a skeleton, she thought, *outside her skin*. 'I've come to ask you for help.'

'Help?' the Lady replied, toying with a goblet that sat on the armrest by her hand. 'I do not deal in help. I deal in *deals*.'

The court tittered before her, but Tuesday didn't spare them a glance. She licked her lips and said, 'A deal, then.'

'Deals and dreams and desires,' the Lady spoke in a singsong tone. She took a long slow swallow from the goblet and put it down. The drink stained her mouth blood-red. 'I could sell you a story that would delight beggars and kings. A dream to enchant a thousand sleepers. A lie more finely crafted than the liesmith himself could ever hope to create.'

'Right,' said Tuesday, 'well, I only want a name – *my* name. What would that cost?'

'And have you forgotten so easily? I would think a name harder to lose than most things.'

Tuesday narrowed her eyes, feeling as if she were being made a fool of, though the Lady met her gaze with an innocent look. '*Of course* I haven't,' she returned. 'My name's Tuesday.'

To her right, Quintalion smacked his forehead with the palm of his hand.

The Lady Fortuna's eyes lit up. 'If you are the same Tuesday whose name I have heard whispered in my streets, then a name might cost more than you can afford to pay, sweetling.'

Tuesday shifted uncomfortably in her stare. The Lady looked through her to the back wall, and it gave her the disconcerting feeling of being invisible. 'I've got money,' she said, and pulled out the purse of coins.

'Hey!' Quintalion spun around on his heel to face the Lady Fortuna. 'That purse was promised to me, milady, and as such, she has no business offering it to you.'

'Be silent, worm,' the Lady hissed, her eyes flashing, 'and I may let you keep your tongue.'

Hester raised her musket in a practised movement, from ground to shoulder in one single sweep.

The guards flanking the Lady Fortuna strode forward, their hands at their hips where swords hung from their belts.

'No!' Tuesday said. The situation was rapidly spiralling out of control. She gently pressed a hand to the barrel of Hester's musket. Hester stubbornly kept it raised for a moment, and then gave way with a sigh, flipping the barrel in her hand and resting it across her shoulders.

'I . . .' Tuesday's voice came out as a croak. She swiped her tongue around the inside of her mouth, but it didn't help. Swallowing, she tried again. 'I'm sorry. I came for your help – for a deal. I don't want any trouble.'

'If you want to avoid trouble, young one,' said the Lady, 'then you should not be travelling with companions such as these.'

'I've got no one else.'

The Lady leaned forward as much as the chair would allow. Her eyes sparkled golden in the light. They were too large, the pupils slit like a cat's. 'Then deal with me directly. If I hear a word from either of them, I'll end your time at this court in a way that will make that traitor's fate seem kind.'

Death. The word hung unspoken in the air. *Or worse . . .*

Quintalion frantically shook his head at her, and Hester's steely glare made her look like she was about three seconds away from breaking the musket in half, but Tuesday took a deep breath and stepped forward.

'I woke up in the Unreality House,' she said simply, 'with no clue who I am other than a letter telling me not to find out. But I can't just walk away.'

She gripped the satchel tightly, the feel of the leather reassuringly real against her fingers. It gave her the courage to continue. 'I chose to walk into that House and die – to become someone different from who I was. I want to know why. And I want to know what I was running from to choose that fate.'

'Ah.' The Lady raised her hand. Her fingernails were like talons. 'The finding of one's true name. There's nothing more important in all the world.'

'Not to me,' Tuesday replied quietly.

The Lady Fortuna nodded suddenly, and motioned to the crowds before her. 'Leave,' she said. 'Scurry away to your dark corners and your nests. I wish to speak to the girl without a thousand eyes upon me.'

The court grumbled, one of them even saying, 'Well, that wasn't half so fun as I'd hoped,' as he shuffled out, but they hurried out of the room in a mass of colour and rustling fabrics, and soon Tuesday, her friends and the Lady were alone with the guards.

'I said leave,' she told them.

The one on the right, a short man with a protruding brow and a helmet that kept slipping down over his eyes, stuttered, 'But, milady . . . what if –'

'Oh, what if, what if.' She waved him away impatiently. 'What if the sky falls and the oceans turn red? What if up is down and left is right? The future is full of what-ifs, and they do not grow less because you voice them.'

The guard frowned at her. Tuesday couldn't tell whether he was angry with his mistress or just hadn't understood what she'd said. 'But . . .'

She sighed. 'I promise the Lady Fortuna shall not die on you, Macklethwaite. Fortune City will not fall this day.'

The guards exchanged a look, but then turned and left, collecting the whimpering Sebastian Sol as they went.

CHAPTER THIRTEEN

'Now,' the Lady Fortuna said once they had disappeared, 'to the deal you wish to strike. I do not deal lightly. If you make a bargain with me, you make it for life and death and beyond, as many have discovered to their peril.'

She raised her eyes, and Tuesday followed her gaze to the bottles and vials that she had barely noticed when she'd first entered the room. Some contained coloured lights, some squirming shapes or locks of hair, and others fogged up at regular intervals, as though an invisible being were breathing inside. One large canticle held a still-beating heart.

I may be out of my depth here, Tuesday thought. 'I'm sorry?' she said aloud.

'The deal. You require your name, and I require payment.'

Tuesday quickly made a mental inventory of the contents of her satchel, but she owned nothing that could possibly interest the Lady. 'Some clothes?' she tried. 'Or I'm sure Hester wouldn't mind giving you some of her food. She has an excellent stock of pomegranates –'

'Which are mine and not to be sold for so little a price as a name,' Hester said quickly, and then, when the Lady raised a perfect eyebrow at her, she added, 'I mean no disrespect, Lady, but some things are worth the risk of death.'

The Lady drummed her fingers against the armrest. *Rattatat, rattatat.* Pipes led away from the chair up into the ceiling, across the walls, wrapping the room in steel, and finally down into the floor. The beat echoed off the pipes, reflecting back at the four of them like laughter.

'I,' the Lady Fortuna said, 'deal in dreams and memories and the shadows of experiences. There is nothing in your imagining that I could not take from you. And you offer me pomegranates?'

Tuesday cringed away from her. She curled in on herself, suddenly feeling very young. 'I . . . I have nothing else to give.'

'Of course you think you don't, if your perception is so limited.' The Lady Fortuna smoothed away the creases in her pleated dress. 'Did I not just say I deal in dreams? There is nothing as dull as someone offering me reality.'

Shifting uncomfortably, Tuesday bit her lip. 'I'm not sure I understand.'

'You're looking for your past, yes?' the Lady said. 'I think it only fair that you should pay for it with your future.'

'My future?' Tuesday shook her head in disbelief. How could she give up her future? That was the whole reason why she was trying to find out who she had been: so that she could forge her own path, safe in the knowledge of where she'd come from.

'That's my price,' the Lady said. 'Take it or leave it.'

'How much of it?' she asked. 'I won't suddenly die tomorrow, will I?'

The Lady Fortuna laughed so hard that the bars of the chair sank into her thin flesh. 'Even I wouldn't be so heartless. I will take a mere sliver of your life, hardly a breath. You'll never miss it.'

Tuesday peered suspiciously at her. 'Why do you want it?'

She shrugged. 'A bit of life is always good to have on hand. I have clients who would sell their own mothers for an extra second.'

Tuesday opened her mouth, but no words came out. If the Lady Fortuna spoke the truth, then the loss of a minute or hour of life could hardly matter in the grand scheme of things. What did it matter if she died on a Wednesday instead of a Thursday … not at all if she'd had the chance to breathe in every little thing that this world had to offer.

She turned to Hester and Quintalion for guidance, but the Lady's threat had bound their lips once more and all they did was stare back at her. A fleeting sense of annoyance arose in her that Hester would break her silence for fruit but not for her, but then she realised that perhaps Hester was purposely keeping quiet. *After all, the choice is mine.*

She took a deep breath. 'All right. But only once I find out who I am. You said it yourself – the future for the past is a fair trade, but I don't have the past yet.'

'Done,' the Lady said. 'Shall we make a pact in the old ways?'

Quintalion shook his head so violently that his hat flew clean off and bounced down the stairs.

Tuesday hesitated.

'It's the old ways or nothing at all, girl-child. Do you want answers or not?'

The little experience she had in the old ways was restricted to the magic that had kept her in her long slumber, and even then she had never actually seen it being wielded, just felt the whisper of power caress her skin as it rocked her back to her dreamless sleep. But she was a child of magic; she knew that as easily as she knew her name was Tuesday.

And what was the alternative? To stumble through life with no purpose or knowledge of why she was even alive? She might as well go straight back to Madame Marisol's House and while the rest of her years away in a state that was not life or death but *in-between*. 'Yes,' she whispered.

'Good!' With one hand, the Lady Fortuna released herself from her bonds, reached up and plucked a hairpin from her dark hair, twisted it open, and then pricked its point deep into the fleshy pad of her index finger, wincing as a drop of blood welled up.

'You would think that I have shed enough of these not to notice one more,' she said quietly. 'But every drop cuts me to the bone.'

'Why do you do it?' Tuesday asked, staring at the blood in fascination.

'Because my city must live,' she replied, 'and I know of no way to pay for life but with life.'

When enough blood had risen to the surface of her skin for it to form a perfectly round bead, the Lady held her finger out over the goblet that still rested by her hand. The drop of blood fell into the liquid with a faint splash. 'One for the mind.'

As Tuesday watched, horrified, the Lady next stabbed the hairpin into her fourth finger and let the blood fall into the goblet. 'One for the heart.'

Finally, she pricked the pad of her little finger, coaxing the blood to rise to the surface by massaging her skin until a drop lay flush and full. 'And one for the body,' she said as she swirled the three drops of blood around in the cup. 'Now you.'

'Me?' Tuesday gulped, staring at the hairpin the Lady held out for her. The end of the metal was brown with drying blood. She took it with a hand that wouldn't stop shaking.

She turned to her friends for support, but Quintalion, who had retreated to fetch his hat, just stared at her mutely and waved his hand in a way that clearly said, *Go on. You've made your bed, now lie in it.* Hester stood by Tuesday's side, stock-still but for her wooden leg, which whirred and clicked as she tapped her foot up and down against the floor.

The Lady was waiting with one eyebrow raised and the goblet extended towards her, so she closed her eyes and jabbed the hairpin into her fingers, wincing as it pierced her flesh, and soon her own three drops of blood, darker than she'd thought they would be, went into the goblet along with the Lady Fortuna's.

The Lady raised the cup to her lips and took a swig, and then offered it to Tuesday for her to do the same.

Her nose wrinkled in disgust, but she took the goblet and forced herself to tilt it back so that the liquid swirled against her lips. Though she took the smallest sip she could, the sour flavour of blood and wine combined hit the back of her mouth. It smelled like the garbage on the streets of Beggars End. Gorge rose in her throat. She grimly swallowed, forcing back the urge to gag, and handed back the cup to the Lady Fortuna.

The Lady held the cup aloft and said, her voice deep and dark in the empty hall, 'In blood, the deal is struck and bound. And not even death shall break the binding.'

In one of Madame Marisol's stories, something momentous would have happened – a bolt of lightning or a great wind whipping up. But now there was only the never-ending hum of the machinery beneath their feet to mark the occasion.

'So it is done,' the Lady said, and sighed as she relaxed back against her seat. The collar smeared blood across the white column of her throat.

Tuesday had the sudden urge to wipe it off, but she held herself still, tight as a wire from the knowledge that – any moment now – the Lady would tell her who she was. She'd promised it – the future for the past. Tuesday wondered whether she had been a great lady at a court, with hoops twice as wide as those on the ladies in Beggars End, or perhaps an adventuress who travelled to all the distant points on Hester's map, while adding more names of her own. Or maybe she had just been a simple farmer or shop assistant: one of the unremarkables that no doubt filled the world. That would have suited her well, too, as long as she had been happy.

And then she remembered the note, and frowned, because happy was obviously the one thing she had not been. *There is nothing in your past but pain and regret. I willingly lay down my life so that you may start a new one. And that is the only promise I would ask you to make: forget about me.* How could she have asked that of herself? To forget, to ignore the fierce hunger that drove her forward with every step . . . she might as well forget to breathe.

She was on her knees before the Lady Fortuna almost without realising what she was doing. 'Please,' she choked out. 'I want to know who I was. Tell me of my past. I beg you.'

The Lady Fortuna chuckled softly. 'Are they always so eager, the young? I do not remember being like you. But then, it was such a long time ago.'

Tuesday glanced up at the woman through her hair. Her skin was almost translucent this close, and she was so delicate that Tuesday imagined a puff of wind might blow the woman away. But her eyes held danger, dark and wild. 'Please ...' she whispered.

'Very well.' The Lady Fortuna clapped her hands together. 'Your past. It stretches out far further than you can imagine, and touches more lives. So I fear, sweetling, that the only clue I can offer you is the Book of Days.'

Confusion swirled through her, and she raised her head with a dozen questions on her lips, the most important of which forced its way through her chattering teeth. 'The Book of Days? That is not a name.'

'I think you'll find we did not drink an oath for a name, girl-child.'

Tuesday shook her head, sure that she'd misunderstood the woman. 'No ... no, that's not right. I asked you for my name. You promised me you'd tell me who I am.'

'And so I have, in my own way. Reality, as I have said, is so very dull.' The Lady's smile showed her teeth, white and sharp.

Tuesday's fingernails dug into her palms as she tried to keep herself upright. The world was tipping, tipping, and she didn't know how to right it. 'But,' she said, still clinging to the hope that the Lady was teasing her, 'that is not *who I am*.'

'I think you'll find I didn't promise it,' the Lady Fortuna replied swiftly. 'I said I would accept the trade of your future for your past, and I have not dealt falsely in this. The Book of Days is key to finding that past. Find the Book and you'll find yourself.'

She'd played her for a fool. Tuesday flushed with anger, pushing herself to her feet with shaking hands. 'You tricked me!'

'If you expected me not to, you are an even bigger innocent than I had thought.' The Lady stared back at her serenely.

Tuesday had a sudden urge to carve out the woman's eyes. *She would not look so beautiful then, with tears of blood.* The desire rose hot within her – it screamed at her to *bite* and *rend* and *slash*. Tuesday's mouth curled down into a snarl.

But then, as quickly as it had consumed her, the fire burned out. She hugged her arms around her middle, taking deep breaths to quell the anger that was even now lurking deep within her. *Where did that come from?*

Hester's hand rested gently on her back, her fingers tightening in the material of Tuesday's dress. 'Very well,' Tuesday said. 'Where can I find this Book?'

'It was last seen on the shores of the Silk Sea, but I shouldn't doubt that it has long passed beyond the borders of our world.' The Lady slipped one arm back into the manacle-like contraption attached to the chair, flinching as the needles within once more pierced her skin.

Tuesday forced down her anger. It wouldn't help now. She had no desire to spend the rest of her days as one of the Lady's pets, kept in a bottle at her leisure. No, she'd had enough of that. 'Beyond the borders of our world,' she repeated, thinking out loud. And then she remembered something. 'Hester said Thaïs disappeared with it. Could she have taken it beyond this world?'

The Lady Fortuna frowned, the lines stark against her pale skin. 'I do not know. But if anyone could, it would be her. Stubborn as a mule, that one.'

'Oh.' Tuesday turned to Hester, wondering if she might know more about the borders of the world, but she just shook her head almost imperceptibly.

'This advice I will offer you for free, though,' the Lady Fortuna said. 'Be careful when seeking the Book. The daybreakers have long desired it – to destroy such an artefact would prove their domination over our way of life – and their leader, Theophilus Sterling, has been pursuing it relentlessly for years. Do not cross him.'

'We already have,' Tuesday said. 'I don't want to again.'

Slipping her other hand free, the Lady took another sip of the wine. 'Perhaps one of your companions would like to persuade you to forget this foolish venture?'

'As a matter of fact, I would,' Quintalion said. 'But first, milady, if you'll allow me the liberty to do this.' He replaced his hat, stopped directly in front of Tuesday and tapped her on the back of the head.

'Ouch!' she said, smoothing down her hair. 'What was that for?'

Quintalion's cheeks were tinged with pink and he spoke so quickly that spittle flew out of his mouth. 'Why do you think I told you to leave the talking to me? Because if you had, you never would have gotten yourself tangled up in one of that witch's deals.' To conclude his tirade, he jabbed his finger at the Lady Fortuna, and then, when her mouth turned down in displeasure, he added begrudgingly, 'No offence,' no doubt to avoid her turning him into a toad.

'I didn't have any choice,' Tuesday told him, feeling the heat in her blood rise. She bit her lip, trying to keep the tears at bay. 'Besides, *you* were the one who brought me here. If you hadn't suggested coming here, I never would have made the deal in the first place.'

Quintalion opened his mouth and closed it again. His face screwed up and he muttered, 'I never thought I'd say it, but I liked you better when you only asked questions.'

'Well, I have one for you now, if you like,' she said. 'Why does Sterling want the Book so much?'

'Actually, no, I don't,' Quintalion revised.

Tuesday rolled her eyes.

'Enough.' Hester cut into the conversation in her usual blunt style. 'Peace, or I will be forced to shoot both of you. And that would ruin my day.'

'Your day?!' Quintalion said, but then Hester raised the musket and he fell silent.

She then turned back to the Lady, who had been watching all of them through half-lidded eyes. 'What do you mean, sending the girl off on this senseless quest? The Book of Days doesn't exist. It is a fairy story, a myth.'

'You are a Saqiran, yes? What would one of your kind know about the most important book in the world?'

'Enough to know that it is a lie!' Hester burst out, her nostrils flaring. 'A book that holds all of the knowledge of your gods? Of life and death itself? Only babes and old men would believe in such a thing.' Her fingers dug into the musket as she took a deep breath to steady herself.

The Lady Fortuna drained the last of her wine. 'I merely offered the girl a clue as to her past. It is her choice whether or not she seeks it.'

But Hester didn't back down. 'You say it was last seen on the shores of the Silk Sea? That is east, through Tantallon. There are a thousand daybreakers between here and the Silk Sea.'

A smile blossomed on the Lady Fortuna's face, but there was no joy in her eyes. 'Then she had better hope you are a good shot.'

CHAPTER FOURTEEN

'The nerve!' Hester said, pacing the floor. 'The absolute gall. *Dalhaka*.'

'Really,' Quintalion said from where he lounged on a low couch in the corner, 'that's a bit harsh, even for you.'

He had hired them a small suite of rooms close to the Lady Fortuna's court, grumbling about the price as though he were spending a king's ransom for the privilege. He'd managed to bargain the owner of the lodging house down from his original asking fee, for which Tuesday was grateful, since her purse of coins was not inexhaustible and, however loudly Quintalion grouched about spending his own buying price, she did feel bad every time he had to dip into his reward.

The rooms were not worth what it would cost to demolish them. They'd rented a suite on the third floor of the Five-Gin Peak, one of the colourfully named towers she'd counted from the *Zephyr*: a bedroom for her and Hester to share, one for Quintalion, who had quickly invaded theirs, and a cramped living space to connect the two rooms, with a moth-eaten carpet, a wood-burning stove in the corner, a table with three legs of varying lengths, and a rusty metal container that Tuesday had been horrified to learn was their commode. The rooms smelled of rot and mould, and the walls sweated, but at least they wouldn't be staying in them for too long. And the cracked washbasin and water jug in the corner gave her the chance to wash off some of the ash from her face and arms.

Hester's constant pacing was making Tuesday dizzy. She'd been fuming ever since the Lady Fortuna dismissed them, and Tuesday had been forced to confiscate her musket for fear that she would do one of the many passers-by an injury on the ride back to the lower levels.

'I made a deal with her,' Tuesday said to try to calm her down, as she scrubbed away at her skin. 'She wouldn't go back on that.'

'A stupid deal,' Quintalion offered, cleaning beneath his fingernails with the tip of a knife.

Tuesday took a deep breath and exhaled it through her nostrils in a snort. 'A stupid deal maybe, but it's done now and there's nothing we can do about it. Besides, she gave us a clue. The answer lies in the Book of Days. We must go to the Silk Sea and find it.'

'We *must* do nothing.' Hester spun around on her heel so quickly that her false leg groaned in protest. 'I do not like being told what I must and must not do. Last time I was ordered to do something, it was my brother who paid the price, I will not be told –'

Twin spots of pink flared in Hester's olive cheeks. She suddenly went very still. 'I should not have spoken in anger. We Saqirans are a passionate people, but that passion should not be directed at you. It is not your fault that *dalhaka-shalut* witch tricked you.'

'Isn't it?' Quintalion prised the last little bit of dirt from beneath his pinkie and leaned back on the couch, crossing his legs. 'I think our dear Lady was entirely transparent in what she wanted from that exchange. Poor little Tuesday here just didn't have the eyes to see.'

'I have eyes,' Tuesday muttered, crossing the room and flopping down on the bed. It sank beneath her, sucking her into its quilted bedspread like some kind of carnivorous plant.

'Perhaps. But not the wisdom or experience to use them.' Quintalion tucked his knife away in an inside pocket and gestured to her, slowing his speech down as though she were a child. 'If the Lady Fortuna is right and the Book of Days has passed beyond this world, then you would be wise to forget it. Just give me that purse of coins and we can all go our separate ways. Perhaps at solstice we can exchange postcards.'

'No!' Tuesday struggled out of the bed-trap. 'If the Book of Days will tell me about my past, then I *am* going to find it. How do you know so much about it, anyway?'

Quintalion shrugged, not meeting her eyes. 'You can hardly stay alive for as long as I have without listening to every little whisper in the night.'

'How old *are* you?'

'A dangerous question,' Hester said. 'You had better hope our friend is not vain or you may yet be in strife. Men have been shot for less in the north.'

Quintalion didn't bother covering up his smirk as he pushed himself up off the couch. 'Fortunately for you, I'm not that much of a peacock –'

'Though your vests would suggest otherwise,' Hester muttered.

'– and I'm happy to tell you that I'll be approaching the vicinity of seven hundred in a couple of months.'

'Seven *hundred*?' Tuesday squeaked. 'I thought thirty, maybe thirty-five at the most.'

'You flatter me.' He gave her a bow that started at his boots and ended with his little finger. 'But as much as I would love to stay and enjoy the compliments that will, no doubt, start flowing like wine from your lips, I must be off. If you insist on this fool trek to the east, we'll need more than a pocketful of helions and luns.'

He rolled his hat up his arm in a complicated and probably entirely unnecessary movement, fixed it on his head, and held his hand out to Tuesday. 'Purse.'

It took her a second to realise what he meant, and she was halfway through digging it out of her satchel, where it always had the uncanny knack of burrowing right to the bottom, when Hester coughed loudly, and Tuesday stopped. 'You're not just going to run off?'

'If I was, would I tell you?' He grinned at her, and then added: 'I'm to the moneylenders. If we're headed east, then we've got to pass through Tantallon, and Tantallon hasn't accepted luns since before my time. Banknotes are what those glorified farmers trade in. No doubt I can scrounge up a few on the black market – for a price.'

'This entire rock is a black market,' Hester said, but she didn't move to stop him.

Tuesday's hand curled around the purse at the bottom of the satchel. She pulled it out and shook a good handful of coins into her palm, and then held the coins out to Quintalion, who grinned in disbelief.

'You really don't trust me, do you?'

'Not with a purse full of coins, no,' she told him.

'Good,' he said, and pocketed the money. 'I'll be back as soon as I can. I don't want to spend longer in one place than we need to.'

A chill curled around Tuesday's spine, and she straightened, her hand tightening around the strap of her satchel. 'Do you think the daybreakers could find us here?'

He waved the question away. 'Not a chance. Sterling would never risk attacking Fortune City. The Lady Fortuna is too powerful. But he's not the only one who would be interested to know that we're hunting for the Book of Days. So stay here, all right? I don't want to have to worry about you too.'

She smiled at the thought of him worrying about her, however unbelievable it might be, and just nodded in reply, watching him stride out of the bedroom and leave her alone with Hester.

Tuesday, however, had absolutely no intention of staying put. Not when there was information to be had. The Lady Fortuna had told her, after all, that the Book of Days was the key to finding out who she was, but how much did she actually know about it? Not much, other than what Quintalion had told her . . . but it was a start. Because books, Tuesday knew, meant libraries. Surely there must be a library somewhere in Fortune City, and she intended to find it. But how to go about it . . .

Now that Quintalion was gone, Hester had transferred all her pent-up anger at the Lady Fortuna into a frenzy of cleaning and polishing: she'd procured a rag from somewhere, most likely not the rooms themselves, since it was clean and had no holes, and had lined up her gun, the disturbingly large collection of knives found about her person, and her disassembled wooden leg on the bed in a neat queue to be scoured.

She spat on the rag, picked up her musket, and began to work the rag up and down the smooth length of the weapon in soft, sure strokes.

Tuesday watched her hand move back and forth, back and forth: Hester was so invested in the motion that she'd started to hum a quiet tune. The bed she sat on was across the room from Tuesday's, and Hester had turned away from her to better grip the gun, held across her knees. Surely she wouldn't notice if Tuesday slipped out of the room. And if she got caught, she could say that she was simply going off to use the commode. She hoped Hester hadn't yet investigated their lodgings thoroughly, for anyone who had gone near the commode would be able to tell that Tuesday was lying.

She inched her way over to the edge of the bed, pausing every time Hester's cleaning caused her to turn in Tuesday's direction.

It felt like it took a lifetime, but finally she was off the bed and standing up as quietly as she could. She silently cursed when the hem of her dress slid off the bedspread with a loud rustle, but Hester never said a word.

Tuesday started the long journey from bed to door. She wished Madame Marisol had packed lighter shoes for her to wear: every time she took a step, her boots thumped on the wooden floor, and she was sure Hester would turn and see her standing there with her foot raised in the air like an idiot, but she made it all the way to the door without incident.

Success! Tuesday congratulated herself as she sidled through the door that Quintalion had left open, only to hear Hester say, 'Where are you going?'

Fantastic. Tuesday popped her head back in the room and gave Hester a sheepish smile. 'A bit of air?'

Hester put her gun down and stared at her. 'And when I next see Sterling, I am going to kiss him on the mouth.'

Tuesday sighed as she leaned against the doorframe. 'All right, fine. I want to find out more about the Book of Days.'

The musket went straight into Hester's belt, the rag disappeared up a sleeve, and the knives were secreted away. 'Why didn't you say so?'

*

'When you said,' Hester remarked, 'that you wanted to find out more about the Book of Days, I did not expect this.'

They stood in the antechamber of Fortune City's only library. It occupied the lowest four floors of a tower called the Washerwoman's Folly, though the Visitor's Folly might have been a better name. Fortune City, apparently, was fonder of cards, vice and firewater than reading, and it took them eight passers-by before one of them was able to point them in the right direction. They'd only found the right entrance with the help of some very friendly ladies who had directed them to the small door round the side, in between catcalling from the windows at passing men.

'Magicians, I would understand,' Hester continued. 'Perhaps one of your fortune tellers who read palms with one hand and steal the gold from your purse with the other. But a library?'

Tuesday tried not to breathe in the layer of dust that hung in the air. It tickled her nose and made her want to sneeze. 'It's a book, Hester,' she said. 'Who knows more about books than librarians?'

'Assistant librarians,' came a voice to their right, 'but don't tell anyone.'

A boy lounged against a stack of books. He was a little shorter than Tuesday, but his unruly brown hair gave him another two inches of height. He was dressed entirely in shades of brown: light-brown shirt pale enough to seem cream in the poor light, corduroy trousers held up by braces, and a threadbare vest with some of the buttons done up in the wrong holes. He looked to be a year or so older than her, and when he smiled at her, his dimples flashed. His face was an explosion of freckles, where it wasn't covered by a large bandage wrapped around his eyes.

'You're . . . you're blind,' Tuesday whispered, taking in the bandages and the staff that he held in one hand. She'd never seen anyone who was blind before, and she had to force herself to stop staring at him, before she realised with a jolt that he probably wouldn't notice.

'Am I?' the boy said, his words light. 'I had no idea. What can I help you with today? We just got a shipment in from Tiamata – some interesting curses in those, let me tell you. I wouldn't recommend reading them if you're an amateur magic practitioner, though . . . you might end up looking like me.'

Tuesday ventured closer to the boy, stopping just beyond the reach of his staff, which he held out horizontally to the ground. Assuming that he was trying to ward them off, she lowered her voice so as not to frighten him. 'I'm Tuesday,' she said.

'Pleased to meet you.' He nudged her with the staff, and then shook it up and down like an extended handshake. 'And the woman with the questionable leg who's loitering by the door?'

'How did you . . . ?' Tuesday spun around, certain that Hester must have done something to give her position away, but the Saqiran was standing stock-still by the door, her hand on the grip of her musket. Wondering whether he was hoaxing her, Tuesday waved a hand in front of his eyes, but he didn't respond.

She snuck around the staff and walked towards the boy as softly as she could, but the moment she was within arm's length of him, he stuck out his hand and said, 'You'll need to breathe a little softer if you want to catch me out, but I don't blame you for trying. My name's Jacobi Heller. Jack to my friends.'

She took his hand and shook it, feeling a blush worm its way up her neck. 'Hello. We're sorry for intruding – me and Hester, that is . . .' she added, waving for Hester to join her.

'Intruding? Not at all. I don't get much company, what with the location, so I'm pleased to meet you.' His nose wrinkled as he frowned. 'I'm pretty sure I said that already, but it's as true now as it was a minute ago.'

'We were wanting to ask you about a book.'

'You've come to the right place, then,' he said. 'Though you might want to let go of my hand first.'

She looked down to find their hands still intertwined, and pulled her arm away with a splutter, tucking an errant strand of hair behind her ear.

'And what about you?' Jacobi said as Hester crossed the room to stand at Tuesday's shoulder. 'We have some good stories from the north. *The Maid and the Fig Tree*, that sort of thing.'

Hester narrowed her eyes at him. 'How do you know I'm from the north?'

Tuesday was wondering the same thing. When Hester spoke, she gave the game away: her accent was almost as distinct as her dress sense. But she hadn't said a word until then, and this boy certainly couldn't see her belled cotton pants and vest with that bandage over his eyes, whether or not he was actually blind.

Jacobi flashed them another brilliant smile. 'It's a gift. Now come, my father would say that I'm not showing you proper hospitality. I've got some tea brewing. You're welcome to share some.'

Looking to Hester for confirmation, Tuesday shrugged and nodded, and then, remembering who she was talking to, added: 'Yes . . . thank you.'

He led them through the library. It was a small tower, filled to bursting with row upon row of musty old books and, occasionally, in the spaces not covered by more stacks of books on the floor, a bench or two to sit on. They were unoccupied, however, and the three of them passed through the empty room in silence.

Tuesday watched him as he walked in front of her. The staff swept out in front of him with each step, but it seemed more for confirmation of his path than anything else; he walked as assuredly as she did.

Every so often he would pause at the head of a row of books, reach up to finger a sign with marks etched into the wood, and continue on. After the third time he did this, Hester said: 'You read our language?'

He nodded. 'I like the way the words feel against my fingers. I never would have thought to, but after the accident . . .'

A small frown appeared on his lips, which he tried to hide by turning away, but Tuesday saw it. 'It's a beautiful library,' she told him, to change the subject.

'Thank you.' He stepped up onto the first stair that wound up into the darkness of the tower, poked his staff at the next one, and then began to ascend more smoothly. 'Father's entrusted me with it while he's away. It smells of sewage in the summer and I have to bang the wall at night when the girls next door get rowdy, but it's home.'

As they climbed, the constant thrum of the city's engines grew fainter until it was only a muffled vibration against the floorboards. The library continued on the other floors of the tower that they passed, with rooms filled to the brim with books, the light that peeked its way through the smoke barely able to penetrate the gloomy interior. Tuesday ran her hand along the spines as she walked. Caught in her wake, dust danced around her arm like tiny moths.

'You must have every book in the world here.' She liked to think of the words surrounding them, sandwiched between leather covers: old words, and new; words that didn't mean what they ought to; and words that carried too much power to even whisper them.

Just like names, she thought. After all, what was *Tuesday*, if not a day of the week? Yet it was her everything.

Jacobi laughed. 'I wouldn't say we have quite that many. But we have a goodly number of the books that are banned in Tantallon and beyond. They're brought here for a second chance at life.'

'And have you read them all?'

He stiffened in front of her. She wanted to kick herself. Of course he hadn't read them all. That was like asking a cripple if he enjoyed running.

Jacobi stopped in front of an open door. 'No,' he said finally. 'But my father reads to me, and I remember quite a lot of it.'

Hester, who had fallen behind to examine the signs written in her language, caught up to them in just enough time to hear Jacobi's last words. 'It is just you and your father, Jacobi Heller?'

Jacobi nodded; the bandage slipped down around his ear. Tuesday itched to straighten it for him. 'My mother died almost ten years ago, just after the accident.'

The hard lines around Hester's eyes softened. 'May Sahir ever water the grave of your mother with rain and fruitfulness. I lost my brother. I know what it is to suffer a parting.'

'Thank you. But why talk of death and gloom when there is tea to be had!'

With his staff, he gestured to the open room in front of him. It was just as full of books as the other rooms, but most of them had been pushed aside to make room for four odd chairs and a table set with tea and buttered bread. Flames sparked in the fireplace behind the table, turning the room cosy and warm.

'So,' Jacobi said, leading them inside, 'why have you come all this way to seek the services of an assistant librarian?'

'All this way?' Tuesday said. 'How do you know we're not from Fortune City?'

'With that accent?' Jacobi sat and spooned some sugar into a cup with one hand on the rim. 'Natives of Fortune City always sound like they have a frog in their throats. I think it's the smoke. Whereas *you* sound like you're from everywhere and nowhere at once. What are you – assassin, spy . . . courtesan?'

Tuesday sucked in a laugh and almost missed the chair as she sank into it. *A courtesan?* 'None of them,' she said once she'd finally cleared her airways. 'I'm nothing.'

'Tuesday,' Hester answered for her, 'did not come here for idle chatter. If she had wanted that, we have a friend who would be more than happy to oblige. She is after information.'

Jacobi threw his hands up in a show of acquiescence, and narrowly missed knocking over the staff that he'd rested against the table. 'Fair enough. And what would someone who is not an assassin, spy or courtesan be wanting to know?'

Tuesday glanced around at the room to check that there weren't any daybreakers hiding in the corners, before whispering, 'The Book of Days. Do you know of it?'

Jacobi sucked in air so quickly that it provoked a coughing fit. He thumped himself on the chest, turned side-on to discreetly extract half a piece of bread from his mouth and threw it into the fire. 'Do I know about the Book of Days? Of course I do. That's where my father went – to find it!'

'What?'

'My father's a librarian. He specialises in books of magic, of the old ways . . . He's been obsessed with the Book of Days for as long as I can remember.' Jacobi narrowly missed smacking Hester in the face as he gestured wildly in time with his increasingly excited speech. 'Up until it went missing, no one's ever been able to study it – the Days guarded it themselves, of course – but now . . .'

'I thought it was last seen on the shores of the Silk Sea,' Hester said, dunking a hunk of bread in the tea and then delicately taking a bite. 'How do you know the Days don't guard it still?'

'That's the thing . . .' He crossed over to the edge of the room in four great strides, where a side table lay up against the wall, covered with scrolls and books and dirty dishes. He ran his hand over each of the scrolls until he found the ones he was looking for, made a pleased sound in his throat and hurried back over to the table, unfurling the largest scroll right on top of the mugs of tea and the plates of bread, which Tuesday hastily cleared away before the scroll got butter all over it.

It was a map, so large that it hung over the edges of the table, and almost identical to the map that Hester kept back on the

Zephyr, except that instead of being completely flat, the features were raised. 'My father,' he continued, trailing his fingers over the map, 'believed that the Silk Sea wasn't the destination. It was the starting point.'

'The starting point for where?' Tuesday asked, and leaned over to study the map. The only thing east of the Silk Sea was a large landmass called Yäel, but it was largely blank, with fanciful depictions of manticores and three-headed snakes on it. 'Yäel?'

Hester, however, was shaking her head. 'You cannot mean the City.' Her voice was reverent.

Jacobi tapped the map in triumph. 'That's exactly where I mean.'

'But the Days would never take it there,' Hester said, crossing over to the window. 'Which means . . .'

'They no longer have it,' Jacobi finished. 'Isn't it perfect? Scholars have been waiting for this for generations. The chance to study the Book of Days itself.'

'But you can't!' Tuesday thrust herself away from the map in a flurry of paper. 'You'll go mad.'

Jacobi's dimples made a return appearance. 'Surely you don't believe that. Superstitious garbage. The Days made that up to keep us from . . .'

His words melted into the background as Tuesday stared down at the table in disbelief. When she'd moved the map, she had accidentally exposed the other scrolls he had collected. And there, partially obscured by a code chart, a likeness of her face stared back at her. The artist had even included the white fingerprints on her cheek.

Harsh black words sat beneath the drawing: *Tuesday*, it said. *Missing. Reward Offered. Contact Your Nearest Daybreaker Outpost.*

'What's this?' she asked, deliberately keeping her voice light.

Jacobi looked up from where he had been excitedly poring over the map. 'You know, the bad thing about being blind is that it comes with the whole not-seeing thing.'

Oh. Right. 'It's a wanted poster,' she explained. 'Of me.'

'So *that's* what that is,' he said. 'Some man handed it to me this morning on my way to the baker's. Clearly, my assassin theories are right on the mark.'

He was grinning at her – a grin that made her feel things she didn't understand – but she couldn't return it, because that meant the daybreakers were closing in.

'They're here,' Hester said suddenly at the window.

Tuesday held the poster up so that her friend could see it. 'I know. Look at this.' Then she thought for a second. 'That explains why the footman seemed to know me.'

Hester didn't even glance in her direction. She clutched at her gun with shaking fingers. 'No,' she said, very deliberately, 'you misunderstand me. The daybreakers are here. Now.'

Tuesday leapt to her feet just in time to see the hulking form of a daybreaker airship break through the smoke.

CHAPTER FIFTEEN

'How did they find us?' Tuesday ran to join her friend at the window, but Hester was already back at the table.

'I do not know, but we must move quickly. We can escape on the *Zephyr*. They will never see us through the smoke.'

'No!' she said. 'We have to find Quintalion.'

There wasn't just a single airship. Tuesday leaned out of the window to scan the skies. At least six airships loomed over the city, and the towers blocked her view to the south and the east, so there could have been even more.

Jacobi stuffed the rest of the papers in his rucksack and crossed over to the window, peering uselessly up at the sky. 'I'm sorry,' he said, 'but did you just say that the daybreakers are here?'

'Indeed.' Hester drained the rest of her tea and swung her gun over to rest against her shoulder. 'And I doubt they're after bread and butter.'

'But they *can't* be.' He gripped his staff tightly, as though he was preparing to fight them off then and there. 'Father said they'd never dare attack the city. Not with the Lady Fortuna protecting us.'

Guilt twisted in Tuesday's stomach. 'I'm so sorry,' she said to him. 'This is my fault. They've come because of me. But if you stay here, you should be safe.'

Papers flew as the city shook. Tuesday gripped the windowsill to steady herself and looked out at the cloud of smoke billowing from the side of one of the daybreaker ships. The top of the closest tower exploded in a thunderclap.

'You have a strange definition of safe,' Jacobi said.

Outside, a flaming arrow bolt flew through the air and plunged deep into the hull of a daybreaker ship with a shriek of metal.

'The defences!' Jacobi cried. 'Each tower has an arrow-bolt station at the top of it. The Lady Fortuna operates them all with magic.'

'Then they'll go after her first. Hester,' she said, crossing to the door, 'find Quintalion. Meet me at the *Zephyr*.' Her heart was making a valiant effort to leap out of her mouth, but she couldn't just leave . . . not without doing something to help.

Jacobi followed her on unsteady feet. 'Great,' he said. 'I'm coming with you.'

'What?' She watched as he scrambled over to the side table, dropped his rucksack onto it and began to fill it with more scrolls and crumpled-up shirts and suspenders from the open drawer.

'You're looking for the Book, that much is obvious. You need my help. No one knows more about it than my father. And since he's not here right now, you'll have to deal with the next best thing – me.'

Another boom as debris flew outside the window.

The daybreakers were probably already at the Lady Fortuna's throne room. Her knee jiggled with impatient energy. 'We don't even know you. How do we know we can trust you?'

'You don't,' he replied cheerfully, and hiked the slipping strap of the rucksack up on his shoulder. 'But do you have any better ideas?'

The question threw Tuesday back to her first meeting with Hester so thoroughly that she could almost smell the rancid hay and smoke on the breeze.

Hester, thankfully, decided to take that moment to save her. 'Yes,' she said, and shifted just enough for the handle of one of her knives to slide into view. 'I could kill you where you stand.'

'Ah.' He blanched, but then recovered quickly. 'What if I ask you very nicely not to?'

There was no time. 'Hester, I trust *you*. If you think we need him, then take him with you. I have to go.'

'Wait,' Hester said. 'Where are you going?'

Tuesday was already out on the landing when she threw the reply over her shoulder: 'I'm going to save Fortune City.'

*

The understreets were strangely empty as Tuesday rounded the final corner to the Lady's court, the carriages all abandoned and hanging motionless from the rails. Word about the daybreaker attack must have reached even the deepest bowels of the city.

She skidded to a stop at the top step. The doors had been blown off their hinges. One of the guards lay slumped half beneath the left door, a gash streaking blood across his forehead and his sightless eyes staring out at her. His helmet, caved in though it was, still covered one ear, and she had the oddest compulsion to straighten it.

But she stopped when she heard the voice.

‘Come, come,’ it said, its pace like a ticking clock, ‘you really must understand how foolish you’re being. Your city is surrounded, defeated. We have won. Why will you not simply give us what we want?’

It was Sterling. Tuesday knew it was the green-eyed daybreaker even without seeing him. She could sense his presence, sweet and yet cloying at the same time. His familiar voice drew her in and she’d taken two steps towards the door before she shook herself out of it and flattened herself behind the wall instead. *What was I thinking?*

Holes speckled the walls and the fallen doors – gunshot or cannon fire, most likely – and they provided her with a perfect view of the Lady Fortuna’s court.

Peeking through a large gap, she could see the Lady lying at the base of her throne, with Sterling’s boot upon her shoulder. Tuesday shuddered and hugged herself, feeling his phantom boot-print on her own back.

The Lady Fortuna shifted weakly. She said something, but it was too soft for Tuesday to hear.

Sterling shook his head. ‘Wrong answer,’ he said, and leaned down onto her.

The Lady shrieked. Something in her shoulder gave way, and then her entire arm hung loosely at her side.

Bile rose in Tuesday’s throat; she swallowed against it, closing her eyes to block out the sight of the Lady writhing on the ground, but she could still hear her breathy moans.

‘It would be so much easier if you just gave in,’ Sterling said. ‘We ask so little of you. All we want is the girl. Give us Tuesday and we’ll leave your city alone.’

Tuesday’s breath was coming so loud that she was sure they would be able to hear her. *Of course* Sterling had come for her, but hearing it from his lips gave it a reality that she didn't want to face. She'd been happy forgetting the events of Beggars End, but now they all came tumbling back, and she realised with a start that she might die here, deep in the abandoned tunnels. *I don't want to die*, she thought. *Not without knowing who I am . . . not ever.*

The Lady had stopped her shudders and was staring at Sterling, clutching her concaved shoulder. The pinprick scars on her face and body had broken open again, and her pale skin was smeared with blood. 'I won't,' she said, and her voice, though quiet, was laced with defiance.

Sterling straightened out his left sleeve, brushing away the dust. He looked almost bored. 'There are a dozen airships surrounding your city. They have orders to fire and bring it to the ground if we do not return by the next hour. This should not be a difficult decision: your city or this traitor girl.'

'Traitor?' the Lady said as she pushed herself up off the ground with hands spotted with red. 'Who has she betrayed? Not us.'

'She killed our love!' he thundered into her face, all composure lost to snarling, red-faced passion. 'One of your Days. Isn't that betrayal enough?'

'As if Thaïs could ever love a heartless cur like you!'

Tuesday reeled against the destroyed wall. Thaïs . . . Thaïs was the woman Sterling thought she had killed? It couldn't be right. It had to be a lie, some trick to get the Lady Fortuna to give her up.

Sterling ground his boot down upon the Lady's wrist, his eyes alight with twisted passion. 'She loved us,' he said in a harsh whisper. 'She *loved* us.'

Tuesday didn't see anything to love in the cold eyes of the man before her: the same eyes that had barely blinked when he'd killed Col. Her neck still ached from the strength of his hand, that day in the marketplace, cutting off her air. She had felt his passion then, when he claimed that she had killed his love – Thaïs. What if he was telling the truth about that as well?

'Time is wasting,' he said, the brief out-of-control moment tucked away again behind his clipped words. 'What is your decision?'

Tuesday braced herself for the Lady to give her up. She was nothing to her, after all, just a traveller the Lady had tricked into going on some foolhardy quest. She supposed the Lady Fortuna had a vested interest in keeping her alive so that she could *claim* that life, but what good would it do her if she were not here to make that claim?

To her surprise, the Lady drew herself up and choked out, 'Never. I will never submit to you.'

And then Tuesday realised that it wasn't about her, not really. It was the east and the west: the old ways standing defiant to the last against the new, even as they battered down her door.

Tuesday felt a fierce swell of pride at the woman on the floor, who spat at Sterling now, the gob of blood and sputum hitting his cheek and rolling down his neck.

He slowly reached up and wiped away the phlegm. 'Last chance,' he said. 'The bells will soon ring for the hour. Will you give up the girl?'

'Not even if the world should turn and the darkness take me.'

He sighed, and if Tuesday didn't know what a monster he was, she could almost have heard regret in his next words: 'Very well. Then you will fall, and so will your precious city.'

She couldn't let him do it. She couldn't let his daybreakers blow up the city – not with the possibility that her friends hadn't yet reached the *Zephyr*. And what was the difference, really, in dying at his hand, and a long, slow fall from a dying city?

She stepped towards the door, but suddenly dark hands wrapped around her mouth and her shoulders, pulling her back, and a streak of purple cloth rushed past her into the room.

'You've done it now, *Dagny*, haven't you?' a voice in her ear said.

'Quintalion!' she huffed the words out against his fingers, which were splayed against her mouth.

'Were you expecting someone different?'

No, she thought, *but I didn't expect to see you again . . . not after I gave you half my coins*. She was prevented from saying this to him out loud, however, by his hands at her mouth and a sharp voice from inside the room.

'Hester,' Sterling said. 'Come to die, have you?'

Tuesday shrugged Quintalion away so that she could move back to her previous vantage point, and peered through the shrapnel hole to see Hester, two curved blades in her hands, pacing in front of Sterling like a desert cat stalking its prey. Tuesday recognised the swords: they had been stored in the mast of the *Zephyr*. Why had Hester come back, if she'd made it to the safety of the ship?

Hester swung the blades through the air; testing the weight and the balance, Tuesday thought, by how she adjusted her stance to compensate for her wooden leg. She kept her eyes fixed on Sterling, who had abandoned the fallen Lady Fortuna and withdrawn his own sword from its scabbard. 'You know why I've come,' she said softly.

'Your precious promise.' He ran a finger along the edge of his sabre, just light enough not to break the skin and release the deadly poison. 'Remind us again how that goes: before the year ends, one of us shall die? Was it something like that? You'll be disappointed to learn, then, that we've already died. We die every day without her by our side. The rest is just a technicality.'

'I would very much like the technicality of slicing your head from your body,' Hester told him.

Tuesday could feel Quintalion breathing beside her as they crowded together to share the spy hole. 'Fool,' he muttered, but made no move to help Hester. 'The plan was to get you and get out. The whole city's surrounded.'

'I know,' she whispered. 'Sterling said they'll fire on us if he doesn't return by the next bell.'

Quintalion rolled his eyes. 'Oh, wonderful. That gives us about ten minutes. Surrounded by daybreakers, seconds ticking away, and *she* decides it's time for a grudge match. You pick them well.'

Tuesday drew herself up as Sterling and Hester circled each other in the throne room. 'If I remember, you were the one who found her, not me. And I'm . . . I'm *glad* you did!' she told him, feeling her face flush with the passion of defending Hester. 'She's been nothing but a friend to us since she rescued me.'

'Among other things,' he muttered darkly. 'And what's your defence for the blind boy currently cluttering up her ship, eh?'

'Jacobi?' She smiled into the back of her hand. 'It was Hester's decision.' *Not that I'm happy he's coming, not at all.* It was a logical decision. Nothing to do with the fact that his smile made parts of Tuesday wobbly.

Quintalion tipped his hat back on his head, most likely so that Tuesday could get a better view of the utterly unimpressed look on his face. 'I'm sure you established a great deal of trust in the . . .' he pulled out his pocket watch from his vest and made a show of checking it, 'two hours you've known him.'

She bit back the curse that came bubbling up from her memory: probably picked up from one of the times when Madame Marisol read too close to the fire and singed off her eyebrows. 'Thank you,' she said instead, turning back to the action inside the throne room, 'I have.'

Sterling and Hester were still circling each other, neither of them paying any heed to the Lady, who had pulled herself up the steps to her throne with a hiss of pain and was watching them both through half-lidded eyes.

'Well?' Sterling said finally. 'Come on. Finish us. Or are you too much like your brother?'

Hester growled at the mention of Narvi, but Sterling wasn't finished yet.

'We've heard he never was much of a soldier,' he said, his sabre at his side. 'Too soft, too much of a dreamer. We are surprised your elders didn't leave him in the sand dunes to die as a babe. Better that than grow to be such a disgrace on his house.'

That was enough. Hester lunged at him.

With a crooked smile on his face, Sterling dodged her first thrust, sweeping her sword away from his body with a circular motion that left him wide open for a second.

Hester took advantage of it, and drew her right sword in a sweeping draw from navel to neck, but he had already stepped away and her blow sliced nothing but air.

They would kill each other. Though they danced around each other with a matched grace, attacking and blocking in equal measure, Tuesday could already see their fight played to the end: Sterling would distract Hester with some verbal barb or another, and she would lose her guard for the moment that it would take for him to nick her with his poison blade. And she, before dying, would rake her swords across his neck and end his life in spurting blood and darkness.

Tuesday stepped forward to intervene, but Quintalion grabbed her arm and held her back.

'What are you doing?' she said, forgetting to whisper in her worry for her friend. 'We have to help her.'

His fingers kneaded against her wrist, but she wouldn't give an inch.

'She's made her choice. We have to go. This whole city is going to start to fall in less than five minutes. Do you want to die?'

Of course she didn't. But she couldn't just leave, knowing that she was letting Hester take the fall for something that was her fault. 'Sterling's here because of me,' she told Quintalion, and felt his hand tighten around her arm in response. 'If we hadn't come here, none of this would have happened. I can't just walk away.'

'Tuesday, no.' She heard the warning in his voice, but she ignored it. Taking a deep breath, she darted forward, breaking his hold on her, and ran out into the throne room.

The sudden space was disorientating. She stumbled, thrown off balance by the lack of Quintalion's restraining hold on her. Then the thrum of the city's engines beneath her feet spurred her forward, and she righted herself in the midst of toppling, letting her momentum carry her further into the room.

Hester and Sterling hadn't yet seen her; they were too busy fighting.

Quintalion called for her, but she ignored him and ran on. She didn't even know what she was going to do when she reached them – jump in the middle of their fight or something equally as stupid. She only knew she had to save Hester, just as Hester had saved her.

The two of them whirled and ducked in the middle of the room, which seemed to be tilting. For one horrible moment Tuesday thought that the pounding in her ears was more cannon fire – that the bells had rung, signalling the daybreakers to destroy the city rather than taking pot shots as they had been previously – but then she realised it was something far worse.

The Lady Fortuna was dying. She'd slipped down from the step, her skin even more translucent than normal. She was still moving her mouth in an attempt to speak, but no sound came out.

What had Quintalion said about the city and her? She remembered him swaggering up the stairs that day on the *Zephyr*, going on about Tuesday getting attached to the world. They were linked, he'd said, the Lady and the city. *If one falls, so does the other.*

The engines – the heart of the city – had slowed to a sporadic beat. Tuesday had to do something . . . now.

Another two steps and she reached Hester and Sterling. She ducked beneath one of Hester's swords, slid her hand into the woman's vest, and pulled out one of her knives, almost dropping it since her hands were so slick with sweat. Then, hardly stopping to drag the blade from the sheath, and paying no attention to Hester's startled cry, she circled around

Sterling's sabre, coming to rest behind him. Hardly breathing, she grabbed a handful of his tunic, tugged him back and rested her knife at his throat.

'Stop this!' she shouted, and was relieved when her voice came out clear and strong.

At the door, Quintalion dropped his head to his hands.

'Ah,' Sterling said, seemingly nonplussed by the knife at his throat, 'just the person we've been waiting for. Tell us, Tuesday, how does it feel to be the cause of an entire city's demise?'

Her hand shook so hard that she almost nicked his skin. 'They're not dead yet.'

'What are you doing?' Hester cried with a grunt of frustration. 'We should kill him.'

'And what then?' Quintalion sauntered over to the three of them as if he was in the middle of a garden party. 'Have you forgotten that his men will blow this place out of the sky the moment he doesn't show?'

Hester tucked one of her swords under her arm, leaned over to tighten a screw on her wooden leg, and then pulled her cotton pants back down to cover the join, her eyes never leaving Sterling's face. She was panting, the barely controlled rage evident in the tight lines around her eyes. 'He killed my brother, my entire battalion. He deserves to die.'

'And *I* might have killed Thaïs.' Blackness crept in at the edge of her vision, a desperate panic that grew with each word. 'Do I deserve to die?'

Yes, she answered for herself. Sterling shifted beneath the knife, but made no attempt to free himself, which was strange, since he was facing death at either their hands or at the hands of his own daybreakers if he didn't return to them, but Tuesday was too horrified at her growing conviction that she was a murderer to give it a second thought.

Quintalion shook his head in confusion. 'What are you talking about? You didn't kill anyone ... you couldn't have. You haven't even been alive a week.'

'Tell them,' Sterling whispered, turning his head so that his breath puffed against her cheek. 'Tell them what happened in the City of Lost Things. Tell them how you must have killed her to escape.'

Hester and Quintalion were looking at him like he was mad, but he couldn't be mad because he made too much sense, and the truth of it burned deep inside her. The floor tilted a little more. 'I don't know,' she said quickly, wishing that her head would stop feeling like it was going to split apart. 'I don't know any of that, but the letter I wrote ...'

It was in her satchel, but she didn't need to read it to remember the words. They were seared into her mind. '*There is nothing in your past but pain and regret*,' she said, and she saw the writing before her as clear as if she was reading from the letter. '*I willingly lay down my life so that you may start a new one ... a future that is finer than your past.*'

'See! See how she writes a confession? The door to the city is only opened by death. Thaïs,' Sterling choked on the word, and then drew himself up tall as if he was ashamed of his weakness. 'We know she entered the city. We waited, but she didn't return. *You* did. You killed her to open the doors and escape ... you killed our love!'

'I ... I couldn't have,' Tuesday spluttered. The world around her blurred. Her hands were tingling. Dimly she felt someone gently take the knife from her as everything grew silent and dark. 'I couldn't have,' she said. Her numb lips made the words bleed together like dripping ink. 'I couldn't have. I'm sorry I'msosorry.'

Somewhere, on the very edge of her consciousness, bells were ringing.

CHAPTER SIXTEEN

The blast tore through the room, sending shrapnel flying. Tuesday found herself on the floor, clutching at her arm, though she didn't remember how she got there.

Thaïs. Sterling. The daybreakers. Memories trickled through her head as if through a siphon. She groaned, and the world came rushing back in.

The cannon shot must have hit the room at an angle: twisted metal fell in rivulets off the far wall, and the blast had torn through the floor and half the throne before continuing deeper into the city – to the engines.

They wouldn't last long. The Lady had escaped the cannon shot, lying sprawled at the steps of her throne, but another burst of ammunition would mean her end, and the city would fall.

Tuesday pushed herself to her feet. The world tilted before righting itself. Warm liquid trickled through her fingers, staining them red. She glanced down at her arm to find an ugly gash splitting the skin just above the elbow. Blood poured from the wound. *Funny,* she thought. *I can't feel anything.*

Hester and Sterling lay to her left, the knife between them. Sterling's forehead scrunched once in pain, but then he relaxed back against the floor. Hester, meanwhile, shook herself awake with a shout and went for the knife.

She'll be fine, Tuesday told herself, and turned her attention to Quintalion.

He lay sprawled on the floor at her feet, right on the edge of a large hole. A hunk of metal was lodged in his chest. Her heart clenched with fear. He had to be dead. No one could survive an injury like that.

When he sighed and murmured to himself, she almost laughed in relief. But then he rolled over on the very edge of the wreckage, his arm dangling in space, and all her relief disappeared. If he moved even an inch to his left, he would fall through the hole in the floor.

She tottered over to Quintalion on unsteady feet. The entire room was tilting to the left. Quintalion shifted on the slippery floor. One leg fell over the edge, and then half his torso. She threw herself at him and managed to grab onto the edge of his greatcoat. She leaned back, heaving with all her might.

Quintalion slipped further.

'Wake up!' she screamed at him. He was too heavy – even with all her strength, his prone body still inched towards the hole, dragging her with him. 'Quintalion, you have to wake up.'

His eyes moved underneath closed eyelids as he groaned and twitched. Wind screamed up through the gap in the floor, and when Tuesday leaned in closer, she caught a glimpse of dark clouds and lights on the ground. The explosion must have ripped all the way through Fortune City.

From far below came the heavy tread of feet and a dull, repetitive sound that she couldn't quite place.

Tuesday tugged on Quintalion's coat. The wool slid between fingers slick with blood. Quintalion's eyes blinked open and his mouth formed silent words beneath the howling wind. Movements unsteady, he turned to his left, almost slipping off the jagged edge.

'No!' she cried out.

She could feel him slipping from her grip. Her feet dug into the floor, but she couldn't find purchase.

And then a pair of hands appeared to her right, hauling on the coat. It was Hester. She had a gash at her hairline that dripped blood into her eyes.

Sterling sat to their left, watching them as the room fell apart around him. No rope bound him, and yet he just sat and stared at Tuesday with those green eyes that made her turn away, back to Quintalion. Fear would have to wait.

'On my count,' Hester huffed in her ear. 'One, two, three . . . heave!'

Tuesday threw herself back from the edge of the hole, Quintalion's coat still caught up in her fingers. She was bleeding on it, she realised as she pulled him back, and wondered whether he would be angry with her for soiling it. And then she laughed at the thought, because Quintalion was back on solid ground, away from the edge, and she didn't care if he yelled at her for the next hundred years. He was alive.

'Ow,' he said, sitting up groggily. His hands went to the piece of debris, poking and prodding. 'Well, would you look at that.'

He got a good grip on the metal and pulled it out with a groan of pain.

'You're all right,' she breathed. She only realised that she was still clinging onto his greatcoat when he took her hands in his and gently moved them back to her lap.

He scrounged around for his hat, found it hooked on a piece of pipe at the edge of the hole, scooped it back up and popped it on his head. 'Of course. You're not going to get rid of me so easily.'

'Pity,' Hester muttered, but she was smiling.

Dizziness flooded over Tuesday as she collapsed backwards. The cut on her arm bled so heavily now that spots of red painted the floor.

'We need to get out of here,' Hester yelled over the wind.

'What's happening?' She clutched at her arm. Some of the adrenalin was beginning to wear off, and it stung as if her whole arm was on fire. Chills ran up and down her body, and she shivered against the wind.

Quintalion looked around. 'I'm no expert, but I believe Fortune City is being reduced to rubble.'

'We must reach the *Zephyr*,' Hester said. 'I have made it ready for us. It is our only hope.'

'What about him?'

Sterling smiled at her, his sharp teeth gleaming in the glow of the smouldering metal.

'I will see to him,' Hester said, her hand on Tuesday's shoulder. 'You check the passageway. We must know if it is blocked.'

The wind whipped her petticoats up around her knees. She struggled to her feet and crossed the room, throwing her arms out wide to stabilise herself against the sloping floor.

Outside the door, rocks shifted against each other. Pebbles and dust cascaded off the boulders.

'It's blocked,' she called back. 'We're trapped!'

Good, a voice said in her ear. *You killed someone. You deserve to die.*

Hester looked up from where she had bound Sterling with his own belt. 'There must be a way out. I will not be defeated by *him*.'

Tuesday glanced around her, swallowing back the rising panic. The exit had been barred by rocks, and yet this was the Lady Fortuna's court. No self-respecting ruler would have only one door to their throne room. What if there was a coup or an angry mob?

In the stories Madame Marisol read her, Aemilia had been trapped in just the same circumstances, and Amiens had rescued her by sneaking in through a secret passage. Tuesday only wished she could remember where it had been hidden.

The Lady Fortuna would know.

Tuesday stumbled across the room towards her. The glass jars and cages that used to hang from the ceiling had all smashed, littering the floor with shards of glass and debris. The ground shuddered again, and she slipped on the slick floor. It reminded her of when she'd first come aboard the *Zephyr*, all wobbling legs and balancing arms, and she wondered, with a pang, whether she'd ever see the ship again.

When she reached the Lady, Tuesday gagged. The stench of burnt skin and death mixed together. Half of the Lady's body was charred and black – the cannon fire must have grazed her. It was a miracle she was still alive at all, but when Tuesday bent down over her body, the Lady's pale eyes opened and she smiled, her mouth tinged with blood.

'Do not worry about me, child,' she gurgled. 'I am of the old ways – immortal. Death is nothing to me. I will rise up in a new body.'

That's good, Tuesday thought, giving a sweeping glance at the damaged skin and the thousand cuts and burns. *Because your old one needs some work.*

'You shall not be rid of our deal so easily.'

The boom of cannons sounded in the distance. 'You may be immortal,' she told the woman, 'but I'm fairly sure I'm not. If we don't get out of here, your deal for my life is going to be worthless.'

The Lady Fortuna's cough stained her lips and chin red with blood. 'Ah,' she breathed, 'you are better at the game than I had thought.'

The city's engines stuttered beneath them, falling silent, and then started again. The Lady Fortuna blinked rapidly as she struggled to stay conscious.

'The way out?' Tuesday said, gripping the woman's shoulder.

Metal shrieked against metal as the room tilted. Far above them came the muted sounds of screams.

'Behind the throne,' she whispered. 'The second knot in the wood panelling.'

'Thank you.' The Lady's hand was cold as ice. Tuesday wrapped her fingers around it in a comforting gesture and then stood.

The Lady Fortuna sighed and, for a moment, Tuesday thought that was the last breath of a worn-out body, but then she seemed to reach down into herself for strength, and her voice lost its breathiness as she said, 'Find the Book, child of two lives. Find it and remember.'

Then her head dropped back against the top step and she was still.

'Er,' Quintalion said, appearing at Tuesday's shoulder, 'I don't want to ruin the moment, but we need to leave. Now.'

She turned to respond, but he just shook his head and put a finger to his lips and then pointed to the floor.

'The engines,' she whispered in horror. 'They've stopped.'

*

They emerged from a manhole cover, their eyes stinging with grime and smoke. The Lady's secret passage had taken them gradually uphill, and when Tuesday looked around, they definitely weren't where they had come in. The edge of the city lay in ruins to her left, and the streets were alive with people shouting and screaming as they pushed past one another, running through the fog and the confusion.

The city trembled beneath their feet. It thudded to the pulsing rhythm of cannon fire from the airships that hung in the skies above them. Every couple of seconds a burst of light erupted from the side of the ship, raking the taller towers with bullets and cannon shot. The attack was so unchangingly precise that Tuesday could almost picture their actions: *shoot, reload, shoot, reload, shoot*. She unconsciously began to mimic the pace with her breaths, and it gave her something other than the chaos around them to focus on. *Breathe, breathe.* As long as she kept breathing, she lived.

'The only reason we're still alive,' Quintalion said as he helped her from the manhole, 'is that they haven't hit all the engines yet. But that won't last long.'

Hester emerged next from the tunnel, dragging the unwilling Sterling. The blood on her forehead had dried into a crusty brown paste that flaked in her hair. 'My ship is ready . . . if that librarian of yours hasn't already made off with it.'

'Assistant librarian,' she said automatically.

Trying to get her bearings, she looked around for a familiar landmark, but all she could see was smoke and flames. A cannonball hit the nearest tower; they raised their arms to shield themselves from the chunks of brick and plaster that rained down onto their heads.

'Where are we?'

'I think that's the Spire,' Quintalion said, pointing at the tower that was still shedding bricks. 'Or at least it was.'

'Then the *Zephyr* is south,' Hester said. 'Come, my friends, we must run.'

Sterling twisted in Hester's grip as she dragged him up out of the manhole. 'No, don't you dare touch us!' He twisted his head from side to side in protest and stared up at the airships. 'We will stay here.'

Tuesday thought Sterling would have been happy to see his daybreakers, but he shied away from the ships and dropped to his knees in the dust, glaring up at Hester when she tugged at his makeshift restraints.

'What are you doing?' Tuesday asked him. 'Get up! The city is going down. You have to get up.'

He stared at her with those mesmerising eyes, and she found herself stunned into silence. '*Solus mayetvos*,' he simply said.

Quintalion, however, wasn't so affected. He leaned over, put one hand on either side of Sterling's shoulders, and lifted him bodily to his feet.

'You,' he said, 'are our ticket out of here. Don't think for one minute that a death wish is going to change that.'

Fortune City lurched down in the darkness. Tuesday's feet were swept out from under her and she hit the ground. A flash of pain burst from her injured arm. Tuesday gasped and slid her hand up past the ruined fabric to cover the wound. Gravel and dirt fell in showers from her arm. She blinked away the tears as the city stabilised itself and their descent was arrested.

Screams drifted through the air. The ground shook and then another section of the city peeled away into the darkness.

'Quickly,' Quintalion said, pulling himself to his feet and pushing Sterling back towards Hester. 'It's all falling apart.'

They ran, unsteady on the listing ground. Though the daybreaker airships still hovered over the city, they had stilled their cannons, and the sudden silence made the absence of the city's engines all too noticeable.

The city was aflame. They ran through streets choked by noxious smoke, the buildings on either side ablaze. She held a sleeve over her face, coughed against the fabric, and ran half-blinded by her streaming and stinging eyes. All she could make out in front of her were three figures, ducking in and out of view in the midst of the smog. She hoped it was her friends and Sterling; she could have been following complete strangers and she wouldn't have been able to tell. The streets were dark as the barely visible skies above her came alive with the sounds of shouted commands and the glow of the last rays of light hitting white sails.

So we're not the only ones with escape on our minds.

After long minutes running, they finally reached the port. It was bordered on three sides by crumbling brick tenements that hadn't yet caught alight, and most of the heavy traders had already left or been cut loose and now waited, drifting on the breeze.

A galleon had just cast off, the skeleton crew releasing the ropes that held it moored to the city. Several sailors frantically tumbled from nearby doorways, trying to catch up to their ship and the shipmates who had abandoned them. They called after them with curses and cajoling, but the captain didn't stop. One of the men left behind took a chance – he leapt out over the void, his fingers scrabbling at the ship's trailing rope. He missed them by a good foot and dropped with a shriek out of sight.

'There!' Hester said, pointing to the right. 'The *Zephyr* waits for us.'

Their ship lay at the furthest berth, its triangular sails unfurled and full. Tuesday caught sight of a familiar bandaged head and smiled. Jacobi was already on board. She'd hoped that Hester would choose to take him with her when she set off for the ship, but she also knew there'd been an equal chance that the Saqiran could have simply pitched him over the side of the city when no one was looking.

A gang of sailors with guns and a small cannon stood on the dock in front of their own ship, a sloop by the name of *Jolly Death*, as several of their fellows scurried up and down a mast and tugged at ropes, trying to get one of its sails unstuck. A couple of them raised their pistols in Hester's direction as she led her group past the ship. Their cannon was primed and aimed directly at the entrance to the harbour. A sailor stood behind it, his hands shaking as he tried to light a match.

'Calm yourselves, gentlemen,' Quintalion said as he walked past. 'We've got our own ship, thank you very much.'

Something was bothering Tuesday, or rather the *lack* of something was bothering Tuesday. She looked up. The airships had fallen back to a safe distance.

'That's not good,' she said.

Suddenly the city plummeted. Tuesday's stomach leapt into her chest. Quintalion's face twisted, his mouth moving, but she couldn't make out the words.

The ships flew into the air, still held aloft by their own power. Some of the mooring lines held, dragging the ships down with the sinking city, and some didn't. A mooring line to Tuesday's left snapped, slapping the ground with a twang that knocked the cannon-sailor off his feet. He stayed down. The ship itself shot up into the atmosphere. The force of the breaking mooring line had shifted its weight and now it listed to the right, throwing the sailors against the side. She watched in horror as one of them plunged over the side and fell like a rag doll in the squall.

Quintalion grabbed her arm and dragged her to the right. He was shouting in her face, though she could only pick up bits and pieces: '. . . make for the . . . go!'

They ran. *The ground can't be far off,* Tuesday thought idly, as she struggled to keep her feet. She looked out over the edge to find it coming up to meet them, strange white markings dotting the green dales.

The wind stole her breath. No matter how hard she tried to suck air into her lungs, it always seemed to get whipped away, and soon Tuesday was panting. Her sides screamed in protest, and her injured arm refused to stop bleeding which, combined with the breathlessness, left her shaking as she ran.

Quintalion reached the ship first, but hung back at the edge of the dock. Tuesday didn't realise why until she caught up to him: the ship's plank lay half off the dock and then, when the city shuddered to the right, slid off into the darkness. The

Zephyr hung a good five feet from the harbour, with only the mooring lines holding it to the city.

Quintalion said something, and though the wind whipped it away, Tuesday could tell it was a curse.

Still half-carrying and half-dragging the uncooperative Sterling, Hester finally joined them. The three of them clutched at each other to keep upright as the city broke apart around them. The wind roared, louder than anything she'd ever heard before.

'. . . we going to do?' It was only when they huddled together that they had any chance of hearing each other over the wind and the screams.

'Trust our luck to fate,' Hester said.

'Fate?' Quintalion screamed back. 'Fate and fortune lie dead. Who are we supposed to trust in now?'

'Me, Quintalion,' Hester said, handing him the belt that bound Sterling. 'You must trust in me.'

Hester's chest heaved – she sucked in a deep breath – and then her leg muscles tensed and she sprang. If Tuesday hadn't been so terrified, it would have been a beautiful thing to see. Hester flew through the air, her body arcing gracefully as she pumped her legs and tensed for the landing. She hit the railing and clung there like a bur, before scuttling up and over the side.

'Ladies first,' Quintalion yelled, but she waved him on.

'You go,' she choked out. 'I'll be right behind you.'

Quintalion was already at the bottom of the mooring line, which was pulled tight as the *Zephyr* plunged down with the falling city. 'Now is not the time to be heroic. Get on the ship – someone has to cut the mooring line free and it's sure as hell not going to be Sterling here.'

She swayed and then smiled at him to cover her exhaustion. The chill had invaded her entire arm. She didn't think she could climb just yet. 'Give me a moment. I'll follow you. I can cut the line.'

'Are you sure?'

Her teeth were chattering too much for her to form words, so she just nodded at him.

Squeezing her uninjured arm, he passed her one of his knives, and then ruined the moment by adding: 'Because I'd hate to have to pick through the wreckage to find my purse of gold.'

She watched as he kicked Sterling to make him go first. The daybreaker glared at him but climbed up the rope, followed shortly by Quintalion, who ascended arm over arm with a catlike grace. The two of them tumbled over the railing and then they were safe on the ship.

The last rays of the sun lit the scene: the falling city, trailing plumes of smoke; the lights of the ships and the airships floating above; and the ground rushing up from below.

Tucking the knife into her satchel, Tuesday leaned out over the edge of the port. Though every jolt sent stabbing pain down her arm, she pulled herself onto the mooring line. The rope bit into her fingers. She tucked her legs around the rope and prayed to whatever gods might be out there that the rope remained taut; that was the only thing keeping her from falling.

The wind roared up from below her, where the moors loomed closer as the city fell through the air. She didn't have long. Three short pulls made barely any progress along the rope. Her arm throbbed in time with her breathing. She glanced down to see the blood from the cut on her arm stain the rope red.

She swayed. She wanted to close her eyes. Exhaustion pressed down on her, but she knew if she gave in to it, she'd fall. Perhaps that was for the best. She'd plunge along with the rest of the dying city, and no one else would have to know that she might have killed someone.

It was only what she deserved.

'Tuesday!' Hester called out, shocking her from her trance. 'Cut the mooring line. We must get free of the city!'

With shaking fingers, she reached down and pulled the knife from her satchel. Blood streamed down her arm. She blinked the sweat from her eyes as she brought the knife up to the thick rope, just behind her body.

'Hurry!' Quintalion screamed.

Her hand shook so badly that she could barely find the mooring line. She slid the blade against it.

Another tower fell, closer this time. It smashed into the harbour and rained debris over them, showering them with dust and bricks. Tuesday shut her eyes against the pain and cried out – the knife was slipping in her blood-slicked fingers. She tried to fix her grip on it, but if she let go of the rope, she would fall, and so all she could do was watch helplessly as the handle fell from her grasp. The knife tumbled through the air and out of sight.

'I'm sorry,' Tuesday whispered. She'd failed. They would die and it was all her fault.

The ground rushed towards her. A loud roar came from behind her, and she turned her head to see the eastern part of Fortune City break free and tumble downwards, towers and carriages and people all falling, before it smashed into the earth.

I won't close my eyes, Tuesday thought. *I will see to the last.*

But then Jacobi leaned out over the ship's railings. 'Tuesday,' he called out to her. 'Grab my staff. I'll pull you up.' He was so far out of the ship that Quintalion had to hold him around the waist to keep him from slipping over the railing.

The staff was almost at her fingertips, but Tuesday couldn't grab it. Her muscles screamed in protest when she tried to inch her way further along the rope. She whimpered softly, and then reached out a hand, shutting her eyes tight when the wind tore at her sleeve and almost pulled her from the rope.

'I can't!' she cried.

Jacobi leaned further over. The wind whipped the bandage from around his head and sent it flying up into the air. 'Trust me,' he yelled. 'I won't let you go.'

Trust you? she wanted to say. *I've barely known you for three hours.* But the funny thing was, she did.

The wind died away just before impact and, for a few dreadful moments, Tuesday could hear both the screams of the people in the city and her own gasps as she reached out towards the staff.

Hester stood with one of her blades ready, but all Tuesday could focus on was Jacobi's face. Brown eyes. He had brown eyes.

Her fingers curled around the staff. 'Please,' she whispered, and let her legs fall from the mooring line, her body still dangling out over the hull.

The rope twanged by her as Hester cut the *Zephyr* free just before the smouldering remains of Fortune City smashed into the ground. Twisted shards of metal fanned out over the grass.

'Right,' said Quintalion, his voice loud in the sudden silence, 'let's never do that again.'

CHAPTER SEVENTEEN

Tuesday's shoulders rolled back and she laughed. It was high and reedy and bordered on hysteria, but she couldn't think of a more appropriate reaction to what had just happened.

The world had literally collapsed around them. If that didn't deserve a moment's laughter while she was hanging off the side of a ship, she didn't know what did.

Below her, pale lights appeared over the horizon. The stomp of boots and horses' hooves wafted through the air.

'Seven sisters,' Quintalion said, grabbing onto Jacobi's staff and attempting to haul it up, with little success. 'It's the Shining Ones.'

Figures started popping up in the smoking wreckage. They staggered from under half-collapsed houses and out of rubble, their faces streaked with smoke and grime. The still-burning fires lit their faces as they stumbled and coughed their way out of their ruined city.

Tuesday had no idea how anyone survived the fall. She supposed the city *had* been quite low to the ground when the last engine failed.

The lights came over the nearest dale. They weren't people carrying lanterns or firebrands, as she had guessed, but rather the light came from the glint of fire off armour. There were maybe fifty or sixty of them, their eyes hollow and bodies decaying.

'It can't be,' she breathed. 'They should have died hundreds of years ago . . .'

Quintalion grimly tugged on Jacobi's staff. 'Ah, but death wasn't part of the spell. Now give me a hand,' he added to Jacobi. 'We need to get her up right now.'

With Jacobi and Quintalion hauling on the staff, Tuesday scrambled up the side of the ship and over the railings with a grunt of pain. She'd been hanging for too long, and at the first change of position pins and needles leapt across her skin.

'What's the hurry?' Tuesday gingerly stretched her arms to the front. Her forearm was numb, and she could barely feel the blood still dripping down her fingers.

Hester finished off the knot that tied Sterling to the mast and crossed over to the helm. 'The massacre,' she said simply.

'I thought you didn't care about the Shining Ones.' She leaned over the railing and watched them curiously, noting the way they gripped their swords, blades pocked and rust-stained, and the swiftness with which they bore down on the fallen city, their movements oddly shambolic.

'I have no care of hornets either, but I do not poke my hand into their nest.'

Pulling on the helm, Hester took the *Zephyr* higher into the clouds, though not so high that they would attract the notice of the daybreaker airships still hanging in the night sky above them. Most of the ships that had fled Fortune City had already disappeared; only a few floated over the crash site, lowering nets and lines into the wreckage.

'Vultures,' Quintalion murmured distastefully.

'I've read about the Shining Ones. They say the very sight of them turns you mad.' Jacobi leaned on his staff next to Tuesday, his face towards the darkness. 'I guess today's my lucky day.'

Hester snorted.

'I'm Jacobi, by the way,' he added, and stuck a hand out in Quintalion's general direction. 'Jacobi Heller. We didn't have the chance for a proper introduction before.'

'Escaping a falling city will do that.' Quintalion smirked, but shook his hand.

'You saved my life,' Tuesday told Jacobi. 'How can I ever repay you?'

He shrugged and ran his hand through his mess of curls. 'You can call me Jack, for a start.'

Jack to my friends. She grinned at him and then the blood rushed to her head and she sagged against him.

'Are you all right?' His eyebrows crinkled in concern, but she couldn't concentrate on his face because it kept wavering in and out of focus.

She pushed herself away from him and turned so that the darkness hid her wound, walked to the edge of the ship and looked down at the scene below. 'I'm fine,' she said. 'It must be the height.'

They'd ascended so high that the people below were barely dark blots against the flames. The few ships that remained by the city retreated to a safe height and heads popped up, outlined in the light of the many lanterns. The sailors watched silently as the Shining Ones swept towards the survivors in the ruined city.

They moved like a hurricane. The flames glistened on the spears and swords and pikes. The riders reached the wreckage before the soldiers on foot. They attacked them, screaming loud enough to tear their throats, and slashed and wheeled their way through the twisted metal, finally doubling around to make another pass. The survivors cowered and limped away from the oncoming army, but most of them were wounded from the fall, and they didn't make it three feet before the Shining Ones converged on them.

When they were finished, they left nothing but rags and the echoes of the soldiers' screams.

Tuesday reeled away from the edge. It didn't seem real, not the blood nor the pikes hitting flesh nor the garbled screams of the dying. She fought the nausea bubbling at the back of her throat and took a shallow breath. *It's just a story*, she told herself.

'What are we supposed to do about him?' Quintalion inclined his head in Sterling's direction.

'Kill him,' Hester said.

'Yes, well, we know your views on the matter, but I'd prefer an opinion that's a little less bloodthirsty.'

Sterling watched them in silence. Hester had tied him to the mast with hanks of rope from shoulder to knee, and there wasn't much he could do but stare.

Leaving the helm, Hester picked up Sterling's sabre, which she had placed in the mizzenmast with the broken sword, and then took the stairs two at a time, her wooden leg clanking with each step. 'I told you. I *will* kill him before the year is out. I will not betray my brother's memory by breaking that promise.'

'Actually,' said Sterling, speaking up for the first time since he'd been brought on board, 'you said one of us would die. Hand us that sabre and we would be more than happy to fulfil that promise.'

'Not likely,' Quintalion countered. 'Do you have a gag anywhere? I'd rather not have him yelling to warn his cronies.'

Sterling shook his head. 'Are you blind?'

'I am!' Jack said helpfully.

Hester rummaged around in one of the chests on deck, probably searching, Tuesday guessed, for the most disgusting used bit of rag she could find. Hopefully one that smelled of feet.

'They will not leave their commander,' Sterling spat out. 'They will board and kill you all.'

'Are you so sure of that?' Quintalion said, pointing.

Tuesday followed his hand, but the night had suddenly grown darker, and she couldn't see what he was pointing out against the blackness that assailed her senses. She wavered, and then felt her legs give out completely, leaving her no choice but to slide down the railing to the deck.

She shivered. It was very cold for this far north. She'd left her cloak on the ship, but she didn't think she had enough energy to go and get it at the moment. Perhaps after she slept for a while.

'Maybe,' Sterling said, his voice cutting through her failing senses, 'given the state of your friend, they'll have one less to gut.'

She blinked against the darkness. Someone gripped her shoulder and she let out a moan of protest when they brushed against the wound on her arm.

'She's hurt!' That was Jack, so close to her that she could feel his stuttered breath against her forehead. 'Hold on, Tuesday. Hold on.'

That was a funny thing to say. *Hold on to what?* She opened her mouth to ask him, but the words got lost on the way, and all that came out was a strangled cry she didn't even realise had come from her until Hester said: 'The gash runs deep. Why did you not tell me you were hurt?'

'Oh, I don't know . . . possibly the fact that we were running for our lives.' Quintalion's words were light, but Tuesday could hear the undercurrent of worry.

'I have to stop the bleeding. Boy, hold her still while I bandage it.'

Hester's voice kept fading in and out. Tuesday wished she would speak up, but she couldn't quite find the strength to tell her.

Then something pressed against her arm and the white-hot agony sent her deeper into the blackness until she remembered no more.

*

Pomegranates. The smell of them lingered on the air, and the tart aroma made her mouth water.

Her friends' voices rang in her ear. She'd been hurt. Her hand shot to her arm, but there was nothing there. No blood. No cut. Just bare skin, tanned by the sun to a copper brown, and the top of a leather sleeve poking out of the metallic shoulder braces she wore.

'That's strange,' she murmured, and then looked around for the first time.

Her heart sank. She was back in the grove, the one from her dream. Sure that she would find Sterling next to her as she had before, she twisted around with her hands in fists to defend herself, but there was no one there, just a quiet field and the sound of the wind through the trees. It ebbed and flowed, and rustled the leaves in a calming rhythm that beat in time with her own heart. Odd . . . the wind never normally sounded like that. It was almost a roar, as though coming from a hundred voices.

She turned. The ocean lay before her, lapping at the sand and so immense that it drew a gasp of delight from Tuesday, who had never seen a body of water larger than the basin she washed her face in.

'What are you doing?' came a voice to her right.

Tuesday spun on her heel to find a young man staring at her with a smile on his handsome face. He was maybe seventeen, and still lanky from growing too quickly, with dark eyes and dimples.

She leaned over to rumple his hair, which caused him to make a face and bat away her hand. 'I am waiting, little one,' she told him, but the voice was not her own.

Her companion threw his hands up in the air. 'Waiting, pah! Why can't we just go? When *I* make my first kill, I'm going to be the greatest soldier the world has ever known. I'll . . . I'll win the whole war with one hand tied behind my back.'

He placed one hand behind his back, drew his sword with the other and stabbed away at the air. Sadly there was nothing on the beach to fight, except a hermit crab near his bare foot, which scuttled away too quickly to provide any real sport. Half-heartedly, he poked at the hole it had left behind.

His antics drew a laugh out of her; it rippled from her throat, deep and rich. 'The war has been over for years. This is a border skirmish, nothing more.' One look at his disappointed face and she added, 'There will be other causes: *better* causes.'

The hole yielded no further hermit crabs. Frowning, the young man slid his sword back into his sheath. 'You,' he told her, 'are welcome to wait for a better cause, while I get all the fame and glory.'

'Then you are looking in the wrong place, brother,' she found herself saying. 'You will not find glory here.'

'But what could be more glorious than a battalion of brave Saqirans sweeping in to save the day?' His eyes were far off, no doubt already imagining the charge. 'We'll send those Voltemande soldiers crawling back into the hole they came from.'

'Yes, dearest,' she said, the words not her own, 'but we would not be here save for the daybreakers' incursion on our land. And we will be ambushing a small scouting party, hardly the entire army.'

'To begin with,' he began, and then stopped suddenly as a trumpet sounded and drowned out his words.

Worry knotted itself around her stomach. She'd heard that trumpet in the last dream, just before the wave of warriors screamed towards her, but whatever control she'd had over her body before had disappeared, and when she tried to run, her legs didn't obey her.

The ground roared. They were coming. Beside her, the young man that she'd named as her brother tensed and crouched down on the balls of his feet, and then straightened up again, the muscles in his arms quivering with tension.

'Here we go, Hassar!' the young man cried. 'Are you ready?'

She shook her head, and dark tendrils of hair snaked over her shoulders. Still not of her own volition, she turned to the side, just in time to see the warriors crest the pomegranate trees and thunder towards them.

'I bet,' the boy called out, uncaring of the soldiers coming closer, 'that I can make it to their camp before you. I was always the faster runner. Remember when we raced around the watering hole?'

'You filed down the sole of one of my slippers so that my gait was uneven and I fell,' she said, amusement creeping into her voice.

'And who got the extra serving of Oma's goat stew for coming first?' He winked at her. 'I cannot help it if I'm clever.'

'No.' She grinned back at him, jumping up and down on her toes, 'and I cannot help it if a scorpion accidentally finds its way into your boot tonight.'

The warriors came closer. They ran in silence, which somehow made it worse: now all Tuesday could hear, besides the soles of their feet slapping against the ground, was the wind and the waves. It was such a beautiful day.

'You can't find a scorpion this far south,' the boy said with certainty. 'Besides, even if you do, it will not matter: I will be the hero of the day, and you will not.'

'We'll see about that!' She may have spoken with bravado, but she could feel the tension humming through her veins. She was afraid. The difference from her first dream shocked her: there, she had been fearless and brimming with excitement, even as the horde ran towards her promising only death and destruction, and *now* the fear chose to assault her?

The warriors thundered by on either side of her towards the edge of the field, where she knew that Sterling would be waiting, though the pomegranate trees currently shielded him from view. All she could see were bare backs and straining legs as men and women raced past her. If she looked into the grove, beyond the branches and the wasps buzzing around the bursting pomegranates, would she come face to face with herself, standing by Sterling?

Curious to find out, Tuesday desperately struggled to gain some control over her own body, but no matter how hard she willed her head to turn or concentrated all her energy into getting even her little finger to twitch, she remained unable to do anything but come along for the ride as she felt herself take a breath and tense.

'This is it, little brother,' she said. Tuesday could sense that whoever she was in this dream wanted to say something else. Her mind hummed with emotions that weren't hers: fear, and duty, and, above everything, love. *I love you.* It lingered on the tip of her tongue, but when she spoke, all she said was: 'I'll try not to let you take first blood.'

The young man just grinned at her and then he was off. He'd made it to the edge of the grove when a great sound like a clap of thunder boomed out from beyond the trees. Tuesday swung around, the gasp caught in her throat, and her hand at the sword on her hip. A spray of dirt appeared above the tops of the fruit trees, and then another, just a little further away.

'Narvi!' The scream tore itself out of her throat, all at once familiar and yet foreign. She *knew* that name.

He paused at the entrance to the grove with his back to her. His shoulder blades drew together and then he ran on into the field without a backwards glance.

Boom! Another shower of dirt kicked up. She ran.

Her heart thudded. In her mind, one thought scrolled over and over again: *not him, not him, please not him.*

Death. The smell of death hung over that field, and she knew with a certainty she couldn't put into words that the vulture-headed god Nephrim would not be far away.

Men and women lay broken and bloody in the black soil, their limbs torn from their bodies and scattered across the churned earth. A platform rested at the edge of the field, with figures waiting beneath the shade cloth, and Tuesday's hand clenched so hard on the sword pommel that her fingerprints indented the leather. There should have been tents here, and soldiers: not a single dais and the silent shadows with their judging eyes. *They knew*, she thought wildly. *They knew of our ambush.*

One woman – a friend of her brother's, who often shared his evening meal – had almost reached the platform. Her long legs pumped against the earth, she drew her sword. It stuck in its scabbard, but she kept running while she yanked at the leather-wrapped handle, and then suddenly it slid free.

She seemed almost surprised, and looked back at the others. The smile died on her lips as the explosion tossed her into the air, and when she came back down to earth, she wasn't the girl who once sewed the flaps of their commander's tent together for fun, she was just a body with a gaping hole where her legs should be, and a mouth still moving in confusion as the light faded from her eyes.

Tuesday skidded to a halt at the edge of the field. 'Narvi!' she yelled.

He stood a little way from the girl who had been his friend, and when he turned back to her, she could see the tears running down his face. He wiped his hand across his eyes to hide them. 'How did they know, sister?' he cried out.

Her eyes flicked to the dais and its shadowy figures. Something had gone very wrong, she could feel it in her bones, and it wasn't just the waste of life as her kinsmen died around her, or the dream that she fervently wished she would wake from, but something she had to remember that kept slipping away from her even as she tried to hold on to it.

'I do not know,' she heard herself saying, and then, desperately, 'Stay there, Narvi! It is . . .'

Landmines. Though Tuesday had never heard the word before, in this dream she knew them intimately. She had seen them used, in the Battle of Bow Ridge, where the daybreakers had sowed them beneath a field and then watched as a thousand de Kena rode to their deaths. A casing of metal and a small measure of gunpowder. When she had accompanied the trade caravans as a young girl, she would never have thought Voltemande capable of creating such a monstrosity from simple saltpetre. Her people had no use for it, and bartered it for silks from over the seas. And now it was being used to kill?

Saqira. Hassar. Narvi. The knowledge of where Tuesday was hit her like a sledgehammer just as Narvi crouched to the ground and took a deep breath, his eyes determined.

'No!' This time, the cry was entirely her own. She'd heard Hester, she knew that her brother had been killed, but now that the smell of smoke and blood lingered in the air, knowing that she couldn't do anything to stop it from playing out in front of her was the cruellest cut of all.

The panic engulfed her, and this time it didn't just belong to Hester but to Tuesday as well, and it was both of them who surged forward onto the landmine-strewn field towards Narvi.

Please, she prayed to the sky and the Days who had left the world to the daybreakers. *Please let it turn out differently. Let her save him.*

He turned back to her for a moment, with his friends dying around him, and smiled. She knew that smile – or rather Hester did – and it made her run even faster, just as it stole the breath from her lungs. It was a smile of goodbye.

With one swift movement, Narvi planted his sword in the dirt at his feet and ran. Her foolish brother was being noble, an undercurrent that had always lurked beneath the jokes and the tricks. The familiar feeling of fond exasperation washed over her until panic swiftly replaced it. He was going to die – willingly – to try to save friends who were probably dead already.

Her vision tunnelled until all she saw was her brother's retreating back as he propelled himself forward and kicked his toes into the dirt, just as he had done since she had taught him to walk all those years ago, and for a second she saw him as he was then, a boy of seven tearing off around the watering hole while she paced herself to let him win.

And then he was gone.

The silence choked her. She kept running, hoping that she would hear his voice as he reappeared, laughing at having won their race, but all she heard was the pounding of the blood in her ears. Dirt flew into her eyes. She glanced down. Half her leg was missing, but it didn't matter. Nothing mattered anymore. He was gone.

And then Tuesday felt herself lurch forward, and she was herself again, watching as Hester collapsed in the dirt not far from where her brother had taken his last stand. A keening cry stuck in her throat; the woman curled herself into a ball and placed one shaking hand on the hilt of Narvi's sword, still anchored into the ground.

The sound came rushing back in as Tuesday stumbled forward on legs she wasn't used to controlling. Hester's cries were loud in her ears, along with the screams of the dying, and the ever-present lull of the waves against the shore . . . and clapping.

'Well done, darling,' came a voice. 'What a wonderful idea. I had no idea it would work, but look . . . the door opens.'

'Of course it worked, Theo. It was my idea, was it not?' The voice was arch, and achingly familiar. Uncaring of the danger, Tuesday walked closer to the shaded platform, wanting to know who the voice belonged to, and dreading it at the same time.

Sterling stepped forward out of the shade of the platform, his hand held out to someone still out of sight. He had fewer lines around his face, and when he smiled, they all smoothed away as his eyes lit up with joy. He had to be twenty at the oldest, a fresh-faced captain wearing a uniform that looked brand new.

'Gladly,' the voice came again, 'but let's not go through the door right now. There's celebrating to be done, my love. It can wait until tomorrow.'

'Whatever you say.' Sterling gestured to the unseen woman again. 'Now take my hand and come see.'

Boots clicked on the wooden floor; the other faceless daybreakers shuffled backwards out of the way, and then the woman stepped into the light. She wore a tunic and riding trousers, and her armour glinted in the late afternoon sunlight.

Tuesday stared at the woman. With a jolt, she realised that she was looking into the face of the woman she had been accused of killing, and she knew before Sterling said the word exactly who it was.

'Thaïs.'

Anger twisted in her gut. She had wanted to think well of Thaïs, to believe that she had had the best of intentions when she had created the Shining Ones. But how could a woman who had stood by and watched a hundred people die be anything but a monster?

Though she had never met her, Tuesday felt the betrayal blur her vision as tears came to her eyes. She'd been so blind when she'd first set forth into the world, thinking that everything was beautiful and new and pure. The Days had been steeped in myth, reminders of a past that had seemed so magnificent to her; they'd been the figureheads of the old ways and the life that Madame Marisol had brought her into. And now to know that it was just a lie, that one of the Days had watched idly as she caused so much destruction – had even stolen the Book of Days itself, if Hester's hearsay was to be believed – well, it took her breath away with its unfairness.

Sterling and Thaïs glanced past her, beyond the bodies that stilled against the soil, and their gaze landed on something out of Tuesday's view. She spun around, wanting to know what they were looking at, what could possibly turn their attention from the destruction they'd wrought together, and then her mouth fell open in awe, for a doorway had appeared out in the waves. It was made of a black wood that had splintered and rotted from the salt water, and its double doors slowly opened, heedless of the waves that battered them from behind.

All this . . . to open a door?

She gagged and dropped to her knees in the dirt, her throat burning as her stomach tried to rid itself of its contents. Were this not a dream, it would most likely have succeeded, but here she could only heave up great gasps of air. The ground rushed up to meet her, and the last thing she saw before she surrendered to the darkness was Thaïs staring at her.

CHAPTER EIGHTEEN

Tuesday bolted straight up with a yelp. Darkness choked her. She was dead, she knew it, she was back in her keeping-house waiting to live, hammering desperately on the glass . . . but then the splinters raked her hands and she knew without looking that it was the door she'd seen in her dream, and no matter how hard she kicked and punched and yelled, it would always remain closed to her, and she would spend the rest of her days in the blackness.

'You're all right. It's all right, Tuesday, you're safe.' The voice was familiar, and enough to draw her away from the worst of the nightmares, but when a dark shadow loomed over her, she instinctively struck out against it. Her fist connected and she heard a grunt.

'Steady on,' came the voice. 'Has anyone ever told you that you have a mean right hook?'

'Jack?' she murmured, still half-lost in her dream.

'The one and only. It sounded like you were having quite a dream, there.'

'Thaïs!' she choked out. 'I saw her and she was the one, the one I killed, but I didn't, it was just the dream. *I* was me. And I ran towards her and – oh, seven sisters – *Hester*. Thaïs killed them all, Jack, she killed them all.'

She clung to Jack like she was drowning, hiccupping and sobbing in her fear as she told him about her dream. She didn't know whether she was making any sense, and though he had tensed up when she first wrapped her arms around him, he let her spill out her sadness in fractured sentences, occasionally murmuring, 'Shh,' or 'There, there,' or other awkward but well-meant reassurances, but mostly just letting her cry.

Eventually she calmed down enough to shake off the last of the dream, and she opened her eyes to find herself clinging to Jack's shirt like a drowning man clings to a raft. He had one hand hovering over her shoulder, as though he didn't quite know whether he should pat her or push her off him, so she saved him the trouble by pulling away from him and coughing awkwardly.

'Sorry,' she said, raking her hand through her hair.

He nodded and gripped his staff tighter. 'Not a problem. I'm used to hysterical girls throwing themselves at me. It's a hazard of the profession.'

The sound she made came out somewhere between a laugh and a hiccup. 'The librarian trade?'

'*Assistant* librarian,' he countered, raising a hand to his uncovered eyes. 'And yes. You'd be surprised.'

He leaned over, felt around on the floor, and thrust a water skin in her direction, which almost hit her in the chest, but she took it in the spirit in which she was sure it was given and drank deeply, happy for an excuse to fall silent.

'It's just water, I'm afraid,' he told her. 'We ran out of your tea. Oh yeah,' he bit his lip, 'sorry about that. You were nearly out of your mind with fever and we were trying to find something to help, so we looked through your satchel. Hester smelled the yarrow and elderberry in the tea and thought it might work.'

'It's fine.' She waved his apologies away. *The tea.* So that was why she'd dreamed of Hester. *It must make you dream of whoever you think of before you fall asleep.* Hester's had been the last voice she'd heard before she slipped into unconsciousness. But she had been thinking of the Shining Ones as well, and that had led to Thaïs, so she supposed it was only natural that the two dreams would mix. Still, it was a pity about the tea. She would have liked to talk to Madame Marisol again. She could use her counsel, now more than ever.

Tuesday took another swallow of water and looked around. They were in a dim room with curved wooden walls, and the only light came from between the wooden slats above them. Several hammocks had been strung up between the posts, along with a bedroll to one side, which Tuesday guessed was Jack's, since she could only imagine how difficult it would be to try to blindly navigate a hammock. It was bad enough for her, as she found out when she tried to untangle herself from the sheets and almost fell flat on her face. She decided not to push her luck and try again, especially when Jack made a face at the yelps of surprise that escaped her lips as the hammock shook and swung at the slightest effort.

Instead, she held herself upright and, with as little movement as possible, poured the remaining water into her palm and splashed her face with it.

Her eyes felt like they'd been scraped with sandpaper, and her nose wouldn't stop running. 'I must be a mess,' she said, and then blushed with mortification when she realised who she'd said it to.

But he just held his hand out for the water skin and said cheerfully, 'You look fine to me.'

'And you must have a fantastic imagination.' Grinning, she raised her right arm and examined the bandage wrapped around it. Hardly any blood had seeped into the linen, which meant that someone must have sewn the gash. 'My arm feels better,' she said to Jack. 'Who stitched it up?'

Biting down on her lip, she flexed and stretched her arm, expecting pain but surprised when she felt nothing but a gentle pull of the knitted flesh stretching. Whoever had tended her had done a good job.

'Hester,' he said. 'It turns out she knows her way around a needle as well as a musket. She told me some stories of her time in the army while you were out cold. I may have to document some of her adventures. I'm no writer, but a good assistant librarian always learns the tricks of the trade . . . Tuesday?'

She barely heard him when he called her name. Hester. Once again she was back in that grove, with the landmines going up all around her and Narvi disappearing in a cloud of smoke. Something brushed against her arm and she flinched, but it was only Jack, who was leaning forward with his hand on her elbow and his eyebrows turned down in worry.

'I'm all right.' She shook him off, not wanting to be touched.

He let her go, and dropped his hand to the edge of the hammock, where he started to play with the loose threads. 'Are you sure?' He shrugged his shoulders. 'Not to be indelicate, but you were crying on my shoulder not ten minutes ago. Do you . . . do you need to talk?'

She swiped a hand across her running nose and sniffed. 'No, it's all right. I'll be fine.'

It was a lie, but it seemed to placate him, and they spent the next couple of minutes sitting together in a comfortable silence as Tuesday contemplated getting up. When she swung her legs out over the hammock, however, she was dismayed to discover how much they shook even if she lifted them an inch. She felt as weak as a kitten.

'Jack,' she said, trying to keep the panic from her voice. 'I don't think I can stand.'

Had she been wounded worse than she'd thought? Visions of never being able to walk again danced through her mind – of never seeing the rest of the world or climbing the mountains she'd seen on Hester's map. She sucked in a sob, but Jack just smiled at her, held out his arm and stood with the help of his staff.

'Of course you can't,' he said. 'You haven't got out of bed for a week. I told you, you were running a pretty bad fever there for a while. Quintalion's hardly left your side.'

'Quintalion?' That didn't seem right. Quintalion wasn't the caring type. The shouting, sarcastic, long-suffering type, yes, but Tuesday couldn't imagine him sitting by her hammock and wiping the sweat from her brow, like one of Madame Marisol's heroes by his damsel's bedside, and she was about to tell Jack that when he continued: 'I ended up having to threaten to hit him with my stick to get him to have a rest. Now take my hand, and we'll have you up in no time.'

Take my hand. The words flashed through her head. Sterling had said that to Thaïs. She frowned, and then decided that she was being stupid. Jack was just trying to help her. Worming her way to the edge of the hammock, she took his offered hand and stood.

Her legs instantly folded.

'Whoa there,' he said. 'It looks like it's worse than I thought.'

She blushed as he wrapped an arm around her and helped her to her feet. Leaning against him more heavily than she wanted to admit, she managed to stand and then begin to walk around the hold.

'You remind me of myself,' Jack told her, sweeping in front of him with his staff so that they didn't fall. 'I got sick, when I was younger. My father would lead me out like this every day so that I got some air. You should have seen us, Tuesday . . .' He paused to chuckle softly. 'He was a head shorter than me, even at that age. I would rest my head on the top of his and we would walk out to the window like that. He said I was the best wig he'd ever owned.'

She laughed at the picture of the two of them, and then snuck a sidelong glance up at Jack. Though he was scrawny, with a leanness that caused his shirt and pants to look a little too big for his frame, he was tall too, and she couldn't imagine him being so sick that he would need his father's help just to walk out to the window. 'What happened?'

'My parents thought it was just a normal childhood fever at first. But I didn't get better. I think that's when I first discovered my love of books. My mother would sneak out books from the library when Father wasn't looking, and read them to me, with me propped up against the pillows. I loved those stories. *Finnegan the Rake*, *The Lamentable Tale of Truesdale Button*, *The Hob-Nob's Treasure*.'

'*The Tales of Amiens and Aemilia*?' Tuesday asked, remembering how she'd lived for those tales, back when she hadn't even known what living was.

'Only when I felt really bad. Mum thought a bit of good old-fashioned romance might make me feel better. I liked the bit about the dragon.'

The dragon? Madame Marisol mustn't have reached that point in the story. Tuesday made a mental note to find the first copy she could.

'How long did it take for you to get better?' Just a week had left her antsy and itching to be up and about, and she'd been asleep for most of it. She couldn't imagine what it must have been like to be bedridden for long enough to need books for company.

Jack kept his arm out rigid beside him for her to lean against, but now she hardly needed it: the blood rushing to her legs had shaken off the last of the weakness, and she was finally beginning to pull herself free of that horrible dream. So she was more interested in the inside of the hold than his answer and, her attention taken up by a small mirror nailed to the hull, she almost missed his hushed reply.

'I didn't.'

'*What?*' She stopped suddenly, pulling at his arm so that he was forced to stop as well, and then stared up into his face.

He chewed at his lip. 'We don't have to talk about it. It was a long time ago. And it's not like I died or anything . . . just, well, almost.'

Almost. He said it so casually, like almost dying happened every day. *Though*, she reflected, thinking back to the last couple of days, *maybe it does.*

'No, I want to know,' she told him. 'I mean, if it's not too . . .' She left the words unsaid, but if truth be told, she probably would have pressed on even if it was too painful for him to discuss, for her curiosity had been woken now.

'Of course not.' He waved her concern away. 'I don't mind. You were probably wondering about the whole seeing *thing* anyway.' He paused, as though gathering his thoughts, but then, just as he opened his mouth to speak again, boots clattered on the stairs and Quintalion appeared, squinting into the comparative darkness of the hold.

'I just had to get away from Hester,' he said. 'If she goes on about how we should slit that daybreaker's throat one more time, I swear I'm going to –'

He caught sight of Tuesday and stopped mid-speech, his mouth hanging open comically. A second passed in silence, and then Quintalion recovered magnificently, saying: 'Oh, you're awake, are you? Good. I was starting to worry that I'd have to make it to the Silk Sea with you slung over my shoulder like a particularly annoying piece of luggage.'

Tuesday smiled. 'It's good to see you too, Quintalion.'

He nodded and made his way over to the mirror and the barrel of water in the corner of the hold, where he wasted no time taking out a small dagger and a pot of something that smelled of musk and starting to shave.

'What's he doing?' Jack whispered to her.

Quintalion scraped off the stubble from cheekbone to chin with one meticulous swipe of his dagger. 'Shaving,' she whispered back.

'Sounds fascinating. Well, someone's got to stop Hester from murdering your reluctant guest. I'll be off.' Jack crossed the hold and climbed the stairs one at a time, with his staff *rat-tat-tatt*ing each step, and then disappeared into the sunshine.

Sterling. She'd forgotten that they'd taken him captive, and for a moment she regretted her actions back in the Lady Fortuna's court. It had seemed like the right thing to do at the time – his daybreakers wouldn't be able to shoot them out of the sky with him as their hostage, after all – but knowing that he was so close to her sent shivers down her spine.

'Are you all right?' Quintalion was watching her through the mirror's reflection.

She schooled her face into what she hoped was an acceptably happy look and nodded. It was so far from the truth it was practically a lie, but she didn't want to talk about her dream again, not when the first time had left her crying on Jack's shoulder.

Thankfully, either she was a better liar than she thought, or Quintalion knew her well enough not to push the issue, because he fell uncharacteristically silent as he continued to shave.

She was grateful for it. Now that Jack had left her, her knees were beginning to wobble again, and she shakily made her way back to the hammock and sat down with a sigh.

If that had really been Thaïs up on the platform, then it was highly likely she'd been working with the daybreakers to open that door, wherever it led to. A heavy feeling settled in the base of her stomach. It was now clear that Sterling must have been telling the truth about him and Thaïs being in love, which meant the other things he said might also be true. Like her killing Thaïs.

She let out all the air in her lungs in a long, slow exhale.

'You know,' Quintalion said, still absorbed in his ablutions, 'you shouldn't listen to what he says. Just because he was right about one thing, doesn't mean anything else he says isn't a crock of –'

'How did you know?' she burst out. She hadn't yet told him about her second dream, and he would have had no way of knowing that she had been seeing through Thaïs's eyes in the first dream, if he even remembered her telling him about it at all, which was highly doubtful given the amount of mead he'd drunk. Most of that night was a happy blank for Tuesday.

Quintalion rubbed the excess lather off his dagger with a piece of fabric that hung from a hook on the hull. 'I'm nearly seven hundred years old, girl,' he said. 'You don't get as old as I am without picking up a few things along the way.'

'That's not an answer.' She crossed her arms and tapped her foot impatiently, just to show him that she meant business, though the fact that she almost fell out of the hammock trying to reach the ground diminished the impression somewhat.

He slapped the fabric back onto the hook. 'You remind me of Thaïs,' he said, and sloshed the basin of soapy water onto the floor, where it turned the wooden beams dark. 'My aunt hated evasive answers. She used to box my ears at the slightest suggestion of glibness.'

'Your aunt?' Tuesday wasn't sure that she'd heard him correctly. He couldn't have been talking about Thaïs.

'Yes,' he said deliberately, 'my aunt.'

If what he said were true, that would mean he was related to the Days themselves. She stared at him as he splashed his face with water, half-expecting him to turn blue or breathe fire or do something else magical now that she knew he was practically a god, but to her great disappointment he stayed the same old Quintalion: yellow waistcoat, mixed-up eyes and a scowl that could scare a general.

Of course, he could be lying. 'So your mother is . . .' she said, and left the end of her sentence unsaid.

He didn't miss a beat.

'Father, actually. He was known by many names, but you would know him as Satyr. He was the patron of all that's wild.'

'Was?' she asked, remembering what he'd told her about the disappearance of the Days.

He lowered his head, and the sunlight filtering through the boards painted his skin golden. 'You're not the only one who wants to find the Book of Days.'

Relief poured over her in waves. Now it all made sense: why he'd woken her, why he was willing to accompany her on her quest with so scant a reward. He wasn't just some opportunistic treasure hunter; he was looking for the Book of Days to find his father.

'So that's why you woke me?' she asked, wanting to hear it confirmed.

'Sorry to disappoint you, but I had no idea who I was waking,' he told her. 'I paid a man to bring me anything he could find on my father. He brought me the invitation, some trinkets and a whole lot of dead ends.'

Wake me when it's safe. The words came rushing back to her. She had known one of the Days, and trusted Satyr at least enough to wake her from her sleep. 'The invitation,' she sputtered out. 'We have to find your father. He'll know who I am.'

Quintalion's face pinched in obvious distress. 'He hasn't been seen in hundreds of years. Why do you think I paid someone to try to track him down? No, Tuesday, I don't think you'll find your answer from a corpse.'

'You think he's dead?'

He shrugged and turned away from her. 'I don't know. I wish I could find answers in that invitation as much as you do, but the Unreality House isn't where you go to find them. It's where you take someone if you want to forget about them.' He paused before adding, so softly that she could barely hear him, 'If only I could take my father there.'

'But that's horrible!' She recoiled away from him.

'Is it?' He perched himself on the water barrel, his face still darkened by shadows. 'Is it? Is it worse than not knowing what happened to someone you once loved with all your heart? Would you really want a life filled with nothing but questions and grief at where they lead you?'

He spat the words out in a furious whisper, and she found herself lowering her voice to placate him.

'Well, no ... but I wouldn't want to forget about them entirely!' She shivered at the thought of all the others she had seen, silent and safe in their keeping-houses. Had they just been left and forgotten about, discarded to live out the rest of eternity alone?

'Yet look at Sterling.'

She raised her eyebrows at that, but Quintalion held his hand up for quiet before she could voice her objections.

'I'm not making excuses for him – the Days know he wouldn't want them from me – but look at what he did in Fortune City.'

'Blew it out of the sky because the Lady Fortuna wouldn't give me up?' Her hand wandered to the bandage on her arm.

'No, that's what his daybreakers did. *He* walked into a hostile city full of people who would be glad to see him dead, knowing that if he didn't return by the next bell with his quarry, he would fall with Fortune City.'

She picked at one edge of her bandage and said, 'I'd be a lot more sympathetic if I wasn't the quarry he was looking for.'

Quintalion blew out an annoyed breath. 'You're missing the point entirely. His grief drove him to that, and when he failed to capture you, he was quite content to let himself die. You're telling me you'd prefer obsession like *that* to forgetting who you lost and living on in happiness?'

She almost laughed, but caught herself before it reached her throat. Quintalion had such a way with words that it wasn't often she was able to score a point in their conversation. '*You* forget who you're talking to. I'm the girl travelling halfway across the world just to find myself. I think I know obsession.'

He opened his mouth, shut it again, and then added in a quiet tone, as though he knew he'd been beaten: 'And a book.'

'And a book,' she allowed, pretending for Quintalion's sake that she didn't only want the Book of Days so she could find out who she was.

And to see whether I have blood on my hands. She didn't voice it, but the thought was always in the back of her head. Since she had woken, however, another thought had taken root. She tried hard to silence it, because if she let it whisper to her for too long, she'd go mad. *Sterling destroyed an entire city just to find you*, it said. *You already have blood on your hands.*

Luckily, she was saved from having to admit her fears by the uneven *thump-clop thump-clop* on the stairs. Hester appeared a second later.

Tuesday smiled to see her safe and well, but Hester didn't return her smile, barely sparing both of them a glance as she stopped at the bottom of the stairs, and instead kept her head half-turned towards the deck above, her fingers drumming against her leg.

'Tuesday, Quintalion,' she said, an edge in her voice. 'I think you had better come on deck.'

CHAPTER NINETEEN

Tuesday burst out into the sunshine and winced as the brightness pierced her eyes. The *Zephyr*, she saw when her eyesight cleared, lay beached on earth that was cracked and scorched. The land was so flat that the sun seemed to hang too large on the distant horizon. A few trees clung to life, their roots breaking up the flaky ground as they dug down deep to find water. The air was so warm that it was like trying to breathe in a clay oven. Tuesday licked her lips to relieve them, but her mouth felt as parched as the dead trees.

Sterling drooped where he stood against the mast. His dark uniform was stained darker still with sweat, and beads of it had broken out on his forehead and gathered at the grimy gag, which now lay around his neck.

'Tell them what you told Jacobi.' Hester nudged Sterling in the ribs with the butt of her musket. His green eyes shuttered and he flinched, but made no cry of pain.

'We do not wish to say anything further.' A bruise above Sterling's eye painted his brow black, and a swollen and puffy lip distorted his words, but when he spotted Tuesday on deck he strained against his bonds and stared at her through his one good eye with an intense gaze that raised goose pimples on her arms.

'She lives, then,' he spat out. 'We are relieved. Her death would have stolen from us the exquisite agony we have in store for her.'

Tuesday shrank behind Quintalion. She didn't trust herself around Sterling. Though she mostly wanted to walk right up to him and slap him, a very small part of her whispered that she should untie his ropes, and what terrified her was how persuasive it was.

'Oh, don't change the topic,' Quintalion said to Sterling, his arms crossed. 'I doubt the good captain called us here to listen to your pathetic threats.'

'I would not have brought you on deck at all, but Jacobi Heller provoked a response in him.'

Jack sat on the steps to the quarterdeck with his sleeves rolled up, his vest tossed to one side and his maps and books spread about him. He wore another piece of cloth covering his eyes, cleaner by far than Sterling's gag, and it gave Tuesday a moment's confusion until she realised that he probably wore it to protect his eyes from the sun, since he wouldn't have been able to tell if he was looking directly at it.

'It's just Jack,' he told her, 'and I didn't mean to. He asked me for some water and I thought, well, it's so hot that it would be cruel not to –'

'He destroyed your home!' Tuesday yelled.

The muscles twitched in his forehead. 'And I would like nothing more than to leave him out here to die, but I was under the impression we brought him with us for a reason.'

Tuesday dug her fingernails into her palm, and then struggled to release the tension that knotted her insides. He was right. She'd stopped Hester from killing him because, as much as it pained her to admit it, she knew he could be useful. With a thousand daybreakers between them and the Silk Sea, having their leader as a hostage might be their only protection. 'I'm sorry,' she said. 'You're right.'

'So we do not kill this *dalhak-shu'uvi*.' Hester's hands tightened around the musket, causing Tuesday to step forward with her hand raised in peace just in case Hester ignored her wishes and shot him anyway, but her eyes flicked up to meet Tuesday's and she slowly reached up over her head and slipped the musket into its holster on her back.

'You are as weak as your brother, Hassar San Khalar.' Sterling turned his blistered face in Hester's direction. 'We knew it the moment you fell before us. Pathetic, the whole lot of you. What we did was nothing more than putting down a pack of rabid dogs.'

The knife was up and at Sterling's throat before Tuesday had a chance to move. 'Say that again, *my lord commander*.' Hester dug the tip of the knife into the hollow of Sterling's throat just enough to draw blood.

'Hester,' Quintalion drawled, 'do you really want his blood all over your deck? It'll be hell to clean.'

Jack was scrambling to his feet in a flurry of papers, but Hester paid him no mind. They were all too far away to do anything but stand and watch if Hester decided to drain the life from their only hope of crossing Voltemandian territory.

'You or me,' the woman whispered to Sterling. 'I do not make promises lightly.'

'Like you promised to destroy us years ago? How many innocent lives got caught in the crossfire? Fifty? Sixty? We read the reports. Millers Row was a peaceful town, but that didn't stop you from burning it to the ground when you thought it was harbouring daybreakers.'

The tip of the knife pressed in deeper, and a thin line of blood dribbled down Sterling's neck. 'I've changed.'

Sterling inched away from Hester and swallowed, squinting against the unrelenting sunlight. 'Says the woman holding a knife to our throat.'

'Says the man trying to make her use it,' Quintalion cut in. 'Give it up, Sterling. If it's a quick death you're looking for, this is the wrong place and we are definitely the wrong people. I do, however, pride myself on my ability to keep a man alive for days without his skin . . . a technique I'd be more than willing to demonstrate on you.'

Sterling's laugh came out as a cross between a cough and a wheeze. Hester removed her knife from his throat and slipped it back in its sheath, but not before nicking him on the cheek in a move that Tuesday was sure she would claim as accidental. He shook against his bonds with the force of his coughing.

'You're all fools,' he said when he was finally able to take a breath.

Quintalion glanced over at Tuesday, and then looked away. 'Tell us something we don't know. Like whatever you said that excited Hester so much she dragged an invalid away from her bed.'

It took Tuesday a moment to realise that he was referring to her, but by then the conversation had already moved on, leaving her to narrow her eyes at Quintalion and hope that he felt the full vitriol of her stare. Given that she was staring at the back of his head, it wasn't as effective as she wanted.

'He's got my father!' Jack burst out. 'He whispered it when I gave him the water, said that I might soon be moving up from being an assistant librarian.' He dropped down to collect the map at his feet and worried at it with shaking hands. 'That's how it's always been in the Heller family – we inherit the title of librarian. How could he know if he doesn't have my father?'

'Why?' Tuesday asked Sterling, moving out from behind Quintalion's shadow. 'Why did you take him?'

'Don't bother asking him,' Quintalion said, 'he's clearly trying to goad us all into killing him here and now. Gag him again and have done with it.'

'His father can open the door,' Sterling said.

'He'll never tell you!' Jack crossed the deck and stopped just before the mast, holding the map so tightly that the paper crinkled. He tilted his head in Sterling's direction, no doubt daring him to say more, but the daybreaker shut his mouth and turned his body away from them as much as the ropes would allow.

'Door,' Quintalion mused. 'How difficult is it to open a door? A good set of lock picks or a heavy boot at a pinch would set it to rights. Unless it's not just any door. Unless it's a door to a certain city . . . he's trying to enter the City of Lost Things.' With a crook of his finger, he gestured for them all to join him as he walked to the upper deck, far out of Sterling's hearing.

Hester leaned against the wheel, useless though it was since the *Zephyr* was grounded. 'But the doors to that city can only be opened by death,' she breathed. 'Surely . . .'

And then she stopped, suddenly turning very pale. 'Oh,' she said softly. 'I had not thought . . . *of course.*'

'Hester?' Tuesday asked.

Hester's eyes were dark in the bright sunlight. 'You know that the daybreakers killed my brother, but you do not know why.

I did not know myself, though I have spent many sleepless nights remembering that day. But now I believe I know.'

'They wanted to enter the City of Lost Things,' Jack said, before adding, 'Sorry. I know that was probably aimed more at Tuesday. It's just that I'm sure you're right. The locals know where the door is – it's a closely guarded secret that my father only learned through months of living with them – and they've been sacrificing people to it since before the Saturday Wars. If the daybreakers know where it is –'

'Tortured some poor soul to get the location, no doubt,' Quintalion broke in darkly.

'– then it stands to reason that they would kill your people, Hester, just on the off-chance it would work.'

'Wait,' Tuesday said. All this talk of cities and doors and sacrifices was completely baffling her. She felt like she was standing in front of a painting that everyone was calling a masterpiece, but she could only see a single squiggle. 'What *is* the City of Lost Things?'

'It is called the Ma-altisilar in the language of my people,' Hester told her.

'The City on the Edge of Forever.' That earned Jack a swift smile from the Saqiran.

'On the Edge of All Time,' she corrected, 'but your translation is better than most. It is the city where the dead gather, the great pasture where the grass always grows, the hereafter.'

'And Sterling wants to go there because . . . ?' But then Tuesday realised that she could answer her own question. It had been staring her in the face for so long. 'Because he wants to bring back Thaïs.'

She was clattering down the steps to the main deck before the others could stop her. 'Why?' she said, stopping in front of Sterling. 'Why do you want to bring her back?'

Sterling cracked open gummed-up eyes. 'Because we love her,' he said simply, 'and you took her from us.'

'I didn't kill her,' she said softly, staring at her feet.

'Yet you ran from us at the gate to the city with the fleetness of the guilty.'

She couldn't meet his eyes. The guilt weighed in her bones, and she bit her lip to keep from crying. She wouldn't give him that. He could have her guilt and her apologies, however meaningless, but not her tears. 'I'm sorry,' she whispered.

'Sorry won't bring her back to us.' He spat at her feet.

Appearing at Tuesday's shoulder, Hester cursed and reached to her hip, but Tuesday just shook her head, and the woman's hand stilled beneath her vest.

'No, that's not what I meant.' Tuesday pressed her hands together behind her back, happy to feel the burn on her forearm as the newly sewn skin stretched, since the pain took her mind off the man before her.

She took a deep breath and hoped that she would be able to keep her voice from shaking. 'I don't know if I killed her. If I did, then that's something I'm going to have to come to terms with . . . but that's one death. How many have you killed? Or *had* killed? All those people in Fortune City . . . Col . . . that day in the pomegranate grove. I'm sorry that Thaïs died, but her life can't be worth *that*.'

'It is every bit worth that,' Sterling said, his words garbled together. 'We would destroy the world and everyone in it just to see her face again! *Solus mayetvos.* There *is* nothing –'

His eyebrows knitted together suddenly, and he stopped mid-tirade. 'Wait . . . how do you know about the pomegranate grove?'

Hester had turned to face her as well, and Tuesday realised with a sinking feeling that she hadn't yet had a chance to explain her dream to her friend.

'I . . . I . . .' she sputtered, feeling all eyes on her. 'I was going to tell you, Hester.'

'You were there?'

Her friend's voice emerged from her as nothing more than a sigh, but Tuesday heard the sorrow and the accusation held within it and turned away so that she didn't have to look at Hester and have all her suspicions confirmed.

'It's not like that. I would never have just done nothing while . . . but I've been having these dreams . . .'

'Being yourself and yet not, helpless to do anything while your enemy ran towards you,' Quintalion said softly. So the drink *hadn't* dimmed his memories.

'Exactly.' She reached for any lifeline thrown her way, anything to help her explain something she still didn't understand herself. 'Like I was looking through someone else's eyes . . . yours, Hester.'

'You know,' Jack said, 'I read that dreams can be the doorways into past lives.'

'Ha!' Quintalion choked on his laugh. 'You mean Hester and Tuesday? Preposterous. Not to mention that Hester, as far as I'm aware, is still alive. You *are* still alive, right, Captain? You haven't drunk any draughts with a skull and crossbones written anywhere on them?'

Jack joined in Quintalion's high spirits with a few chuckles of his own, but from the way he forced them out of his chest in a barking cough, Tuesday got the feeling that he was only doing it out of politeness.

'No, it's not that.' Tuesday pulled tight on her satchel as she tried to explain. 'Madame Marisol gave me some tea. She told me to drink it if I ever needed her, but it actually makes you dream of the last person you were thinking of, and I must have been thinking of Thaïs and Hester at the same time and . . . it worked a little too well,' she finished lamely.

Sterling stood there, watching her with his head tilted to one side, but as this was rapidly becoming his default position, she figured he would soon tire of it and ignored him, turning instead to Hester, who had wrapped her arms around her chest and angled her body away from the rest of them.

'Hester?' She hesitated with a hand hovering above the other woman's back, not expecting a response.

'What did he look like?'

'What?' Tuesday edged her way around the smaller woman, but Hester kept herself guarded, her eyes searching the barren horizon.

'What,' she replied after a pause, her words sharp, 'did he look like?'

The others had retreated to a respectful distance, Quintalion ducking down to help Jack gather his scattered maps before the wind blew them away. Sterling watched the women silently.

'Who?'

'My brother,' Hester said, and swallowed thickly. 'I do not close my eyes at night without sending up a prayer to the gods of my ancestors to give me the strength to rain down vengeance upon all those who took him from me . . . but I find when my thoughts turn to him I can no longer see his face. Perhaps it is for the best. No doubt he would weep to see what has become of his beloved sister.'

Tuesday's throat grew tight. The day, hot as it was, suddenly turned cold, and she shivered. *Build a new life, a better life. A life filled with love that is not oppressive, dreams that do not warp and turn bitter, and a future that is finer than your past.* Isn't that what she had told herself? And yet here she was, with an entire city's blood on her hands, just because she couldn't let go of a past she didn't remember. It was a fate sorrier than Hester's: at least she was fighting for someone.

'His eyes,' she said softly, staring at Hester's back. 'They were as dark as the night, but so full of life. And his smile . . . it held the promise of mischief. His hair was a mess of curls. I think it would probably eat any comb that tried to come near it. In the dream I, uh, I could feel everything you felt. I know how much you loved him.'

Hester continued to stare out at the twisted and burnt ground surrounding them. A hot breeze ruffled her hair and she slowly, almost imperceptibly, nodded. 'He was . . . my everything.'

Her hand came down on Tuesday's shoulder and squeezed, and Tuesday held herself very still, as though in the presence of a wild creature, fearing that any movement would startle the woman back into the Hester she knew, the one with the uncanny ability to hide knives in places where it shouldn't even be physically possible, to spit out insults in two different languages, but Hester only let her hand rest on Tuesday's shoulder for a moment, and then stumped off across the deck towards her cabin.

'That's it?' Sterling laughed as he rested his head back against the mast, his face twisted with exhaustion. 'She was in your mind, saw your people die and did nothing . . . and you're just going to walk away? We knew you were weak.'

Hester stopped, her back tensing beneath the light shirt. She turned around slowly, and Tuesday shrank back against Quintalion at the look in her eyes. 'I am *not* weak. Every second that you still draw breath proves how strong I am.'

Then she turned away, stalked back to the cabin and shut the door without another word.

'Kill us then!' Sterling snarled out the words. His lips cracked and bled, but he ignored the blood streaked around his mouth and strained against his bonds hard enough to draw matching lines of red around both wrists. 'Our life will not save you. Our men are already at the city, and when we have Thaïs, she will bring us the Book of Days, and we will read you out of existence and laugh as every speck of you floats away on the breeze.'

It was the ravings of a man baked in the sun and deprived of water for too long, and Tuesday would have left him to his bitterness had Quintalion not stood up straighter beside her and said: 'What did you say?'

'Don't listen to him, Quintalion,' Jack tried, stepping forward with his staff in one hand and a pile of papers in the other. 'It is the lack of water that speaks, not him.'

Quintalion launched himself across the deck and grabbed hold of the front of Sterling's sweat-stained tunic, pulling him as far forward as the ropes would allow so that they were bare inches apart. His face was twisted in panic. 'What,' he ground out, 'did you say?'

Sterling's tongue darted out to taste the blood on his lips. 'Did you really think we would be so foolish as to walk into Fortune City without a plan? We knew that witch would not abandon her city without a fight. So we told our men –'

'What?' The force of Quintalion's shake rattled Sterling's teeth together. 'What did you tell them?'

If she didn't know him, she would have assumed he spoke in anger, but she could see the little tremors shivering over his skin – Sterling's words had clearly rattled him.

Jack crept forward to hear his response, and Tuesday found herself moving closer as well, and the closer she came, the more her gaze was drawn to Sterling's right hand, and the waxy and scarred skin that painted it a lifeless white.

She swallowed against the buzzing revulsion at the back of her throat.

'We told them . . . we told them . . .'

With a pinch, Quintalion closed off Sterling's air supply. Sterling's eyes bulged as his chest heaved uselessly, unable to funnel air from his throat to his lungs. 'You told them . . .' he prompted.

Sterling's eyes lost their focus just as Quintalion released his throat, and he collapsed back against the mast, coughs shaking his thin frame. His frantic gasps for breath made his words erupt from him in a wheeze. 'Kill us. We welcome it.'

'Not today, I think. You see, you're far more useful to us alive. Maybe, if you're lucky, when you've told us what your men are up to, I'll slit your throat cleanly.'

'Quintalion, no!' Tuesday cried out. Sterling had killed thousands of people, yes, but she couldn't just stand by and let him be murdered in front of her. *Not again*, a voice whispered.

'You promise?' Sterling shifted against the mast so that he could look directly into Quintalion's face, and after a few moments, Quintalion nodded.

Tuesday couldn't believe what she was hearing. 'You can't!'

Quintalion turned on her, and his face was a thundercloud of emotion, driving her back across the deck and away from him so that she didn't get caught in the storm. 'You forget,' he said in a voice quiet with the promise of soon-to-be-released rage, 'what this man stands for, what they've *taken* from me. A clean death is more than fair.'

It was the first time since she'd met him that Tuesday truly saw the depth of pain and anger in his eyes, and it struck her dumb.

'What about what he's taken from *me*?' Jack chimed in, somewhere near Tuesday's shoulder. 'Do I get a say in this? Come to mention it, what about Hester?'

'The captain,' Quintalion muttered, his focus again on Sterling, 'is not here. I am. And I give you my word, daybreaker, that if you tell us what your men have planned, I'll send you to your beloved Thaïs.'

Sterling licked his lips and drew in a deep breath. 'Our men were given orders back at that rat hole you have the audacity to call a city –'

'Yes, yes, kindly skip the insults. You hate us, we hate you. We're not exactly covering new ground here.'

Sterling snorted and rolled his eyes towards the sky, but continued: 'If we were to fall, their instructions were to proceed directly to the door to the City of Lost Things. No doubt they are there already.'

Quintalion's brow pursed and he loosened his hold of Sterling's shirt, his gaze turning thoughtful as he spoke almost to himself. 'We can't fight an entire army. What would be the point of that? Two hundred men twiddling their thumbs on the shores of the sea? Planning to do a spot of fishing, are they?'

'The doors can only be opened by death,' Jack said, stepping closer to Tuesday. 'All the stories agree. The City of Lost Things belongs to the dead. Even if they somehow found the door, they could wade into the sea itself and be no closer to the city than if they were a hundred leagues away.'

The blood dripping onto Sterling's pale hand drew Tuesday's attention. It ran across the back of his hand and pooled in the channels between blue-red veins and the hollows of his fingers. Would the skin be cold, the life long fled? Or, if she wrapped her hand around his, could her warmth return the flush of health back into those long fingers?

Sterling's voice pulled her back from her daydream into harsh reality. 'Not if,' he said, 'we have a willing victim. A father, desperate to save the life of his son.'

Jack stiffened beside her, but Sterling hadn't finished.

'Were you not listening before, Jacobi Heller? We were not lying when we said your father knew how to open the door. It's amazing what a man will do to save his child.'

The staff slipped from Jack's slackened fingers and he surged forward, scattering the papers around him as he charged towards Sterling. Not wanting to see Sterling beaten to death in front of her, Tuesday reached out and grabbed at Jack's shirt when he rushed by her, and dug her fingers into the soft cloth to hold him back.

He settled at her touch, but his mouth was still a taut line, so Tuesday whispered to him: 'Don't. It's what he wants.'

'Maybe.' She hadn't meant for her words to reach Sterling, but he looked over at her. 'You know our desires.'

Though the heat of the day plastered her hair to her forehead with sweat, she shivered.

'Or,' he continued, 'perhaps we just wish to see the looks on your faces when you realise there's no way for you to win. Our daybreakers will reach the City of Lost Things, and we will dance with our love while they tear out the pages of the Book and end the old ways once and for all.'

Quintalion snorted, released his hold on Sterling's tunic, and then patted him on the shoulder. 'I hate to tell you, but you're veering dangerously close to cliché. *End the old ways once and for all?* You can do better than that.'

'Wait.' Tuesday held up her hand for silence. Something Sterling said had leapt out at her as wrong, but now it was fading along with the rest of the words. She screwed her face up in concentration, not caring how odd she must have looked, and tried to block out everything going on around her, the rustle of wind, a door opening to her left. *And there it is.*

Her eyes shot open in triumph. 'You said your daybreakers will reach the city … *will*. That means they're not there yet. There's still time to stop them, to rescue Jack's father and find the Book of Days.'

'Then what are we waiting for?' Hester stood in the doorway to her cabin. She had strapped two curved swords to her belt, the broken tiger-headed blade peeked out at the top of her wooden leg, and the pearl handles of several smaller blades gleamed in the sun. Her musket was in its customary position on her back, and she carried a flaming torch. 'Let's go save the world.'

CHAPTER TWENTY

'Anything you want to keep,' Hester said as they stared at her, 'bring it with you. The *Zephyr* is no use to us now.'

With a final frown in Sterling's direction, Jack gently peeled Tuesday's fingers off his shirt and bent down to pick up his staff, collecting his papers at the same time, and then disappeared into the hold.

'But Hester,' Tuesday said as Quintalion forced the gag back up into Sterling's mouth, 'won't we need it if we're to get to the Silk Sea before the daybreakers?'

Hester raised the torch. The waves of heat pouring off it made the already scorching day unbearable. 'My ship was damaged in the fall of Fortune City. Look there! The sails lie shredded and useless.'

Tuesday looked up at the main mast: the sails hung in tatters, flittering uselessly in the light wind. Hester must have fought to land the ship safely when Tuesday was unconscious, which explained why they were beached in such a desolate place. Several of the chests were missing as well, and Tuesday wondered whether they had been lost in the rough landing or whether Hester had been right to doubt the honesty of the harbour master in Fortune City.

Hester laid her hand against the mast and sighed. 'She has served me well all these years. I would have liked to send her to her sleep beneath the waves of the sacred La'Haiia, but since that sea lies many miles to the north and we have no time for the journey, I must make do with a burial of fire and hope the gods are merciful.'

'The gods?' Tuesday asked. She knew it wasn't the time, but she couldn't help herself.

'My people do not follow your Days.' Hester regarded her coolly as she held the firebrand closer to Sterling's face than was strictly necessary. 'No, my gods were already ancient when yours were written into being. My people hold two things above all others: the night and the rain, and according to tradition, any burial must include both. But come. We have not the time for a history lesson. Get your things and prepare to leave.'

Perhaps Jack will be able to tell me more. He'd learned their language, after all, so it stood to reason that he'd know some of their stories. She was just heading down into the hold to ask him, when she met him as he ascended the stairs, with his rucksack stuffed full and the straps tight across his arms. When his staff tapped into her boot, he nodded at her, eased past and up onto the deck without a word.

She continued down the stairs and paused at the bottom to let her eyes adjust to the darkness. A dark Quintalion-sized blur paced across the floor, throwing things over his shoulder and muttering.

'What are you looking for?' she asked him, journeying further into the hold.

He paused briefly and then spun around on his heel and continued in the opposite direction.

When Tuesday's eyes finally adjusted to the dim light, she saw that he was rooting around in one of the barrels tied off against the side of the ship, and the things he had been throwing were actually pouches that rattled when they hit the planks.

'You'd think,' he said, fumbling with the knot on one of the pouches, 'that a pirate would have some decent weapons around here, but no!'

Tuesday crossed the hold and bent down to pick up the pouch that Quintalion had abandoned. Flipping the rope tie off, she uncorked the pouch and poured the contents into her hand. 'Rice,' she said, her mind supplying her with the word.

'Yes, rice.' Quintalion poured his pouch onto the floor. 'I'm sure it'll be oh-so-helpful when we're surrounded by two hundred daybreakers.'

There wasn't time to argue with him. A constant flow of footsteps came from above, joined by the occasional thud of heavier things hitting the deck, which she could only assume was either Hester killing Sterling and disposing of his body, or she and Jack preparing for their journey. She corked the rice and held on to it, planning on putting it in her satchel when she had a chance.

Quintalion regarded her. 'Of course, we *could* eat it.'

'I thought I might,' she replied archly.

He threw her a couple more of the pouches, followed by several biscuits that refused to break, even when she flung one against the floor, and the four water skins that he'd filled at the barrel by the mirror. She collected everything in her skirt and looked around to see whether there was anything else they might be able to use, gaping in disbelief that Quintalion remained silent.

By the Days, she thought, *I've had the last word.* It happened so rarely with him that, if they hadn't been in a hurry, she would have been inclined to hold a party or at least open a bottle of Hester's Tiamatan wine.

Quintalion was rigging up some kind of rucksack, similar to Jack's, only twice as large and with considerably more rope holding it all together. As he threaded four tin cups to one of the straps, he said, so softly that Tuesday almost missed it: 'I'd prefer a hand cannon.'

She huffed out a laugh that she fervently hoped he didn't hear and crossed the room to her hammock, dumped the food on the floor, where she spied her satchel, and started to undo the hammock from its hooks.

'Friends,' Hester called out from above them. 'Gather your supplies and make ready. The morning draws on and we must be gone before the heat grows too great.'

Quintalion shucked his greatcoat off, rolled it and carefully placed it in his rucksack. He then checked his pocket watch. 'Ten o'clock? We've less time than I thought.'

'We *are* trying to beat the daybreakers to the City of Lost Things,' she reminded him. 'I imagine they've quite the head start.'

'According to my calculations, we should be about a week behind them,' he said. 'But their ships are slow. *You* try lobbing around twelve working cannons and four arrow-bolt towers and see how fast you can travel. They could probably hit a hundred and twenty miles a day at most, and with us somewhere near the border of Saqira if this accursed heat is anything to go by . . . well, we may just be able to catch up.'

'On foot?' No matter how slow the cannons made the daybreakers' airships, they couldn't possibly be slower than walking.

'Ah!' He winked at her. 'I didn't say that, did I?'

Pushing down the annoyance that threatened to spill over, Tuesday told him, 'You're not exactly making this easy for me.'

'It's not my job to make things easy for you. It's my job to get you to the City of Lost Things and let you have your epiphanies on your own.'

She sighed in frustration at his obstinacy. 'Or you could just tell me everything *now* and save me asking you later.'

'Where's the fun in that?'

She dropped the flattened hammock to the ground and piled the food and supplies onto it. 'I didn't think you found any of this fun.'

'Indeed I don't.' He hefted the make-shift rucksack onto his back and grimaced, shouldering the weight. 'But the company is better than some ventures I've been on – don't take that as a compliment, because you'd be saying the same thing if you'd once spent a trip down the Mallowmere tied to a barrel and a dead man named Bob – and the reward is sufficiently decent to make this little jaunt of ours worthwhile.'

'Yes, well, don't worry,' she said, rolling the hammock over the supplies, 'you'll get your coins.'

'Good,' he said, his voice tight. 'I just hope it's worth it.'

*

They met Hester and Jack up on deck just in time. Hester had piled everything around the main mast: chests, barrels, nets and ropes, the torn-off helm, and even the useless sails. She'd tied Sterling's hands together and kept him on a short rope, though the way she glared at him, Tuesday had no doubt that she would have preferred to leave him behind for the bonfire.

As it was, she seemed to be using him as some sort of pack mule: she'd slung three large bags over his shoulders, and his tunic was damp from the water skins hanging from them. She'd even placed his sabre on a rope around his neck; its scabbard smacked into his chest and hands with each step he took, but the ropes trussing him gave him no way to use it. No doubt she had intended that too: a powerful reminder of his helplessness.

'Very well,' Hester said, clearing her throat. 'It is time.'

'Do you want to say something? A goodbye?' It would be hard for Hester to part with the ship, she knew, especially since it carried the image of her brother as its figurehead.

Hester nodded. 'I would give her a eulogy that would outshine the stars were there enough time, but there is not. So I must content myself with thanks. She has been a true and steady vessel. I will miss her. I will not say sorry for what I am about to do, but I will say that I wish it did not have to be so. Goodbye, old friend.'

Torch in hand, she stroked the helm gently, and then threw the firebrand into the middle of the pile around the main mast. It hissed and popped, lapping at the wood, and soon it caught the cloth and the sails went up with a ferocity that drew them all back and away to the rope that Hester had hung from the side of the ship.

Hester led them from the wreck as the *Zephyr* burned behind them, and not once did she look back.

The wood cracked and warped as the fire chewed it up. Tuesday dug her fingernails into her palms and tried not to listen.

'Did we have to burn her?' she asked Hester.

'We are in the northeast. I would rather commend her to the sky than see her in the hands of a daybreaker.'

Silence fell, but for the rush of flames and the tread of their feet on the dry earth. They walked until the ship faded from view. A column of smoke still rose high into the sky, marking the site of the *Zephyr*'s burial.

The day grew hotter. Tuesday shed one petticoat, and then the second, and left them sitting on the black rocks that had begun to dot the landscape, splashes of darkness against the dull tawny and yellow sand. The rocks were twisted and sharp. They cut her hand when she bent down to pick one up, and though she slipped it into her satchel for further study, she was careful never to brush up against one as she picked her way through them. They looked like black glass, and reflected the heat of the sun so there was no escaping it: it assaulted them from above and below. Soon enough Tuesday pulled Hester aside to help her, and her pair of stays came off along with the last traces of her decorum. *Madame Marisol*, she thought, *would be shocked.*

'I am surprised,' Hester said, watching to make sure none of the men turned around, since she had threatened them with a painful death if they did, 'that you wore stays at all.'

Jack, who had been allowed to help on the grounds that since he couldn't actually see there would be no impropriety, blushed from his chest to the roots of his hair.

Tuesday shrugged her arms back into the ragged blue dress, and then began to do up the buttons on the front. 'Madame

Marisol dressed me like this – probably to discourage adventuring. Is it very odd?'

Jack spluttered and started coughing, so Tuesday patted his back and took the stays from him. It had been cruel of Hester to make him hold them.

'Not odd at all,' Hester said, 'in the east. I am just wondering why your Madame Marisol dressed you as a daybreaker's paramour.'

Paramour? She didn't recognise the word, but she understood Hester's connotation, and it was her turn to blush. 'I don't believe,' she said hotly, 'she had any intention of the sort.'

'Marisol?' Jack said, his voice strange. '*Madame* Marisol?'

Tuesday distastefully dropped the offending garment and took great delight in kicking it onto one of the black rocks, where it snagged and tore, waving in the wind like some kind of deviant flag. 'That's her name,' she said. 'Do you know of her?'

'Yes,' he choked out. 'I stayed in her Unreality House.'

Tuesday couldn't stop herself from laughing. She hadn't meant to, but what he said was ridiculous. 'But you couldn't possibly have done that . . . you'd have had to be . . .'

'Dead,' he filled in for her.

The story he had been telling her came rushing back: how his father walked him out to the window, how his mother read to him, and how he didn't get better . . .

'Well, look at that,' Hester said suddenly. 'Quintalion is leading us in the wrong direction. I had better go and correct him before we find ourselves back at the *Zephyr*.'

It wasn't a very subtle attempt at excusing herself, but as Hester left the two of them alone to go yell at Quintalion, Tuesday found she appreciated it.

'Dead,' she repeated. Or *almost* dead.

'But I wasn't.' Jack ran his fingers through his hair, his rucksack rustling with the movement. 'I mean, it was pretty bad there for a while, but I'm better now,' he added, with just a little too much jollity in his voice for Tuesday to believe it was real.

'What happened?'

He shrugged and started walking after the others, slowly enough so that Tuesday was able to match his pace after a few steps. 'You know most of it already. The healers thought it was a wasting disease. It's funny . . . I don't actually remember, well, almost dying, but I do remember my mother crying in the darkness, but when I tried to comfort her, I couldn't reach her. Is that possible?'

Tuesday shook her head. She couldn't give him an answer.

'Next thing I know I'm waking up and everything's black and I can't see and Father's saying, "Welcome back, my boy," but his voice is strained and I know something's wrong.'

Using his staff, he hit one of the rocks away from his path with enough force to send it flying.

'Your parents brought you back?' It was like there was a hole inside her; she felt very cold, and she found she was shaking. A stranger had woken *her*.

'The way my father explains it, they couldn't take it after I . . .' He paused and licked his lips. 'So they took me to Madame Marisol's to forget about me. It's the best place for it, you know.'

His voice was hard and he kept his face away from her, but Tuesday could tell by the tension in his shoulders and the silent shakes that he was holding back tears. Hesitantly, she slipped her hand in his. 'But they came back,' she reminded him.

His hand gripped hers, and she blushed.

'They did. Father says that even though they couldn't remember me, they knew they were missing something in their lives. It's enough to drive anyone mad. So they took the invitation that Madame Marisol had given them and came back for me.'

'But you're better,' she said, looking him up and down. 'You don't look like you've got a wasting disease.'

'I don't.' He shrugged. 'I guess being in the House gave my body enough time to rest and heal itself, because I woke up feeling fine. Well, until I realised something was wrong.'

'They got you back. Your parents got you back.' She smiled a little at the thought of how it could have been different for her: the hand of her loved one on her cheek, gently pulling her out of sleep, the familiar green eyes greeting her as she looked around for the first time, someone to cover her with a blanket and keep her on her feet. 'Wait . . . you said you knew something was wrong.'

He pulled his hand away from hers, and she shuddered at the sudden loss of warmth.

'My father was the one who put me in the keeping-house, see. You have to be woken by the person who puts you in the keeping-house.'

She hadn't known that, and it posed some interesting questions she'd have to ask Quintalion later on, but for the moment Jack needed her more. She rested her hand on his arm, her fingers working against the rough cloth of his sleeve in tiny patterns, and said: 'But you're here, so surely he did, unless . . .'

He made a great show of batting the rocks aside from his path, and when he next spoke, his voice was rough. 'My mother, she . . . Father said she was so overwhelmed at seeing me again – remembering me – she didn't think. She reached out to me before Father could stop her . . . brushed her hand across my eyes.'

Tuesday rested the back of her hand against her cheek, against her own mark from being woken. She didn't need a mirror to know that the imprints of Quintalion's fingerprints lay stark and white on her skin. 'But you're all right,' she said to him. 'You're here. Your mother?'

The hole inside her grew bigger.

Jack gripped his staff with both hands and sent another rock flying. 'She, uh, she didn't . . .'

'I'm so sorry.' It was the right thing to say in the situation, but now, walking next to a friend who wouldn't even turn his head in her direction, it felt so inadequate. She couldn't think of anything better to say, so she just squeezed his hand and they walked on in silence.

They'd almost caught up to the others when she said quietly, 'Is that why you're blind? Your mother died bringing you back and you . . .'

'Came back wrong.' He gave her a tight smile. 'But it's all right – I still have my father.'

His face clouded over, making Tuesday want to kick herself for starting the conversation, but then he said: 'So you were a guest of Madame Marisol's as well. I've never met another almost dead person before.'

She laughed, the tension leaving her shoulders. 'You don't *have* to be almost dead to be in the Unreality House. I mean, I don't think I was; just . . . different.'

'Still,' he said, his usual jovial tone returning, 'it's a pleasure to meet you, fellow Unreality House dweller.'

He released her hand and then held out his right hand to shake hers, and Tuesday, muffling her laughter, shook it.

'So why are you different, exactly?'

It would be a long story, but he looked so earnestly keen to hear it that she took a deep breath and began – she told him all about the letter she'd sent herself, and wanting to know who she was and who she had been, and Quintalion waking her up to a world she'd never seen. He *oohed* and *aahed* and asked questions when she stopped to draw breath, and insisted that she get the letter out, running his fingers over every inch of the paper and declaring that it hadn't come from any paper mill he was familiar with, and by the time they stopped for lunch with the others, Tuesday felt as though she could tell him anything.

CHAPTER TWENTY-ONE

'We are here,' Hester said. She pointed to a spot on the map seemingly in the middle of nowhere. 'In the dragonsbreath wastelands just south of my country.'

'Dragons?' Tuesday interrupted breathlessly. 'Are there dragons here?'

'Only runts that do not deserve the name. But once there were fire breathers, great giants of the sky. This was their territory.'

'I've heard the Shining Ones roam here now.' Quintalion sucked an errant crumb off his pinkie. 'So I suggest we don't camp here for the night. I've no desire to have my head part company with my body . . . though at points in this trip it's felt like it already has.'

Hester threw a hard tack biscuit at Sterling and grinned when it bounced off his leg and rolled away. He reached for it, but the sabre he wore around his neck snagged in the dirt, the pommel smacking him in the face, and he glowered at all of them as he tried to scoop the biscuit up with one leg.

'It may be, but they don't travel this far east,' Hester said. 'The soldiers of Bittertongue are well disciplined. They keep them away from the city's borders.'

'With the city supplying half of Voltemande's iron, I don't doubt they're paid well to protect it. I've heard you can taste the metal on the air for two hundred miles.'

Jack took a swig from the water skin and then held it out to Tuesday, who took it but paused with it halfway to her mouth, too engrossed in the stories of new places to remember to drink.

Sterling had dragged the biscuit into range and now held it cupped in both hands, struggling to remove his gag without losing the biscuit or hitting himself in the cheek again, which was already sporting a mark, red against the grime. Crumbs rained down on his tunic before Hester finally clucked with annoyance and loosened his gag for him.

'You talk, you die,' she told him.

Tuesday thought that he would ignore her and begin to weave his honeyed words. He had a death wish, after all, and seemed to delight in vexing them. But he kept his peace and nibbled at the biscuit without comment.

Hester turned back to the map and pointed to a dot tucked in against the curve of the river. 'Bittertongue is our destination. There are three hundred miles of open country between us and the city, so we must make haste.'

'Make haste?' Quintalion said. 'The daybreakers will be at the Silk Sea in a few days, maybe less if they push the engines through the night. It'll take us ten days just to reach Bittertongue. I've got us covered once we hit civilisation, but how are we going to make it in time?'

Hester's dark eyes flashed and she rolled up the map with a flourish. 'Follow me and I'll show you.'

*

They walked through the afternoon and into the night, eating their meagre rations as they went, with Hester allowing them to stop only when one of them was about to fall to the ground. To her shame, it was usually Tuesday, and by the time the second morning dawned after a fitful night's sleep, she walked silently at the back of the group, too proud to ask for a break and too tired to do much else than keep moving forward, watching the ground so that she didn't fall in exhaustion.

The further east they walked, the wilder the landscape grew. The black rocks changed from the size of a fist to the size of a ship, and they walked in silence through frozen waves of dark glass, and the twisted shapes of trees consumed by flames.

'Dragonsbreath,' Hester told them when Jack asked how something could be so smooth. 'It burns and freezes at the same time. My people make weapons out of it. Nothing sings as prettily as a dragonsbreath blade.'

The gag silenced Sterling, but Tuesday caught his eyes flicking down to the sabre hanging around his neck.

Walking among the tangled shapes, Tuesday wouldn't want to have met the creatures capable of making such fire. They travelled past so many pale trees that the land must have been a forest before the dragons came; now it was nothing more than sand and charred wood.

Witnessing the destruction that the dragons had caused, Tuesday could only imagine what they looked like, and the picture that it left her with robbed her of her sleep for much of that night as she searched for eyes in the darkness.

'You should be asleep.'

Tuesday bolted upright. Her cloak slid off her shoulders and pooled in her lap. Quintalion stared at her, his body half-lit by the firelight that also reflected in his eyes.

'Oh,' she said, mostly to stall for time so that her heart would have a chance to slow to its proper rhythm. 'I thought you were a –'

'A daybreaker?' he said. 'No, there's none of them to be found out here. We are in lonely territory now. Only wild things allowed.' His mouth split open into a grin and he slowly ran his tongue over his sharp teeth.

A dragon. She caught the words before they escaped her, but then the sight of Quintalion, outlined against the fire and smiling like the wild things he spoke of, drew a question out of her. 'Are you really seven hundred years old?'

'Are you really less than two weeks old?' he countered.

'I suppose I must be.' Had it really only been a fortnight? It seemed like so much longer since she'd first set out from Madame Marisol's on that cold and drizzly evening. She'd learned so much that she felt like a different person from the wide-eyed girl who had stumbled out of that door and looked up at the sky in amazement, but she supposed it was to be expected. She had once been someone else, after all: someone with enough sorrow in her heart and hope for the future to write herself a letter to never look back.

She glanced over at Jack, who had made a pillow of his rucksack, which rustled every time his breath caught in a snore. 'Jack told me that people bring their loved ones to the Unreality House to forget them, that it was a rare thing for his parents to come back and wake him. Do you think that's what happened with me? Do you think I was meant to be forgotten?'

She'd expected Quintalion either to brush off her comment or immediately offer up a reassurance couched in an insult, but to her surprise, he did neither. The seconds lengthened as he stoked the fire, prodding it with a branch he'd broken off one of the petrified trees, and staring into the flames as they sparked and leapt into the air. 'I don't know,' he said finally, and it was so unlike him to admit he didn't know something that Tuesday sat up and scrambled closer so she could hear him better.

'Maybe you were. My father was never known for his attentiveness. You might have caught his interest one day and been forgotten the next.' He speared his branch into the heart of the fire and the flames popped and sizzled in response. 'And once upon a time, I would have thought that was the way it should be, but now . . .'

She twirled the edge of her cloak around her fingers and waited, breathless, for him to continue speaking. Here in the darkness he had a weariness she hadn't seen before: his shoulders slumped as though he was holding up the sky, and when he spoke, his voice was hoarse and his words stumbling and unrehearsed.

'Now?' she prompted.

He raised his head to the sky, which was brilliant with stars, and sighed. 'Now I know you.'

Sterling muttered in his sleep, and turned onto his side, the rope that tied the sabre around his neck tightening as he moved, and then he frowned, said a single name, and went back to sleep with the gag hanging half off his face.

The others slept too, in various states of fitfulness, so Tuesday lowered her voice, not wanting to disturb them. 'What does that mean?'

Quintalion threw a handful of sand into the fire and the shadows grew. 'It means that there might be a reason for you to be in this world beyond finding out who you were. The past doesn't matter, girl. You . . .' He hesitated, and then said, barely loud enough for her to hear, 'You shouldn't enter the City of Lost Things. There's nothing but death there, and I . . . I worry.'

His words filled her with a strange happiness that she couldn't place, but she decided to have mercy on him and ignore what he'd said. While he'd confessed his fear as though it tasted bitter in his mouth, she was enjoying their heart-to-heart so much that she didn't want to snap him back to his normal self by acknowledging it. So she played dumb.

'It's where the Book of Days is,' she protested. 'So that's where I have to go. It's the only way to find out who I was.'

Quintalion turned his face from her, and doubt began to pool in the pit of her stomach. 'It *is* the only way to find out who I was, right?'

'Why does it matter to you so much?' he asked her, and his tone held some of the Quintalion that she knew, who could switch from charm to disdain in the blink of an eye.

Though she knew he'd probably make fun of her for it, here in the dark she could hold no secrets. 'Because it's all I have,' she told him quietly. 'Without it, I'm nothing but a ghost of a girl who doesn't know she's dead.'

'You could build a new life. You have friends, people who care about you.' He gestured to the others sleeping round the fire and then slowly, as though it caused him great pain, rested his hand over the breast of his waistcoat.

Tuesday turned away so that he wouldn't see her smile. Warmth flooded through her. 'I know,' she said, 'But I have to do this. I just *have* to.'

She couldn't explain what drew her to the Book of Days and the promises it held, but she could feel it pulling her onward with every breath she took. It had driven her forward these past two days, when Hester had walked them for so long she wanted to collapse, and it beat like a drum in the back of her head, calling her towards the sea and the secrets that lay within the city.

She was only thankful that she wasn't going there alone. 'Oh!' she said, and then clamped her hand over her mouth.

Jack let out a snort, snuffled out something that sounded foreign, and then his breath evened out into the slow rhythm of sleep.

'Sorry,' she whispered, 'but I forgot about your reward.'

Quintalion's left eyebrow quirked. 'What?' he mouthed.

'Your reward . . . your payment. I know I said I'd give it to you after you've protected me from the daybreakers, but after all that I've put you through, I think you deserve it now.'

She riffled through the satchel until she found the purse of coins, tucked between a pair of drawers and a piece of squashed cake wrapped in brown paper, and held it out to him.

His eyes flicked to the fire, to her, and then to the fire again. 'You shouldn't give me that.'

'But I want to. If you haven't pushed me off a building or sold me to the highest bidder yet, I don't think you're about to start now.'

He flashed her a smile that was all teeth. 'Don't be so sure about that.'

Tuesday ignored him. They were friends. He'd just told her he cared about her, that he worried for her – not that he'd probably admit to it if asked in the morning – and he wouldn't betray her now.

So she threw the purse. It arced high, lost for a second in the night sky, and then Quintalion's hand snatched out and caught it.

He didn't say anything after that, and soon Tuesday tired of waiting and went back to sleep, and dreamed of eyes in the darkness, one blue and one brown, and woke more exhausted than she had been the day before.

*

Hester drove them on without mercy. On the afternoon of the third day, they left the towering glass formations behind, and as they headed further east, the ground underfoot turned from sand to parched earth, and the sky from blue to grey.

'It's the smoke from the factories,' Quintalion told her, pulling at the collar of his shirt, which was damp with sweat. 'The skies above Tantallon are always grey.'

He didn't say anything after that. Walking beside him, Tuesday tried not to notice the grim lines painted around his eyes or the way his mouth turned down into a grimace when he caught his foot in one of the fissures in the earth.

Only Jack remained cheerful. Tuesday had taken to linking her arm with his, since the frequent holes and cracks made it difficult for him to keep up with the rest of them, and as she guided him along the safest route, he would tell her about his childhood, living in one of the border towns along the river Widowmere, or he would recite fragments of poems and stories that he had been told, or espouse the virtues of properly brewed tea, and once, in one of their few breaks, he even attempted to make a cup, though the water wasn't boiled and they drank it straight from a water skin, with the dregs clogging up the neck and the bitterness seeping through. Tuesday didn't want to hurt his feelings, so she pretended to enjoy the lukewarm drink, and it was worth picking out bits of tea leaves from her teeth to see him smile and recommend other flavours to her, even if his smile *did* wobble at the edges and his enthusiastic tirade petered out into silence before long.

On the morning of the fourth day, they came across a Saqiran trade caravan, the long line of camels weighed down with crates and bales of hay and small tents with silk hangings that fluttered in the breeze. Hester grew very excited, and talked to the leader of the caravan for a long time in Saqiran, while Sterling stood sullenly by wearing Quintalion's greatcoat and hat that Hester had dressed him in to avoid his being recognised. Quintalion, with his shirtsleeves rolled up, eyed off the guards, while Jack took Tuesday to meet her first camel. It spat a hunk of partially digested hay at her, but when one of the caravan attendants showed her how to pat its long neck, it lowered its head and let her scratch its shaggy fur.

The sun tracked across the sky and still Hester's negotiations continued. She'd laid three knives and one of her swords on the ground in front of her, and the leader of the caravan, a swarthy man swallowed up in sweat-stained linen, made a great show of examining them, and Tuesday didn't need to understand Saqiran to know that he was pointing out the flaws in the workmanship.

While the negotiations continued on, the younger men of the caravan brought them luncheon: dates and plums, three different kinds of bread with jams to spread over them that tasted like fruit and honey combined, cream fresh from an obliging goat, and spiced wine to wash it all down. The traders had just returned from Belborough, one of the women explained, where they had received a good deal on the jewels and weapons they traded, and so they laid out their best platter for their guests according to the will of Sahir, one of their two main gods, as Jack excitedly whispered to her.

Tuesday silently thanked the god. After a couple of days eating nothing but tack, this new Saqiran food was a welcome relief, and even just getting the chance to sit down for more than half a bell at a time felt like luxury. They ate dishes off napery embroidered lavishly with tigers and camels and other creatures with too many legs or fangs that Tuesday couldn't name; when she described them to Jack, he gleefully told her all about them. Djinns, and chimeras, and sphinxes: apparently in Saqira magic had not dimmed as it had in the rest of the world, and these mythical beasts still roamed free in the deserts.

'I've even heard stories of a great northern land where up is down,' he said, and then licked the last trace of goat's cream off his fingers with relish. 'I'd like to find it one day.'

'Why don't you?' She took another sip of the spiced wine. It burned the back of her throat as it went down.

'What dear Jacobi is neglecting to tell you is that the Seething Sea lies between him and his precious northern land.' Quintalion tore off a hunk of flatbread, dipped it into one of the fruit preserves that had been laid out before them, rolled it and bit off a mouthful.

'So?' She'd only seen the sea in her dream, but she was pretty sure that was what boats were for.

'It's *seething*,' Quintalion told her. 'Roiling, boiling, smouldering and churning. The only boats that could cross are iron.

But look – here comes Hester. Any luck in your enquiries, Captain?'

Hester walked with her head held high and her shoulders thrown back, dignity personified despite the scorched earth giving her some trouble with her wooden leg, which kept getting caught in the holes.

'Indeed I did,' she said, and yanked Sterling's bonds so hard that he tripped and almost fell. 'Come and see.'

She led them to the end of the caravan, where three chariots sat, their wheels high and stained with dirt and their yokes empty. They were cracked in several places, and the sun had faded their paint to a dull blue and rust.

'You traded your knives for *those*?' Quintalion asked, his voice dripping with disdain.

Hester slapped one of the chariots and paint chips flaked into the air. 'They may not be pretty, but neither am I, and I have not failed you so far, have I?'

'I don't know,' Quintalion said, 'you're not a total loss. A bath and a dark room . . .'

Her fingers twitched, but the gun remained, thankfully, on her back in its holster. 'And these are not all I bargained for.'

A strange kind of yipping was coming from a set of covered boxes behind one of the camels. Smoke eked out from under the cloth.

'You didn't . . .' Quintalion said.

'What is it?' Jack whispered, craning his head to the side.

'These are the descendants of the great wyrms in the old tales,' Hester said. 'What you, Jacobi Heller, might call dragons.'

She whipped the cover off like she was doing a magic trick, to reveal six scaly, growling beasts. They were as sleek as cats, but four times as large as the biggest Tuesday had ever seen – a tomcat scrounging around the alleyways of Beggars End – and covered entirely in scales: two as red as flame and the other four varying shades of blues and greens. They yowled like angry alley cats as well, and threw themselves up against the side of their cages, opening their mouths to emit high-pitched whines, and shook their heads furiously, making the metal clasps of their collars rattle against the bars. Their horns and fangs had been filed back, but they looked as though they could pack a nasty head-butt.

'*Those* are dragons?' Tuesday wrinkled her nose. The dragons she'd heard of in tales were as tall as Fortune City's towers: wrathful beasts that breathed fire and snatched away maidens to take back to their piles of gold. These little things couldn't *carry* a maiden, let alone take her back to their lair. 'Can they even fly?'

'Of course not. None but the great wyrms could. And though they may be small, they are fast. This is what we need, yes?' Hester unlatched the cage and six screaming bundles of bad attitude streaked out into the sunshine. Her hand darted this way and that, and before the dragons knew what was happening, they'd been leashed and muzzled. One of them let out a confused whine.

'The chariots can fit two people,' Hester said, tying the cantankerous beasts to the yoke. 'I will take the daybreaker. Quintalion, you drive Jacobi Heller, and Tuesday, you will have to ride alone. Do you think you can manage?'

Tuesday stared at the chariot. There was a small place to stand; the front was raised high and curved to throw off any rocks that might be flung into their path; the wheels were spoked and almost as high as the front, and a long set of reins dangled over the top edge of the chariot, leading to the two dragons that had been hitched to the yoke. *It can't be that hard, right? Just flick the reins and then tug left and right for directions.*

Besides, it didn't matter whether she thought she could do it or not. She would have to. She didn't think she could take another day of walking at the pace Hester set, and any slower guaranteed they'd never reach the City of Lost Things before Sterling's daybreakers sacrificed Jack's father.

'I'll do it,' she said.

Hester showed them all how to tug on the reins if they needed to stop, and the best way to stand to keep their balance. She helped Jack up into the chariot behind Quintalion and directed him to wrap his arms around Quintalion's chest, which drew complaints from both of them. Then she mounted her own chariot and they were off.

At first Tuesday's dragons refused to budge, and when they stared back at her with smoke coiling out of their mouths, it wasn't hard to imagine them grinning at her inexperience. But then she pictured Jack's father locked up on one of the daybreaker airships, being taken to his death, and she twitched the reins with enough force that the surprised dragons surged forward, tripping over their own feet in their haste.

The chariot skimmed over the hard ground, as light as a feather. The trade caravan soon faded into the distance, leaving nothing but open land before them, wide and flat and ready to be discovered. Tuesday's hair streamed back, the speed made her stomach do flip-flops, and the wind flung her skirts high around her legs. *If only Madame Marisol could see me now.* A laugh bubbled out of her throat and she turned her head to see Quintalion joining her in her mirth, his shoulders shaking with silent laughter and his eyes lit up in excitement. He looked at once old and young: the scion of an ancient and wild house.

Behind him, Jack had stopped holding on around Quintalion's chest and now grabbed only two handfuls of the back of his shirt to steady himself, his staff tucked between their bodies. The wrapping around his eyes was coming loose and his papers fluttered in the slipstream, but he didn't seem to care.

Once the dragons had warmed up, they responded to every twitch of Tuesday's reins. She urged them forward and soon she caught up to Hester, who piloted her craft with a grim determination. Sterling rode behind her; his hands, which had previously been tied together, were now also secured by a long rope to the railing that ran the length of the chariot's front. He kept the rope loose and stood with his feet planted firmly apart as if he had no care for his safety.

She laughed in his face, the joy of the moment overwhelming her. He couldn't hurt her now. They would rescue Jack's father and find the Book of Days, and she would finally know who she was. Everything would be perfect.

Drunk on her soon-to-be victory, Tuesday flicked the reins once again and the pair of beasts surged onwards, their flanks glistening with sweat that arced off their folded-up wings in sheets. Soon she'd overtaken Hester's chariot, but she drove her dragons faster still, not caring whether she was going in the right direction, but laughing and hollering out the mad whirl of joy that consumed her.

It's going to be all right, she thought. *It's all going to be marvellous.*

Hester let her lead for a good half-hour, but when the pale grey clouds had enveloped most of the sky, she overtook Tuesday, and set the pace at a slower run, stopping once or twice to water the exhausted dragons.

'I thought you had turned mad,' she told Tuesday the first time they stopped, as she showed her how to pour the water into the dragon's mouths while keeping her fingers far away from their sharp teeth.

'Oh, she's always been mad,' Quintalion said helpfully, but Jack asked her to describe the landscape before she could come up with a suitable retort.

As they headed east, the land grew more forgiving. Grass sprouted up amid the cracks in the ground, though it was short, bristly and sharp enough that even the dragons turned their noses up at it. The last of the dragonsbreath disappeared, and Tuesday stopped worrying that she'd hit one of the rocks and it would get stuck in the spokes of her wheels and cause her to crash. They occasionally rode close to towns that were mostly abandoned – the houses charred and long since deserted – and those that were occupied were ringed with walls so high that, even standing on her tiptoes in the chariot, Tuesday could only see the very tops of the chimneys.

'They say a war never really ends,' Quintalion reminded her from the next chariot.

After another couple of miles, roads started to appear, though they were little more than dirt tracks, lousy with potholes and furloughs from carts, but they spoke of things to come, and Tuesday found herself snatching glances out to the side of her chariot, certain that a daybreaker ship would be looming behind the next cloud.

They travelled into the night without any sign of trouble, but as they went further east, more and more people began to join them on the road, their faces obscured by hoods and their lanterns held high. They travelled in carts, on horseback or by foot, and regarded the chariots with suspicion. It wasn't long before Hester called for silence, and they rode the rest of the way with only the whir of the wheels and the snort of the dragons for company.

Sometime after midnight, they limped into Bittertongue. It was a town of mining folk, with the houses and scarce shops resting in a valley below the mines themselves, which lit up the hills even at that time of night. A constant stream of horses and carts made its way down from the mines, through the main streets, and disappeared beyond the crooked eaves of a large marketplace just visible at the edge of the city.

'That is our destination,' Hester said. 'I have got us to your civilisation, Quintalion. It is your turn from here.'

Tuesday sagged against the front of the chariot. Every few seconds her eyes kept trying to close, and she had to force herself to stay awake by pinching her arms until they bruised. The others didn't look much better; only Sterling stood straight and tall behind Hester, making Tuesday suspect that he'd discovered how to sleep standing up.

'Right.' Quintalion clapped his hands together. 'You may know the desert, but the city is mine. I'll take it from here.'

They sold the dragons and the chariots for a pittance to a caravan heading the way they'd come and continued into the city on foot, Jack and Tuesday propping each other up as they competed to see who could yawn the largest. The mine folk didn't spare them a second glance; they led their nags on through the streets with their heads down and their eyes on the cobblestones in front of them.

The air was too close here in the city, filled with smoke and bitterness foul enough that Tuesday was forced to spit onto the side of the street just to rid her mouth of the taste. The city rang with the sound of the mines: men shouting, the thud of horses' hooves on metal, and a dull roar that reminded her of the engines at the heart of Fortune City.

As they travelled closer towards the marketplace, she realised that the sound wasn't coming from the mines at all, but rather a piece of machinery large and loud and half-hidden behind the curve of the market building's open doors. It let out a roar like the call of a dozen dragons, and smoke shot up out of the chimney at the front of the metal beast.

'By the gods, Quintalion,' Hester tutted in disapproval, 'surely you are not planning on making us get on that thing. It's barbaric!'

'What is it?' Tuesday whispered to Jack.

Quintalion drew himself into a mock bow. 'But of course. It runs right through the middle of Tantallon and goes all the way to the port cities. From there we should be able to make our own way up the coast to the doors before the daybreakers even know we're there. Provided, of course, that Mr Heller is happy to show us the way. Am I brilliant or am I brilliant?'

'It sounds like a train,' Jack whispered back to her, his voice tinged with awe. 'I heard one a couple of years ago, when Father took me with him to Tantallon to collect some books, but I've never actually seen one up close. What's it like?'

So Tuesday described it to him: the brass trimmings on the compartments, shining like gold in the streetlights; the plumes of smoke; the people milling around in their sombre coats and plain gowns, so different to the style and exuberance of the west; its great height, almost tall enough to block out the stars; and its length, as long as fifty carriages combined; and finally, the long tracks that stretched out further than the eye could see. Men with soot streaks on their faces unloaded their cargo from the horses and carts and hefted the sacks onto an open-topped compartment of the train, like a big bucket, and nodded to the guard standing watch over it.

The whole town was so different from any Tuesday had seen before, and she knew she should hate it. This was Sterling's territory, after all, and that of his daybreakers. But she couldn't stop the feeling of excitement deep inside her. It pulsed brighter and hotter at every new detail, from the women getting out of what looked like a clockwork carriage, to the men playing cards while they waited for the train, their bowler hats all stacked in a pile.

A shrill whistle sounded. The men and women around the train stopped their conversations and poured into the open doors of the compartments. The card players scattered in a flurry of cards, grabbing their bowler hats and dispersing to different ends of the train.

She wasn't surprised when Quintalion produced five tickets without money ever exchanging hands, nor when he directed them to the fanciest of the compartments, with plush leather seats, its own attendants dressed in their braided and buttoned uniforms, and enough brass filigree to sink a ship.

He winked at her. 'I ride in style.'

The horn sounded again, drowning out the clatter of the mines, and then they were off, slowly at first, and then building up steam. Leaning her head out of the window, Tuesday watched the lights of Bittertongue disappear through the open window, and then they were on their way towards the Silk Sea and the City of Lost Things.

CHAPTER TWENTY-TWO

Quintalion set them up in their own little suite, with sliding doors that hid them from the rest of the passengers, a table that winched down from the ceiling, and a series of tubes attached to a speaking apparatus that they could apparently use to contact the attendants if they needed anything.

The opulence was wonderful after their time in the wilderness, but Tuesday particularly appreciated the large copper bath with its plentiful supply of hot water and its own room so that she could wash in privacy. She luxuriated in it for at least two bells, scrubbing herself all over with the cake of soap that smelled of lilies, and trying out each scented perfume and lotion. Only when she was blisteringly clean and dressed in a yellow frock that she'd found in her satchel did she emerge to let the others have their turn.

She spent the rest of the morning curled up on one of the seats, rather daringly using her bustle pad as a pillow as she was lulled into a drowse by the sun streaming through the open window. The others joined her eventually, in various degrees of cleanliness, from Jack's apparent hands-and-face-only bath to Quintalion's resplendent appearance in a new peacock-green waistcoat and a shirt run through with gold threads, smelling of oranges and spices.

It wasn't long before he and Hester were reminiscing about the old days, while an odd rustle of pages came from Jack's direction, where he'd spread out one of his maps and periodically explored the surface with his fingers. But apart from the hiss of steam and the chug of wheels as their train glided south, the world was hazy and quiet. Tuesday occasionally let her eyes open, surveying the miles of neatly tilled earth, but mostly she watched the play of light behind her eyelids and dozed, content with the knowledge that they were speeding towards their destination.

When the train stopped momentarily for more coal at a town so small it fit neatly along the single main road, Tuesday shook herself out of her nap and, hearing shouting coming from outside the train, eased past Jack and stuck her head out of the window to see what was going on. Three or four youths wandered up and down the length of the platform wearing ill-fitting tweed suits and carrying trays around their necks.

'Pheasant pie!' one of them called out. 'Sandwiches, lemonade, mulled wine.'

The second lad, a tall and gangly youth with teeth as black as the coal being loaded on board, soon took up the cry. 'Cushions, reading glasses, books. Don't spend your trip bored and uncomfortable! I've got the latest edition of Worth's *Lacrimosa: A Lamentable Tale of Tragedy and Betrayal* right here. Just a single ration ticket, and cheap at half the price.'

At Tuesday's insistence, Quintalion reluctantly gave her one of the notes he'd changed over in Fortune City, and she bought the first boy out of his stock, plus something extra another lad had been selling that caught her eye. As they watched the town give way to more farmland, they feasted on cold chicken and sandwiches and pies so hot that the steam poured out in waves when Hester cracked open the pastry.

Once they had drunk the last of the lemonade, even giving Sterling a taste, Tuesday shyly passed Jack the wrapped package she'd bought, under the table so that no one else could see.

'I thought you might like them,' she whispered to him, and then pretended to be very interested in reading the lemonade label so that she wouldn't have to look at him when he opened it.

He let out a small gasp as the last of the paper came away and explored the item with his fingers, cocking his head to one side as he held up the glasses.

'They're tinted,' she told him. 'I thought you might like a break from the bandages.'

'Aren't you sweet,' Quintalion said, missing nothing despite having his hat pulled down over his eyes.

Jack rolled the brown paper between his fingers for so long that Tuesday was worried he didn't like the gift. Had she offended him? She hadn't meant to; when she'd seen the pair of metal spectacles, her only thought had been how perfect they would be for him – he must be tired of the feeling of cloth wrapped around his face – but perhaps she'd made a mistake. She knew so little of how things were done, and what if giving a blind man glasses was like giving a man with no legs a pair of shoes?

She tucked her hair behind her ear and said, 'You don't have to wear them . . . I mean, if you don't like them.'

He ran a finger around one rim and coughed, and when he next spoke, his voice was husky. 'They're . . . I . . . *Thank you.*'

Warmth flooding her, she helped him undo the bandages and unwind them from around his face. He breathed a sigh of relief when the final layer fell away and he angled his face up towards the sun, his brown eyes blinking against the light. He slipped the glasses onto his face and grinned.

'Appropriate,' Quintalion said, as Tuesday returned Jack's smile, and even Hester nodded in approval.

*

The mood soured not long afterwards. The sunlight disappeared under a thick cloud of smoke that hung low in the sky, and with it went Tuesday's good humour. They'd travelled deep into farming country. At first she had sat up at the window, eager to study the ploughs and horses and different types of grain that Hester pointed out to her. But as they went further south, the jovial farmers who had waved at them as they went past grew fewer and fewer in number, until the only ones left stared at the train with pinched faces and distrust in their eyes.

Quintalion had bought a paper from one of the attendants, and read the main stories out loud, hardly able to keep the laughter from his voice: *Unsurpassed Prosperity!*, the headlines read, and *Machines Lead Us into a Golden Age*. When he read the article proclaiming *Voltemande and Tantallon Stand United Against the Superstitions of the Old Ways*, he choked and had to be rescued by Hester reaching over Sterling and slapping him on the back.

'Propaganda,' he said. 'The lot of it. Do they look prosperous to you?'

He jerked a thumb out the window, where they were passing through a small city, with smokestacks reaching towards the sky and carriages clattering along cobblestone roads.

The houses next to the train tracks were little more than hovels: crumbling brick shanties with boarded-up windows and doors hanging off their hinges. Soot-streaked washing hung between the walls that segregated the weed-strewn alleyways that were their gardens, and men and women drifted in and out of the open doors like ghosts.

With faces hollowed out by hunger, they clutched their squalling babies to their breasts. They didn't beg or plead, just stared in stony silence at the train as it went by, their black clothes making them look like a flock of crows just landed on a fresh corpse. Behind them, plastered on every exposed brick factory and house, were slogans, stencilled in white paint: *Hail the Council of Equals*, and *Industry Saves*.

After that, Tuesday turned her face away and drew the blinds whenever they approached a town, but even closing the window couldn't stop the stench that seeped into their carriage: the heady smell of livestock as they were driven into town to be slaughtered, the fire from the train's engine mixing with the soot and the smoke from the machinery, and unwashed clothes. The bells rang constantly. The shrill sound mixed together with the factory whistles and the screams of children, loud enough to cause Tuesday to clamp her hands over her ears.

The things she had seen in the west may have been vicious – the de Kena and the stories of their savagery in battle, the corruption of Fortune City, the ferocity of the Shining Ones descending on survivors – but they were nothing compared to the systematic misery of the townspeople in this supposedly civilised country. No wonder Sterling was so remorseless; she doubted anyone could survive growing up surrounded by this unhappiness without developing a streak of iron in their soul.

The next day, the train was stopped at its first checkpoint. A sour-faced young guard in bottle-green burst into their compartment demanding to see their tickets and identification papers, and Tuesday, who was still caught in the throes of sleep, almost fell out of her foldaway bunk bed. Quintalion, however, was ready with a smile and a pleasant conversation about *the unseasonable weather we've been having lately*, and the guard did little more than check their papers, stamp them, give a cursory once-over around the room while begrudgingly apologising for disturbing them, and leave as abruptly as he had appeared.

'Damnable greencoats,' Quintalion muttered when the guard had left and the train began to speed on its way again. 'Give a man an inch of power and he's swanning all over the place like he's a bleeding general.'

He helped Tuesday descend the metal ladder, tucked the bed back into the wall, and handed her back the identification papers, which he must have taken from her satchel while she was still waking up. She shivered in her shift and smoothed her thumb over the stamp. It left a streak of maroon and gold across her skin.

'What *was* that?' she asked. She was still too shocked to quite take in the fact that she was dressed only in her shift in front of three men: one of whom wanted to kill her; one she thought of as her protector; and one that she blushed to think of seeing her in this state of disarray, even though she needn't have worried.

'Mandatory checkpoint.' Quintalion's own undoubtedly forged papers disappeared into the inner pocket of his waistcoat. 'Ever since Voltemande's daybreakers *liberated* it from the old ways, Tantallon's been a country under lock and key. We're lucky we got on at Bittertongue – the soldiers tend to leave it to itself because it's so close to the Saqiran border. If we'd tried to board any further south, I doubt our bones would still be unbroken.'

'But that's horrible.' The gaunt faces she'd seen from the window flashed through her head. 'Didn't the people fight back?'

Quintalion threw Tuesday his coat, and she slid it on, the sleeves reaching down past her fingertips, and then rummaged around in her satchel for the new clothes he had bought her from a peddler the night before, claiming that he wouldn't have her looking 'provincial' in the big smoke.

'Of course,' he said. 'But after the first few massacres – oh, forgive me . . . *strategic culling of the undesirables*,' he mimicked, 'all of the dissenters headed east to the safety of the bipartisan tri-cities. Well, all but the most idealistic or foolish.'

'Same thing,' Hester interrupted, leaning forward with her elbows resting on the table. She'd slept sitting up, and looked just as pristine as always. Tuesday was half-convinced that she woke up in the middle of the night to brush her hair and do her laundry, but that was ridiculous. She'd tried to stay awake, just in case.

Jack swung his legs down off the seat and swivelled his body so that he sat upright. He'd taken off his brown vest to sleep, and half of the buttons on his shirt had come undone.

'And now an entire country lives as virtual prisoners. It's very depressing. I'm glad we're not staying for long,' Quintalion said flippantly. 'Who's up for breakfast?'

Sterling shook his head, mumbling against the gag in his mouth that kept him silent.

'Oh,' Quintalion jerked his head in Sterling's direction, 'he wants to speak now, does he? I hope I didn't hurt his feelings.'

'Be silent,' Hester hissed at Sterling.

The fear rose in Tuesday's throat, hot and thick, making it hard to breathe. 'Don't let him. Please, Quintalion, don't let him talk.' She shoved her arm into the sleeve of her blouse, wishing that she could articulate her fears.

She knew she was being irrational, that there could be no harm in words, but she was terrified that she would listen to him and suddenly everything he was saying would make sense. It had happened before: a tug on the edge of her consciousness, urging her to listen to the man, that he could be trusted and meant her no harm, and it had felt so good to give in to the feeling that now she had to put all her attention towards doing up the buttons on her high-waisted navy skirt just to stop her hands from shaking.

'Please, Quintalion,' she said.

Quintalion's eyebrows furrowed into a frown as he glanced at her, but then he shrugged and leaned forward to yank the gag out of Sterling's mouth. 'I want to hear what the daybreaker has to say. We could use a little amusement.'

Sterling coughed and ran his tongue around his cracked lips. 'You're wrong,' he rasped, his voice rough from disuse.

'About breakfast?' Quintalion asked him. 'You're right – I think it's closer to brunch.'

'We only desire peace.' Sterling flexed his hands against the rope tying them together.

'You've got a funny way of showing it.' Quintalion took out a pack of cards and shuffled them with ease, keeping his attention on the spinning pieces of pasteboard and his voice light. 'I doubt the dead of Fortune City consider what you did an act of peace.'

'We gave the Lady a choice. It is not our fault she was . . . unreasonable.'

Doing up the final button with one hand, Tuesday passed Quintalion back his coat and collapsed on the seat next to Jack.

'You bombed her city,' Quintalion said incredulously.

'Only because she didn't give up the girl. Had she surrendered her, we would have left that floating abomination in peace.'

'What do you want from me?' Tuesday burst out.

He fixed her with his green eyes. The intensity of his stare raised the hair on her arms. 'We want her back,' he said simply. 'You are merely the road that leads us to her.'

'Thaïs?' There it was again: that thrill of familiarity running down her spine. *No*, she told herself. *I can't have killed her. I won't believe it.*

'There is no one else. *Solus mayetvos.*'

There were those words again, the ones she'd first seen engraved on his sabre, and they piqued her curiosity enough for her to consider asking him what they meant, but she couldn't risk antagonising him into silence once more, not when they could use this opportunity to learn more about his plans.

'I thought you said you were after the Book of Days,' she said instead, keeping her tone neutral so that she didn't provoke him. 'I *heard* you. You sent your daybreakers ahead to find it. But why?'

Sterling slammed his fists down on the table, the movement so quick and unexpected that she flinched back from him, and even Hester paused for a moment, dumbstruck, before her hand went to the curved blade at her hip.

'You know nothing!'

Quintalion calmly dropped the cards to the table and covered Sterling's unharmed hand with his own, and when his fingernails dug into the flesh, it drew a wince from Sterling's throat. 'You're scaring the lady,' he said.

Blood welled up from beneath his nails as the two of them stared at each other, neither willing to be the first to break eye contact, even when Quintalion pressed deep enough for the blood to trail down Sterling's fingers and pool on the wooden table.

'You think you have us where you want us.' Sterling spoke through gritted teeth. 'You are wrong.'

'Maybe,' Quintalion drawled, 'but I'm not the one about to get two inches of cold steel in my belly.' He nodded at Hester, who held one of her knives pressed just beneath Sterling's rib cage.

'What's that saying again? There are two kinds of people in life you should never cross: Saqirans and women.' Quintalion patted the back of his hand. 'Looks like it's not your lucky day.'

'Actually,' Jack interrupted, 'the original phrase is *Never trust those that both give life and take it away*, but the translation's been somewhat lost over the centuries. There's a fascinating paper on its supposed origins; I think I might have it with me.'

He dove into his rucksack in a flurry of papers.

Sterling raised an eyebrow. 'Touched?' he said, gesturing to his head.

Quintalion snorted. 'Librarian.'

'Assistant librarian,' Hester and Tuesday said at the same time.

'No doubt the boy's heard about the power of the Book of Days from his father,' Sterling said, appraising him.

Jack stopped his riffling and stared in Sterling's direction, his mouth pulled down into a scowl. 'Don't even *think* that I'm going to tell you anything about it. You've got my father.'

'And if we promised that no harm would come to him?'

Jack bit his lip and then frowned again, but his words were certain. 'You kidnapped my father, you destroyed my home, my library. You've already told me you're planning on killing him to open the door. Why in the name of the Days would you think I'd trust you now?'

'I like him,' Quintalion mouthed to Tuesday.

'Because we have never lied.' Sterling wrenched his hand away from Quintalion's and cradled it against his breast; the blood trickled onto his uniform, staining it in patches of dark maroon.

She saw Col, kneeling in the dirt while he pleaded for his life, and then the look of surprise in his eyes as Sterling's bullet stole his breath. 'No, that's not right.' She couldn't bear looking into those eyes again and so she stared down at her lap instead. 'In Beggars End, the first time we met. You promised Col money, and then . . . and then you killed him.'

'Yes, we promised him money, and money we gave him. It was not our fault he didn't ask for his life as well. We said we were honest, girl, not merciful.'

She took a deep breath that whistled in the back of her throat. 'Honest,' she repeated. 'Then tell me truthfully: what do you plan to do to me? What do you want from me?'

The smile stole over his face, and his eyes glittered in the sunlight streaming in through the window; once more, Tuesday was back in the dream, with his hand on hers and his voice singing in her ears, only this time his smile didn't melt away the lines of his face, it hardened them.

'We will drag you into the city of the dead itself and slit your throat over the Book of Days. Only by your death can our love live again.'

*

He subsided into silence after that, leaving Tuesday alone with her thoughts as the bells on the train chimed the hours and the weather grew colder as the day drew on. She'd seen Sterling's face: he meant every word. He would kill her if he got the chance. She didn't know how her death was supposed to bring Thaïs back, but there was a lot she didn't know, and whether or not there was a purpose, she would still be just as dead. *What did I do to deserve such hatred?* she wondered. *Did I really kill Thaïs before I sought refuge in Madame Marisol's House?*

Staring at the ground, her identification papers caught her eye. They must have fallen when she got her clothes out of her bag. She scooped them up. *Dagny*, the name read. It was as much of a truth as *Tuesday*, so why did it feel so wrong?

She pulled the letter out of her satchel and unfolded it, staring at the flowing writing. How different it was from the officially printed identification papers, with their stamps and their seals. She gently fingered the looped writing, and sighed.

The identification papers might be a lie, but who was to say that the letter wasn't as well: perhaps not the words themselves, like the forged papers, but the gaps between the lines. She'd created a whole narrative out of what the letter didn't say, an imagined possibility wilder than any story Madame Marisol had ever read, and it was beginning to pull her under. So many different paths leading to the girl she had become: murderess, victim, lover, or liar. And the key to her past was the Book of Days, just out of her reach.

A loud knock startled her from her thoughts. She slid both pieces of paper into her satchel, dug the heels of her hands into the leather seat and pushed herself upright, shaking her head to brush away the sudden picture flashing through her head: eyes, green eyes, in the darkness. Sterling stared at her.

Quintalion stepped away from the porthole in the sliding door; his face was panicked. 'We may,' he said, 'be in trouble.'

'Open up in there!' The knock came again, louder this time. There was a flash of navy and then a hard face pressed itself up against the glass. It was a daybreaker.

'Hide him,' Quintalion whispered out of the side of his mouth, smiling and nodding at the daybreaker peering into their cabin.

Hester, who sat next to Sterling, hissed, 'Is it not a little late for that?'

She sliced through the gag's material with one of her knives, stuffed the grimy fabric down the back of the chair, and tore Sterling's sabre from around his neck, sliding it behind his back so that only the hint of a hilt was visible. It would work as long as the daybreaker didn't look too closely.

The daybreaker thumped on the door again and then the doorknob rattled as it jiggled from left to right. Quintalion grabbed the knob without a word.

'Open up in the name of Voltemande!'

Tuesday suddenly sat up straight, an idea formulating in her head. 'Why are we hiding him?'

Quintalion's face grimaced in a pantomime of helplessness as he pretended to fumble with the lock holding the door closed and shrugged at the daybreaker. 'Because we don't want to be lined up against a wall and shot, that's why.'

'What is in your head, little one?' Hester asked her.

'Why *are* we hiding him?' Tuesday repeated, brimming with a mixture of excitement and fear. 'I didn't save his life back on Fortune City so that we could drag him around like some kind of animal. There are a thousand daybreakers between us and the Silk Sea, that's what the Lady Fortuna said. But if we have their leader . . .'

'A hostage,' Jack breathed.

'No.' Tuesday grinned at him. 'A friend.'

*

'So you see,' Sterling said. 'This is all a big misunderstanding. These people are travelling with me as my guests. I trust we will not be bothered again?'

The daybreaker took in all of them – Jack sitting innocently by the window, Hester and Quintalion at Sterling's shoulders, and finally Tuesday, smiling widely as she leaned against the table – and nodded. 'Of course you won't be, sir. It's just . . .' he hesitated.

'What is it, man? Spit it out.'

The daybreaker took a deep breath. 'We've had reports that you were dead, fallen in Fortune City.'

Sterling stood up straighter, but only Tuesday could see that it wasn't from impatience but rather to escape the knife that Hester pressed against his back. 'Do I look dead to you?' His words dripped with sarcasm.

Shrugging, the daybreaker said, 'You can't be too careful . . . *sir*.'

Sterling tensed at his inferior's tone, but then his shoulders relaxed. 'Quite right.'

'There was even some suggestion that you'd lost your mind in your grief,' the daybreaker continued, looking him up and down with a deliberately calculating look. 'But that can't be right. After all, you couldn't very well lead the daybreakers if that was the case now, could you?'

'Of . . . of course not.' Sterling swallowed and tugged his tunic down over his torso, straightening the creases, and in doing so exposed his bleeding hand.

'Sir?' the daybreaker said.

Hester's knife dug further into Sterling's back.

'A scratch,' he said quickly. 'I must have scraped it when I was boarding. I assure you I'm completely fine.'

The daybreaker's hand strayed to the blunderbuss at his hip, and he gave the room another once-over, scratching at his stubble as he surveyed the four of them. They must have looked a sight – four identical grins wide enough that you'd have thought they were meeting the Days themselves – but the man just nodded to Sterling and turned to leave.

With a last bow to his commander, the daybreaker left the five of them alone. Quintalion closed the door, locked it and collapsed against it.

'Well done,' he said to Sterling, and patted his cheek, laughing when Sterling wrenched his head away. 'You get to keep your tongue.'

So that the daybreaker wouldn't be suspicious, Hester had attached Sterling's sabre to his belt before they opened the door. Sterling's hand wandered over to it. He gripped the hilt, but Hester had her blade at his throat before he could draw the sword.

'Do not entertain such notions,' she told him. 'They do not end well for you.'

He removed his hand from the hilt. 'Dear lady, we had no such inclination.'

She led him back over to the long seat and shoved him down onto it, the leather squeaking as it took his weight, and then she fetched up the rope that she had hidden beneath the table, brought his wrists together and began to wind the cord around his skin.

He sat there in silence with a placid smile on his face as Hester drew the rope tight across his flesh, which was red and raw from previous bindings, and even when she roughly withdrew his sabre from his belt and looped it around his neck again, his smile remained in place. Tuesday couldn't help but think that something was wrong. It was the ultimate mockery: leaving his sabre within reach while he was helpless to use it, a reminder of whose mercy he was relying on. He had been held hostage, dragged across the desert and forced to help someone who might possibly have killed his lover; if she were in his situation, she would not be sitting there looking as content as a cat who had just caught a mouse.

Sterling waited until Hester was done with the ropes before slowly reaching up with his bound hands and smoothing an errant strand of brown hair out of his eyes.

'Something's not right,' Jack said suddenly. He sat bolt upright and placed his hands flat on the table, which shuddered beneath them from the movement of the train.

'We don't know what the blind boy means,' Sterling said, his eyes wide. 'We did as you asked, did we not?'

There was something obvious she was missing. It hovered just out of her reach, darting away every time she almost had it. *Think*, she told herself. *Think!*

Quintalion flopped onto the end of the seat, launching Hester a good two inches into the air. She hit the leather with an unimpressed snort, which he ignored, resting one leg on top of his knee and sliding his hat back over his eyes. 'It's fine. The daybreakers are probably toasting their commander's health right about now. Give it a half-bell and they'll be belting out "My Good Time Girl" and reminiscing about the war.'

Sterling should *not* have looked so pleased. He'd been acting strangely since he opened the door to the daybreaker, but if anyone had asked her in what way, she wouldn't have been able to tell them. It wasn't his words, delivered as they were in his customary clipped tone, but something that lingered beneath them, hidden behind a door to which she didn't have the key.

Jack gripped his staff with both hands and turned his head towards the window, where the breeze pushed his dark curls back from his sightless eyes. His brow furrowed. 'We need to leave. Now.'

'Not a chance, Mr Heller,' Quintalion told him. 'There's a good two days travelling yet, and I may want to lighten the pockets of a few drunk daybreakers.'

Jack shook his head. 'I don't think you can.'

'Oh,' Quintalion said, hooking his thumbs over the clasps of his waistcoat. 'You doubt my skills? I'd be glad to oblige you with a demonstration if you have a couple of coins you're happy to part with.'

When Jack turned his head back from the window, his face was pale. 'My *doubt*,' he said, 'is less due to your skills, and more to the squadron of daybreakers coming straight for us.'

CHAPTER TWENTY-THREE

Boots clattered outside in the corridor. Quintalion was out of his seat and pulling down the shade on the door to their compartment before he hissed, 'Daybreakers. How in the seven sisters' names did you know?'

'I'm blind, not deaf,' Jack remarked.

'How did they find us?' Quintalion pressed his entire body weight against the door. '*He* sent them away, I heard him. Unless . . .'

Sterling grinned at Tuesday, and suddenly she *knew*. The missing piece of the puzzle slotted together to reveal the terrible truth. 'Did he?' she said, fingers drumming on the table in her haste to spit the words out. 'I mean, yes, he said the words, but I'm more worried about how he said them.'

Hester's musket thumped onto the table as she rose swiftly. 'Now is the time for plain speaking.'

Her brain felt like it was travelling faster than the steam train – it was so *obvious*, why hadn't she seen it before? – and her mouth struggled to keep up, tripping over words in her haste. 'What's . . . what's the last thing Sterling said? We did as you asked . . . *we* did.'

The door shuddered against the weight of the daybreakers on the other side. 'Can we not quibble over quirks of speech right now?' Quintalion shouted.

Rising comprehension dawned on Hester's face. 'When he spoke to the daybreaker, he said *I*.'

'Exactly!' Tuesday smacked the table in triumph. 'He never speaks like that, only in my dream. The daybreaker would have known something was wrong.'

'The girl is smarter than she looks,' Sterling said. 'But it will not save her.'

The door strained at its hinges.

'Down!' Hester reached for her musket.

Quintalion hit the ground and covered his head. The musket shot splintered through the wood and then a muffled groan came from outside, followed by the thump of a body against the floor. Somebody cursed.

'The door will not hold for long enough to allow me to reload,' Hester said, slinging the musket back into its holster.

'In that case, I'd say it's time to go.' Quintalion crossed to the table and pulled the lever, sending it shooting back up into the ceiling amidst Jack's cries of protest as his papers flew everywhere.

Ignoring him, Quintalion flung the window open and said, 'Ladies first.'

Tuesday looked from the window to the ground rushing below and then back at Quintalion. 'I don't think so.'

'Do you have a better idea?'

A chunk of the door exploded inwards, showering them with shards of wood.

'No,' she said in a small voice and joined him at the window. The farmland streaked by in a dizzying pattern of yellows and greens.

'Open up in there!' one of the daybreakers shouted. 'In the name of the Council.'

'Not likely,' Quintalion said, and helped Tuesday up onto the leather chair.

She was fine until she stepped onto the wide window ledge, and then all her strength crumpled away and she collapsed against Quintalion, clinging to his coat, her fingernails digging into his sleeve. The cold air whipped past her. She couldn't open her eyes. If she opened her eyes, she'd fall. She whimpered deep in her throat.

'Look at me,' Quintalion said gently, and then, when she shook her head against his breast, repeated the words with a note of command in his voice. His thumb tucked under her chin and tilted her head up.

She reluctantly obeyed and met his mismatched eyes. His face was an oasis of calm.

'It's going to be all right,' he told her. 'There should be a ladder just to the right of the window. Climb up it onto the roof. I'll be right behind you.'

She wanted to tell him that he was crazy, that there was no way she could climb a ladder on the side of a moving train, and if he thought she could then he had greatly overestimated her, but the only thing that emerged from her mouth was a half-hearted squeak of fear.

He rested his large hand over her cheek. 'You can do this,' he told her quietly. 'I know you can. Do you want to know why?'

She sniffed and nodded.

'Because,' he said, and his fingers traced the patterns they had left on her skin when he woke her, 'I know you, Tuesday. Who you were in the past – who you'll be in the future – none of it matters. All that matters is who you are now. And the girl you are now can do this.'

He said it with such conviction that she actually believed him, and she squeezed his arm in thanks for pulling her back from her doubts.

'Also, the man *I* am now will push you out the damned window if you don't get a move on.'

Choking on her laughter, she let him ease her further out onto the ledge, gathering up her skirt so that she didn't trip on it, her eyes never leaving his as her hand clutched the air until her fingers closed over a ladder rung.

'You've got it?' he asked her.

Her teeth chattered too much for her to speak, so she just nodded.

'Good. Then climb, Tuesday, climb for your life.'

Behind him, Hester fired off another shot through the door. The hinges shrieked in protest and then buckled, and the daybreakers poured into the room.

With no warning, Quintalion pushed her off the ledge. Tuesday fell, her left arm flailing wildly and her heart in her throat. Her boots thudded against the rungs as she desperately tried to find purchase on the slick metal. She gasped and closed her eyes, but the expected pain didn't arrive.

She opened her eyes to find herself clinging to the ladder, standing on shaking legs at the final rung, and with her right arm holding her body close to the train. Despite this closeness, her skirt flapped around her legs, the sheer strength of the wind threatening to tear her from the ladder at any moment.

I can do this, she told herself. *If I can climb the walls of Beggars End, I can climb a little train.*

She took each step slowly, and when she was halfway up, she heard Jack's voice below her.

'Tuesday?' he yelled. He sounded worried.

'I'm here,' she tried to call back, staring down at him, but the cold wind seeped into her throat and she could only manage a wheezing reply that was torn away before it reached him.

Still, his head whipped up in her direction. 'Can I join you? Only, Hester's right behind me with Sterling and there's a high chance she's going to start jabbing me with her sword if I don't move soon.'

She moved up another rung. The ladder was bolted to the train and didn't give an inch, even in the wind, so it ought to be safe for the two of them to be on it at once. 'Of course!' she shouted back.

He climbed with one hand on the rungs and one clutching his staff, his mouth a determined slash in his face. When his head bumped against the sole of her boot, around halfway up, he gave a murmur of surprise.

'Do you think you can go any faster? I don't know how long Quintalion can hold them off.'

Her arms feeling like lead weights, she scrambled up the side of the train and collapsed against the roof. A bullet whooshed past her head in a hail of metal fragments. Gasping, she pulled herself forward until she lay in the middle of the roof, and lowered herself down so that her cheek was pressed against the metal, her breath fogging the top of the train in little clouds as she panted from fear and triumph. *I made it. I made it.*

A thump and then the warmth of a body pressed against hers alerted her to Jack's presence. His shoulders heaved and he grinned at her, tucking his glasses into his pocket so that the wind wouldn't tear them from his face.

'What a story this would make, huh?'

The laughter bubbled up from her unexpectedly. Here they were, on top of a moving train to escape men who wanted to kill them, and all Jack could think about was stories. How like a librarian. *Assistant*, her mind supplied automatically.

She supposed that, really, everyone was living their own story, whether it was immortalised in the grand histories or just passed down from mother to daughter by the fireside . . . She only doubted whether she'd live to tell her own.

She rolled over on her back to tell Jack this when she saw Sterling climbing onto the top of the train with Hester following closely behind him. She'd untied his hands to allow him to climb, and as she was preoccupied with unhooking her wooden leg from the filigree at the top of the ladder, Sterling stumbled, going down on his knees.

With a growl of impatience, Hester leaned over to drag him to his feet, only to rear back suddenly when he withdrew his sabre and brandished it at her.

'You really,' he said, slipping the scabbard over his head and sliding it back into his belt, 'shouldn't have untied us.'

Hester's eyes danced. She leapt back out of the way of his sword, pulling her own blades from their sheaths and twirling them in her hands. 'Let's finish this,' she said, 'you and I.'

They crashed against each other in a whirl of blades. They moved on steady feet, untroubled by the train moving beneath them, their attention entirely focused on each other as they stabbed and thrust, gave ground and took it, and parried each other's blows.

'Uh,' said Jack, sitting up beside her. 'What are they doing?'

'Fighting,' she replied.

'Is now really the best time?'

Hester forced Sterling back with well-aimed blows that rained off his sabre. He stumbled backwards with his blade raised in front of him, the only thing protecting him from Hester's furious attack. They teetered at the edge of the carriage. There was nowhere else for Sterling to go; he would fight back or he would fall, but Hester's precise cuts left no openings, and he soon found himself with his heels against the edge of the drop.

'Fall,' Tuesday whispered. '*Fall*.'

Another barrage from Hester sent Sterling's arms flailing wildly to stabilise himself, all attempts at defence forgotten, but before Hester could dive in for the kill, Sterling leapt from the carriage. His long legs easily propelled him to the next compartment, and he hit the roof at a run, turning and crooking his fingers at his opponent to invite her to join him.

She gathered herself and jumped, but she was too short to make the distance, and she hit the front of the carriage, scrabbling against the metal to find purchase with her legs dangling over the lip. Her curved swords rolled to a stop in front of Sterling's feet along with the broken tiger's head blade, which had been jostled loose by Hester's leap. He kicked the curved swords off the side of the train, sheathed his blade and bent down to pick it up, his head tilting as he examined the broken blade.

'Beautiful,' he shouted to Hester, still struggling to pull herself up over the edge of the carriage. 'We'd wager it belonged to your brother judging by its uselessness. A fine sword to die by, indeed.'

'My brother died by your hand, not his sword,' Hester huffed. The lower half of her body swung through the air, buffeted by the wind, and she slid further down with every second.

'Wrong!' Sterling crouched down by her struggling body, smoothed his fingers through her hair, and tugged back on her head hard, forcing her to look at him. 'The moment you attacked our men you died by your swords. You brought your end upon yourselves. And now we're going to send you to your brother.'

He pulled her up by her hair with one hand. Hester struck out at him, but he seemed not to feel her blows, and Tuesday, watching in horrified silence from the next compartment, remembered his cold hand wrapped around her throat that first time she'd met him in Beggars End.

'No!' she shouted, throwing herself to her feet, her skirts making movement difficult. The train rumbled beneath her, but she didn't care. All that mattered was saving Hester as she'd once saved her. But Tuesday wasn't Hester, with her combat skills and her musket and knives. She was just plain old Tuesday, the girl without a past, and she reached the conclusion that she was running straight into danger without anyone else to protect her around the same time she realised she didn't care.

Sterling paused with Narvi's blade held against Hester's throat. 'Come to beg for mercy for the savage?'

'Do you want to know what Thaïs said to me before she died?' It was a low blow, but Tuesday only had to look at the sword hovering by Hester's throat for all guilt to disappear.

'*What?*' he choked out. His grip loosened.

She laughed in his face. 'You're right. You've always been right. I killed Thaïs. She was there in the City of Lost Things, and I wanted nothing more than to be free, so I wrapped my hands around her neck and squeezed. A life for a life, that's how you get out of the City. And do you want to know what she whispered to me as the light died in her eyes?'

The words came out in a jumble of fragments and lies that she hoped sounded the tiniest bit plausible. Sterling was transfixed by her, to the point where he didn't notice Hester slipping out of his grasp.

'What did she say?' His voice was so soft and plaintive that Tuesday would have felt sorry for him had he not been dangling her friend off the side of a train.

As it was, she leaned forward and shouted the two worst words she could think of, something that she knew would pierce his heart more deeply than Hester's blades ever could: 'Thank you.'

His face crumpled, and for a moment she longed to take back the lies, but it was too late: Hester wrenched herself from his grip and swung her legs up and over the lip of the train, flipping forward to collect her sword as she rose.

She advanced upon him. 'I'm going to send *you* to your lover . . . if she still wants you.'

His mouth turned down in a snarl and he was up off his knees, drawing his sabre from its scabbard with a shout as he threw himself at Hester and the fight began again.

A shadow blocked out the few rays of sunlight that made it through the smoke, and Tuesday spun with her hands balled into fists, ready to attack, but it was just Quintalion.

His close-cropped hair was sticky with blood, and his waistcoat had a tear in it from belly to ornamental pocket. She didn't know why, but the sight of the golden embroidery fraying at the edge of the slit green silk sent a jolt of anger through her.

'That was fun,' Quintalion said, wiping the sweat from his brow.

'You're alive,' she said, and then flung herself at him, hugging him around the waist and probably tearing his waistcoat even more.

He coughed and awkwardly patted her on the back. 'Yes, well, that's enough of that ... what in the seven sisters are *they* doing?'

'Fighting to the death,' she mumbled against his chest, though she doubted he would have been able to hear her with her mouth pressed against the silk. She was leaning her head away from him to tell him again when the train turned on the tracks.

She stumbled. Only Quintalion's hand on her elbow saved her from falling over the edge.

'Stay down low.' He crouched with his feet wide apart. 'Like this.'

'What about Jack?' she said, copying his stance.

Jack had moved to the other end of the carriage and stood clutching his staff in front of him. Several daybreakers climbed up onto the roof right behind him. He tilted his head, his hair ruffling in the breeze, seemingly oblivious to the danger he was in. Tuesday opened her mouth to warn him, but Quintalion shook his head and gestured for her to watch. The first daybreaker onto the roof of the train chuckled and pointed at Jack, mere feet away. Jack's arm muscles were taut beneath his rolled-up sleeves. He stood as still as a statue until three of the daybreakers came within reach, and then the staff whipped out and he turned. He smacked the first daybreaker over the head, used the momentum to carry the staff through to crack the second on the shoulder, who collapsed with a yowl of pain, and then, when the third swore loudly, he flicked his staff out and pushed. The daybreaker lost his footing – he stumbled, his arms flailing wildly – and then he was over the edge of the train.

'I think he'll be fine,' Quintalion said.

On the next carriage, Hester and Sterling were a blur of movement, their blades flashing wildly. With a blow that drew sparks when it glanced off her broken sword, Sterling forced Hester backwards. He pressed his advantage, cutting and slashing and forcing Hester to throw her sword up to cover her naked arms. Her blocks grew weaker as she stumbled on the slick surface of the train. Her wooden leg caught in a groove and she tripped, hitting the roof hard.

Sterling raised his sabre.

'Look out!' Tuesday screamed.

Hester's foot darted out and she swept Sterling's leg from under him. He rolled, tucking his sabre under one arm, and stood in one swift movement, but by then Hester had regained her footing, and they faced each other again.

A bullet whistled through the air and hit the roof mere inches in front of her. Tuesday ducked and swivelled around to find another daybreaker jumping across onto their carriage.

'How inconvenient,' said Quintalion. 'I thought I'd killed you all.'

He stalked towards the daybreaker along the flat bar that ran the length of the compartment, his face split in a grin and his coat streaming out behind him in the wind.

'Come on!' he yelled. 'You've got me in your sights. What are you waiting for?'

The daybreaker cracked off another shot from his blunderbuss, and then another. They flew wide of Quintalion, hitting the roof instead, and the man's hands shook as he raised his weapon once more, but Quintalion was upon him before he had the chance. He whispered a word that Tuesday couldn't hear, rested his hand over the man's heart, and *pulled*, and something bloody and sinewy appeared in his grip for a second, before Quintalion threw it over the side of the train. The daybreaker's face drained of all blood, the blunderbuss fell from his grip, and his mouth moved in a silent scream.

Quintalion poked him with a bloody finger and he crumpled, the slipstream sending him down the side of the carriage and over the edge.

'That,' Quintalion said, catching the gun with his foot before it disappeared over the side, 'is for the Lady Fortuna.'

He chucked the blunderbuss over his shoulder in her direction. It bounced in her palm once, but she caught it on the second go.

'There,' he said, loading his pistol with gunpowder and shot. 'If a daybreaker grabs you, crack him over the head with it.'

She stared at the weapon in her hand. *I couldn't possibly . . . not again.*

But Tuesday didn't have time for doubts, because four more daybreakers swarmed up the side of the carriage. She shifted the gun experimentally from hand to hand.

The men hesitated, but they were steadier on their feet than their fallen companions had been, spreading their legs out wide to balance their weight as the train shifted from side to side, and it wasn't long before they advanced on them.

'I thought you killed them all,' she screamed at Quintalion.

'So did I.' He took out the first daybreaker with a shot to the neck that sprayed blood in an arc across the next closest daybreaker's face, and the man crumpled, clutching at his jaw. 'Evidently not.'

The train lurched just as he fired his pistol again, and the bullet went wide over the second daybreaker's shoulder. Quintalion cursed and raised his pistol, but it was too late: the second daybreaker floored him with a fist to his face.

'Quintalion!' she cried.

Her friend struggled to rise, but the daybreaker stepped on his back and crushed him into the metal. The man kicked the pistol from Quintalion's hand. It skittered across the roof and over the edge.

'So this is the famous Quintalion?' the man yelled, the other two daybreakers fanning out around him to leer down at the man in the greatcoat.

'Not so tough now, is he?' One of them spat on Quintalion's back.

He moved beneath the daybreaker's boot sluggishly, as if he wasn't quite awake, and when he gracelessly moved his head to the right to reveal the oozing cut on his cheek from where the daybreaker had punched him, anger flared up inside Tuesday, drowning out the fear.

She surged forward, shifting the blunderbuss in her hands. 'Leave him alone!'

'Who's this?' One of the daybreakers whistled at her like she was a runaway dog, and the others laughed. 'C'mere, girl. C'mere.'

'She's no fun.' The third daybreaker was a weaselly little man with a wheezing laugh that sounded like it came out of only one nostril, which it did, the other being completely missing from his face, along with half his nose. 'Toss her to the tracks and have done with it.'

Please don't die, please don't die, please don't die. She was so close now that she could see the cold, dead gaze in their eyes, and her muscles tensed to run, but she had no choice. The second daybreaker was pointing his blunderbuss at Quintalion's head, and the weasel stretched out his claw-like fingers for her neck. She sidestepped him, closed her eyes and swung the blunderbuss as hard as she could. There was a sickening crunch.

She opened her eyes to find the second daybreaker collapsed onto Quintalion, senseless, and the others staring at him in disbelief.

'You little . . .' the weasel said, but a hand reached out and grabbed his ankle, and he didn't get a chance to finish his curse before he was sliding over the edge of the carriage with a nasally wail.

'Well done, Tuesday.' Quintalion stood shakily.

She looped her arm in his to support him as he pressed a hand against the cut on his cheek.

The other daybreaker hung back. The train was gathering speed, and the smoke that billowed from its funnel filled the air with so much blinding ash and choking fumes that she could barely see Sterling and Hester on top of the next carriage.

'Time to go,' Quintalion said, and he darted back, grabbed Jack's arm, narrowly avoiding being clobbered by his staff, and tugged the boy forward so that the three of them stood shoulder to shoulder against the daybreakers. More and more climbed up the ladders on the sides of the carriage until at least twenty faced them. Too many to fight off.

'What,' Tuesday called out, 'do we do now?'

The smoke stung her eyes, forcing hot tears to roll down her face. She angrily scrubbed them away, but that just made it worse, and she stumbled to keep her footing, her vision gone dark. *Is this what it's like for Jack?*

A hand closed around her arm. She jerked away, but then the familiar smell of tea and must filled her nostrils and she leaned into Jack. 'Take my staff,' he told her, taking the blunderbuss from her and replacing it with the end of the stick. 'Quintalion has a plan.'

Eyes streaming, she saw Quintalion outlined against the smoke. He dug around for something inside his greatcoat and then raised his hand to his mouth, his fist closed tightly around something.

'Want to see us disappear?' he asked the daybreakers, and then opened his hand and *blew*. The smoke grew black, roiling like a thundercloud, before covering them completely. It smelled like oranges.

It was so dark. There was a tug on the staff and then she was tripping and running forward with only the wail of the wind and the sound of footsteps in her ear. *Oh no*, she thought, as she realised what Quintalion's plan was, but it was too late.

They smashed into the daybreakers, and though the men let out shocked exclamations and calls for their guns, the three of them kept going, pushing forward on the staff as they went, and the daybreakers scattered before them. A flash of blue through the smoke, an arm flailing in the air, and they were clear, but Quintalion wasn't done yet.

'Jump!' he yelled.

Before Tuesday could open her mouth in protest, the staff pulled her forward and she had just enough time to tense for the leap before she was yanked out over the breach between train compartments. The tracks flew by in the haze of smoke; she swore she'd live a quiet life in a house by the sea if the Days only let her survive the jump, and then she was clear, skidding to a stop on top of the next compartment, where the smoke dissipated almost immediately to reveal Quintalion calmly handing Jack back his staff.

'Thanks,' he said casually.

Brakes squealed, sending the three of them tumbling forward onto their knees. Hester and Sterling remained standing, though even they paused with their swords in mid-air, only continuing their deadly dance once the train started to slow down.

'I think this is our stop,' said Quintalion. 'Over the rest of the train and climb down the back to freedom – I've done this move so many times they should name it after me.'

But Tuesday wasn't listening to him. She was too busy staring at the reason they were slowing down. Six airships were hovering around the train, their massive gun turrets all pointed at them.

CHAPTER TWENTY-FOUR

Tuesday's legs started to shake and she sank down on the roof while her skirt billowed up around her.

'What's the matter with you . . . ?' Quintalion began, before turning and seeing the daybreaker airships surrounding them. 'Oh,' he finished lamely.

How did they find us? They'd kept to themselves during the train ride, and the ticket inspectors had seemed satisfied with their tickets and papers, admittedly fake as they both were, and there had been no time for the daybreakers they had defeated to call in reinforcements. Panic clawed through Tuesday's mind as she desperately tried to think of a way out, but there was nowhere they could go. It was hopeless, nothing to be done, they'd lost, and she cried out for the cool darkness of her keeping-house where nothing could hurt her.

She could feel it scratching at the corners of her mind: that desire to let go and fall back into the safety of oblivion, to become an un-girl again, and she scrabbled against the comfortable, blank bliss, fighting with all her might to keep the dark spots from crowding out her vision.

Someone was saying something in her ear, a word she recognised better than any other, and she grabbed hold of that sound like a lifeline, willing it to pull her back from the edge. Cool fingers stroked her hair, and traced lines down her face. Were they trying to wake her up? Would they leave pale marks to join the fingerprints on her cheek?

'Tuesday!' the sound came again, and this time she recognised it for what it was: her name.

The darkness around her dissipated, and she found herself looking up into Jack's worried face. 'Jack.'

'Thank the Days,' he breathed out.

'Indeed,' Quintalion murmured with his hands held high in surrender. 'He was going to kiss you next.'

Twin spots of red appeared on Jack's cheeks. 'I would *never*! I mean, not that I wouldn't want to . . . uh, that's how they wake them in the tales, but . . . well, I wouldn't presume to think *we* were anything like Amiens and Aemilia, but . . .'

She wrapped him in a hug before he could embarrass them both any further, and nuzzled her head deep into his shoulder, inhaling the warm, familiar smell of him.

'Right,' he said, and hugged her back.

'Touching,' came a voice. 'We hate to interrupt, but there's something you might want to see.'

She stiffened in Jack's embrace and raised her head.

Sterling stood with one arm locked around Hester's stomach, pinning her in place against his body, his sabre at her throat.

'It looks like we win.'

'Don't,' she whispered, and now that the train had finally slowed to a stop, the word travelled easily through the air.

'But it is our right,' he said. 'We defeated her in combat and we shall taste the sweet victory of plunging our blade through her heart.'

Hester squirmed in his grip, but he was too strong. She had been stripped of her knives and her musket and they now lay kicked to one side in a pile.

'I have no heart,' Hester muttered. 'You tore it out when you killed Narvi.'

Sterling's gaze turned to Quintalion and Jack, already on their feet but helpless to do anything, and then she felt it land on her, and she shrunk away from it as though he'd struck her.

'That's not entirely true, is it?' With his blade, Sterling angled Hester's head so that she was forced to look at the three of them. 'You may have locked it away all these years, but *now*.' He tutted. 'Strange how a liar, a blind boy and a murderess could win over the heart of a member of the legendary San Khalars.'

'Let her go, Sterling.' Tuesday's legs wobbled when she tried to push herself up, but on the second try they held firm and she straightened, staring at him defiantly, entirely grateful that he couldn't see how her hands shook behind her back.

'We don't think you're in a position to bargain.'

She shrugged, and hoped the panic didn't show in her voice. 'Maybe not, but we just took out a squadron of daybreakers. I think that deserves your attention.'

Quintalion and Jack took out a squadron of daybreakers, a little voice inside her pointed out. She ignored it.

The sabre brushed against Hester's cheek. She winced and turned her face away. *One scratch . . .*

'Please,' Tuesday tried again. 'I'll come with you. Just let her go.'

Quintalion pulled her around roughly to face him. 'You can't! I kept you safe, you foolish child, and now you want to throw your life away? He'll *kill* you.'

She rested a hand on his cheek. His eyes were filled with tears. 'I know,' she said, and turned to Jack.

'I *will* get your father back, safe and sound. I promise.'

This was her fault. They wouldn't even be here if it wasn't for her. But unlike after Fortune City, where the realisation plummeted her into despair, this time she drew strength from it. She'd allowed others to lead her for far too long – first Madame Marisol, as she ventured out into the world, and then Quintalion, and even Sterling in his strange way, always driving her forward, away from his eyes and his words – but these last few steps were hers and hers alone. She'd got them into this mess, and now she was going to get them out of it.

Taking a deep breath, she crossed the roof and came to a stop before Sterling, her arms raised in defeat.

'Well, this *is* amusing,' Sterling said. 'The girl comes to us willingly? What does she think she has to offer?'

Days and nights not yet lived, years flashing before her eyes, laughter and tears, and roads yet untaken. 'My life,' she said simply.

He hummed in his throat, turning his head to the side in a show of considering her offer. 'We were planning on taking that anyway.'

'And you could kill me right now,' she agreed, 'but I know you won't.'

The sabre moved away from Hester's cheek, who breathed a sigh of relief that was only perceptible to Tuesday because she'd been studying her face, hoping that she was all right.

'Why won't we?'

Well, for one he'd already told her that he was going to spill her blood over the Book of Days, but that was just logistics. She needed to give him a reason before he changed his mind and killed her where she stood. She cleared her throat and prayed to the Days that her hunch was right. 'Because you say *we* instead of *I*, and I know why.'

He huffed out a breath. 'An affectation, nothing more.'

'Perhaps,' she allowed. 'Or perhaps it's because it's the only way you can pretend she's still here with you. Thaïs. I know you loved her. If you let my friends go, I'll tell you why she thanked me when I killed her.'

Lies, more lies, but she'd told this one forcefully enough that it was starting to imprint on her like a second skin. Tuesday: the girl who killed a Day. As much as she knew it was a lie, she was starting to feel like there could be a grain of truth buried somewhere in all the deception.

Sterling forced his words out through gritted teeth. 'If what you say is true, then we'll ask her when we wake her.'

'Do you think she'll tell you?' Quintalion cut in. 'When they're dying, people say things they'd never normally dare. Trust me, I know.'

She shot Quintalion a grateful look and continued. 'Leave my friends alone and I'll tell you *everything*.'

Sterling's grip on the sabre wavered. His eyes darted up to the airships above him. 'You swear it?'

He was going to agree; she saw it in the curve of his mouth and the way his pale hand unclenched at his side. If she ever met this mysterious Thaïs, she'd have to thank her.

'On my life and the life I can't remember,' she promised.

He nodded to one of the airships and suddenly the air was filled with the clang of metal as its arrow-bolt tower blazed into life, preparing to lower a bolt. She drew back, uncertain, but the chain descended slowly, stopping just behind Sterling with little shudders of tension.

'We have a deal,' Sterling said.

'No!' Jack cried out, but the sound of the gun towers swinging in his direction quickly silenced him.

She turned back to him, willing a smile to her frozen lips, more for Quintalion's benefit than Jack's, for he had stepped forward with his hand hidden in his coat, and Tuesday had no doubt that he was seconds away from his own destruction.

'Please,' she told them both, 'let me do this.'

Quintalion's jaw was tight as he shook his head. Jack had a death grip on his staff, and looked like he wanted very much to use it, but he *couldn't*. She wouldn't see her friends die because of her.

'Do you remember what you asked me on the first day I met you?' she addressed Quintalion, trying and failing for a jocular tone. 'You asked me whether I was stubborn. And I am, I know that now. I'm doing this with or without your blessing. But I don't want our last conversation to be an argument.'

'Why break the habit of a lifetime?' He laughed, and then his face screwed up and the laugh turned into a choked-off sob, which he quickly stifled with his hand.

'Come, come,' Sterling interrupted. 'We tire of this display of sentiment. Say your goodbyes and make peace with your fate.'

Say my goodbyes. Now that it came to it, Tuesday couldn't force the words past her lips. There was so much to say to the three of them. She'd only known them a short time, but already they'd carved a place in her heart: Quintalion, with his tricks and his cleverness, which he wasn't shy about proclaiming to all he met; Hester, who kept all her passion locked up tight behind a calm exterior, except when she thought no one could see; and Jack . . . oh, *Jack*.

She made her way back to them, still unsure what she was going to say, but Jack didn't give her the chance.

'You're not going with him,' he told her. 'We'll fight him, we'll pay him, I'll bean him in the head with one of my books, but I'm not letting you give yourself up for our sake.'

She swallowed against the lump in her throat. 'Don't you see? I have to go. Not just for you, but for me. Would you get your sight back if you could?'

He seemed confused about the turn the conversation had taken, and thought for a second or two before saying, 'I . . . yes, I mean . . . I don't . . . no, I don't know. It's a part of me now.'

'Exactly,' she told him. 'And my life before I woke is a part of me. I can't just walk away.'

'We *could* fight.' Quintalion glanced at the airships circling above them. Though there were no men visible on their decks, she had no doubt that they were waiting for someone to make a move.

'No,' she said gently. 'We can't.'

'Then this is really it, isn't it?' Quintalion ran a hand over his head and snorted. 'I'm finally free of you.'

When she'd first met him, she would have been hurt by this flippant farewell. But she knew him now, and she knew how much pain was hidden behind those words, so she wrapped her arms around him in a hug, her cheek against his neck, his pulse thudding against the fingerprints he had let behind on her skin.

'Thank you,' she whispered to him.

And then she went to meet her fate.

A self-satisfied smile touched the corners of Sterling's mouth as she came to him. He loosened his grip on Hester.

'You cannot do this.' Hester's voice was hard. 'You cannot let him win.'

'He *has* won,' Tuesday told her, averting her eyes so that she didn't have to look into Hester's disappointed face. 'Don't you see? I . . . I'm just trying to get us all out of this alive. Well, most of us,' she added, when she remembered the plans Sterling had for her.

Determination steeled Hester's gaze. 'Then I am sorry. I am truly sorry.'

Her boot lashed out, catching Sterling on the ankle. He dropped, cursing. 'Go!' she screamed, but it was too late. Sterling was on his feet again.

The sabre slashed through the air. Hester jumped back, and Tuesday thought she had managed to avoid the blade until a line of red blossomed on her shirt.

'A single cut,' Sterling whispered.

Oh Days no. What have I done? The world swam around Tuesday as she watched Hester give them one last defiant look before sinking to her knees with her hands covering her midsection. It couldn't be true. Sterling had been lying, or exaggerating. The cut wasn't deep. Hester would be fine. She didn't realise she was babbling all of this out loud until Sterling pulled her away from Hester, and she looked in horror at the blood covering Hester's hands.

'On second thought,' he said, 'kill them all!'

'No!' The shriek tore itself out of her soul. Everything was spinning, train and sky and airships, and she no longer knew which way was up. Sterling whispered something in her ear, but her world had gone silent and grey, and nothing but her own harsh breaths penetrated the fog that had descended. Her body was moving, lifting, and somewhere in the back of her head she knew that it was wrong, that she had to *fight*, but what was the point if her friends were already dead? She let herself go limp.

Her mind was already racing back across the Whispering Plains, to Madame Marisol's House, where it was safe and quiet.

CHAPTER TWENTY-FIVE

'Whoa there, lass,' came a voice. 'You're all right. Nothing will harm you, I swear it.'

Hands followed the voice, gently but firmly lowering her arms from where she had been unconsciously tugging at her hair, and then trailing down to set her own hands together and rub them briskly.

'There you are,' the voice said again, as one might speak to a skittish colt. 'You're coming back to us, I can tell. Take your time.'

Time. Time was something she didn't have. They had to make it to the Silk Sea before . . . before *what*? It had been very clear to her a second ago, but now it slipped away, and she whimpered.

'I won't let that brute in here if that's what you're worried about,' the voice said. 'I'll give him a piece of my mind, and if there's any justice in the world, he'll choke on it. What was he thinking, scaring a poor innocent girl half to death?'

Not half to death, she wanted to tell him, *dying*. Dead. And not me, never me, but someone who smelled like pomegranates and fresh, clean air.

'Ah, I never should have embarked on the expedition,' the voice exhaled, tinged with regret. The hands stilled against her skin, and she allowed her arms to fall back into her lap.

'Jack told me not to. He wanted to go instead of me, but I wouldn't listen. "They won't want a boy who's not even a full librarian yet," I told him. "Best let your old man go instead. One final adventure."'

Why did that name sound familiar? It brought to mind a voice not unlike the one speaking to her now, and a face with kind brown eyes. She wanted to remember, to ask the voice and the hands how she knew this Jack and why his name sent sparks of light to shine in the darkness.

The voice continued, though she didn't think it was speaking to her anymore. 'It was all for him, that's what I wish I could have told him. If we found the Book . . . I've pored over every secondary resource, every legend and scrap of hearsay, and they all state that the Book has the power to change the world.' The voice hitched in a sob. 'I just want to bring my poor boy's sight back, that's all. Surely the Days wouldn't deny a father that.'

She was blind. Of course, that was it. It all made sense now: why she was trapped in the darkness, and why a voice and a cool cloth against her forehead meant so much to her. But no, that wasn't right. *She* wasn't blind, but someone she knew was, and she dug her fingers deeper into her temples to clear away the murk that hid the truth, but the voice shushed her and anchored her back to the present.

'Hush, lass, hush. You stop that. Just lie quiet.'

But she didn't want to lie quiet. The darkness wrapped around her too tightly, like a pall, and the keeping-house became a coffin. She beat against it with her hands, and cracks appeared in the glass.

'I wish you could tell me your name,' the voice said. 'I'd dearly love to know it.'

She had a name, but the name came with a history that caused the cracks to spider-web across the glass. It was too much. *Madame Marisol, help me!* She lashed out with all her might. Sections of the glass began to plane away to reveal scenes playing out before her eyes in glorious colour: a city falling, walking through purple grass as tall as a house, four friends sharing a meal together.

Friends. There could be no friends here in the darkness, and so she turned her face against the night and *pushed*. Every crack and splinter allowed more and more memories to rush into the holes left behind, and she breathed in the fresh air for the first time in what felt like forever. Hester returned, and then Jack, and finally Quintalion following along behind with his usual swagger.

Tears streamed down her face. She felt like she was drowning only to be dragged onto dry ground, and she gasped in relief at each new memory that came back to her, so overwhelmed that she barely noticed the hands pulling her up so that her back was once again resting against the wall, or the euphoric commands to *keep going, you're almost there, my girl.*

She beat against the glass with all the strength she possessed, and the cracks widened until she remembered waking and walking and singing and light, and she laughed, not caring if she sounded mad because how could she not be, with an entire lifetime trying to cram itself back inside her mind? She saw one more flash, a vision of her staring at herself, but different somehow, and then the glass shattered, and she shot out into the light with a gasp.

Hands eased her up and rubbed circles on her back so that she could breathe again, but they were no longer single points of comfort in the darkness: now they belonged to a tiny old man, whose white hair seemed to delight in growing anywhere but his head, and who stared down at her through a thick pair of glasses with something akin to hope lighting up his features.

'Tuesday,' she said to him when her breathing returned to its normal pattern. 'My name is Tuesday.'

'Augustus Heller,' the man replied, 'and it is very good to finally meet you, my dear.'

She wanted to tell him so many things, that she knew his son, and how relieved Jack would have been to know that he was still alive, but before she'd even opened her mouth there was the sound of a key being turned in a lock, and the door to their cell swung open, drenching them in harsh gaslight.

Sterling stood outlined against the light. He had changed into a fresh uniform, and Tuesday felt herself tensing automatically to rise, wanting to rip the buttons off and tear great holes in the cloth, because how *dare* he appear before her refreshed and spotless, as though by taking off his old blood-encrusted uniform he could simply sweep away the memory of the lives he'd destroyed.

Two other daybreakers entered the room before she had the chance, carrying chains and looking to Sterling for confirmation as they came to a halt before Tuesday and Augustus. Sterling nodded. They dragged them both upright, and Tuesday was forced to hunch over while they undid the shackles that bolted them to the wall, the metal chafing against her skin when one of the daybreakers carelessly shoved her to one side to get better access to the keyhole. Once the old shackles were off, she barely had enough time to knead her thumb into the tender skin at her wrist before they clapped on the new set of irons, and before long she stood facing Sterling with her hands locked together in front of her.

Sterling looked over the two of them, side by side in their chains, and nodded. 'We're here.'

*

The pomegranate trees stretched their branches towards the sky like old bones. The oncoming winter had stripped them of their greenery, and the only pomegranates left on the bare branches were shrivelled, the frost leaching their colour to a blood red.

It's fitting, Tuesday thought as she stared around her. She hadn't thought she'd ever see the grove again, but knowing the bones that were hidden beneath her feet, it somehow felt right that the trees were dead.

Augustus Heller shuffled down the gangway of the idling airship and adjusted his glasses. 'Well, I'll be . . .'

He had been on an expedition to find the City of Lost Things, she remembered, when the daybreakers had caught him. Anger flared up within her when she realised that he would never get his wish; if Sterling had his way, the man who had looked after her as if she were his own child would fall before the door of the city.

'If you have the chance,' she whispered to him, mindful of the daybreakers holding their chains, 'run. Just go.'

'And why would I do that, my dear?' the old man asked.

'They'll kill you!' she burst out. 'The door to the City of Lost Things can only be opened by death. Do you want to die?'

'They have my boy – my Jacobi. They promised they'd let him go if I show them the way into the city.' Though the chains weighed him down, Augustus lifted his hands to her face and gently patted her cheek, standing on tiptoe to reach her. 'Oh, my brave lass,' he said. 'What father would do less for his son?'

He's dead. She wanted to scream it out, to let it float away on the breeze so that she could forget she'd ever met him, and then maybe she would be able to get the two simple words past her lips, instead of choking on them.

'He's . . .' she began, her voice thick with grief, but before she could tell Augustus what had happened to his son, a pale hand appeared on the edge of her vision and someone shoved a cloth in her mouth. She gagged on the fabric pressing against her tongue as the knots were tied off tightly against her hair.

'That's just about enough of that,' Sterling said. 'Don't make this any harder for him.'

Any harder for him? She slid her tongue underneath the gag, wanting to pull it out so that she could scream or cry or at least call Sterling every one of the swearwords she'd learned from Quintalion and Hester, but he had tied it tightly, and no matter how much she worked it, it refused to come free.

One of the daybreakers shoved her forward, and they started to walk. The airship's engines were ticking down now as the ship cooled, but over the steady thud came the faint sound of laughter and music. The gaps in the trees revealed glimpses of the beach, where a carnival looked to be in full swing: brightly dressed people zipped in and out of painted caravans, and a few couples had started up an impromptu dance, right there on the sand.

'Sergeant Daines,' Sterling said, his voice clipped. 'Explain.'

The sergeant had been chatting with one of the men, but when he heard his name, he exchanged a look with the others and stepped forward to match Sterling's pace. 'The city's been . . . er, throwing a lot of things out lately, sir. It's become a bit of a pilgrimage site for the locals who've lost things.'

'Throwing things out?'

'Yessir,' he said. 'Bowler hats, old pets, my Great Aunt Nellie, though truth be told I wish I could put her back in, the old bag.' He straightened when he caught sight of Sterling's unimpressed face, and added, 'Sorry, sir. But I'd bet my good teeth there's something in there taking up too much room. Like trying to close a cupboard door when it's too full.'

Sterling didn't reply, just pursed his lips and walked out onto the sand with his hand on his sabre.

Despite herself, Tuesday couldn't help but gasp when she caught sight of the sea. The sun sparkled on the water, turning the waves a shade of aqua so bright that only the purples and pinks of the fish darting through the swells eclipsed it. The waves rolled to shore in perfect sets, and suddenly it made sense to her to call it the Silk Sea, because she felt that if she dipped a foot into it, the water would caress her toes like the finest silk slippers. She closed her eyes and breathed in the sea air, and even through the gag she could taste the salt on her lips.

The door lay just out to sea, closer to shore than she had remembered . . . but then everything in that dream had felt slightly off kilter and out of focus. Unlike the pomegranate trees, the passing years hadn't touched it. If anything, the wood looked less rotted, and the double doors had a pearlescent sheen to them that she hadn't seen in her dream. A long line of people waded into the waves with baskets of flowers or incense, leaving the tide to carry their offerings out when the water grew too deep for them to go any further.

Tuesday let out a muffled cry for help, but the crowd was too far out to hear.

A little way from her, Sterling massaged his head, the pulse point in one temple jumping alarmingly. 'This isn't right,' he murmured.

'Sir?' Sergeant Daines said uncertainly.

Sterling immediately straightened. 'Clear out the area,' he said. 'It has to be perfect. We want this rabble dealt with in the next ten minutes or it'll be your badge.'

A weary look flitted across Daines's face, but he simply nodded, clicked his heels together, and moved towards his men.

'Cracked in the head, he is,' the daybreaker holding Tuesday said as the sergeant joined them. 'I thought he'd get over that tart he was walking out with, but he gets worse every day.'

Augustus's guard spat out a stream of tobacco and ground it into the sand. 'We should have bolted while we had the chance. That lot from the *Stormrazer* had the right idea. They're probably halfway to Ravens Reach by now.'

'Too right. I knew we were in for trouble when he started going on about *her*.' Tuesday flinched as her daybreaker shoved her roughly. 'Not a word the whole time I've served under him and suddenly it's *Tuesday* this and *revenge!* that. He's bloody mad, I say.'

'He's still your commander,' Daines reminded him. 'The Council gave him control over the flying corps, and *as such*, you owe him your allegiance.'

His voice was sharp, but it did nothing to quell the mutters of the two daybreakers. Tuesday had to hide her smile. If there was dissension in the ranks, then maybe there was hope that both she and Jack's father could get out of this alive.

Sterling, meanwhile, had pulled out a pocket watch and alternated between staring at it and staring at his men. She was surprised that he carried one; he had always struck her as the kind of man to instinctively know the time to a second. His pale hand beat a drum against his leg.

'Keep your chin up, lass,' Augustus whispered to her when they were jostled together in the sand. 'If I've learned anything as a librarian, it's that it's always darkest before something truly magnificent happens.'

But this wasn't one of his books, safe in their musty library. She'd thought that's what life would be like, back when she'd left Madame Marisol, and had journeyed out with no expectations other than that everything would work out right in the end – that the story of her life would end with *and they lived blessedly and contentedly by the grace of the Days.* But then stories and possibilities were all she had left that House with; there was no way she could have known what life would be like. It was cruel and cold, and people died without fanfare.

She watched the daybreakers disperse the gathering with their blunderbusses and harsh words, and the beach was deserted sooner than she hoped, save for them and a still-burning fire, which crackled and lapped at a pole about halfway down the beach. The pole sat on a wooden platform now being devoured by the flames, with steps leading up to it. Tuesday reeled back, her heart thudding too loudly in her ears, drowning out the flames and the pull of the tide. This fire wasn't built for warmth, as she had assumed, but for death. Someone had walked up those steps and screamed as the flames took them, and their killers had watched them die, just as Sterling and Thaïs had watched Hester's brother die. Just as she would soon be forced to watch Augustus die, and it would keep going, on and on, this never-ending parade of death in the name of grief and a desire to hold on to something that was already lost.

Someone was keening softly, and it was only when rough hands pulled her back to her feet where she had fallen in the sand that she realised that terrible wail came from her own mouth. She had to stop this, or it would go on forever.

'Get her moving,' Sterling said from somewhere near her ear. 'It's time.'

As they waded out into the ocean, the icy water numbing her skin, Tuesday worked the gag with her tongue, back and forth, back and forth. If they were going to kill Augustus, she would *not* stand by as a mute witness, frozen by shock or circumstances as she had been the last two times she'd seen someone die. He deserved to know that the son for whom he willingly walked to his death had reached the City of Lost Things before him.

The water was deeper now, lapping at their legs. Sterling kept up a punishing pace, and since he forced them along in front of him with the flat of his sabre, there was nothing for them to do but match his stride or risk drowning. He stopped only once to unhook the scabbard from his belt so that the saltwater didn't ruin it, and then continued to stride deeper into the surf, until they were up to their waists. Poor Augustus, being so much shorter than both Sterling and Tuesday, was almost knocked over every time a wave pounded into them.

The tide was pulling some of the offerings back to land now, and they stood surrounded by the flower baskets, with the scent of sea and incense in their noses. About ten feet from the door, Sterling suddenly halted. This was it. Tuesday furiously worked her tongue beneath the cloth. It was wet with spit now, and only a thin section remained in her mouth; she'd managed to slide the rest of it down onto her chin.

With his sabre brandished in front of him, Sterling gave Augustus the handcuff key and watched with his attention half on Augustus and half on the door as the old man calmly unlocked his handcuffs and let the chains fall from around his wrists.

Tuesday took advantage of Sterling's distracted state to fiddle with the knots holding the gag closed, but they had been tied tightly, and she had only just loosened them when Sterling swung around to face them again.

Augustus removed his glasses and slipped them into his pocket. 'I should have given those to my boy long ago,' he murmured. 'Not that he'd have much use for them, but they're ceremonial. The tools of my trade, you know. A librarian's only as good as his glasses. I suppose he'll get them when he finds my . . .'

He choked on the word then, and Tuesday gripped his shoulder, the only comfort she could give him. 'Make sure he does?' he asked her.

She nodded, not trusting herself to speak even if the gag would allow it. This was wrong. The injustice of it burned through her veins, and she tugged at her chains in frustration.

Sterling's gaze was once more on the door, the sabre wavering in his hands. If she was quick, she could wrap the chain around his throat and end him now. White-hot needles of anticipation prickled against her skin. It would be so easy. Just loop the chain around that white neck and pull. Or perhaps he would sink beneath the waves and she would watch his chest heave for air that he'd never breathe again . . .

Panting, she swallowed down the rage. She didn't know where it had come from, and that worried her more than she was willing to admit. Her fingers unclenched from where they had been curled around the cool metal.

Sterling shook his head, as though clearing it, and turned back to them. The chance was lost. He positioned himself in front of Augustus and began to speak, his words solemn.

'Augustus Heller, librarian of Fortune City,' he said. 'For posterity's sake and for the sake of the honour that binds us, do you go to your death freely?'

The solemnity of his oath threw Tuesday abruptly back to Fortune City and the deal that she had made with the Lady Fortuna. Strange how Sterling came from a culture that decried the barbarity and superstitions of the old ways yet followed his own traditions just as solemn and binding. Sterling and Augustus might not be drinking a draught of their own blood, but the ceremony was no less formal. She would have laughed had it not been so serious.

'I do,' Augustus replied.

Sterling surged forward. Tuesday heard herself cry out. It was too quick; she hadn't yet freed herself. *This can't be happening.*

The tip of the sabre was inches away from Augustus's heart when the man spoke again, staying Sterling's hand. 'Wait! I have one request for you.'

Eyes darting to the door, Sterling sighed and then inclined his head. 'It seems only fair for the man who will restore our happiness.'

Tuesday bristled. He was all grace when he was victorious, but she'd seen the storm clouds in those green eyes, and she knew the anger that rippled beneath his skin.

Augustus licked his lips. 'Don't let the lass see this. She's only a child. Don't make her carry my death for the rest of her life.'

'She's seen worse, we assure you,' Sterling said.

Tuesday poked at the gag with her tongue. Almost there. She could feel the fabric slipping over her lips, and let out an experimental cry of, 'Don't. Please, don't,' but though her voice was loud and clear, the men didn't even glance in her direction. She frantically worked the gag further out of her mouth.

The men stared at each other, Sterling with his sabre a hair's breadth from Augustus's heart, and Augustus calmly facing him. The waves smashed against him – he was shivering, great tremors that ran up his spine each time the cold water drenched him – but he didn't falter.

'She may have seen worse,' Augustus said, 'but I know there is honour in you. Allow a dead man his trifles.'

The cloth slipped out of Tuesday's mouth. Tuesday briefly closed her eyes in a prayer of thanks, protests against this injustice spilling from her lips, but Sterling was already nodding, and as if from a great way off, his voice funnelled down to her.

'Very well.'

He grabbed her shoulder and suddenly the water closed over her head. She gagged and coughed, fighting against the hand that held her beneath the waves, but everything was churning and she didn't know which way was up. She breathed in deeply, desperate for air, but dragged in a lungful of seawater instead. Bright spots flashed before her eyes. It had all been a trick. He was never going to kill Augustus. It had always been her.

She lashed out wildly, but none of her blows connected, and soon she felt her muscles relaxing as her mind screamed for air. Everything was quiet beneath the water, the world growing distant and hazy. The darkness closed over her, and though she struggled against it, she couldn't stop the wave of tiredness. Someone was humming in her ear, a lilting tune that kept time with her faltering heartbeat, and their fingers carded through her hair. *Madame Marisol?*

And then the darkness receded and she was being hauled out onto dry land. Her body automatically gulped in the fresh air, even as her mind yelled that this was wrong, that she should be dead, and as soon as she could lift her head she looked around to find the reason for her salvation. Had Sterling had second thoughts?

That was when she caught sight of Augustus lying in the sand, his sightless eyes staring out at the sky as a crimson stain spread over his shirt. The scream tore itself from her and she flung herself at the old man, but strong hands pulled her away and then the world tilted and she was being carried, but it didn't matter anymore because she'd failed Jack and she'd failed his father, so she let herself slump in Sterling's arms as he walked along the channel of suddenly dry land and through the open door into the City of Lost Things.

CHAPTER TWENTY-SIX

Tuesday lay in the middle of a crossroads, the four paths branching out in opposite directions until they disappeared into the distance. The sign at the centre of the crossroads read: *Here*, *There*, *Somewhere Else*, and *Entirely the Wrong Way*.

Am I dreaming? She sat up, and the blood rushed to her head and sent her groaning back to the ground. A school of fish darted in and out of her sight. She was fairly certain fish weren't supposed to fly, at least none she'd ever heard of, so she was quite willing to write their existence off as a dream of her dying mind as she struggled for air beneath the waves . . . Only, when she blinked to clear her vision, Sterling loomed over her.

She was sitting up before she had a chance to think, her body taking in blessed gasps of air. The fogginess receded, and as the last couple of minutes washed over her, the truth of what had happened stole the air from her lungs.

'Augustus,' she choked out. 'You killed him.'

'You're remarkably cognisant for having spent the last hour unconscious. At least, we believe it has been an hour. Our watch doesn't work in this abominable place.'

So they'd made it to the City of Lost Things then. She vaguely remembered the archway above her as they stepped through the doors, but everything after that was black. It was lucky that she hadn't eaten since luncheon, because she didn't think she'd be able to keep anything down. Sterling had paid for their entrance with blood. *Only death can open the door.*

Sterling held out his hand for her, to help her from the ground.

She stared at it incredulously. 'I'm not going anywhere with you.'

He must have removed the handcuffs from her while she slept, and she felt almost insulted. Did he think that now they were in the City, she was just going to blithely follow him to her death? He may have killed everyone she ever held dear, and it might be a long way to Thaïs, but she wasn't going to join her friends without a fight. Meekly allowing Sterling to kill her would be an insult to their memories.

Then there was the Book of Days to think about. Sterling wanted it and hated it in equal measure – he desired it as a means to bring back Thaïs, and yet loathed it for that very power because it came from the Days. And as long as Tuesday still had life left in her body, she would thwart his plans.

So she sighed and let Sterling pull her to her feet, shivering in her damp clothes. He stared at her as if he hadn't expected her to be so cooperative, and she almost laughed in his face. *If only you knew . . .*

Her fear of him melted away, leaving only bitterness and hatred. He had taken her friends from her. He had destroyed their lives. There was nothing more that he could do to her. Death was the only card he held now, but even that did not frighten her. If she died, she would see her friends again, and that was *good.*

She must have been smiling, because Sterling drew back from her with doubt in his eyes. 'What is it?'

A giggle escaped. She clamped her hand over her mouth and spoke through her fingers, trying to hold the laughter inside, because if she let it out, she'd never stop. 'You,' she said. 'You think you're so powerful, but inside . . . inside you have *nothing*. Your men are deserting you, Thaïs left you, you don't even know who you are anymore.'

From the way his hand twitched at the hilt of his sabre, she could tell it took great self-control for him not to kill her now – spilt blood at a crossroads, wasn't there a curse for that? – but all he did was say, 'And how, pray tell, is that any different from you? You are a thief of life. You don't deserve to be alive. And nothing that you can say will ever make us look at you and not see the woman you murdered.'

'But at least *I* don't define myself by a romance that was dead long before Thaïs was,' she spat out. She took another deep breath and the words seemed to flow from her like wine, and she hardly knew where they were all coming from, only that she had to get them out or she would explode.

'She was going to leave you, Sterling, that's why she stole into the city in the night. She had the Book, didn't you know that? I bet she told you that it was hidden in the city, but the truth was that she was going to hide it there herself. She was making sure you could never reach the Book of Days, because she knew – she *knew* – what the world would be like if you used its power – darkness and smoke and death!'

She was panting, heaving in great gasps of air, and so she almost missed the look of incredulity that crossed Sterling's face until he said, his voice soft: 'How could you possibly know that?'

'Of course I know that, I . . .' She paused when she realised what she had said. It had come from deep inside. She had just wanted to silence him and the words had jumped obligingly into her mind, but now that she tried to pin them down, they flitted out of her reach. She'd never even met Thaïs, at least not that she remembered, so how could she know what the Day had done? 'I . . . I don't know.'

Sterling spurred her forward and they walked in silence after that, Tuesday too confused to want to antagonise Sterling further, and Sterling stumbling beside her as though he didn't see the ground. Every so often he would mumble to himself, snippets of silent conversations: 'No,' or, 'That can't be right.'

Time didn't seem to hold any sway over this strange city. The days and nights passed in seconds, and for a long stretch of their journey both the sun and the stars and crescent moon hung in the sky, as if the city couldn't decide what hour it wanted to be. No matter how long they walked, Tuesday never grew tired or hungry. Perhaps the dead had no business with such trivial matters, but she found herself missing it, like something unremembered until it's lost. It wasn't *right* to walk for so long without tiring; it made her feel strangely unreal.

'There is no logic to this land,' Sterling muttered.

She shrugged, not inclined to humour him after what he had said about her. 'Death isn't logical. You of all people should know that.'

'Why us?'

She was about to say, *Because you've sent enough people here*, but something stayed her tongue. It wasn't pity – she had no pity for the monster that stood before her – but perhaps it was a sad kind of empathy. She knew what it was to be lost, to be chasing something distant and unattainable, and despite everything he'd done, she couldn't bring herself to taunt him for it.

'Because you've been here before,' she settled on saying, 'with Thaïs.'

It started to rain; big fat drops out of an orange sky. 'We haven't,' he said in a small voice.

That can't be right. She had seen the door to the city open herself, in her dream. She'd heard them rejoice at its opening as Hester's people lay dying before them. 'But the pomegranate grove,' she said. 'The door . . . I saw it open.'

'We were going to enter the city together, triumphant. But the night was coming and she told us it would be better to wait until morning, and then . . .'

'She left in the night?' she said, remembering her recent revelations. The arch, laughing creature that Tuesday had seen in her dream wasn't one to be caged, she could tell, and the cage that Sterling had bound her in, despite her initially entering it of her own free will, would have been suffocating.

'We did not realise until it was almost too late. We ran to the door just as she was stepping through. We called out, but . . .' he took a shuddering breath, 'she didn't look back.'

The thick rain hid his face from her. It soaked into the skin of Sterling's pale hand as he cursed and threw it up over his head. Blue veins wormed their way from his wrist up to his fingers.

'What happened?' she asked. 'To your hand, I mean.'

He snorted. Tuesday thought he wasn't going to tell her, but then he cleared his throat and said: 'By the time we reached the door, she was almost gone. We . . . we did not wish to lose her, so we grabbed hold of her shirt, but the city of the dead was not meant for the living, and it slipped through our fingers.'

She started back, surprised. He had actually reached into the City of Lost Things itself, and it had rejected him, leaving him with a hand as pale as a corpse, but why? The door opened only to death, and they had given it a whole grove.

When she asked him why, he laughed bitterly. 'We did not know then that it does not open for any death – why do you think none of those local sacrifices worked? It opens only to a *willing* death.'

'So it was Narvi,' she whispered, remembering the determined look in the young man's eyes before he ran further into the minefield. 'His battalion was dying, his *friends* were dying. He probably didn't see much difference between a victory in battle and a victory in death.'

Sterling nodded. 'We knew that, what with how those savages value honour, one of them was bound to wish for death at being faced with such a dishonourable defeat.'

'So that's why you told Augustus that you had Jack.'

'What father wouldn't go to his grave to protect his son? And now we are here, we will find our lost love, and we will be able to breathe again.'

How dare he? She lashed out at him, too furious to realise how stupid it was, only wanting to release some of the wild anger coursing through her. He easily blocked her punch, and held on to her wrist so that she couldn't try again, which just made her struggle harder.

'How many lives have you ruined?' she said, straining against his grip. 'Mine? My friends'? For what? Chasing some dream, some . . . some . . . *fantasy* of love?'

'She loved us.' His grip tightened on her wrist, drawing a hiss of pain from her. 'She *loved* us. And when we silence your fool mouth, she will come back to us, and together we will build the world we always dreamed of.'

'With the Book of Days?' She struggled against him, but he wouldn't let go of her arm. They clung together in the rain.

'Yes, with the Book,' he grunted. 'And then we will burn it, and the old ways will crumble into dust. We will bring order and peace to the barbaric west. We will bring cities and factories and doctors, and the world will move forward as it should, with us at its helm.'

'What if they don't *want* those things?' she asked, gritting her teeth as she fought against him. 'They're happy as they are.'

With a swift move, he pinned both her arms by her side and drew close to her so that their bodies were almost touching. A jolt rippled through her.

'You speak for them all?'

It was risky and utterly untrue, but then truths had never held her back, and so she simply replied, 'Yes.'

He let her go and turned away. 'Then you are a bigger fool than we thought.'

*

She wandered along the lonely road with Sterling her only shadow. The rain had long ago disappeared, and the sky was grey with clouds. She wished the city would make up its mind and pick a time, preferably night. The dark wreathed everything in mystery, whereas the daylight showed things for what they really were, and she would rather not face the truth of her situation until she had to. As a lost girl who had sent her friends to their deaths in pursuit of a book and the name it would lead her to, and who now walked to her own ending, if she dwelled on her situation, she doubted she would be able to put one foot in front of the other.

Still, it seemed the city was dwelling on it for her. The colour drained from the landscape until only dull black trees stretched their crooked branches towards a pale sky. Tuesday reached out a hand: the colour had also leeched from her skin, and the navy-blue dress became just *the dress*.

Words have power, she thought.

Each step became harder to take than the one before. Tuesday looked behind her to find her footprints laid out in white, a path to all that she knew. For a moment she toyed with the idea of turning and going back the way she had come. Could Sterling really harm her here?

He walked beside her with his head drooped almost to his chest, and his eyes focused on the ground beneath his feet. She doubted that he would notice in time if she made a run for it, but then what was the point? What was there to run to? Madame Marisol would welcome her back, but Tuesday was a different person now. She'd seen such terrible and wonderful things. When she'd trailed her fingers through the tops of the clouds, how could she go back to watching them through a window?

So she walked, even when the path grew sparse before disappearing completely. They travelled through curling mist so thick that sometimes she lost sight of Sterling altogether, only to have him reappear at her elbow with his sabre out, ready for a fight. He said nothing when she just looked at him and continued on, but a muscle in his jaw kept twitching as they travelled further into the mist.

Soon Tuesday began to think she heard voices calling out to her. They were faint at first, and she walked for a while believing that she had only imagined them, but they grew louder and more distinct as the mist thickened. They called out her name.

'Did you hear that?' she finally asked, after hearing a voice that sounded like Quintalion's.

Sterling spun in her direction, and only drew his sword back at the last minute, after Tuesday had stepped away from him in fear. 'We hear nothing,' he said tersely.

The piercing cry rang out once more. 'There it is again,' she told him. 'Can't you hear it?'

His brows knitted together, and he turned his head towards the sound. 'No . . . *no*. It was nothing but the wind.'

'There is no wind.'

This time the sound of her name was unmistakeable. It faded away into whispered pleadings from a voice she knew too well.

'It's Hester,' Tuesday gasped. 'And my friends. I can hear them . . . I have to help.'

She darted onto the path before Sterling could react. The mist swallowed her, but she didn't need to see where she was going, because she could follow her friends' shouts. They were just through the mist, calling to her, and if she only ran a little further she'd see them. They'd be on board the *Zephyr*, waiting for her. Hester would clap her on the back and proclaim that she'd had a marvellous adventure, worthy of the gods themselves; Jack would show her all the places he'd been on his map and then blush when he realised he'd been talking for too long; and Quintalion would smirk at her in that way he had, so she knew that, underneath it all, he was pleased. Together again, and this time no one could separate them.

'Tuesday!' Jack cried. He sounded a long way off . . . and yet so close that Tuesday spun around, certain she would find her friend standing behind her, but it was only Sterling breaking through the mist.

'You simpleton,' he said, puffing. 'Something is not right.'

'Help me. Please, help me!'

A strange look crossed Sterling's face. He spun around, his eyes wild, but the mist twined around them ever tighter, and though he slashed at it with his sabre, the sword did little more than stir tendrils of mist through the air in spiral flurries. 'It is Thaïs,' he said. 'It is our love.'

He must have been imagining it. Thaïs was not calling for help, it was Tuesday's friends, and they were lost and alone and frightened. They needed her help. She had failed them in every other way, but she would *not* fail them now.

'I'm coming!' she called out. 'Just hold on.'

She had to find them. The thought pounded through her brain in time with her steps: *find my friends, find my friends, find my friends.* Her foot caught something and she tumbled, hitting the ground with a thump, but she pulled herself up before she even had time to register the pain. Her friends needed her.

She didn't know what had happened to Sterling, but right now she didn't care. All that mattered were her friends' increasingly loud voices.

'We're here,' they called. 'Please save us, Tuesday.'

Her mind played out scene after scene of death and destruction. *They're dying,* she thought. *They're dying again and it's all my fault.*

Up ahead of her, the mist cleared, and she stumbled out of it to find Madame Marisol standing there with her arms outstretched.

'Hello, my dear,' she said. Her pink dress was the only thing not bleached of colour, and it stood out in the grey world like a beacon.

Tuesday hung back at the edge of the wall of mist. She couldn't be real. She was back safe in her House, many hundreds of miles away, with nothing to disturb her but the occasional visitor. There was no way she could be here in the city as well.

As if sensing her hesitation, Madame Marisol clucked her tongue. 'Come here this instant, child. Are you going to make an old lady wait?'

She sounded like the Madame Marisol she'd known, and she certainly looked like her. As Tuesday allowed her feet to carry her forward, she even caught a whiff of the cloyingly sweet perfume that always hung in a cloud around her. It had to be her. 'Are you . . . are you really here?'

'Of course I am, duckie. You needed me so I came. I'm so proud of you, Tuesday. You've built such a life for yourself.' Madame Marisol opened her arms out to her.

The last of her doubts laid to rest, Tuesday ran to her embrace with a glad heart, but when she reached Madame Marisol, she disappeared, and her arms closed around cold mist.

'You killed me.' The voice came from behind her. She spun around. The Lady Fortuna stood before her, the blood pouring from her face and arms staining her pale dress copper brown, all the more garish against the black and white world surrounding her.

'*What?*' Nothing made sense anymore. Madame Marisol had been right there, right where she stood. She'd felt the ghost of her touch right before she disappeared.

'You killed me,' the Lady repeated. 'If you hadn't come to my city, I would never have died. You bring death in your wake.'

Tuesday heaved in a great breath. 'I'm sorry. I didn't mean to.'

'It's too late.' The woman stared at her distantly. She paid no heed to the blood, though so much had flowed out of her that her skin was translucent, every vein mapping out a path across her body. 'It's too late and now all will come to darkness.'

'No!' Tuesday choked out. 'I won't let it.'

'You can't stop it, sweetling.' The blood dripped down the Lady Fortuna's arms, over her hands, and pooled at the woman's bare feet. 'It has already begun. You will wake the darkness, and there's nothing you can do to stop yourself.'

'I won't.' She sank to her knees, heedless of the shallow scrapes that crisscrossed her skin. This was it. She was going mad. The words bubbled out of her, full of the pain and fear that she'd been holding in for so long. 'I'm sorry . . . I didn't want to hurt anyone. I promise I'll make everything right. I'll make it better. I swore an *oath*.'

'Oaths do not matter in death,' the Lady Fortuna said. 'Only the darkness as the daylight fades.'

'I'm sorry,' she said. 'I'm so sorry.' She slumped forward on her hands, filled with an exhaustion that ached in her bones.

The Lady Fortuna's voice grey softer, each word fading away as she did: 'Only the darkness.'

Tuesday didn't know how long she lay there, curled up on the ground with her hands pressed against her ears, but by the time she became aware again, the landscape had shifted once more. She sat up shakily and brushed the clinging tendrils of mist away from her. Fine silk carpets cushioned her seat, and a lazy breeze played with the open flaps of the tent she now found herself in. From outside came the sound of waves lapping against the sand. A fire burned in the brazier in the centre of the room, and the smoke coiled around the top of the low-hanging ceiling.

'Do you really think we should do this?'

The voice came from the next room, which was hidden from her sight by a tapestry of a unicorn. It sounded familiar, and Tuesday sat up straighter, sure she had heard the voice before.

'Of course we should, my darling.' That voice was unmistakeable. Sterling was there, she knew it, and she tensed to run, but something about the way he spoke kept her seated. 'Besides, this is all for us. With the Book gone, the old ways will fall, and we can create the world the way we want it to be. No more war between the old ways and the new. Just peace.'

'Peace that comes from bloodshed is never truly peace. Must you really destroy the Book?'

'It's the only thing standing between us and a glorious future. Surely you can see that.'

'But my brothers and sisters . . .' the voice hesitated.

'You don't need them. You've never needed them. You're Thaïs. You are everything. You're my day and my night, and we will rule the world together as is our right. *Solus mayetvos.*'

Tuesday squirmed. There was something awkward about eavesdropping on a man she sincerely wished dead wooing a woman she had quite possibly killed. But something was wrong. This wasn't some dream, where the events of the past paraded in front of her; this was real. She was in the middle of the City of Lost Things, and whether Tuesday had killed her or not, she'd bet all the money she'd given to Quintalion that whatever was in that tent with Sterling wasn't Thaïs.

She pushed herself to her feet, torn between running and staying. It would be so easy to leave Sterling. He deserved whatever fate this thing, this shape-shifter, had in store for him, but then what would that make her? She had hidden behind people all her life – first Madame Marisol, and then Quintalion – but now it was just her and the truth of who she was staring back at her, and she found she didn't like what she saw.

'Seven sisters,' she muttered, and dashed into the second room.

Sterling and Thaïs were locked together in an embrace. When Thaïs pulled away, Tuesday got her first close-up look of the woman. Thaïs's hair was golden, her figure all curves, she was tall and broad of shoulder, and there was something in the arrogant tilt of her head as she stared at Tuesday that suddenly made it obvious she and Quintalion were related.

Tuesday's mouth moved, but no words came out.

'Tuesday.' She could tell from Sterling's terse greeting that she wasn't welcome, but she was too busy gaping at Thaïs sitting placidly next to him to care.

'Who is that?' she said, finally finding her voice.

'Are you an idiot, child? This is Thaïs. I would have thought you'd know the woman you killed.'

Tuesday shook her head and backed away. It had to be the mist playing tricks with her again. She'd seen Thaïs in her dream; she'd apparently *killed* Thaïs. There was no way the woman sitting next to Sterling could be her.

'Get away from her,' she said, feeling her hands begin to shake. 'She's not real, this isn't real.'

'What are you talking about, girl?' Sterling ran his hand down Thaïs's arm, sending slivers of mist twining around them, and just for a moment, when he had buried his face in her neck, Thaïs's image flickered to reveal something monstrous . . .

something with horns and teeth and rage. It only lasted a second, but it was enough.

Tuesday tugged on his arm. He strained against her, still gazing lovingly into Thaïs's eyes, and Tuesday had to force down the feeling of contentment, because it wasn't *right*, and she wouldn't allow it. It was the mist or the place, nothing more.

'Come on,' she said to him. 'We have to go.'

'If you're lucky, we may let you live now that we have our love back,' he said idly.

'She's not real.' Tuesday pulled on his arm again, vainly trying to get him away.

'What does she say, Sterling?' Thaïs said. 'I'm real. I'm here. Can't you see that?'

A look of pain flickered over Sterling's face. He shrank back from her. 'You never called us Sterling,' he said softly. 'We made a rule. There would be no formalities between us. Just you and me.'

'But it's *me*.' Thaïs's voice held a note of desperation. 'I'm right here. Don't you dare ignore me! Don't shut me out. It's not my fault,' she whined. 'It wasn't my fault.'

Sterling's lip quivered and he dragged in a deep breath, shutting his eyes briefly before saying, 'We *will* find you, Thaïs. You know that. We will spend our life and death looking.' With a barely audible whimper, he allowed Tuesday to pull him to his feet and away from the woman. 'But we have not found you yet.'

'I'm right here, darling. Look at me. Look at me!' Thaïs's face twisted. Fangs erupted from a mouth still screaming at Sterling, two gleaming horns spouted from her golden head of hair, and her skin split and burst, revealing a growing mass underneath, until all that was left of Thaïs was a pair of grey inscrutable eyes watching them.

The monster stood before them, at least six feet tall from the tip of its horns to its padded feet. It was a thing of nightmares, an unholy mix of beasts that made Tuesday want to run and never look back. It had the face of a lion, its teeth caked with gore as it growled at them menacingly. The grey eyes were somehow ancient. The bristly fur did nothing to cover the many scars and open wounds that littered its bulky body, which was muscled like an ox and trembling with pent-up power. The hind legs were sleeker and made for running. Its mane shook with the strength of its roar, and the front leg came forward like a challenge, the pad of its paw almost as large as Tuesday's head and wickedly clawed. Flecks of ash rained down on them as it flexed wings of fire. Its tail lashed out, and Tuesday saw that it was coiled like a snake, with a stinger bulging at the end.

'We think,' Sterling said, 'we may be in trouble.'

CHAPTER TWENTY-SEVEN

'What is it?' she whispered. They backed away from the creature, which stamped at the ground and snorted, the hangings of the tent already beginning to catch fire from its wings, and as they burned, the illusion melted away to the greys and blacks of the faded world.

The creature spoke, its voice deep and rumbling, like stone scraping against stone, and yet whispering in her head as well. Tuesday clutched her hands to her ears.

'I am Il-dakul, the stallion that snatches de Kena babes from their cradles. I am the nightmare that slithers from the cracks in the ground to steal the water bearer away. I am the reckoner.'

There was the sound of metal against leather as Sterling pulled his sabre from its sheath. 'What do you want from us?'

'Your death,' it replied simply. 'You are wrong. You dare enter here while still alive. There must always be a balance. You tip the scales and you must die.'

Tuesday would have responded, but the creature took three great steps towards her and she lost all reason except for a primal urge to get away.

It stopped just before her, huffing out a hot breath against her skin. The scent of decaying meat and spices assaulted her. 'You,' it said, 'are neither mortal nor immortal. What *are* you?'

'I . . . I don't know,' she stammered. 'I'm nothing. I'm Tuesday.'

The creature sat back on its haunches and regarded her silently. 'That is not nothing.'

The tent burned away to ashes around them, and though the flames licked at her arms and head, all she felt was a gentle puff of hot air. The brazier melted to her right, and the metal dripping out of it caught her eye just in time for her to see a flash of peacock green in the darkness.

But there is no colour here, she thought.

Sterling's sabre slashed through the air, carving a black line into the creature's flesh. 'Withdraw now,' he said, 'and we will let you live. If not, then by the fair rules of war, we're within our rights to kill you.'

Il-dakul laughed. The ground shook with its mirth. 'This mayfly thinks itself a viper. It is nothing to me. I have brought entire armies to their knees.'

There it was again: the glimpse of green in the mist, and then the glint of a curved sword.

'Like the de Kena?' she asked, trying to keep its attention focused on her. A desperate hope was starting to rekindle within her; she cradled it against her heart, terrified that a single breath of air would extinguish it forever.

The creature inclined its head. 'I come for everyone in time.'

'We thought there had to be a balance.' From the way Sterling's eyes skittered to the right every couple of seconds, Tuesday knew he had seen them too, and she thanked the Days that he had decided to be reasonable and pick his battles.

'This land is not only of death. There is the promise of life also. Your coming here threatens not just the lost.'

'Then take me to the Book of Days,' Tuesday said, hoping that none of her fear made it into her voice, 'and I'll leave.'

Il-dakul's tongue lapped at its fangs as it stared at her. 'You seek the Book? Its resting place has not long been in this city, and yet you are not the first. Many have fallen in such a quest. What makes you any different?'

The barrel of a musket broke through the mist. The spark of hope that she'd been guarding flickered to life.

Tuesday looked right into its gaping maw and said, 'Because I've got friends.'

The bullet tore a chunk out of the creature's ear. It roared in pain as Quintalion burst through the mist, already firing the pistol in his other hand. The next two bullets hit Il-dakul in its shoulder. It lunged forward.

Tuesday yelped and staggered back out of reach of its claws. The creature advanced on her. Gore matted the fur on its shoulder, dripped down its powerful leg, and she was reminded for a moment of its impression of Fortuna, blood-red and white.

Sterling charged at it with his sabre held high. It batted him aside with ease, and he fell, unmoving, to the ground.

Il-dakul opened its mouth to speak again, but it was beyond words now, and all that came out was a garbled roar, instantly muffled by another round as Hester burst out of the gloom.

Tuesday's heart leapt. Sterling must have been lying about the poison on his blade, for here was Hester as large as life. He had been lying, she decided, and the others had escaped from the daybreakers somehow and come to find her. She couldn't keep the smile from her face, but there was no time to celebrate, for the shots had gone wide, and though they scoured furrows in the creature's flank, they didn't bring it down.

She ducked as the claws raked through the air, so close that her hair fluttered in the breeze they made. Il-dakul limped towards her, and she backed up, feeling the raw power emanating from it. This was something primal and dark, something she'd only ever felt once before, in the seconds after she'd woken up at Madame Marisol's, but then it had vanished as quickly as a scent on the breeze.

This time, however, the power didn't vanish. It washed over her in waves, thick and suffocating. Her eyes dimmed – she could hear Quintalion shouting at her to run, but her legs no longer had the strength. She hit the ground hard and collapsed onto her back.

A shadow fell above her. 'I will enjoy destroying you, unnatural girl.'

Il-dakul's voice was the cold at the edge of oblivion. It would take her back there, she knew it, back to the chill and the void and the endless waiting. She screamed, but no sound emerged from her chattering lips.

She would die here.

A small voice echoed through her mind. *No!* it cried out. *You will not die here.* She wanted to ignore it, but it kept repeating the words, faster and faster, until they hummed through her frozen body, filling it with life.

'No,' she said out loud now. 'No.'

'Plead, little girl.' The creature stood over her. 'Beg for your life as countless others have done before.'

Quintalion sprayed the creature's hide with bullets, but it didn't seem to feel them. There was a *boom* of sound as Hester released the rifle's arsenal into its right side.

'I won't,' Tuesday said suddenly.

'What?' Il-dakul leaned down, its face close to hers.

Danger amplified every sense: the gritty sand, the creature's fetid breath as it panted above her, the roar of the guns firing uselessly. 'I won't beg.'

'Why not?' It placed a paw on her chest, almost gently, as though it was playing with her. The claws were so long that she had to angle her head up to avoid them puncturing her throat. 'If you do, I might even have mercy.'

'I won't beg,' she said slowly as the beast leaned over close to her, 'because I'm not done yet.'

Twisting out from under Il-dakul's paw, she jabbed her thumbs into its eyes with all her strength. It let out an unearthly shriek and scuttled back. She crawled away from it as quickly as her shaking legs would go, hoping that she'd managed to blind it.

Too close, she thought. *Still too close.*

Its head whipped in her direction. 'I may not be able to see you,' it said, 'but I can still hear you.'

'Tell me about it,' Jack said, and darted forward out of the mist. His staff whirled and Il-dakul's leg gave out and it dropped to the earth with a yowl of pain.

There was no time for thanks though, for almost as quickly as it had fallen, the creature was back on its feet. It dragged its crippled leg behind it as it rounded on Hester and Quintalion.

Tuesday scrambled off the ground and threw herself towards Il-dakul, but Jack grabbed her around the waist. 'Don't! It'll kill you.'

'It'll kill *them*!' She twisted in his grasp, but he wouldn't let go.

'They can look after themselves. I don't want you hurt.'

You might, she thought bitterly, *if you knew what I let Sterling do to your father.*

Hester raised the rifle to her shoulder and fired. The bullet hit Il-dakul square in its forehead, right between the two horns, but still it didn't drop.

She cursed, threw the rifle to one side, and went for her sword. It stuck in its scabbard. She tugged at it desperately, but it wouldn't pull free.

Sterling surged past Tuesday with his sword drawn. She had thought him dead, but now he planted himself in front of the struggling Hester. The claw marks gouged into his arm and the bruise painting his jaw black did nothing to dampen his determination as he thrust the sabre at Il-dakul with a tightly controlled grunt of effort. It tore through the smouldering wing and buried itself in the beast's side up to the hilt. Black blood spurted from beneath the sword. Il-dakul groaned and twisted, trying to reach the sword with its mouth.

'Why?' Hester hissed at Sterling.

He wrenched his sabre from the beast and fell back as it snarled uselessly at him. Sterling's mouth was a grim slash in his face. 'What is the point of letting a dead woman die?'

'Dead?' Tuesday squirmed out of Jack's hold and ran to Hester. The hope she had kindled so carefully was blowing out in that single word. 'You were safe . . . you were fine. Sterling lied about the poison, and you all escaped from the daybreakers. You came to rescue me.'

She sounded like a child, but she didn't care. For one glorious moment, she thought she had been wrong. Everything was supposed to be all right, and she felt a deep sense of injustice that it wasn't.

'How do you think we got into the city?' Hester asked gently. 'It needs a willing sacrifice.'

'I don't know. I thought . . . oh, Hester, you can't be dead!' She didn't realise that the tears were escaping her eyes until Hester brushed them away with her sleeve.

'Hush, child,' she said. 'Do not weep for me. I am where I must be. Narvi will be waiting for me.'

'Narvi?' Il-dakul grunted.

Tuesday had forgotten about the creature. It had eased itself back on its hind legs and sat lapping at its wounds, speaking between the swipes of its tongue. 'I have not received a Narvi into this city for a hundred years.'

Hester swayed, her wooden leg the only thing keeping her from sinking to the ground. 'You would not have. We are Saqiran,' she said desperately. 'This is not where we lay our heads to rest at the end of our long day.'

Il-dakul, the reckoner, let out a great laugh. 'Creeds and gods and technicalities matter not to me. I balance the scales for all the realms of the dead, from the Summer Kings of Ormonde to the eternal portraits of the Yäelani. And I tell you that your Narvi has not crossed my borders.'

'You lie,' Hester whispered. The curved sword slipped through her fingers and hit the sand.

'Death is the only truth.' The creature gathered itself up and lunged, its fangs bared for the kill . . . and suddenly Hester's sword was at its throat, held steady by a panting, terrified Tuesday.

'Try it,' she said, forcing down the tremor in her voice.

'You will not kill me.' Its dead eyes stared back at her, filmy with blood and grime. It had been sagging, on the verge of collapse, but now it drew itself up to its full height, magnificent and still deadly despite its wounds.

She moved the sword to the base of the creature's throat and hoped that she wasn't about to make the worst mistake of her life. 'Just a scratch from that sabre Sterling stuck you with will kill. Even now you must feel the poison swirling through your veins. If you want to see the scales balanced before you die, take me to whatever is tipping the scale.'

'Us too, naturally,' Quintalion said, shooting her a look.

She took a deep breath that caught in her throat and continued. 'I know it's not just us. The city was shedding things long before we came through the door. So take us to the problem and I *will* make things right.'

Il-dakul's laugh ended in a wet gurgle. 'You think yourself a reckoner?'

It stood a good two heads higher than Tuesday – she had to reach up to hold the sword steady at its throat – and, despite its grievous wounds, it was still easy to picture its gigantic mouth closing around her head. The sword wobbled.

'No,' she said. 'I know what I am. I'm Tuesday. I like stories and rain and biscuits with tea, and I swear to you if you don't obey me I will plunge this sword through your throat and end your reckoning.'

Sweat glistened on the creature's hide. It let out a single shuddering breath and then, with a roar, it leapt.

Tuesday shut her eyes, expecting to feel the clamp of jaws around her throat, but there was nothing but an intense wave of heat and voices all around her, echoing in her ears, and then she staggered and opened her eyes to find herself in front of a place she never thought she'd see again. Madame Marisol's Unreality House.

CHAPTER TWENTY-EIGHT

Most people believe the best way to forget someone is to throw them down a well. Or lock them in a room with eight keys, or bury them at a crossroad in the thirteenth hour. But they're wrong. The best way to forget someone is for them never to have existed in the first place.

Madame Marisol's Unreality House was where you brought people to make that happen.

'H . . . how?' she stuttered. She turned to Il-dakul for answers, but it had disappeared, leaving the five of them alone. Her hands clenched at her side; she had to concentrate hard not to pinch herself, because the longer she stared at the little house, the more like a dream it seemed. Smoke curled from the chimneys, and a hint of light touched one of the first-floor windows, bathing the veranda with a warm glow. Someone was home.

Her heart surged with the hope of seeing Madame Marisol again. Despite her adventure, she had missed the woman who had cared for her all those years, and she was walking forward when Quintalion put his hand on her shoulder.

'She won't be there,' he said softly.

'What?' She spun around to face him. 'But it's her House, I know it is.'

'It may be her House, but she won't be waiting inside.' He took a deep breath and ran his hand over his head. 'The Unreality House is what you might call a unique piece of architecture. It exists in both our world and the hereafter. How do you think her guests remain alive and yet not alive?'

She frowned. 'I hadn't thought of that.'

Quintalion smoothed down the lines of his green waistcoat. 'That is the shadow House, the link that Madame Marisol's House retains with the City of Lost Things. And unless I'm mistaken, which I never am, it's where you'll find the Book of Days.'

She longed to race forward on light feet, even if it was only to a shadow of the House she knew so well, but all the fear and hopelessness she'd felt on her long walk with Sterling came together into a tangle deep inside her, and she sagged, almost falling to the ground, except Jack caught her in his arms.

She sank into his chest and breathed in the familiar woollen vest, its fibres tickling her nose. 'I'm sorry,' she said, hiccupping as her voice caught with sobs. 'I'm so sorry. Jack, your father . . .'

He mopped up her tears with his thumb, and gently traced the curve of her cheekbone and the fingerprints embedded in her skin. She leaned into his touch.

'Hey,' he said. 'Hey, there now. It wasn't your fault.'

'But he would never have died if I didn't . . .'

'If not him, then the daybreakers would have just found someone else. He wouldn't have wanted that.'

Though his words were comforting, she heard the pain echoed in his voice, and stared up at him, wishing that he would strike out at her or tell her he hated her . . . anything but his brave attempts to console her. She didn't deserve them. When she told him that, he shook his head and ran his hand over her hair.

'Of course you do,' he said. His eyes, though, were dark with grief. The glasses Tuesday had bought him sat in the breast pocket of his shirt, and he had replaced them with his father's spectacles, still flecked with sand.

Tuesday decided to accept his assurances, whether or not she believed them, and gently wiped the sand away from the frames with a shy smile. 'I guess that means you're not an assistant librarian anymore.'

His hands tightened around her shoulders. 'I don't really know *what* I am anymore.'

But that meant . . . All the hope that had been kindled into life was extinguished in those words. She had thought it was only Hester who had died, that the others had somehow found their way free from the daybreakers, but now the reality of her situation crushed her beneath its heel. Jack and Quintalion were dead as well. There would be no more long afternoons spent talking, laughing, and occasionally being insulted, no more sharing meals or listening to Quintalion's snores and his louder avowals when he woke that he didn't snore. She had meant to ask Hester and Jack to teach her how to read Saqiran.

She caught the wail before it escaped her throat, but Jack rubbed at her cold arms anyway.

'What is it?' he asked. 'What's wrong?'

Oh, everything, she wanted to say. 'Nothing. I'm fine, really.'

'Good.' Jack straightened his shirt as though shoring himself up from his sorrow. 'Because my father always said that a wise man shouldn't focus on the army on the horizon when an assassin's sneaking in through his window.'

'He came up with that from life, did he?' Quintalion asked.

'A book, my dear fellow,' Jack said. 'They are the windows into other lives.'

'We trust that we are the assassin you're referring to.'

She looked over Jack's shoulder to see Sterling staring at the two of them. He was wiping the blunt edge of his sabre on his pants, Il-dakul's black blood darkening the material, but when he noticed that Tuesday's eyes were on him, he smoothly slid the sword back into its scabbard and added: 'The boy is wise to fear us, for the presence of your friends will not save you. Whether they are dead or alive, we will still find our love and end your pathetic existence to set her free.'

The words were haughty, but his voice was tinged with sadness and a touch of desperation. His dead hand – the one he had sacrificed to stop Thaïs from leaving him – drummed out a silent beat against his leg.

Tuesday turned to him with a sigh. 'I won't run. Don't you know by now that I won't run? You can walk right into that House with me, but don't think for a moment that you'll be walking out with the Book of Days. Not without my blood on your hands.'

'That is an acceptable arrangement,' Sterling replied.

Of course it is. Tuesday ignored him. 'It's not the blood on your hands I'm worried about, it's the blood on *mine*.'

The Whispering Plains stretched out to the horizon in every direction, as real as she remembered; a sea of grass, waving in the wind, and so familiar that she coughed against the tears clogging her throat as she addressed Hester, whose silence had only served to remind Tuesday of what she'd done to the Saqiran. 'You *died*, Hester. You would still be alive if you hadn't met me.'

'And mayhap I would be bitter and friendless and seething with rage,' Hester said with a little shrug. 'Would that have eased your conscience?'

'No,' she blurted out. 'Of course not. But you'd still be alive, all of you . . . It's my fault you're dead. Jack, you should have been a librarian, but now you're just . . . just . . .'

Dead. She couldn't bring herself to repeat the word; it tasted too bitter on her tongue.

They'd saved her – even in death they'd saved her – but it didn't change the fact that even if she made it out alive, she'd be walking out of the City of Lost Things alone. New paths and new possibilities called to her, the roads that she hadn't yet taken, but she had thought she would be travelling them with friends, and now the prospect of a lonely, never-ending journey terrified her.

Quintalion's eyebrows knitted together and then comprehension bloomed on his face. 'Do I look dead to you, you cloth-headed girl?'

He looked as he always had: the same arrogant pose and predatory leanness; his accustomed greatcoat worn high on his shoulders, the collar turned up against the wind; the mismatched eyes, and the grin that made her feel like she'd missed the joke. 'Not exactly,' she said. 'But neither does Hester, and I *know* she's dead.'

Hester silently pulled her slashed shirt open. A single cut ran from the bottom of her breastbone to above her navel, angry red lines curling out from it around her torso.

'And yet I'm still standing.'

Jack frowned slightly when Tuesday reluctantly eased herself from his embrace and crossed over to Hester, lightly tracing the length of the fatal cut. 'Does it hurt?'

Hester snorted, and gave her a look. 'I am dead, child. I feel nothing.'

'I'm so sorry.' She pulled her hand back, unwilling to meet Hester's eyes.

'Do not grieve for me. I was dead from the moment I lost my brother –'

'But still she talks,' Sterling muttered.

'Rejoice instead,' Hester said over the top of him, 'that Quintalion and Jacobi Heller yet live.'

But she'd *heard* Sterling give the word for his men to kill them, had seen the gun turrets swing in their direction. There was no way they could still be alive . . . and yet they were standing here, whole and unblemished, and Tuesday didn't know whether to laugh or cry or hit them for scaring her like that.

'Then both of you, you're not . . . ? You're really . . . ?' She didn't want to believe it for fear that the truth would snatch away the pleasant fiction. She would blink and they'd disappear and she'd be alone.

'Perfectly well,' Jack said, 'for a stretched definition of *well*.'

Tuesday couldn't help it. She flung herself at both of them, throwing her arms around their necks and pulling them in for a hug, which Quintalion only put up with for a moment before prising her away and saying: 'Are you trying to finish the job? Air, Tuesday. It's generally a good idea.'

Picking up Jack's staff, which she had accidentally knocked from his hands in her wild leap, she passed it back to him and said, '*How?*'

'Our thoughts exactly,' said Sterling. 'We ordered our men to kill you, did we not?' The tic – that *tap, tap, tap* of fingers against chest – was the only part of Sterling moving but for a vein in his forehead that had joined it, beating out a rhythm against his skin.

'Captain Theophilus Sterling has yet to realise that just because he orders something done, it doesn't mean anyone's going to do it,' Quintalion said. 'He could order us to strip down to our undergarments and dance a waltz, but I highly doubt he'd get more than a punch on the nose for his troubles.'

A smile tugged at the corner of Jack's mouth. 'I never pegged you as one to shy away from some good old-fashioned exhibitionism.'

'The point is,' Quintalion continued smoothly, 'that orders are only useful when you have the power to see them carried out. And our dear commander no longer has that power.'

'They disobeyed us?' Sterling whispered, turning away. *Tap, tap, tap* went his fingers.

Suddenly the soldiers' gossip made sense. *We should have bolted while we had the chance. That lot from the* Stormrazer *had the right idea.* She had thrown it in Sterling's face without even knowing what it meant for him, but now that she understood, she almost wished she hadn't.

'And there was no one waiting on the shores of the Silk Sea either,' Quintalion said, and then gave a little gasp, as though he were shocked. 'You didn't misplace a troop of daybreakers, did you? Better be careful, Sterling. They'll want to take that out of your wages.'

Sterling smoothed down his tunic. Il-dakul's blood stained his pale hand. 'We sent them away. We . . . we didn't want to waste resources.'

'Of course you did.' Quintalion's grin almost eclipsed his face. 'And I'm a dance-hall performer called Wee Jock.'

'What you do in your private life is nobody's business,' Jack said.

Quintalion was too busy gloating to notice Sterling draw his sword. Hester let out a cry of warning, already going for her weapons, but at the last second he changed course, and Tuesday felt his fingers close around her shoulder as he pulled her back against his chest.

'The girl is coming with us,' Sterling panted, his breath hot against her neck.

It felt like time was repeating, as if it ran in an endless loop and she had suddenly found herself back at the beginning of her story. Only this time she wasn't a scared girl, barely in the world a day. This time she'd brought down a city and bested a beast. She was Aemilia incarnate, and she was *angry*.

The sabre wobbled in Sterling's grip. Tuesday batted it away from her neck and took two steps forward, stopping and turning just at the end of the sword's reach.

Sterling recovered quickly and pressed his blade against her heart.

'Do it,' she said. 'If you honestly think that killing me is going to bring Thaïs back, then just do it now.'

Fury roiled in her head, cold and dark and deep. She should be frightened of how swiftly the rage had erupted, she knew – any other time she would have fought against it – but now she was tired and frustrated, and she'd had enough.

'Do it,' she repeated with her hands held up in defeat. 'Because if you don't, I'll walk into that House, find the Book of Days, and tear it apart page by page in front of you so you'll never see her again.'

Sterling recoiled. 'You wouldn't . . .'

'Wouldn't I?' The laugh bubbled up from deep inside her, unbidden and wild.

'Tuesday . . .' Quintalion cautioned, but the buzzing in her head drowned out his words. He didn't matter. This was between Sterling and her; it had *always* been between Sterling and her. From the moment he had called out to her in the streets of Beggars End they had danced around each other, pursuing and retreating, back and forth, a routine that was almost comfortable in its familiarity. She had been running from him so long that she'd forgotten what it was like to run *to* something, but now that the Book of Days was within her reach, it all came back to her: that thrill of new discovery, the impatience to find out what was around the next corner. The Book of Days was her chance to find her name, her *self*, and she wouldn't let him take that away from her.

'All I wanted was to find out who I was . . . and I guess I still don't know. But I know all about you, Theophilus Sterling.'

He flinched at the sound of his name, but the tip of the blade against her chest dug into her skin, urging her to continue, whatever the consequences.

'You cling to your uniform, and your honour, and your rules,' she continued, 'because beneath all of that – beneath the power and the title – you're nothing but a sad little man who can't let go of the past.'

And there it was: that tremor running down his arm, making the sabre quiver in his grip. She'd won. Even if he killed her now, she'd won.

Tuesday let out a breathy, rueful laugh. 'I never thought I'd find out who *I* am when everything gets stripped away, but now I think I know. I'm the girl who's walking away from you.'

She stepped back out of the blade's reach, took a deep breath, and began to walk towards the House. Each step she took she expected to feel the sabre piercing her skin, but as the distance between them grew larger and Sterling still hadn't come after her, her confidence grew. She released some of the tension in her back that she didn't realise she'd been holding, and snuck a glance over her shoulder. Sterling stared at her retreating figure. As he watched, the sword slipped from his fingers and thudded into the ground.

'Thank you,' she whispered to the Days, and opened the gate and walked up the path and into the House.

*

When she slipped into the House, closing the door behind her, she leaned back against the wood in relief. She was home.

'Madame Marisol!' she called out.

Everything was as she remembered: the rug and the cherubs and the fireplace, though she could have sworn that it had been on the other side of the entrance hall. The sitting room was on the wrong side of the House, too. The pianola and the armchairs peeked out of a room to the right of the entrance hall, not the left. Worry clenched around her stomach.

She ventured a few steps further into the House, hoping to pick up the scents that felt so much like home to her: bread baking in the oven; the sharp smell of hundreds of years of wood polish; Madame Marisol's perfume, finding its way into every nook and cranny. But there was nothing but the smell of must and decay.

'Madame Marisol?' she tried again, a tremor in her voice.

Footsteps sounded from a room upstairs. Tuesday eagerly walked forward, certain this was all a misunderstanding. She had remembered the House wrong. The fire wasn't lit in the grate and the gaslights weren't on because Madame Marisol was sick or tired, and Tuesday would make soup for her and everything would go back to the way it should be.

The footsteps came closer. A shadowy figure emerged out of the closest room to the stairs and hesitated at the top of the landing, letting out a gasp that could either have been delight or fear.

'You're here,' the figure said.

Tuesday's heart fell. It wasn't Madame Marisol. She longed to run back to her friends; only the promise of the Book of Days kept her in position by the door.

'What have you done with Madame Marisol?' Tuesday asked, sounding braver than she felt.

'I told you to forget about me,' the voice said, ignoring her question. 'Although I suppose we both know that was never going to happen.'

The figure began to descend the stairs on light feet. '*And that is the only promise I would ask you to make*,' the voice said. 'I remember the words so well. I must have penned them a dozen times before I was happy with them, though the memories of my old life had nearly faded away. *Forget me. Build a new life, a better life.*'

Those were the words from her letter. Madame Marisol said Tuesday had written it to herself, before she had forgotten who she was, so how could this person know those words so dear to her heart? Unless . . .

She staggered back; her head was filled with noise, a maelstrom that threatened to overwhelm her.

'Did you, I wonder?' The figure reached the bottom of the stairs. Tuesday saw the boots first, high-cut and covering a pair of tight riding trousers, and then the embroidered tunic and the engraved breastplate. She knew who it was before she reached the woman's face; she had seen the figure in her dreams, had lived inside her skin.

'Thaïs,' she breathed.

CHAPTER TWENTY-NINE

The older woman gave a little bow. 'The very same. And what should I call you, besides myself?'

It couldn't be possible. *How* could it be? The ocean waves rushed through her head and above the sound of water breaking on the shore, she heard herself distantly say, 'Tuesday.'

'I was born on a Tuesday,' Thaïs said with a smile. 'Second oldest of my kin. I suppose even with a new life you couldn't escape who you were.'

'But . . . but . . . we can't be the same person,' she found herself stuttering. Her fingers raked through her tangled hair, each jolt of pain welcome as it gave her something to focus on beyond this unimaginable new reality. 'We *can't* be. You're standing right in front of me.'

'Nothing but a shadow and a memory, I'm afraid.' Thaïs's voice was soft and sad. 'But you, Tuesday, are a *possibility* . . . and that is a greater thing by far.'

'How?' she said. She didn't want to believe it, but the truth was quite literally staring her in the face. It was the woman she had seen with Sterling, back on the beach, and in the tent that very day. For a moment she tensed, afraid that Il-dakul had returned, but then common sense crept back in: the creature was dead or had gone to lick its wounds, and she knew that with Sterling's poison coursing through its veins, it wouldn't be causing mischief any time soon.

But the woman remained. They were close enough alike that they could have passed for sisters, and for the first time Tuesday felt like a shadow compared to what she could become. Everything about her was *less*, while Thaïs, even in this diminished form of a memory as she claimed herself to be, was more: taller, more beautiful, surer on her feet when she stepped closer, and with a light in her grey eyes that illuminated her face.

Tuesday was the shadow, not Thaïs, and as she gazed back at her, it was all she could do to choke out, '*Why?*'

'Come with me and I'll tell you everything.'

*

Thaïs led her through the entrance hall and down the little corridor at the back of the House, past the mirror, and through the ruby-handled door into the room containing the keeping-houses. It was a journey Tuesday had taken before, only in reverse, when she'd first woken to Madame Marisol's face. She wished the old woman was here with her now, but she had to face this walk alone, or worse . . . with herself.

Tuesday paused at the threshold of the room. Every nerve screamed at her to run back the way she'd come. Thaïs would take her back into the darkness and the cold, and she would freeze and burn at the same time, trapped forever in the not-world of her own unlived life. Her heart thumped wildly in her chest.

No, she told herself. *I am Tuesday. I've touched the sky and seen dragons. She can't take that away from me.*

Thaïs didn't bother with any of the rushlights; the glow from the keeping-houses lit their way. They followed a twisted path, but Tuesday knew where they were headed. She had sensed it the minute they walked into the room.

'I knew that Theo – that Sterling,' Thaïs corrected herself as she led Tuesday further through the maze of sleeping figures, 'would never give up on his quest to find the Book of Days. He's a very determined man. It's one of the reasons I love him. But I also knew that he must never find it. He would fashion the world in our glory, would destroy whole cities as a monument to our love, and everyone would suffer.'

She couldn't believe what she was hearing. 'But Hester's people – her brother. *They* suffered.'

Thaïs twirled her hands, one in front of the other, as she walked. 'Necessary sacrifices, I'm afraid. I needed a way to get into the City of Lost Things without arousing his suspicion. We travelled everywhere together in those days, even shared a saddle.'

'You killed them.' *I killed them*. The faces . . . the contorted mouths as they coughed out their last breaths, or begged for loved ones they would never see again. Tuesday didn't think she'd ever be able to get their faces out of her head . . . and now it turned out that, in some twisted way, she'd been the one to order their deaths?

Her legs gave way and she dropped to the floor with a thump. Bile rose through her throat, hot and choking. She dropped her head to the cool tiles, her world suddenly shrinking to the room, her own breaths, inhaled through her nose to hold the nausea at bay, and the hand on her shoulder. She shrugged it away violently.

'I'm not proud of what I did,' Thaïs said. 'Believe me, I've had ten years to regret it. I was a different person with Theo. He was so young, and so passionate. He brought out something wild and reckless in me.'

'*Dreams that warp and turn bitter*,' Tuesday whispered.

'And they did turn bitter. Every word I wrote is true. But you have to believe me when I say that I did what I could to save the Book of Days and our way of life.'

Thaïs's questing fingers found her shoulder again, but this time when Tuesday tried to move away, Thaïs clung to her with a light but insistent grip.

'So you left him,' Tuesday said when she realised Thaïs wasn't going to let go. 'But he followed you.'

The sigh rippled out of Thaïs's throat. 'I should've known that he would. He tried to hold me back, to stop me from entering. His poor hand . . . Tell me, and tell me true: does he live still? No mortal can enter the City of Lost Things and live. Even I could feel its pull, tugging at the edges of my life, and I had immortality on my side.'

Yes, and he's been pursuing me this entire time, hungry for my death. She didn't think she should tell Thaïs – herself, she realised with a jolt – the whole story, so she settled for breathing out, 'He does.'

Thaïs's hand tightened on her shoulder. 'Thank you.'

'I don't understand,' Tuesday said. 'I thought you ran from him.'

'That doesn't mean I don't love him.'

The coolness of the tiles was a blessed relief against Tuesday's fevered forehead. She drew in a deep breath experimentally, hoping that the worst of the nausea had passed, and when no urge to be sick tickled against her throat, she held out a hand and allowed Thaïs to help her up.

'I'm sorry,' she said to the woman, suddenly understanding. 'I have friends. I know how hard it must have been to leave him.'

If Tuesday had been in her place, having to leave Hester or Jack or even Quintalion for the greater good, she didn't think she could have done it, and though she may have hated Sterling for all he had done to her, she couldn't blame Thaïs for who she loved. *Or who I loved*, she thought, still trying to get used to the idea.

Thaïs nodded in acceptance and drew her on through the keeping-houses with her arm looped in Tuesday's, offering her support. 'Once I entered the city, I knew I wouldn't have long,' she continued, looking around her. 'This place – this world – is meant only for the lost and, as a Day, that was something I could never be. So the city destroyed me.

'I could feel my memories fading from the moment I stepped through the doors. It was the most exquisite kind of agony, to feel bits of yourself melting away but to be unable to stop it, or even remember what you had lost.'

'But I thought you were –'

'Immortal, yes. But imagine living forever, never knowing who you are. By the time I ventured far enough into the city for the Book to be safe, I barely remembered my own name.'

'But does that mean I'm immortal?'

Thaïs fixed her with a hard look. 'I don't know. Would you really want to be?'

Tuesday thought she heard footsteps echoing in the room, just out of rhythm with their own, but when she looked behind her, there was nothing there, just the peaceful faces of the souls asleep in their keeping-houses. If this House was some kind of mirror, she wondered, did that mean the people weren't real? Perhaps this was all the city's doing, creating a familiar landscape for her as it had so many times before on their journey, and she would end as Thaïs had, a shell of herself with her memories no longer her own, just continuing on forever with no end in sight. She shuddered. 'No.'

Thaïs continued: 'I was foolish to think that I could somehow best the city, that I could stroll in and leave the Book of Days in its care without it taking something in return. But sometimes you do things because you have no other choice.'

'I understand,' Tuesday replied, thinking about her time in Fortune City. 'I made a deal with the Lady Fortuna to find out who I was. I had to drink an–'

'Fortuna?' Thaïs whirled on her with concern in her eyes. 'Even Satyr shunned her, and he taunted dragons for fun. The Lady was here in the darkness before the Days. Some say she turned the Mora back when it first tried to cross into our world. She is far more ancient than anything I've seen. And you dealt with her? You're – *I'm* – either very brave or very stupid.'

Thaïs was searching her face, but Tuesday squirmed away from her gaze, suddenly feeling very young. 'She saved my life,' she countered. 'She let her city fall . . .'

'At what cost?' Thaïs sounded very old, and very tired. 'The Lady never does anything for nothing. Ah, but I suppose I cannot chide you. I gave up everything – the Book of Days, my family, even my life – so that I would finally be safe from my feelings for him.'

Tuesday was beginning to realise that there was only ever one *him* when it came to Thaïs; just as Sterling did not think himself whole without her, Thaïs's thoughts seemed to be always on him. They were each other's world.

She had felt the pull, that strange desire to be near him, the first moment she saw him, and even now his green eyes seared her soul. The feelings disgusted her, so she buried them deep within, telling herself they came from someone she no longer was, and focused instead on what Thaïs had said.

'What did you do?'

Thaïs took a deep breath. 'I took the Book somewhere safe. But with the last of my failing memory, I used its powers one last time: I gave myself a second chance. The Book stripped away the years, took me back to when I had everything before me. Changed me to you. But *his* name still haunted my thoughts. I had to go somewhere he would forget me as I was forgetting him.'

'The Unreality House,' Tuesday breathed.

'He was waiting for me at the door to the City of Lost Things. By that time I had almost forgotten his face. When he called out, I wanted to tell him who I was, but I *couldn't*.'

Tuesday shook her head, too shocked by the pieces of her life coming together to care that her mouth hung open and tears painted her cheeks. 'He said he saw me. He saw me come out of the city instead of you. He thought I'd killed you to escape. That's why he's been after me since I left the House.'

'I'm so sorry,' Thaïs said. 'I knew that the best way to forget someone is to bring them to the Unreality House. If I went there, if I gave myself up to the darkness and the cold, then Sterling would forget me. I didn't think what it could mean for you.'

'He killed my friend. Because of you – of me – she's dead.'

Thaïs let out a sob, and then covered her mouth with the back of her hand. 'I did what I thought was best. If he forgot me, Theo would have no reason to pursue the Book of Days, and it would be safe. But even better . . . I would forget myself.'

Thaïs's words, and the realisation of what she had done, jolted Tuesday back into the terrible darkness. She gasped, but no matter how much her chest heaved, no air filled her lungs. She was back there, in her keeping-house, and just as all of her memories were trickling out of her and the blackness covered her completely, she drew herself up and said, 'No.'

Thaïs's voice was an echo of her own. 'No?'

She wasn't back in her keeping-house. She wouldn't let herself go back there. But to willingly forget everything . . . all the memories, good and bad, the way she liked her eggs and the colour she saw behind her eyes before she went to sleep at night. She had known that once, and Thaïs had taken it away from her. She moaned softly. 'How could you? How could *I*?'

'I've lived a longer life than you could even imagine, Tuesday. I've done terrible and wonderful things. It was time for me to let go. It was your time.'

Thaïs finally came to a stop in front of the thing Tuesday had known they were walking towards. The sprays of fir etched into the wood had chipped; the brass plate bearing her name was fogged with grime, and the whole thing was smaller than she remembered, but it was definitely her keeping-house.

'When I came to this House,' Thaïs said, her eyes on the wooden box in front of her, 'I willingly surrendered all that I was . . . for you. You're all that's left of me. You must carry on my legacy. You must protect the Book of Days.'

Thaïs swung open the door to the keeping-house. There, lying open on the wooden floor, was the Book of Days, the light from Tuesday's keeping-house casting an otherworldly glow on its pages.

The writing was foreign to her, though beautiful, and the script flowed evenly over the pages, leaving space only for a detailed map or illustration before joining again in its close lines. Tuesday wanted to touch the soft vellum, but she held herself back, her hand hovering just above the open page.

She felt as though she was in the presence of something ancient and unknowable, something that had seen the creation of the world. It would be wrong to disturb such a tome, and yet there was a deep ache inside her, a longing to slide her fingers over the ink and lose herself in the story.

It grew stronger every second that she remained standing there, and soon her hand dipped closer to the page, and closer, until she gave herself up to her urges and rested her palm against the Book.

Something jolted her, sending ripples of pleasure down her spine. A single shocked cry forced its way from her lips and then she was tumbling into the Book itself, falling headlong into the words and the names and the stories . . .

'Whoa,' she said, shaking her head to clear it. 'What was that?'

'That, my dearest, was *time*. It was the first laugh and the last star winking out at the end of a long night. My siblings and I created this Book as a repository of our knowledge, and as I was its last keeper, it belongs to you now.'

'I couldn't possibly . . .' The echoes of power still curled inside her head, whispers of the long dead and not yet born. With just a word from this Book, she could topple mountains or send every daybreaker airship plummeting into the sea. The world would be safe then, and exactly the way she wanted it: every road open for her to explore without fear or hesitation. She could raise Fortune City to the skies once more. She could raise Hester from her *grave*.

She'd grabbed the Book of Days before she realised what she was doing, and held it pressed against her chest. She could do it. She could make the world better, as it hadn't been for a thousand years, back when the old ways still burned strong in the hearts of men. The dragons would hunt again, the under elders would venture from their dark forests, and the wild ocean folk would build bonfires at the end of glorious summers that would be seen from the Seething Sea to the ice floes of the south.

Thaïs's gentle touch on her cheek jolted her back from the world she'd been creating in her head. 'I wish it could be so,' she said, 'but you *can't*. How else do you think Sterling started but with whispers of the way things could be?'

'But . . . but . . .' She clutched the Book tighter against her; the leather cover pressed into her arms, leaving pale lines like the fingerprints on her cheek. 'I could make things so much better.'

She wouldn't be like Sterling. She wouldn't dream of war and destruction in the name of progress. Thaïs had ruled over roads and the journey and so would she, and she would be fair and kind and make *everything* fair and kind.

The slap rang out, loud in the silence, and Tuesday felt the sting against her cheek. She raised her hand to her face in shock.

Thaïs was staring at her, her eyes as stormy as the Silk Sea. 'Promise me,' she whispered furiously. 'Promise me you won't ever use it. Promise me you'll keep it safe from those that would.'

Tuesday hesitated, the Book of Days clasped tightly to her breast.

'Promise me!' Thaïs repeated.

'I promise,' she said, and fought against the wild ambition that had gripped her moments before. She had not been made for such power; it left her head pounding and clouded over with memories that didn't belong to her, and while part of her clung to the lives she had been denied, Tuesday realised that they weren't hers to claim, and she reluctantly let them go.

Thaïs smiled in relief. 'My brothers and sisters are still out there somewhere, I know it. They will help you fight the temptation even if I cannot.'

She remembered Quintalion, and his quest to find his father. 'But they died, didn't they? The strain of creating the Book was too much for them.'

'No.' Thaïs drew her hair back as she shook her head, and traced the fir leaves on Tuesday's keeping-house. 'Weakened, perhaps, and less than they were. But we are Days, and wherever there is light and laughter, there we will be.'

'*You* sent the invitation to Satyr,' Tuesday said. *My brother.* He must have been alive for Thaïs to entrust her care to him. 'Quintalion had it. He was the one who woke me.'

The older woman slid her fingers over the pale fingerprints on Tuesday's cheek. For a second her expression darkened in worry, but then the grey eyes cleared and she said, 'Yes. And now I can go to my rest, knowing that Quintalion is watching out for you even as my brother always cared for me. The Book will be safe in your hands.'

'In *our* hands,' Tuesday told her. They were one and the same, and though she had no memory of her life before she woke up in the Unreality House, she'd found out the truth of who she was and had been, and it warmed her to see herself reflected in Thaïs's eyes.

'No!' The word was choked and hoarse and filled with despair.

Out from the shadows of the nearest keeping-house, his sabre held in front of him, came Sterling.

CHAPTER THIRTY

'All this time,' Sterling said. The colour drained from his face. A streak of white hair had bloomed at his temple. 'All this time. Why would you want me to forget you? I would sooner forget my own name.'

'Theo,' Thaïs said, her eyes wide with surprise.

'I waited for you. I waited for you and when you didn't come ... when that girl, that *thing*, came through the doors instead,' he pointed at Tuesday with his sword, 'I knew something terrible had happened.'

'I'm so sorry, my love.' Thaïs held her arms out for him but he flinched away from her embrace. The pain of the rejection drove the breath from Tuesday's body.

'How could you leave me?' The fingers played out their rhythm against Sterling's forehead, *tap-tap tap-tap*, the sound of two hearts beating as one.

Thaïs opened her mouth, but no words came out.

'She had to,' Tuesday said, holding the Book to her chest.

'You!' Sterling staggered around to face her. A lock of hair pulled free from his ponytail and tumbled over his face, shuttering those green eyes. 'You ruined everything.'

'No, my love, no,' Thaïs whimpered.

Sterling advanced with his sabre held before him, forcing Tuesday to retreat, stepping backwards until her back hit the glass door of the keeping-house, and the force of it swung the door closed behind her.

'Give me the Book,' he demanded.

Tuesday shook her head.

'I promised I would slit your throat over the Book of Days,' he said. 'And I never lie. Now give it to me.'

'Never!' Tuesday spat out. Fear coursed through her, tying her stomach in knots, but she ignored it. She had a job to do. She'd promised Thaïs that she would protect the Book of Days, and she'd do it now or die trying. *All those paths I haven't travelled*, a small voice in her lamented.

He would kill her; she saw it in his eyes. His desperation was clear in every line of his body, in every tremor and exhaled breath. He would kill her and that would be the end of her journey.

'If you kill me,' she said, pressing herself against the keeping-house, 'you'll be killing Thaïs too. I'm all . . . I'm all that's left of her.'

He wiped the sweat from his forehead. 'You lie,' he hissed.

'She doesn't,' Thaïs said with some of her old fire, 'and if you think she does, then you're a fool.'

'You're standing right in front of me. This . . .' his voice shook, 'this is a ploy to save the girl. But it's all in vain. You always were too merciful, darling.'

'No ploy, Theo. No trick.' She smiled at him sadly. 'I'm nothing, just a memory held in Tuesday's head. If you kill her, I'll disappear, and it will be worse than it was last time, because this time you'll remember that your blade brought an end to all that you claim to love.'

His eyes tightened. His fingers twitched against his head as his mouth contorted in a silent scream. His gaze went from Tuesday to Thaïs and back again, and he nodded to himself, as though making up his mind. When he spoke, his words were empty. 'I thought she had killed you . . . in a way, she did. And now she has killed me too.'

The sabre flashed in his hands. Tuesday cringed back against the keeping-house. *I'm sorry, Madame Marisol.*

She expected to feel the chill of steel slipping between her ribs, but Sterling flipped the sabre at the last second, and then Thaïs screamed and there was blood and confusion and the darkness rushing into her head.

My name is Tuesday, she thought to herself, *and I won't go back there.* But that wasn't right. She was *already* back there. The cold glass pressed against her skin. She was in the keeping-house and she'd never wake again. But then she felt the comfortable weight of the Book of Days in her arms, solid and real, and she knew she was still alive.

When the darkness receded, Tuesday exhaled in relief. Her throat felt like cotton, all dry and scratchy. The sounds of the room gradually filtered back in. Someone was keening close by, and she opened her eyes to find Thaïs on the floor, cradling Sterling in her arms. The sword lay beside him. His tunic was dark with blood.

'What have you done?' She dropped to her knees next to him.

Sterling's eyes flickered to her for a second and then he turned his gaze back to Thaïs, who had him clutched against her chest.

'*Why?*' The word eased out of Thaïs like a prayer.

Sterling shuddered in her arms. 'Without you, I die. Every *day* is another death. Now I will sleep.'

Thaïs shook her head, lowering her forehead so that it touched his. 'But I would have you live, my love.'

'Not without you,' he breathed, his eyes fluttering shut.

Thaïs shook him gently, and then, when he didn't respond, again with greater force; his head lolled against her neck. 'Save him!'

Tuesday backed away from the two of them, Thaïs cradling Sterling in arms that were streaked with blood. 'I can't,' she said. 'You made me *promise*.'

'I won't see him die.' She clamped her hands down on his wound, but the blood bubbled up too fiercely for her to slow, and he slumped against her, resting his head on her chest.

He blinked three times, and then his eyelids dipped. 'Now,' he breathed. 'Now I am finally whole.'

'No, love, no . . . you will *not* die. I won't let you.'

Tuesday sank back against the keeping-house, watching the scene with horror. This was the man who had dogged her every step – who had *killed* Hester. She should be celebrating as he took his last breaths. But she could feel Thaïs's pain and desperation as she fought to keep him alive. Tears sprang to her eyes.

A part of her, in the tiniest corner of her heart, remembered the love she had felt for Sterling back in the life before her life, and shared it. It had drawn her to him from the moment she first saw him, and no matter how hard she tried to stamp it out with every breath, she couldn't deny something that was a part of her.

And now he was dying.

He had stilled in Thaïs's arms, his head lolling against her neck, with his chest barely rising and falling at all as he struggled to pull air into his body.

Thaïs stroked his hair back from his eyes. Her face was twisted with grief, but no tears fell. Perhaps, as nothing but a memory, she had no tears to give him.

'*Solus mayetvos*, my love,' she whispered, caressing his cheek. 'Forever and always.'

'*Solus mayetvos*.' His lips only just moved, the sound eking out from between them nothing more than a breath of air, but Tuesday heard it anyway, and made her decision.

'The keeping-house,' she said suddenly, springing to her feet. 'Put him in my keeping-house.'

Thaïs stared up at her, hope written clearly on her face. 'It's too late,' she said. 'Isn't it?'

She didn't know why she was doing this. He deserved death. She ground her teeth, fighting against the desire to just let him die in front of her. 'For Hester,' she would whisper as he took his last breath. But Thaïs looked up at her with those familiar grey eyes, and instead she found herself saying: 'Not if he's still breathing. It saved me, it saved Jack. It can save him as well.'

Tuesday dropped the Book of Days, ignoring the loneliness that washed over her as she lost contact with the thousands of lives and stories the Book contained, and slid her arm under Sterling's shoulder. With Thaïs supporting his neck and chest, the two of them heaved the dying man over to Tuesday's keeping-house, Tuesday nudging the door open with her foot, and eased him back against the wood.

Thaïs groaned when his knees buckled and he slumped forward. 'It didn't work,' she despaired.

'Wait,' Tuesday said, shutting the door to stop his fall and hoping that she was right.

Her faith was rewarded when the light within the keeping-house pulsated brighter and brighter and caught him in its rays, pulling him upright, straightening his limbs, and raising his head so that he hung suspended within it, just another of the sleeping souls caught forever like flies in amber.

Tuesday eased out a breath and held her hand against the glass, unsurprised when, a moment later, Thaïs placed her hand next to hers.

'You saved him.'

Slowly, Tuesday slid her hand across the keeping-house and, pausing to give the other woman plenty of time to pull away, rested it on top of Thaïs's. Her skin was ice cold and not quite solid, shifting beneath her own, but they matched perfectly, and the two of them stood there with their hands held over the heart of the man that one of them had loved and both had left.

'What will you do now?' Tuesday asked her.

Thaïs stared into Sterling's face. A streak of blood marred the pale forehead, but it was already fading to brown. 'As long as you carry me in your memory, I will live . . . even if just as a shadow. So I will stay here. *Solus mayetvos*.'

'I've heard Sterling say that so many times,' Tuesday said. 'What does it mean?'

Thaïs huffed out a laugh that ended in a sob. 'Only us,' she breathed.

And now it would truly only be them, hidden away together in the House that wasn't a house, just two more lost souls for the city of the lost. 'I won't forget you,' Tuesday told her. 'Both of you. I promise.'

Thaïs's hand moved under hers. 'Thank you.'

The armour clinked as Thaïs drew herself up. She slipped her hand out from underneath Tuesday's and straightened her vambraces with such a busy interest that Tuesday knew she was holding back her emotion, because it was exactly what she would have done.

Happiness sparked in her heart. She'd found out who she was, and though she would always be Tuesday, she would be Thaïs also. She would walk the roads for both of them, and her future had never held more promise.

'So,' Thaïs said finally, her voice light, 'what will *you* do now?'

Tuesday remembered the words from her letter, and smiled. 'I think I'll live.'

She bent down and picked up the Book of Days. Then she walked out of the room without a backward glance, through the entrance hall, and out into the sunlight, where a librarian, a warrior and a charlatan waited for her. And, oh, the possibilities . . .

The End